CITIZEN

Charlie Brooks left Eton to become a stable lad for racing legend Fred Winter. After riding in the Grand National, and winning the Cheltenham Festival as an amateur jockey, he became the youngest racehorse trainer in England. He has broadcast for Radio Five and Bloomberg TV and hosted his own sports programme, 'The Charlie Brooks Show'. He is a columnist for the *Daily Telegraph* and lives on his farm in the Cotswolds. His autobiography, *Crossing the Line*, was widely acclaimed.

Also by Charlie Brooks

Crossing the Line

CHARLIE BROOKS

Citizen

HARPER

This novel is entirely a work of fiction.
The names, characters and incidents portrayed in it are
the work of the author's imagination. Any resemblance to
actual persons, living or dead, events or localities is
entirely coincidental.

Harper
An imprint of HarperCollins*Publishers*
77–85 Fulham Palace Road,
Hammersmith, London W6 8JB

www.harpercollins.co.uk

A Paperback Original 2009
1

Copyright © Charlie Brooks 2009

Charlie Brooks asserts the moral right to
be identified as the author of this work

A catalogue record for this book
is available from the British Library

ISBN 978 0 00 728640 9

Mixed Sources
Product group from well-managed
forests and other controlled sources
www.fsc.org Cert no. SW-COC-1806
© 1996 Forest Stewardship Council

FSC is a non-profit international organisation established
to promote the responsible management of the world's forests.
Products carrying the FSC label are independently certified
to assure consumers that they come from forests that are managed
to meet the social, economic and ecological needs
of present and future generations.

Find out more about HarperCollins and the environment at
www.harpercollins.co.uk/green

To my mother, Caroline.
Thank God someone in our family can spell.

PART ONE

1

Tipper knew that Ireland was the Emerald Isle; but he'd never seen a real emerald. Ma owned a necklace made of green stones, which, his father had once told him solemnly, were mined straight out of the Mountains of Mourne. Da was a drunk. But when he said that was why they called it the Emerald Isle, Tipper believed him. The uplands of the country, said Da, were stuffed with emeralds like currants in a slice of barmbrack. There were places you only had to take a spade to the ground and you'd turn up a couple of handfuls. It was later, long after Da had disappeared to England, that Ma let on. As far as she knew there wasn't an emerald ever found in Irish ground, and her necklace was only paste from Woolworths. A pure emerald would be something else, she said, with all the different shades of green glowing and gleaming inside of it. People like us would only dream of owning such a thing, she said.

Some of the colours Tipper was seeing now,

through the dirty window of the local CIE bus, matched his mother's idea of the gem. There were greens of every description here with yellows and golden colours mixed in. The hedgerows bobbed with red fuchsia and there were scarlet poppies in the oats. This part of Tipperary was called the Golden Vale and after the place Tipper had come from, it lifted his spirits. He saw no concrete tower blocks on rubble-strewn land, no charred shells of stolen cars, vandalized bus shelters or overflowing rubbish bins. Here the land sparkled in the summer sunlight. It may not have had buried gemstones, but it was a rich land, and an ancient one.

Then there were the horses. The road passed field after field of patient mares grazing, attended by their spindle-legged foals. Every second farm in the Irish midlands was also a stud farm, and every other farmer a horseman whose only desire was to breed a Grand National or a Derby legend. Tipper was heading to one of these stud farms, and he was beginning to sense he'd feel at home there. The open spaces of the midlands might be a novelty to him, but horses were not. He already knew something about them.

'They want me in the hospital,' Ma had told him abruptly, a few days back. 'I got to have an operation and it might be weeks before I can look after myself, let alone you.'

'Jesus, I'll be all right, Ma. What sort of operation?'

'Never mind what sort. And you will *not* be all right. Your brother will be leading you into temptation. So I fixed it with your uncle Pat in the country – he'll have you for the summer.'

As a matter of fact, she was spot on about Tipper's brother Liam. When they grew up there had been nothing to do on the estate but kick a football or get into trouble, and you couldn't play soccer all day every day. So trouble it had been, and that was how Tipper learned he could ride.

Liam had bought a pony for a few pounds at the old Smithfield market in central Dublin. They kept it tethered on some waste ground between two tower blocks. It was the only decent thing Liam ever did. They say that everyone has good in them, but they were wrong when it came to Liam.

They never got round to naming the pony. He was just referred to as 'Himself' and, in the O'Reilly family, it was Tipper that got on best with Himself. Bareback, and with nothing more than a head collar and string reins, he would ride races against the other boys' ponies, never showing a trace of fear. Tipper also developed a talent for cowboy rope tricks. He would put a bucket on top of a gate-post then gallop towards it and lasso the bucket with a length of clothesline. When he tired of a stationary target he lassoed stray dogs. He never missed.

Liam couldn't ride one side of Himself and he resented his younger brother being such a natural.

He enjoyed throwing his weight around once his Da had gone. When he got a few cans inside him he cuffed Tipper hard enough to hurt him. In a playful sort of way.

Tipper and Himself would jump fences made from abandoned supermarket trolleys. But Liam had better use for his brother's talents. He'd get Tipper to ride Himself into the actual supermarket and create a diversion whilst he helped himself under the cover of confusion.

When Tipper was about nine, Liam developed a new interest – joyriding. Tipper went along with it. Faint praise from his brother was better than a smack. They'd trek across town to an affluent area and pick a side street without too much traffic. Tipper would lie spread-eagled on the tarmac with Himself – who knew how to play his part – seemingly lying on top of him, while Liam lurked nearby waiting for a driver to stop his car and investigate the apparent riding accident. While walking up to Tipper, these Good Samaritans would soon enough hear the screech of tyres as Liam reversed their car away at speed. It was the cue for Tipper and Himself to jump up and get the hell out of it.

But inevitably the scam came to an end. One particular driver was too quick for Tipper and collared him before he could mount up. The result was a visit to the Juvenile Court, and an ultimatum from his mother; Himself must go back to Smithfield Market.

And now, years down the line, it felt like a different world to Tipper as the bus rattled into Fethard, an old town still ringed by its medieval defensive walls. Tipper stepped down into a wide Main Street with his bulging luggage. All his things stuffed into the big loop-handled bag that Ma always used to take washing to the launderette. His cousin Sam was supposed to meet him, but Tipper saw no sign of him. Not that he had a clue what he looked like. Instead he found McCarthy's, a famous pub that Sam had said everyone knew. It stood on Main Street, in view of the church. And as Tipper settled himself to wait on a low wall opposite the pub, he watched a funeral procession forming up outside the churchyard gate.

'All right, Tipper?'

It was Sam, sauntering up on Tipper's blind side. Tipper swung round and nodded.

'Yourself?' he smiled. Tipper was immediately struck by Sam's strength. He wasn't particularly tall, but he was solid.

'I'm grand. See the pub?'

He nodded towards McCarthy's.

'What about it?'

'It's haunted. Every time one of the family's going to snuff it, a picture falls off the wall. See that funeral?'

'Yeah.'

'That's the McCarthys too. They have the undertakers as well as the pub.'

'That's warped.'

7

'It's good business. They do the funeral and the wake all in one package. Come on. We've got to walk.'

The funeral cortege was just passing, led by the coffin borne in a smart Mercedes hearse, with wreaths and bouquets piled on the roof. Grim-faced mourners flanked it or trailed behind on foot. Sam and Tipper kept pace as the procession crawled towards the top of the town where, at the end of Main Street, a sign pointed the way to the cemetery, up a street to the left. But the funeral turned right.

'They're going the wrong way,' observed Tipper.

'No funeral in Fethard ever goes the right way.'

Sam nodded towards the street that had been avoided.

'That's Barrack Street. Cromwell came in that way, and the funerals have never used it since. They turn right here, and take the long way down Burke Street and round the back.'

Sam and Tipper left the funeral marchers and forked right by the Castle Inn.

'See those walls there?'

Sam indicated with a wave of his arm.

'They're only the oldest complete town walls in Europe.'

'How d'you know that? Jesus, you're like a guide book.'

'Me Da tells me. He knows all the history. Come here, there's something I'll show you.'

He led Tipper to a place under the town wall and pointed mid way up the stonework.

'See? There's an old witch in this wall.'

Set into the stonework Tipper could just make out a distorted head, grinning with a gap-toothed mouth, above a decayed body and arms that reached down below the stomach. Heavy weathering made it difficult to make out the detail of the carving.

'She's called Sheela Nagig,' said Sam. 'There's little statues of her all over Ireland. Nobody knows who she is. Come on, we've miles to walk.'

He led the way to the stone bridge across the Clashawley River, and set his course along the Kilsheelan road. They took turns to carry Tipper's unwieldy bag. Sam was setting a fast pace but Tipper found himself constantly slowing down, so he could take in the scene: the geese inspecting the river bank, the horses loose in the fields or tethered to a stake on the roadside, the birdsong in the air and yellow wild flowers billowing from crevices in the drystone walls. They stopped to look at the imposing ivied ruins of Kiltinan Castle, and again to view the shell of an old church by the roadside.

'Cromwell,' said Sam. 'He knocked the shite out of everything.'

After ten minutes they turned into a boreen leading towards the escarpment of a steep ridge that seemed to climb up into the clouds. It was laid out in a patchwork of hedged fields in which horses, sheep and cows grazed, the shining grass patched here and there with clumps of brilliant yellow gorse. This pasture rose as far as a thick belt of pine trees, above which lay an expanse of moorland that stretched up to and beyond the horizon. Sam stopped at last and leaned on a gate to look fondly at this view. Coming up behind, Tipper joined him, his eyes tracing the network of hedges on the hillside, strong barriers of beech, laurel and whitethorn, bursting their buds as they flowered.

'Jesus,' he said. 'This is some place.'

Sam's response was reverent.

'This is the Golden Vale,' he said. 'The home of champions and God's Own Country.'

2

Nikolai Nikolayev, universally known as Nico, sat on a chrome bar stool in the Voile Rouge. The beachside restaurant was heaving. Its tender rushed busily from the small pier on Pampelonne Beach out to the floating gin palaces that had cruised round from St Tropez. The music was beginning to step up a beat and the 'models' from the fashion boutique next door were provocatively working the tables.

At the other end of the bar an overweight, euro-trash rich kid made some desperate girl go down on her knees while he poured Louis Roederer Cristal over her face; he laughed loudly for atten-tion. Nico gave him a sycophantic smile of approval and deftly nodded his head. The girl pretended she was having a good time and squealed. That was what she was paid to do. Her team-mate clapped, yelled and tossed her hair over her shoulder. And adjusted her loose fitting top, so her nipples were visible if you'd paid to be that close.

Nico spooned up the last scrapings of his favourite hangover cure: a lemon sorbet heavily laced with Italian bitters. His predatory eyes flicked between the guy he was talking to on the next stool, a Bolivian gigolo named Ramon, and the entrance. Nico had long cultivated the habit of noting every new arrival at the beach bar. The males were quickly assessed in terms of their influence or wealth; the females for any hint of availability; and both for their vulnerabilities, for the most advantageous angles of attack.

It was how Nico lived, how he funded the Jensen and the five-star hotels and vintage champagnes which were the keynotes of his life. With no capital or inherited standing in the world, he might superficially be bracketed with a *pique-assiette* like Ramon. Yet he stood apart from the hangers-on of his acquaintance, the gigolos, barflies and male models that infested the Riviera. For one thing, he looked different. With his puny physique and polecat face, he had to get by without the standard obvious good looks of those to whom freeloading came easy. Minus that confident jaw, lacking those soulful eyes, Nico compensated by growing a neat beard, wearing designer shades and working considerably harder, and with deeper insight, to access the playboy yachts, private tables and penthouse party circuits that all of them depended on. Nico would have it no other way. He was not, he considered, a Ramon, an expendable accessory, a pawn. He was a player. And he was clever.

His quick brain had even taken him to Harvard. The public Parisian school system prepared him well, but his father, proprietor of a modest food shop in the French capital's 6ème Arrondissement, could never have afforded college in America. So Nico won a scholarship and took himself across the Atlantic to learn all about the drug habits and compulsive spending of the East Coast Preppy, the Texas Oilboy and the Jewish Princess. With this preliminary social research under his belt, Nico set forth.

He'd been recruited by Reitchel-Litvinoff, the trouble-shooting New York tax accountants, who found many uses for his chameleon social skills, undoubted numeracy and ability to bluff in six languages – including both American and British. For half a decade he shimmied from country to country on behalf of clients anxious to keep their wealth out of the clutches of the taxman. Whenever it was necessary to sidestep the electronic banking system, Nico was on hand. Here he picked up bearer bonds, title-deeds and attaché cases filled with large denomination bills. There he made discreet trades, deposits in numbered offshore accounts and deliveries at the clients' Swiss chalets and Mustique beach houses.

Yet he featured nowhere in Reitchel-Litvinoff's employment register. He was paid in cash, or in kind, and was impregnably deniable if things went wrong. Finally things did. The IRS picked Nico up on its radar, and suddenly the United States was an exclusion zone. Within a few days, his contact at Reitchel-Litvinoff no longer returned Nico's increasingly desperate calls.

So he had landed, like a hopeful turtle, on the Côte d'Azur, and set about foraging for deals and new contacts. It was a perfect habitat for him. Where rich people took their pleasure they also did business, and Nico found the Riviera a natural base from which to haunt the pleasure domes of Europe. Shopping in Rue de Rivoli and New Bond Street, golf at the K Club, opera at La Scala and going 'Banco' at Monte Carlo's baccarat tables. He convinced himself that he really was one of the high rollers. His skill in manipulating currency for other people frequently came in handy; often that currency was narcotic, equally often erotic; and so he negotiated his way through life, with money enough to pull on a hand-made Italian suit and drive a hand-made English car.

Ramon was half way through some story which involved one of the most beautiful girls in the world falling in love with his body. All of his stories were in this vein, and Nico was only half listening. His attention was caught by a party of Russians, who had clearly just come ashore from a private yacht. They were a couple of girls, chic and silky-blonde, a shiny-suited aide-de-camp and some kind of minder, all bossed by a thickset man with short grizzled hair and a pock-marked face. Apparently unable to speak more than a few words of French, the boss called for blinis and lemon vodka by jabbing the menu with a blunt fore-finger. His hands looked like they'd spent most of their lives working on a pipeline in Siberia.

When the food arrived he ignored the little pancakes and shovelled quantities of caviar and sour cream directly into his mouth. Nico could hear his fellow countryman growling comments about the bar staff's inability to speak Russian. From his accent and behaviour, Nico knew this was no White Russian émigré like himself. The man had emerged from Moscow in the Soviet era, and clearly not in a state of poverty.

The Bolivian was still droning on.

'Di was becoming a nuisance. She was obsessed with me. And Pam didn't like it. Pam was driving me crazy too. She just couldn't get enough of me and that loser of a boyfriend was always on the phone. She's got no brain, you know. I can't stick these girls with no brain, I don't care who they are.'

Nico produced a thin smile, nodded in agree-ment, slid from the stool and patted Ramon lightly on the shoulder.

'Back in a minute, Ramon,' he said.

Then he crossed to the Russians' table, bowing slightly from the waist as the boss-man turned to him. 'I wonder if I might be of service to a fellow countryman,' Nico said smoothly.

3

Sam's family lived in a cottage within the confines of a stud farm. It was among the most prosperous in the area. This was not one of the thousands of rackety micro-studs that litter the Irish hinterland, the kind of small farm where, just for the love and romance of it, a couple of mares would share the grass and the outbuildings with a dairy herd or a couple of breeding sows. The enterprise Sam's father worked for was owned by rich people in Dublin. They expected the stud's progeny to be the best, and to win Grade One races from Ascot and Longchamp to Happy Valley and Churchill Downs. And to generate big returns from yearling sales. The stud itself was a demesne of beautifully maintained, white-railed paddocks, shaded by huge chestnut trees and linked via a network of sandy bridleways to various functional and fanatically well ordered buildings: the boxes, covering sheds, tack-rooms and feed stores.

His father Pat, the stud groom, was a wiry

countryman with a broken nose that whistled when he exerted himself. He had no intention of this being a summer holiday for his nephew. He expected Tipper to make himself useful; sweeping out barns and stables and feeding horses. It was all new to the boy. The first week felt like a lot like hard work, but as soon as he was allowed to get off the end of a broom and handle the horses Tipper began to enjoy himself.

A couple of weeks into his stay, Tipper came in for his tea and found Sam alone.

'Where's your Da and Ma gone to?' he asked.

'Gone off in a hurry to Dublin.'

'What for?'

Sam shrugged. 'Don't know. They didn't say.'

Tipper found out why later in the evening. The stud manager, a remote figure called Mr Power, whom the boys rarely spoke to, sent word for Tipper to come up to the house.

'I have something to tell you,' he said in an unnaturally hollow voice when Tipper presented himself. 'It's about your mother.'

'Oh, right! What about her? Is she okay?'

Without immediately replying, Mr Power ushered Tipper into the hall of his house, a large gloomy space hung with racing prints and photographs of horses. He carefully shut the door behind the boy, then turned to face him. Tipper felt uncomfortable in this strange environment.

'No, I'm afraid that's the point. She is not okay. As a matter of fact.'

17

Tipper could tell he was having trouble spitting it out, whatever it was. He waited silently.

'The thing is,' Mr Power went on, 'I've had a phone call from your uncle who went up to Dublin with your aunt this morning. They went to the hospital, and the thing *is*, she's died, Tipper. I'm sorry.'

Tipper didn't take this in. He was confused. None of it was making sense.

'Who's died? My aunt? I don't get it.'

'No, not your aunt. Your mother. Your mother's died, son. She never got over the operation. She was beyond help, apparently.'

Slowly, like water seeping into a sinking boat, Tipper grasped what Mr Power was saying. His Ma was dead. His Ma. He would never see her alive again.

Tipper didn't speak or move, but stared at Mr Power transfixed. Then after a few moments he found the ability to walk, and brushed past the stud manager. He opened the front door and quietly closed it behind him. He hoped Mr Power wouldn't come after him. He hurled himself down the steps and started running, pelting down the drive that stretched to the road. He pounded across the tarmac, leapt a stone wall and plunged into the small wood on the other side. It was hard fighting his way through the undergrowth, but he didn't think about it. At last he found a small clearing and his flight ended. He needed to be by himself. He didn't even want to see Sam. Tears were streaming down his cheeks. He didn't want to see anyone.

In his misery he sat on a fallen bough and propped his elbows on his knees. His emotions were randomly churning around inside him. It was incomprehensible that he'd never see his mother again. Ever. He hadn't said good-bye to her. He'd just walked out of the door without a care in the world. What had she thought about that? Why hadn't he taken more notice? Why hadn't he seen that she was ill? What could he have done? He would never again see Ma. Never pinch another bouquet of flowers from the cemetery to give her. Never eat her rashers and beans, or watch the English soaps with her. These things seemed enormously important. They were a part of his life that had all of a sudden been detonated and blown away.

His eyes were hot and throbbing. He stared at the ground; it was covered with decayed leaves and rabbit droppings. Now his mind was empty of thought. He totally lost track of time. He had no idea how long he'd been there when he realized that he was freezing cold and it was nearly dark. He thought about Sam. He'd have to talk to him about Ma; it was the last thing he'd want to do. He couldn't bear the thought of talking to anyone about her. Tears started streaming down his cheeks again. Then he got up, wiped his cheeks and brushed his backside. He'd never forget Ma, that wouldn't change. But everything else had.

He just had no idea how he was going to cope. No idea what was going to happen to him.

The next month of Tipper's life was shrouded in a dark cloud of misery. He couldn't get his mother out of his mind. Why had he been denied the chance to say good-bye to her? Maybe if he had it wouldn't have felt so bad. He surprised himself by wanting to talk to Sam incessantly about her. Sam was brilliant. He wasn't embarrassed like Tipper thought he'd be. He asked Tipper all about her and Tipper told him. He loved telling him and he was so grateful to Sam for listening. His uncle and aunt just clammed up and carried on as if nothing had happened. But when Tipper was on his own a black cloud descended on him.

Tipper threw himself into the work on the stud. He had nothing else. He listened to Uncle Pat who taught him that the thoroughbred horse is a man-made creature, the result of three centuries of carefully selected breeding. With a set of rules worked out in the eighteenth century and never varied since. The racecourse rule demanded that all horses are proven racers, or at least the offspring of proven racers. The intercourse rule ensures that every mating is a true one, witnessed, recorded and verifiable. Artificial insemination is abominated in this world, unlike in cattle breeding. The thoroughbred stud is an establishment dedicated to natural procreation as nature intended.

Tipper loved working with the foals, which at

this time of year meant getting them to walk properly on a leading rein. He chatted away to them about his Ma as he walked them up and down the sandy lanes and somehow felt his soul was restored in the process.

'Just watch their front legs, son,' Uncle Pat told him. 'A foal's not like a grown horse, who kicks behind. It's the front legs that are most dangerous in a foal.'

Tipper looked at the youngster he was leading, as if to say, you wouldn't want to hurt me, now would you? And it seemed he didn't. Tipper was confident, comfortable in his handling of the foals, and they responded. Uncle Pat was impressed by his nephew's natural instinct.

'He's got a gift with these foals,' he informed Mr Power. 'But he just doesn't know it yet. He'll be grand.'

Tipper's favourite foal was a high-strung little filly with an unusual dark reddish, almost mahogany coloured coat. When he had time on his hands and no-one was about Tipper would take her into one of the barns, sliding shut the big door before turning her loose. Usually a foal at this stage of its development is nervous of anyone that doesn't smell of its mother, and flighty to catch. Red had always been especially neurotic and Tipper set himself the task of making her biddable. He got down on his hands and knees, reckoning that foals were no different from children – intimidated by anyone that loomed over

21

them. Little by little Red came nearer, smelling his hand, chewing his coat, and in that way the two of them got to know each other. Next he took a long rope and attached it to a halter loosely hanging round her nose and neck. If she wanted to back off, he let her, but he would then tease her in again, like an angler playing a fish, rubbing her neck before loosening the line once more. Gradually Tipper was mastering Red, but without ever imposing on her or making demands. Her education proceeded only as fast as she herself wanted.

Red remained fearful when out in the open, and that was almost her undoing one afternoon, when Tipper and Sam were left on their own in charge of the paddocks.

'Lads, be sure to get the foals in if the rain comes,' Uncle Pat had told them.

The storm came in suddenly on a southerly wind. The sun was still shining but the sky in the south was black. The wind stiffened, tossing straw and sacking around the yard. At the first almighty clap of thunder the boys rushed out carrying ropes to bring in the foals. As soon as they opened the gate and began calling, the herd walked obediently towards them. All of them, that is, except Red, who hung back. They decided to bring in the others and come back for Red. But as they unhooked the gate a second time, another thunderclap split the air and immediately the frightened foal took off, careering away from them towards the far end of the paddock, where she collided with a railing post. She staggered back and hopped unnaturally on three legs. The fourth was streaming blood.

'Jesus, Sam, will you look at that?' shouted Tipper. 'There's blood pouring out of her.' The rain was now hosing down and they were getting soaked.

Sam yanked the gate shut behind him and the boys ran over to investigate. Red shied and tried to hop away as they approached. Tipper held Sam back.

'Stop,' he said. 'She's dead scared. She might hurt herself more.'

Sam looked terrified himself. He was wiping the rain off his face. The consequences if anything should happen to this valuable filly would be dire.

'Christ on a bike, we're in the shite!' he said. 'Is the leg broken or what?'

'Hang on. Let me go to her myself.'

Tipper stepped quietly up to Red, praying that she wouldn't jink away from him. The injury was in the lower part of the off foreleg, which was pumping bright red blood at an alarming rate.

'Come on Red, we got to get you in,' he murmured, slowly putting out his hand and threading a rope through the ring in her head collar. He gave her drenched neck a pat. Then he crept backwards, exerting the slightest pressure on the rope.

'Come on, Red. Come on, littlun,' he urged.

Slowly, the injured creature hobbled with him towards the gate. They got her into the barn and knelt to look closely at the leg.

'It's a big gash she's got, right down to the tendon,' said Sam knowledgably, pulling a cleanish tea towel he'd found somewhere about out of his pocket. 'It bleeds worse there than anywhere.'

'Jesus. What'll we do?' Tipper asked frantically. This was their fault. They would really be for it.

'We better get the bloody vet to stitch her up. And in the meantime we got to get this towel wrapped around, or she'll bleed to death.'

The storm was in full spate now, hammering rain on the barn roof. Red rolled her eyes, hating the sound.

'She's spooked by this bloody weather,' said Sam. 'How'll we get near enough and not get kicked?'

'I'll do it,' said Tipper, peeling off his water-logged coat. 'Hold her head for me.'

He started by rubbing her wet forehead, quietly talking to her all the time. Then he let his hand slip down her neck, then on down the leg towards the gash. Red started to snatch up the leg and Tipper patiently went back to her forehead and repeated the routine until she accepted his touch on the leg. Finally he was able to wrap the towel tightly around the wound, cinching it tight with some twine to make it act as a tourniquet. The blood stopped pouring out.

The vet was an hour coming.

'Well done, lads,' he said, as he bent to clean the wound with antiseptic. 'She'd be dead by now if you'd not got that dressing on her. No easy job, that. Which one of you managed it?'

'We both did,' said Tipper.

'Tipper did,' corrected Sam. 'I just kept hold of her head.'

The vet looked up, peering over his glasses at Tipper with new interest.

'Tipper? Aren't you the boy from the city – Pat's nephew? Well, judging by what I've seen today, you could make a career for yourself, if you want one. You did well, d'you know that?'

Tipper cradled Red's head and rubbed behind her ears while the vet put in the stitches. Suddenly he felt fantastically good. No teacher or authority figure of any kind had ever said such a thing to him. He had lived fourteen years without hearing a word of praise, not from anyone except his Ma. He was proud. She'd have been proud too . . .

'Now for Christ's sake,' said the vet as he packed up his bag. 'Will you both go and put some dry clothes on? Or it won't be this foal that might not see the morning.'

It had been only a couple of months after Tipper's Ma died that Uncle Pat dropped another bomb-shell on him.

'I've been talking to a pal of mine. Joe Kerly. He's Head Lad at Thaddeus Doyle's place on the

Curragh. He says to me they'll take you on for your apprenticeship.'

Tipper's mouth fell open. This news had come out of nowhere. The Curragh was a couple of hours' drive from the stud. But it could have been on another continent as far as Tipper was concerned. And he wouldn't know anyone there. The whole prospect frightened him.

'Jesus, Uncle Pat. Why can't I stay on here? I like it here.'

Uncle Pat shook his head lugubriously.

'No way in the world, son. Sorry. Mr Power says we're overstaffed already. And anyway' – he winked conspiratorially – 'Doyle's a top trainer; he's a lot of good horses. And you never know. He might make a jockey out of you. You've a great way with the young horses, I don't mind telling you. I had me doubts to start with but you've done grand.'

4

Retired General Stanislav Shalakov, the soldier-son of peasants, ideally preferred an entourage of real men; men who could be relied on to fall on a live grenade, or shove a bayonet deep into a Chechen belly. So he would not, under normal circumstances, have associated with an opportunist civilian like Nico. In his eyes – well-practiced at the game of assessing human character – the younger man's sunglasses and doorknocker beard failed to conceal manifest weaknesses: the effete *belo-emigrant* background and the ingratiating cupidity. But while Shalakov had uncounted billions of roubles at his disposal, his yacht had only recently embarked on the seaways of western-style opulence. He knew instinctively how a Nico Nikolayev could be useful to him.

Shalakov's power base in the Red Army had been neither a fighting division nor a high-profile piece of window-dressing such as the cosmonaut programme. Unglamorously, but far more profitably, Shalakov had been head of the Catering Corps.

In terms of manpower, the Red Army had been probably the largest organization in the world and Shalakov's position gave him extraordinary hidden leverage. Only the most foolhardy of his fellow generals ever crossed him, and they quickly discovered their mistake. The time would come, on campaign or exercise, when the food supply chain inexplicably broke down. On the Chinese border fifty troops starved to death after their rations failed to come through. In Kandahar food poisoning decimated a battalion. Shalakov had ways of making sure such disasters were not laid at his door; instead they invariably caused the general in the field to be summoned to Moscow and stripped of his rank.

With the coming of Gorbachev, then Yeltsin and Putin, Shalakov eased into a political role. Having ridden out the storms that wrecked the Soviet empire, he began to construct a private conglomerate of his own, bringing to the task the same ruthlessness he'd employed as a soldier. He oversaw the privatization of the army's vast network of ranches and farms, meat-packing plants and fish canneries, orchards and wheat prairies, making sure the pick of them ended up in his personal ownership; and for a fraction of their true worth. The resulting conglomerate's sheer size and strategic importance gave Shalakov behind-the-scenes influence. The Minister of Agriculture was his personal nominee. He dined once a week with the Minister of Finance and the head of the Bank of Moscow. He out-drank Boris Yeltsin and spent holidays at the Black Sea dacha of 'Vovochka' Putin.

Yet increasingly he understood that the state needed Shalakov more than Shalakov needed the state. And so his acquisitive eyes turned abroad, to the hot spots of the world. Shalakov had decided to go international.

Nico found out that it wasn't so easy to get inside Shalakov's camp. But he kept appearing here and there and never missed a chance to pay his respects to the Russian general whenever possible. He sidled up to Shalakov's blackjack table in London. He effected an introduction to a Grand Prix driver in Monte Carlo. But he was struggling to get on the pay roll. Until, a good two years after Nico had sidled up to his table in the Voile Rouge, Shalakov invited him for drinks aboard his yacht, *Rosebud*. Bought during the 2009 financial crash from a hedgefund owner, she was a substantial vessel, with eight staterooms and a crew of thirty. As usual Shalakov made an oblique approach to the subject he wanted to discuss.

'Do you know how many stud farms the Red Army had for horse breeding?'

Nico, who thought cavalry had gone out with the Charge of the Light Brigade, shrugged.

'I didn't know they had any. It's all tanks and humvees now, isn't it?'

Shalakov gave Nico a look of sarcastic pity.

'You don't know the Red Army doctrine of horse warfare. I was taught this as a cadet in Budenyi Cavalry Academy in Moscow. Never mind the mechanized age, cavalry units are still an important independent arm of war and can be deployed in many ways.'

He began counting the ways on his fingers.

'They can be used for reconnaissance, counter-reconnaissance and patrols, but they are essentially raiders. They can attack at speed, silently and with minimum preparation. They can operate at night, cross narrow mountain passes and swim rivers.'

He spat over the side into the silky-smooth water of the marina.

'Horses. We should have made more use of them in Afghanistan.'

'So how many studs were there?'

'At their peak, during the Great Patriotic War, there were forty-seven. Half that number by my own time, and most of those were then sold off by Yeltsin. They were geographically separated right across the Soviet Union, so that we got a spread of animals biologically suited to different kinds of terrain. In the cavalry we did much research into this.'

'I didn't know you were a cavalry man.'

'Not for many years. But I always kept a few horses. And I bought six of the stud farms from the government. The best ones, of course. Now we are creating a new hippodrome in Moscow. One day it will be the greatest centre in the world for racing horses.'

Nico was used to this kind of talk. With Shalakov everything he touched would one day be the greatest, the priciest, the ultimate in grandeur.

'That *would* be something, General,' he agreed.

Shalakov motioned for the steward to refill Nico's champagne flute and followed up by asking, almost casually,

'You know this market well? I mean the race-horse market, here in the west?'

So this was the reason Shalakov had invited Nico today: he had a new project in mind.

'Oh yes,' said Nico blithely. 'I know it inside out.'

He sipped thoughtfully from his glass. It was not strictly true, but since he regularly attended the cream of Europe's race meetings – Deauville, Ascot, the Curragh – he knew people who'd be only too willing to feed him the inside track on classic breeding, bloodstock sales and top trainers.

'And are you contemplating a particularly *large* investment, General?'

'I never do anything by halves. And, as you well know, I deal only in the finest.'

By the time Nico went ashore he had agreed to make enquiries about how Shalakov could acquire and manage a string of the best racehorses in Western Europe.

5

Uncle Pat had been right about Doyle's yard: it was a fair operation, with a staff of fifty or more. But that made it all the harder for Tipper. Now he didn't even have Sam to talk to. He didn't know anyone or anything in this new world. He was back to square one. He didn't even have Red to look forward to every morning. Hardly a day went by when he wasn't bollocked for doing something wrong.

For the first two years he was just one of twenty indentured slaves, sixteen-year-olds kicked out of their beds at four-thirty every morning, seven days a week, riding work, mucking-out, grooming, and feeding. If they weren't required at the races they would get a few hours to themselves in the afternoon; and then it was back to mucking out at evening stables. One afternoon a fortnight was all they got off.

A little of Tipper's riding ability was noted on the gallops, and as time passed he even got a few rides on no-hopers at country race meetings. But he was so withdrawn. The black cloud that had descended on him after his Ma died hadn't entirely lifted. He was painfully unsure of himself and made scant impression. He hated sharing a room with three other boys. He was always having the mickey ripped out of him, and hadn't yet learned how to rip it back. In bed at night he lay under the sheets wishing he could be back at the stud coaxing Red.

Tipper's loneliness was all the more intense because he'd begun thinking about girls. His were hopeless fantasies, alternating between the sexual and the impossibly romantic. None of the girls in the village would ever talk to Tipper, let alone dream of going out with him. He earned a pittance in wages, and for a year he looked like a tramp, not being possessed of a single good garment to wear. He spent the first twelve months saving for just one thing – a cheap suit to go to the races in, or the pub, or maybe even a club. Until then he had only the clobber he worked in, and that stank because, when it rained, the wet muck-sacks he carried across the yard leaked all over him. No girl would let him near, even if he'd had the courage to go up and ask for a date.

Tipper had been slaving at Doyle's for two years when, during the winter off-season, word got around the yard that an interesting new two-year-old filly with a pedigree like royalty was coming to them. She'd had a disastrous start to her career on the oval US dirt-tracks and been picked up cheap in New York by Rupert Robinson, a pal of Doyle's. Robinson, the youngest son of a hereditary English peer, thought of himself as a society playboy. Though he liked a gamble, he usually lost; a trend which his more astute friends thought unlikely to be reversed by this new acquisition.

'She's got the temper of an alley-cat,' said her handler to Doyle when the fractious filly arrived in the yard. 'She doesn't like you anywhere close and she'd scratch your face to ribbons if she had claws.'

Watching from a distance, Tipper said nothing. But at lunchtime, as soon as the yard was quiet, he went to her stable, stood in front of the half-door and whispered her name: not the name chalked on the board by the door, Stella Maris, but his name for her. For Tipper had known her from the moment she'd jinked and propped her way down the ramp of the transporter.

'Red!' he whispered. 'It's me. Remember me?'

The filly's first reaction was to lay her ears flat and try to bite his head. He dodged the attempt and, sliding the bolt open, slipped inside the stable. At once Red turned her back on him and let fly with one of her hind legs. She was anticipating a smack. So that was the trouble, Tipper thought. Some twat had been thrashing her, thinking it would bring her to hand. Naturally, it had had the opposite effect.

Quietly reciting her name over and over, he stooped and lowered himself until he was kneeling.

Slowly, very slowly, he began inching towards Red, uttering calming words in a light singsong. Praying that she wouldn't lash out again. If she did, and caught him on the head, she could kill him. But because he had crouched down he didn't pose a threat to her. By the time he was a couple of yards from her he saw, maybe, a glimmer of recognition in her eyes. He slowly turned away and moved towards the door of the box. The straw behind him rustled. Then he felt the filly's nose gently exploring his back, and he knew it had happened. She'd remembered him.

Five minutes later Tipper was standing at her head, rubbing her ears; for the first time since he'd arrived at Doyle's, he began to feel hope. In fact it was stronger than that. He felt a tinge of excitement.

Tipper was straight onto the phone to Sam at lunchtime.

'Sam. You're not going to believe this. You won't guess who walked into the yard this morning. You won't believe it!'

'Okay I'll go for Lester Piggott. Or maybe Shergar. I know. Lester Piggott riding Shergar.'

'Fock off Sam. It was Red. You remember Red?'

'No. Can't say I do. Some mare we met in the pub?'

'Sam, stop messing with me. Red. You know the filly that we had on the stud. Who cut her leg. She's here at Doyle's. She's called Stella Maris now.'

'No way. That can't be right. She went to America for Christ sake.'

'Well she's back Sam, and she hasn't changed. She's not easy, but by Christ is she a good sort.'

'Please, Mr Kerly,' he said a couple of days later to the Head Lad. 'Let me ride the new filly's work. I know her. I looked after her when she was a foal at Fethard. She was always a bit nervous, like, but we got on famously. Ask my uncle. You seen that scar on her leg? I was there when she got that, see?'

In his anxiety to get through to Kerly he was gabbling. He took a breath and went on more slowly.

'I saved her life, the vet said, with a tourniquet. She's a bit difficult all right, but I can quieten her. I can handle her.'

Stella Maris may have exasperated her American owners, but her genes wore diamond tiaras, and Doyle and her new owner, the Hon. Rupert Robinson, hoped that, by returning to the wide galloping turf tracks of home, and with the correct handling, she might soon be worth her weight in jewellery. So Kerly's eyes widened in disbelief at Tipper's request to take responsibility for this potential turf princess. He fired a gob of spit at the ground and told him straight.

'Give it up, Tipper. Jesus this is a valuable filly. She's got a hell of a pedigree. Now don't be bothering me.'

Kerly soon learned how wrong he was. The

new filly was so unbiddable she wouldn't even walk out into the yard. When a lad went into her stable she'd sulk in the back of it and then lash out at him in self-defence. For a week Tipper looked on in mounting frustration, until he could bear it no longer. One morning, without dwelling on the consequences, he skipped breakfast and went down to the stable block. He let himself into Red's box, hurriedly tacked her up and took her out for a hack.

Half an hour later they came trotting in again under perfect control. Joe Kerly was at the gate waiting. Tipper got the bollocking of his life, but he'd proved the point. Red became his ride every day.

6

Nico began his research in London. England was the cradle of the thoroughbred horse, and English racing retained just the right mixture of glamour, snobbery, chicanery and big money to satisfy a man like Shalakov. He stepped from a cab in Wardour Street and strolled through to Berwick Street market. Pushing his way through the throng of shoppers and market traders, Nico selected a number on his phone and, when it was answered, spoke briefly. It was only a short walk from here to his destination, a large basement club with a thick carpet and a dozen different ways of losing money, ranging from one-arm bandits to roulette and blackjack. Flitting between the tables were leggy hostesses in smart burgundy uniforms. The place was pretty empty bar a few excitable Chinese swarming round a roulette table like bees round a hive. A sallow-faced Arab sat expressionless near the roulette wheel, looking glumly at the table.

This dive was called the Piranha Club.

Nico was greeted at the bar by a figure known to his circle as the Duke. Aged somewhere in his fifties, the Duke looked innocuous enough. He had the slack, tapering body of a taxi driver, with fish-like hands, slightly grey skin and thinning straw coloured hair. A pair of large gold-framed bi-focals lived on the tip of his nose giving him a slightly studious look. But the benign appearance, as Nico knew, was seriously deceptive. Not only did the Duke own the Piranha Club, he was one of the largest private bookmakers in London.

'All right, Nico my son? It's been a while.'

'Delighted to see you again, Duke.'

It was pretty well five years since Nico had first met the Duke. He'd needed to buy some marching powder for a client and had been sent in the Duke's direction.

'Vodka's your tipple isn't it?'

Nico rather wanted a champagne cocktail but that would have upset the Duke's sense of what was proper. Nico was a Russian, and Russians drank vodka. Turning to the barman he ordered a bottle of Uluvka and a shot-glass. The Duke never drank himself, but he liked debilitating others.

'So, to what do we owe the pleasure?' he said, pouring a preliminary shot and watching while Nico obediently drained the glass in one gulp. 'We don't usually see you in the dark days of winter.'

'I'm on a bit of business. Thought you might be able to steer me in the right direction.'

'Anything to oblige an old mate, Nico. Let's go over there, where we can talk.'

Carrying the strangely shaped bottle with him, the Duke led Nico towards a table in a quiet booth.

An hour later Nico stumbled out into a rainy night, his head fuddled and spinning from the vodka. He meandered up to Broadwick Street in the hope of a taxi and stood on the curb shivering and peering up and down the street. One after another, black cabs sluiced past, not one of them with its yellow beacon lit. His hair, and the shoulders of his fair-weather suit, were soaked by the time a taxi pulled up.

The soaking and the cold had the effect of sobering Nico up a little. He concentrated on what the Duke had told him and tried to decipher the notes he'd written on the paper napkin as the cab passed under the street lights.

At the top of the napkin he'd scribbled:

The Partridge – Johnny the Fish.

Under that he'd written:

David Sinclair – bit of a chin – training plenty of winners. Posh.

At the bottom of the napkin was a third name:

Shug Shaunsheys – a few dodgy habits but sharp. Will find the goods.

7

Red was straight away in harmony with Tipper and making good progress, until the day she had to re-acquaint herself with the starting stalls. This is always an ordeal for temperamental animals. Each stall is fitted with two sets of gates. The back gates are shut individually behind the horses as the handlers load them; the ones in front are instantaneously flipped open by the starter, to release an explosion of horseflesh as the race begins. The practice drill should have involved Red merely walking up to, into and through the stalls, with both sets of gates open. It looked like a simple task, but it wasn't for her. Tipper presented her to the stalls and a group of handlers – the same handlers that assist at every course on race day – crowded round her back end to heave her in, while one of them led her by a rope threaded through the bridle. They got her half way in and then she baulked.

'Go gentle, go gentle lads!' pleaded Tipper, perched up on her back.

Like hell they would. The handler at her head, Eamonn, yanked hard, while one of the others gave her a whack on the quarters. She immediately plunged backwards out of the stall, then reared, pulling the rope from Eamonn's hand and almost flipping over backwards. Tipper slithered perilously to the ground beneath her. As he lay there, expecting any moment to be trodden on, he heard the men's curses.

'The dirty cow,' snarled Eamonn. 'Gimme that fuckin' hood.'

Picking himself up, Tipper saw him brandishing the blindfold that would go over Red's eyes, and prevent her from seeing where she was going.

'Leave off that!' Tipper yelled. 'Let me do this. Give us some space, lads.'

When it came to dealing with Red, Tipper could assert himself in a way he would have never have done in any other situation. Momentarily abashed the men shuffled backwards and ducked under the rails that enclosed the loading area. Tipper removed Red's bridle and took a length of leading-rope, which he looped around the horse's neck. He attached this to the end of a ball of string he got out of his pocket. The handlers, leaning on the rails to watch, sniggered.

'If this one gets loose, boy,' called Eamonn, 'you'll be stacking fuckin' shelves at the super-market for the rest of your life.'

Tipper paid no heed. He allowed Red to go back as far away as she liked from the line of stalls.

Then he went into one of them and knelt down. Oblivious to the derisive snorts of his audience, he reeled in the string and, slowly and hesitantly, Red began moving towards him. It was like that time in the barn at Fethard when he'd first won her confidence. A couple of times, as she got to within ten feet of him, she spun away in panic and he had to start all over again. The handlers grew bored with taking the piss. They left the rail and, sitting down in a ring on the turf, got a card school going.

Six hands of brag later, they didn't notice that Red had found the courage to get her nose into the stall, where she was nibbling Tipper's coat. Tipper now turned and carefully slid out of the front of the stall. He sat on his heels ten feet away, with his back to his filly. His eyes remained fixed on a spot down the track, where by the trick of perspective the two white rails seemed to intersect. But all the time his mind was on what Red was doing behind him. At first she did nothing. A long time passed. The laughter and curses of the card players drifted towards them on the wind. Then, infinitesimally at first, Tipper felt the horse's warm breath on the nape of his neck, and the hesitant prod of her velvet nose.

Eamonn looked up from his hand of cards.

'Christ Jesus, will you look at that, lads?' he shouted. 'The kid's only bloody done it. She's walked all the way through by herself.'

The others swung round to look.

'It must be love,' said one of the others.

'Well if it is, that's the only fuckin' pull he'll be making,' Eamonn retorted.

But the second man might almost have been right. Red had done this difficult thing of her own free will, because she trusted Tipper, and she wanted to be with him.

When the time came to try her at last on the race track, Thaddeus Doyle was in a quandary. He wanted to put up his retained stable jockey, his son-in-law Dermot Quigley, who'd been champion jockey five times. Doyle had seen Stella Maris on the gallops, ridden by Tipper, make mincemeat of prized members of his string, and he asked himself what on earth she would do with a real jock on her back. In the event, he never found out. When they tried working Red with Quigley up, she carted him three times round the yard and threw him sprawling to the ground. As he picked himself up in front of Doyle's staff Quigley tried to hide his humiliation with anger.

'That one's not temperamental. She's mental. I'd rather ride a barrel over the Niagara bloody Falls.'

So it had to be Tipper on Stella Maris; no one else could get near her.

8

Shug Shaunsheys, bloodstock agent, was sitting in front of his computer screen, his watery eyes transfixed by what they saw. Every now and then, his long pink and grey tongue slid out to moisten his lips. Shaunsheys always licked his lips when he was surfing the net. He clicked the mouse to bring up a new picture. He lived alone. There was no one else in the flat to disturb him, no one to stop him enjoying himself. The prospect of a long, self gratifying evening stretched pleasantly ahead of him. Until his phone rang.

His ringtone was *The Teddy Bears' Picnic*. With a muttered curse he groped for it, pressing the receive button and interrupting the tone as it got to 'in for a big surprise'.

'Shaunsheys,' he grunted.

'Shug. It's Johnny the Fish. You busy?'

'No. Just, erm, watching telly.'

'Then I suggest you get your arse out to the

Partridge double-quick. There's someone important been asking for you.'

Shaunsheys was still distracted by the screen in front of him.

'Oh yeah?' he said. 'What about?'

'Horses, you mug. What else would it be about?' Johnny said.

Shaunsheys clicked the mouse to advance the online slideshow. His eyes widened, then blinked. *Jesus Christ!*

'Oh, look Johnny,' he mumbled as he shifted on his chair. 'I don't think tonight –'

'Don't be a prat, Shug. There's a Russian punter in town. So if you know what's good for you get your arse over here *now*.'

The Partridge was a large pub and restaurant that stood some two miles outside Newmarket on the London road. Johnny the Fish, its licensee, was the town's premier racing information exchange. In his time he'd had a spell in the army, and another managing a stud farm. Now he was a genial Mine Host to the trainers, jockeys, and work riders of Newmarket, matching them drink for drink and in the process gathering the kind of intelligence certain people will pay good money for. The Partridge had the look and feel of a club rather than a pub. Deep leather chairs huddled round the fire in the main bar. The walls were festooned with pictures of local heroes; human and equine. And fresh lilies stood proudly in a vase on the end of the bar.

When Shaunsheys walked into the bar fifteen minutes after the phone call, Shelley was the only sign of life, aimlessly polishing glasses. Shelley was sexy and she knew it. She was wearing a tight white T-shirt that didn't quite reach her waist. It accentuated her breasts which were the perfect size for going without a bra. Shelley was born and bred in Newmarket. By the time she was sixteen she'd been around a bit in more senses than one. But she was of no interest to Shaunsheys.

'Johnny around?' he asked abruptly.

'Probably,' she replied in as unhelpful a tone as she could muster. Shelley expected men to have a good look at her. She liked that. Shaunsheys didn't even make eye contact.

'Well where is he?' Shaunsheys asked bluntly.

'Office probably,' Shelley countered.

'Well can you tell him I'm here then?'

Shelley tottered off to find the Fish.

Shaunsheys was on the whole a loner who had no proper friends. He'd been sniffing around the bloodstock world for most of his adult life, and was now formally operating as a freelance blood-stock agent, matching buyers with sellers and vice versa. But he lacked the social skills that would ensure real success in this role, and much of the time he was forced to make ends meet as a stooge in the sales ring. Shaunsheys would help bid up lots on occasions when there would be only one prospective buyer and, consequently, the danger of a low sale price. In return for a substantial 'drink' he would take up a prominent position at the side of the ring and call entirely fictional bids, if necessary against an accomplice posted elsewhere. They would only go up to an agreed level and then drop out, leaving the genuine bidder paying an artificially inflated price.

The trick was to know how far you could push it, and that meant knowing the market, and the target buyers. Shaunsheys was a natural spy. He spent a good deal of time shadowing prospective bidders around the sales grounds, overhearing their comments and counting how often they came back 'for just one more look' at a yearling.

Technically illegal though all this was, the bloodstock world pretty much turned a blind eye. Shaunsheys was, after all, an agent; his fake bids could plausibly be passed off as those of a confidential client; and it all added up to more currency trickling onto racing's cash carousel.

Johnny the Fish appeared behind the bar, smart in brass-buttoned blazer and yellow bow tie, with matching silk handkerchief overflowing his breast pocket.

'Glad you could make it, Shug,' he said rather condescendingly.

Shaunsheys was not his type but the Fish nevertheless had a feeling, however reluctantly, that they were going to be confederates; that they would be playing on the same team with this one. He picked up a glass and put it to the whisky optic.

'So what's this all about, Johnny?' asked

Shaunsheys plaintively. 'I was just putting my feet up for a quiet night in.'

In a swift single movement, Johnny the Fish drained his glass and applied it to the optic again. Then he turned back to Shaunsheys.

'Come through to the office. You never know who's going to walk in to this place.'

Shaunsheys picked up his pint and followed the landlord to a small untidy room dominated by a big knee-hole desk, whose surface was littered with unpaid bills, files and form books. Johnny the Fish sat down in his revolving leather-covered chair and beckoned to Shaunsheys to sit opposite.

'It's like this, Shug,' he began. 'I had a call from our old friend the Duke.'

Shug fingered his pint glass.

'I hope you haven't got me out here to meet him.'

'No. I told you. There's a Russian guy that wants to meet you. He's been sent our way by the Duke. He's called Nico. He's the side kick of some Russian oligarch.'

'And?'

'They want to buy some horses. The Duke has put you in.'

Shaunsheys took a considered pull on his pint.

'What sort of oligarch? Roman Abramovich?' Shug asked patronizingly.

'Look are you interested, or not?' Johnny was getting the hump with Shaunsheys' abruptness.

'*Obviously* I'm interested. But how did my name

come up in the first place? I mean, it's been a while since I had anything to do with the Duke; not since he froze my account, the bastard.'

'He's probably hoping you'll make enough out of this to pay him.'

'So how will I do that, exactly?'

Johnny the Fish bent forward confidentially.

'This guy wants to place a couple of good horses with a Newmarket trainer, but that's just to test the water. He's got more long-term plans. You mentioned Abramovich. Nico – the side kick – he reckons this guy wants to be the *next* Abramovich, but in racing instead of football. And if that's right, I don't have to tell you he'll be thinking very big. Big string. Big breeding operation. Big brown envelopes. They've already picked a trainer – David Sinclair – but they want an agent.'

Shaunsheys was still puzzled.

'Okay, I'm with you so far. But it'll be Sinclair who'll buy him his horses, or produce a couple from his yard that he hasn't sold on. He won't particularly want to work with me.'

'No, you're getting me wrong, Shug. Your role's nothing to do with Sinclair. The thing is, they also want a top-class brood mare. That's where you come in . . .' Johnny stopped in mid-sentence as the door swung open.

'There's a bloke in the bar, Johnny. Wants to see you,' Shelley mumbled in her monotone voice. Shelley liked the Fish but she wasn't a bloody messenger girl.

'That, if I'm not mistaken, will be Nico. One thing Shug. You'll need to look after me in this deal.'

'Yeah. Of course,' Shaunsheys concurred with a wave of his hand. In your fucking dreams, he thought, as they walked back to the bar.

9

During the preliminaries of the Irish Oaks at the Curragh, Tipper, who'd only just turned eighteen, had wondered if things could get any better if he lived to be a hundred. The tension at the start was almost suffocating. But, as Stella Maris jig-jogged around with the other horses, he felt elated rather than nervous. This was the most important fillies' classic in the Irish flat racing calendar, and he was riding the most beautiful horse in the field.

She was not just a beauty; she was arguably the best too. The Hon. Rupert Robinson had hardly been able to believe his luck watching her skip home in her two preparatory contests. If she could now land a classic, he could sell her to stud and make back ten times what he'd put in.

It had all seemed a long-shot when she'd arrived at Doyle's place. The word had got around that she'd needed tranquillizers just to load her into the horse-transporter. She kicked behind, she bit in front and bolted whenever she could. So what made the difference? At the Oaks Doyle was asked that very question by RTE.

'It's a great team I've got,' he told the television presenter smugly. 'Everyone's played their part to get her here, you know?'

He was lying, of course: the real difference was Tipper O'Reilly.

And as Stella Maris became a hot topic in racing circles in the weeks leading up to the Oaks, Tipper had been showing what a useful jockey he was all round; able to judge pace, keep a horse balanced in a packed field and time a run to the line. As a result he'd begun to get rides from other stables. Some were even on winners and, before long, he found himself leading the field for the apprentice jockeys' championship. But claimers – jockeys so inexperienced they get a weight advantage of seven, five or three pounds – are hardly ever entrusted with runners in Group One races. So the question round every bar table on the course was, could this downy-cheeked boy of eighteen beat the grizzled and hardened men, and take a classic?

As the horses began to go forward and into the starting stalls, Tipper hung back, as he quickly ran through in his mind what Doyle had told him to do.

'Don't let them box you in. Try and sit handy and make your move at the last moment. Be the last one to play your hand. And, whatever you do, don't sit too far back.'

Doyle knew that, overall, he had the best horse in the race. But she was a galloping type, who'd done all her winning over a mile and a half, and there were some useful mile and a quarter horses in this contest who could box Red in and then outpace her to the line if they got the chance.

'They've got a pacemaker in,' he warned. 'He might try and dictate a false pace. Don't fall for it. You can make the running if you absolutely have to, if they go no pace at all. And don't get boxed in on the inside. Go wide on the last bend. And more important than anything, for Christ's sake *don't give her too much to do*.'

Watching them load horse after horse into the stalls, Tipper remembered the day on the Curragh when the handlers played brag while he'd coaxed Red through her first lesson in stalls entry. After that there had always been a residue of tension at the starting gate, but he'd never failed to get her in yet. Still, he knew better than take it for granted. Horses are specialists in making a fool of you.

Dancing a little on her toes Red was the last to approach the line of stalls. Tipper sensed her hesitancy and clicked his tongue as a reminder that he was there. She seemed to make up her mind then, walking sweetly forwards and in. Tipper heard the rear gates close with a click behind her tail. At least, that's what he thought.

Aside from normal riding tactics, neither Doyle nor Tipper were on the look out for any foul play.

But stalls handlers are far from the best paid people in racing and the opposition had not been averse to laying out a few euros in the hope of lowering Red's colours. Eamonn – the brag player who'd once predicted Tipper's future as a shelf-stacker – was the handler charged with shutting the gate behind Red. The previous evening, in the pub, he hadn't needed much persuasion that Tipper was a cocky little shit who thought he could make eejits out of the professionals. So, as Eamonn eased Red's gates shut, he made sure her tail was well and truly wedged between them. It was an easy mistake to make – and well paid enough to get him and Mrs Eamonn a flight to Lanzarote. The starter had no chance of seeing what had been done and nor had Tipper. When you go in last, there's no time to be looking behind you.

Tipper was relaxed as he waited for the stalls to burst open. He was sure of Red now, sure she would be delighted as always to get the hell out of the stalls as quick as she could. 'Jockeys!' the starter roared, indicating that he was about to let them go. And then, almost immediately, came the crash as the gates sprang open. Red lunged towards freedom but immediately she felt the stinging tug on her tail and instinct made her plant. Tipper, leaning into her neck to anticipate their forward momentum, almost went over Red's ears as she threw back her head and smacked him in the face. Blood from his nose splattered onto the goggles. Christ! Tipper kicked Red's flanks as her instinct to bolt from pain drove her forward again. This time the tail freed itself and they were out.

But it was too late. Red was ten lengths adrift of the field and Tipper's head was still ringing from the blow to his nose. At the same time some of the words uttered by Doyle in the paddock reverberated through his mind. 'Lay handy. Don't give her too much to do.' That plan had just gone for a Burton.

In the grandstand, Red's owner lowered his binoculars and turned to the trainer beside him.

'What the fuck happened there?' wailed Robinson.

'Fucked if I know,' said Doyle in despair. 'She's never dwelt before. And now the race is as good as over, for Christ's sake.'

If the field had gone no gallop, Tipper could have made up his ground painlessly enough and the damage might have been minimal. But the pacemaker, in the colours of the man who had given Eamonn his summer holidays, went off like it had a chilli-pepper up its arse. All Tipper could see were rumps, human and equine, at some distance in front of him. Don't panic, he told himself as he used his gloves to wipe the blood from his goggles. Don't try to make up the ground too soon, you'll blow her engine.

The field streamed away down the back straight as Tipper frantically formulated a plan to rescue the situation. It would have to be the reverse of the one he had agreed with Doyle. Instead of sitting handy and swinging wide off the bend, as if using it like a sling shot, he would have to hug the rail, saving every inch of ground as he gradually caught them up, then gamble on holding his position round the long bend into the straight. If at that stage any of the horses running the rail in front of him started going back through the field he would be sunk. But it was probably his only chance.

Up ahead the ferocious pace was stringing the field out while Tipper, riding as patiently as he knew how, let Red's strong, easy stride inch her back into contention. He was still four lengths adrift of the tail enders when he spotted the elbows on one of the jockey's flailing. The horse had blown up and, despite his efforts, there was nothing his rider could do. Luckily there was room to ease Red to his outside and glide past him, before angling back to the rail. That's the only horse I can go outside of, Tipper told himself.

On the bend his luck held and Red had enough gears to thread through a narrowing gap on the inside of another two struggling horses. The jockeys shouted some uncomplimentary remarks at him for sneaking up their inside, but he was already past them before they could close the gap. With the straight approaching Red was still fifteen lengths off the leaders, but she was moving well, devouring the ground. Then, as he'd known he might, Tipper found himself closing on some more closely-packed traffic. The inside route was blocked by two runners having a fruitless battle with each other. Should he go wide and round them? No. Sit and suffer and try and get up their inner in the straight. Tipper tightened his reins and steadied Red.

Doyle, who had begun to hope again, was plunged back into renewed despair. 'What the fuck's he doing?' he yelled. 'He's taken a pull.'

Tipper wasn't enjoying himself but he kept his head: be calm, don't panic. As the two beaten horses battled into the straight they did what Tipper had gambled on. Tiring and losing their balance, they rolled wide, so that Tipper was able to grab hold of Red, make sure she was balanced and then throw her into the gap along the rail. She seemed to punch her way through, but there were still twelve lengths to make up.

'She's got the break,' Robinson shouted.

'Too late,' Doyle muttered, putting his binoculars down to stare blankly out at the track. He'd thrown the towel in; but Red hadn't. Tipper gave her a slap down the neck and bellowed at her. As if needing to be told, she dropped her head, lengthened her stride and passed three more horses. Ahead of them, a furlong from home, there were still two runners going like hell side by side, and four lengths for Red to make up. Tipper could see the leading jockeys' whips flailing, and heard the crack as they connected. He was rapidly gaining on them, though it couldn't be said they were stopping. He looked for a gap on the rail, but there was only half of one. Tipper knew there was no time to pull wide. He'd have to go for the diminutive gap.

The post was fifty yards ahead, and Tipper had no more than three seconds to play with. Red was all but biting the quarters of the front two when, suddenly, the gap between one of them and the rail widened a fraction. Red seemed to lengthen her neck as well as her stride as she dived through it. All three horses crossed the line together. Tipper didn't know if he'd got up. A length after the line Red was clearly in front, but actually *on* the line? It would be decided on the nod of a head.

'I think we got there!' Robinson shrieked, jumping up and down in frantic ecstasy.

'Did we fuck,' Doyle growled. 'How in Christ's name he lost that I'll never know.'

'No, no,' insisted the owner, 'I think O'Reilly might have got her up.'

But Doyle was cursing through gritted teeth.

'The bollocks! The little shite! I'll cut the tripes out of him when I see him.'

Tipper pulled Red up. They were both exhausted. His breath was heaving, and Red's nostrils were working like bellows to suck in the air. She had pushed herself a long way through the pain barrier in the last furlong, and she was still hurting.

The race result was imminent and Tipper knew he was either a hero or a villain. No one would be interested in excuses. As far as the grandstand jockeys would be concerned he'd either ridden a tactical race of genius, or he'd blown it. And not many promising young careers would come back after blowing an Irish Oaks. But his fate was now in the hands – or the eye – of the judge, who was studying a freeze-frame of the finish. Coming down from his adrenaline rush, Tipper could not even recall the number they were carrying. As Doyle's lad dodged out of the crowd and took Red's head, Tipper looked back at the cloth under his saddle. Number six.

'Please, God, let him call out six,' Tipper prayed.

Unlike the early days of photo-finishes there was no need now to develop a print. Video technology makes it possible to decide close results almost instantaneously, except in the very hardest cases. And this was one of those, because as Tipper walked Red off the track and entered the walkway that led to the winner's enclosure, there had still been no announcement.

The delay was long enough for a betting market to develop on the result. From somewhere in the tightly packed crowd he heard a bookie shouting odds, but missed which of the three finishers he was taking money on. Meanwhile the lad was chattering away at him, convinced they'd won. Tipper was too exhausted to answer. Looking ahead he saw a TV reporter with a microphone trying to interview the rider of one of the others in the finish. He saw the jockey's head shake: did that mean he'd lost, or he didn't know?

Tipper saw Sam leaning against the rail as he was led towards the unsaddling enclosure. Tipper looked at Sam's expression to get some re-assurance. But there was none there. Sam's face was blank. He shrugged both shoulders and held both hands out flat in front of him.

As they reached the winner's enclosure, with its berths reserved for the first, second and third horses, there had still been no announcement. The place was surrounded by an unnatural hush. Usually there would have been a roar from the crowd, but everyone seemed to be collectively holding their breath. In the enclosure none of the three jockeys knew where to go and, unwilling to tempt fate, they hung back. They slipped from their saddles and began attending to the girth straps. Tipper had just lifted the saddled from Red's back when the PA system briefly crackled. He froze.

'The result of the photograph,' the announcer said, before pausing dramatically.

Tipper looked round. There was Kerly, the Head Lad, and Doyle. Both looked grim. But Red's owner, with a daft artificial smile on his face, was giving Tipper the thumbs-up. He waited. The PA crackled again.

'First, number six . . .'

The order in which the others had finished was drowned in the gigantic roar of the crowd. They didn't care who was second, and nor did Tipper.

10

Nico had a few drinks with Johnny the Fish after Shaunsheys left the Partridge, and then accepted Johnny's offer of a bed. The rooms in the Partridge weren't up to Nico's normal haunts, but he decided a little time spent in reconnaissance might not be wasted.

He was up with the lark and in the public car park at the top of Warren Hill gallops before any of the horses were out on the Heath. When Sinclair's horses came along, they weren't difficult to spot with DS initialled on the horses' blankets. Nico was impressed. Sinclair's string looked the business. It was easy to pick Sinclair out on his hack, slightly detached from his horses, barking instructions at lads who didn't say much back. Sinclair had a slightly fat face, biggish nose and dark hair sticking out of the back of his riding helmet. He looked generally overweight and his facial complexion was just a little redder than it should have been.

Nico picked out a moody looking woman at the back of the string who definitely wasn't a stable lass. Mrs Sinclair, he thought to himself. Her jodhpurs looked like they'd been spray-painted onto her large thighs.

He then followed Sinclair's string back to his yard at a safe distance. There was a convenient wood along one side of it to give him some cover. Nico peered through the hedge into the yard. Again, he was impressed and re-assured. If Shalakov ever comes to look round this place, he'll be happy, he thought to himself. Shalakov's military brain will like the order of this place. The lawns had stripes in them, the stable doors were white and gleaming, and there were men everywhere with brooms sweeping up. Nico was happy as he trudged back up the hill to his car.

Nico spent the rest of the day in Cambridge. He was half interested in familiarizing himself with the place, in case he ever had to pass himself off as a graduate; and he was curious to see what a gram of coke was being knocked out for there. It was as good a way as any to kill time before he formally met Sinclair in the Partridge.

Shelley was in her normal spot when Nico got back to the pub. Nico had a furtive look around to check there were no prying ears.

'I think we have a friend in common,' he said to Shelley smoothly.

'Really?'

'The Duke told me to pass on his compliments. Said you'd be sure to look after me.' He smiled leaving the innuendo hanging in the air.

'Did he just,' Shelley replied frostily.

Before the conversation went any further Sinclair came breezing in. Shelley couldn't stand him. As far as she was concerned he was an arrogant prick. And she hated the way he mentally undressed her. But as he and Nico slid into the armchairs by the fire she had food for thought.

'So, I understand you have a man,' Sinclair smiled, cutting straight to the chase. 'And he wants some horses.'

'Yes,' said Nico smoothly. 'That's the situation. And I am told you may be the person to handle it.'

'Absolutely. But I understand you're also thinking of appointing Shug Shaunsheys? The point is, you really don't need him. I'll get you the horses myself. In fact I've already got one in the yard, a beautifully bred colt, who –'

Nico held up his hand.

'Let me stop you there. The gentleman I act for, Mr Stanislav Shalakov, has many interests. One of them is racing, another is breeding. He has a passion for this. We are thinking that Mr Shaunsheys will help on the breeding side, while a reputable trainer such as yourself will look after the racing. There should be no conflict of interest. No need for you to work together at all.'

'Hmm. I see. But are you sure about Shaunsheys? He's a bit of a dubious character.'

'I'm sure you won't mind if we make up our own minds about that, Mr Sinclair.'

'All right. Suit yourself. As long as I don't have anything to do with him.'

'You won't.'

Nico mentally adjusted. He had thought these people would work amicably together. Obviously he was wrong. But it wasn't necessarily a bad thing, as far as he was concerned. At least they wouldn't be conspiring together.

'Since you have been so frank with me,' he went on, 'there's one thing just between ourselves. I'm doing you a bit of a favour putting you in touch with my client, and I have no doubt you'll be wanting to gratify me in return. You could, well . . . I suppose you make sure I am informed when your horses win and lose – that is, *before* their races are run.'

Sinclair raised his glass.

'Of course. Just between ourselves. If we do come to an agreement, that will present no problem at all. Now, what will you eat?'

Sinclair had a rather smug, triumphal air about him as he raised his arm towards Shelley.

An hour and a half and three bottles of Gevry Chambertin later, Sinclair was driving back to the yard well satisfied with the evening's work. He'd told Nico a string of outrageous lies: the Sinclair yard was 'solid as a rock', 'business was booming', he and Alison were 'a creative partnership focused on success', Shalakov's prospects of quick success on the track, with the two horses Sinclair would initially provide for him, were 'massive'.

'You see, Nico, it's a family business, in the best sense of the word. We're a great team, Alison and I. My yard is all about team spirit.'

Sinclair had always been able to talk the talk, and Nico seemed to swallow these fantasies like a trout attacking a mayfly. Yet the reality of Sinclair's situation was a little different. 'My' yard was not his but, by the grace and money of her father, entirely Alison's. Seven years ago, not trusting his new son-in-law for a moment, Sir Godfrey had drawn up and made Sinclair sign a pre-nuptial agreement whereby, if he and Alison ever broke up, he would walk away with nothing. Whatever the old boy had originally intended, the pre-nup had done more to preserve their relationship than a year of counselling. It kept David and Alison in a marriage that otherwise had all the stickability of wet cardboard. They almost never had sex, there were no children, they were both flagrantly unfaithful, and when they got drunk they fought like cats in a sack.

When he got home he found Alison in the kitchen, rubber-gloved and gutting a pheasant. She often did this sort of thing late at night. He thought it put her in the mood for bed.

'Where the hell have you been?' she demanded as he came swaying in. The worktop in front of her was covered in feathers and she was now sawing the plucked carcase open with a heavy butcher's knife. 'I've had to spend all night answering the phone to sodding owners.'

She pointed with the knife.

'*Your* job, David.'

'Matter of fact I've been at the Partridge with a prospective new one – or at least his representative.'

The last word came out as 'repssntive'. Alison repeated it.

'His "repssntive"? You're pissed.'

'That's as maybe. But I think I've landed him. This could be the big one, I'm telling you.'

Alison put down the knife and used her fingers to scoop out the intestines onto some sheets of old newspaper. She'd heard her husband talk like this before.

'Oh yes? Hope it turns out better than that crappy boy band you had such high hopes of, until they split up three weeks after you bought them a horse. Not to mention – who was it you found before that? Oh yes, the Luton car dealer. Last known address Wormwood Scrubs.'

'This is different, Alison. This guy wants two horses, but that's just for starters. He's a rich Russian, for Christ's sake.'

She emitted a scoffing laugh.

'Oh yeah? He'd better be. Because I'll tell you something, I'm not paying your debts any more.'

With a certain unnerving relish Alison picked up a pair of butcher's jointing clippers and cracked off the bird's legs.

11

Tipper was flying after the Irish Oaks. He persuaded Sam to stay up for the night and they got properly lashed up. But his joy was cruelly cut short the next morning as he made his befuddled way into the yard.

'That filly's knackered,' Dermot Quigley sneered as Tipper approached her stable. 'Near fore tendon. She won't race again. Think you gave her enough to do yesterday?'

Tipper wanted to smack his head off, but he just ignored the chippy little bastard and pushed past him into Red's stable. Her front legs were bandaged up so there was nothing to see. But Tipper realized she was in pain when she turned towards him. Tipper felt sick. He knew there and then that Quigley was right and her career was over. He felt gutted. His stomach tightened up like it had when Mr Power had told him about his Ma. Like something was being ripped out of him. As soon as he was on his own he rang Sam.

'Jesus Sam, you won't believe it. The filly's got a leg. Done her tendon. It's my fault. I was too hard on her yesterday,' Tipper whispered into the phone.

'Don't be ridiculous. A race is a race. You have to ask for everything. Okay it's a fucker. But you won an Oaks on her and no-one can ever take that away from you. Shit happens Tipper, but that filly has made you.'

Thaddeus Doyle barely congratulated Tipper after the race. The only remark he passed was something like 'you got out of jail there'. The injury was no fault of his and Doyle knew that. But Quigley took the opportunity to poison Tipper's pill. He really hated Tipper. It had begun when Red dumped Quigley on the ground. Now Quigley made it his mission to make sure that, champion apprentice or not, there would be no more Group race appearances for this boy, who dared to succeed where he had failed. Tipper would in future be legged-up on nothing but also-rans.

'Let me give you the lowdown on that little shite,' Quigley told Doyle. 'You can't trust him. None of the lads like him. He grew up in a Dublin slum and, from what I hear, he got himself a criminal record as long as the River Shannon. It wouldn't surprise me now if he's off with the bookies all the time getting backhanders. Come to think of it, I've a notion that late jump-off in the Oaks was him trying to throw the race, only the horse was too good on the day to be stopped. And there's another thing.' Quigley held up his finger to emphasize a clinching argument. 'The little runt can't hold his drink.'

None of these facts were true, except the last. But Doyle didn't want to get on the wrong side of Quigley – or, more to the point, of his daughter Mrs Quigley – so he silently restricted Tipper to rides at third-rate meetings till the end of the season. Irish racing has its glittering prizes, but a lot of it is small-time. Tipper still got some winners – and he still emerged top apprentice on his tally of overall victories in the season. But, without the glamour of Red to console him, kicking a series of low-rated scrubbers round Listowel or Kilbeggan started to get him down.

Red's injury had not been life threatening and after a couple of weeks Tipper had learnt that she was to be shipped to England to get ready for a career at stud. When it came to getting her up the loading ramp onto the lorry, Red was having none of it. Tipper had wanted to make himself scarce. Having not had the chance to say good-bye to the only other person in the world he'd ever loved, he now didn't want to say good-bye to Red. Well, not in front of a load of impatient lads. But without his re-assurance she was going nowhere. So he had to lend a hand.

'Come on littlun,' he whispered into her ear. 'Don't be messing me about. You'll be grand where you're going.' He was lying. He feared for her wherever she went. Because he was the only person she trusted. And now he had to mislead her. There was nothing else he could do.

It should have helped that, by the standards of the Dublin estate where he'd grown up, he had a few euros in his pocket. After the Oaks he'd moved out of the stable lads' hostel and bought himself a complete new wardrobe of clothes; and the flashiest Harley Davidson motorbike the Curragh had ever seen. He even found a girl in town who'd joyfully ride pillion. But in spite of that the black cloud that had lifted thanks to Red now descended on him again. He suddenly felt like he was going to be a one hit wonder. He couldn't see anything good on the horizon.

One night after evening stables he parked his bike inside the gate of his digs, behind a hedge where no-one could see it from the road. As he took his helmet off a voice out of the darkness frightened the hell out of him.

'Well, little brother, you've done brilliant for yourself, so you have! Look at that bike.'

The voice was unmistakable.

'Liam?'

A passing set of headlights lit up the shadows and, leaning laconically against the wall, the figure of a young man was swept by light.

'Jesus, Liam! Is it you?'

'It sure is little brother.'

'Jesus. Last I heard, you was in the Mountjoy.'

Liam stepped forward into the streetlight, dressed in a shiny old suit, carrying a full supermarket bag.

'Long time no see little brother. So life's treating you well. Quite a little star I hear you are.'

Tipper felt unrelaxed. There was a hard, nasty edge to his brother's voice. Just like there'd always been. He wasn't congratulating him. He was accusing him.

'Well it's not a bed of roses Liam. I can tell you that. In fact I've got a few problems . . .'

'Yeah. Well haven't we all. Enough of you. I need to borrow that bike. Just for a few days, like.'

'Jesus Liam. Well. Well I need it right now. I . . .'

'Look little brother, I'm not going to go down on my fockin knees okay. You'll get it back. You always were bloody spoilt.' Liam walked towards Tipper and put his hand out flat. He glared at Tipper in the street light with all the malice of a sworn enemy.

Tipper thought about it. His mind took him back to his childhood. To all of the belts that he'd had from Liam. None of them had ever injured him physically but they'd lodged in his mind. He didn't hate Liam. He just wanted nothing to do with him. He thought about legging it down the street. He'd out run his brother anytime. He thought about having a swing at him. But there wasn't an ounce of his body that wanted to do either. So he just gave Liam the keys.

'Cheers little brother. Like I said. You'll get it back.'

Tipper knew he wouldn't. He didn't bother to say a word. He just turned his back and fished his door keys out of his pocket.

'Something a bit interesting,' Sinclair suggested to his wife one evening at about the same time. 'Nico's phoned to ask me about Tipper O'Reilly.'

'O'Reilly?'

'Yes. He asked if he could ride for us next season. Says he saw O'Reilly win the Irish Oaks on Stella Maris and his man would like the kid riding his horses. Thinks he's the most promising young rider in Ireland.'

Alison snorted.

'God, they've not been in the game five minutes and they're already trying to tell us who to put on their horses.'

Taking a cheroot from a tin in her pocket, she lit up.

'Anyway how would you tempt O'Reilly to come over here? He's with Thady Doyle. Why should he come and work for a pillock like you?'

'May I remind you, last time I looked, we were in the top ten flat yards in England? And actually O'Reilly could be the answer to one of our problems. We need a really good lightweight rider, and there doesn't seem much doubt he's useful in the saddle. He'll be heading for a dead end at Doyle's. Dermot Quigley will see to that, I've heard. What d'you think – should I give him a call? Someone else will grab him sooner rather than later.'

Sinclair hated asking her but he knew that it gave her a sense of power. Alison considered the suggestion as she took a deep drag of smoke. She'd seen Tipper O'Reilly in the flesh, on the day he'd ridden Stella Maris at the Curragh. He was a pretty lad all right, fresh-faced, pale skin, just the choir-boy type that she liked best.

'Yes,' she said judiciously. 'Yes, all right, why not? Let's get Tipper O'Reilly over to ride for us.'

She took another satisfying drag and exhaled slowly. She loved reminding her pathetically weak husband that she was in control.

Nico had been bullshitting of course. He hadn't seen the Irish Oaks. He'd never even heard of Tipper O'Reilly until the Duke had rung him and 'strongly advised' him to get O'Reilly over to ride for them.

'Don't worry Nico,' the Duke had re-assured him. 'We'll keep an eye on him for you when he comes over.'

Tipper faced a gloomy end to the flat-racing season. It felt like it was set to be a bloody long, wet winter. His black cloud of depression had intensi-fied as rapidly as his pillion girl had vanished when there was no bike to ride. Then, out of the blue he got a phone call. He didn't know what to make of it; but he knew Sam would.

'I'd a phone call from a feller in Newmarket

in England. Says he'll give me a job riding for him.'

'Sounds great. Who is it?'

'David Sinclair.'

Sam whistled.

'Jeeze, that might not be bad. Big stable. You'd get some awesome rides. What did you say?'

'Said I don't know. Said I need to think about it. But he wants an answer in a couple of days maximum.'

'I'd have bloody jumped at it already.'

'See, I want to go right enough. But I'm pissing myself about being in England. I won't know a bloody soul there.'

Sam phoned Tipper back the next morning.

'What have you done about England, boy?'

'Nothing. I'm still thinking.'

'Well me Da says he'll stand me the fare to go with you; he thinks I've got the experience and I'll easily walk into a stud job over there. So what do you say? Will we go together and try our luck with the Newmarket girls?'

'Are you sure?'

'Sure I'm sure. I'll miss the hurling. But my knee's playing up so I'm probably bollocksed there anyway.'

Sam's Da had seen a change in his son. He could see there were going to be some wild oats strewn about. And he didn't want them seeding in his neighbourhood. So he'd been only too happy to get him across the water.

Tipper did no more thinking. What did he have to lose?

'You're on,' he said.

Newmarket is a lonely, wind-swept place to the shy newcomer. Tipper had been right to have had concerns.

Settling in mid-November into a two room flat off the High Street, he and his cousin looked around for other lads to meet and talk to. In the past a young Irishman would have found that half the population of the town was from back home. Not any more. Sinclair's yard, like most big racing stables, was a Babel of east European and Latin American tongues. They were full of Croats and Cubans, Czechs and Chileans, Ukrainians, Bolivians, Poles and Paraguayans. They were good horsemen, but not such good linguists. The English language was being pushed into third place behind Spanish and the favourite second language of eastern Europe, Russian.

At least there was Tipper's immediate boss, Sinclair's Head Lad Jim Delaney. Delaney was originally from County Donegal and a horseman of the old school. They could talk hurling and football and always, of course, horses. Delaney would sometimes have a pint of stout with Tipper and Sam at the Waggon and Horses or the Golden Lion in the evening. He took an avuncular interest in their well-being, and warned them about any moral pitfalls they might encounter.

'Let me give you two a bit of advice, lads. Keep

your lip buttoned about yard business. This here is a terrible town for gambling. Bookies have their spies everywhere, touts and scouts are always watching and listening. Never get too close to a bookie, or any chancer that might be playing the internet betting exchanges. They'll always be screwing you for information.'

'We're more interested in the girls, Mr Delaney,' put in Sam. 'Where can we meet some?'

'How would I know that? Amn't I a married man? But there's clubs for the likes of you single young fellers. I don't mind what you do with the birds, anyway. But keep out of the way of people who want information. They're vultures.'

Sam had landed a job on a stud outside town, owned by an Irish billionaire called Dermot O'Callaghan. O'Callaghan had made his money developing software that translated text and email messages into any language in the world. He'd invested heavily in bloodstock and developed an impressive stud near Newmarket, which was still the headquarters of the European bloodstock industry.

Sam was built for man-handling stroppy foals and difficult, reluctant mares rather than riding racehorses, and his job on the stud put him one step from the actual training of winners and losers. Tipper, though, was plumb in the path of temptation. What Delaney, Sam and Tipper didn't know was that one of the vultures had engineered Tipper's path to Newmarket in the first place: the Duke.

12

Newmarket is a town controlled by numerous cabals and factions, difficult to break into unless you know the keys and codes of the place. The biggest and most powerful of them is the Jockey Club.Their building dominates the upper end of the High Street. This is not the preserve of jockeys, but of rich and privileged racehorse owners. However, jockeys are to be found at many of the other, lower-order groups, from the freemasons and the golf club down to the small drinking and gambling circles, that meet more or less informally in the pubs and clubs of the town. Although Tipper didn't know it, it wouldn't be long before he was coerced into one of them.

Sam had suggested meeting for a pint after morning stables, at a roadside pub near O'Callaghan's stud.

'It's a nice place,' he'd said. 'Landlord's called Johnny the Fish. He's great craic. They do posh food at one end, but you can get chips in the bar.'

Sam had not yet arrived when Tipper walked in. He went straight up to the counter.

In her tight, white T-shirt, as usual, Shelley was polishing glasses.

'How you doing?' Tipper asked quietly without making eye contact.

'Not bad,' she smiled, alerted by his Irish accent. 'You new around here?'

'Yeah. I've just come over with my cousin Sam. Working for David Sinclair, like.'

Shelley gave Tipper her biggest smile. He was cute. Very cute. This wasn't going to be a hardship at all. When the Duke had told her she had to do 'whatever it takes' to get the new Irish jockey into the Covey Club she was expecting the worst. She fixed Tipper with her green eyes.

'It'll be nice to have a new guy around. God the men in this place are such tossers.'

'Is that right?' Tipper asked still trying to avoid eye contact. This bird wasn't his type at all. He was mighty relieved to see Sam coming through the door.

'Hey. How you doing, jockey?' Sam laughed. Then he saw Shelley. Now she *was* his type. Tipper dragged Sam away from the bar as soon as they'd got their drinks.

'Jesus, Tipper, she is a goddess . . . did you see . . .'

'Give over Sam, will you? She's a right old mare.'

'Well. Aren't you a great judge? I don't exactly

79

see a trail of them after you. She's sex on wheels man.'

Johnny the Fish shimmied out from his office. Sam had filled him in on his up and coming cousin.

'Ah. This is a pleasure,' he said expansively. 'Welcome to Newmarket's haven of tranquillity and restfulness . . . well, not sure about the second bit. Not when the chef's around, any way.'

Tipper and Sam nodded and mumbled something. The Fish was about to sit down and join them when an intermittent stream of oldish, jockey-sized guys ambled past and disappeared through a door which had 'snug' written above it.

'Ah ha,' the Fish smiled. 'The Covey Club. Very punctual today,' he continued without explanation. Sam took the bait.

'The Covey Club? What's that, Johnny? A disco club?' he added mischievously.

'Oh, they talk, have a drink. It's social. Frankness and honesty is what they're about. Being open with each other, if you know what I mean.'

Tipper didn't know. He continued to look puzzled.

'I'll spell it out,' said the Fish conspiratorially. 'For your ears only. They pool information about horses in the yards where they work. Obviously the information's got to be kosher, or it won't be worth much. But there are people who'll pay for really accurate reports.'

Tipper began to comprehend.

'Ah, yeah! I'm with you. You mean anyone having a bet, like.'

The Fish arched his shoulders and screwed his eyes up a bit. 'Anyone having a bet' – that covered professional punters, and bookies too, if you looked at it in a certain way.

'Ye-es. That's it. A bit like that. People having a bet. But it's just a bit of relaxation, a fun way of supplementing the wages, which, as we all know, are miserly round here.'

'Jesus, is that allowed, Johnny?' Tipper asked.

'Well. Strictly speaking it's frowned on,' the Fish reluctantly admitted. 'But it's all innocent fun. It's fine as long as everyone keeps a lid on it. Know what I mean!'

Sam knew exactly what he meant. And he saw an opening for his talented cousin.

'Do they have a man in Sinclair's yard, Johnny?'

'Well as it happens they don't.'

'Well, maybe we have the right man here?' Sam suggested pointing his left finger obviously at Tipper.

'Jesus, hang on a minute, Sam. I'm not sure I should be getting involved with that,' Tipper protested.

'Well, there could be an opening for you, young Tipper,' Johnny persisted. 'No harm in it.'

'You'll have great craic, boy. And you'll get to know a few people. That won't do you any harm,' Sam pointed out.

'Jesus, boys. I'm not so sure.'

13

'How long have you been in London?' Shalakov asked the prostitute sitting nervously on his sofa.

Like all tycoons General Stanislav Shalakov had many calls on his time. With economic interests ranging from Albanian artichokes to Zambian zinc, he travelled continually. His private pleasures didn't receive as much of his attention as he would like. But he tried to devote one Saturday night every fortnight to their indulgence, usually in London, usually in the penthouse apartment he owned in Cadogan Square.

He never had the same girl twice. He quoted a peasant proverb from his youth: you only peel a potato once. By the time a girl had spent the night with Shalakov, she had invariably lost, in his eyes, the fresh bloom, the trembling aura of innocence that had made her attractive to him in the first place.

The shyness, the innocent aura, were all too likely to be a pose anyway, a carefully worked illusion. Most of the girls were in reality more-or-less hardened young hookers handpicked by his security chief, Harrison, for their ability to sham that precious commodity of innocence. Depending on Shalakov's mood, they came in drafts of one, two or three at a time, and they had to be Russian speakers. He insisted on that. Shalakov's English had been passable ever since the Red Army put him and his fellow officers through an intensive language course in the 1950s – part of the Soviet Union's preparation for war with America. But he found it impossible to talk dirty in any language other than his own. And, in any case, he needed clarity, the knowledge that his particular requirements were precisely communicated and understood.

Ana had never intended to leave Moscow. But her mother had been made a very good offer by an agency for Ana to work in London as a secretary. And her mother needed the money to buy kidney dialysis treatment. Ana had nervously gone along with it. For the sake of her mother.

Not surprisingly, she seemed to Shalakov a good deal less calloused by her profession than many of the others.

'How long have you been in London?'

He didn't hear her murmured reply.

'Speak up, girl!'

Ana had been given two options by the men who controlled her when she arrived in London. This or a beating. She was now feeling sick as she contemplated what was in store for her. And she was terrified it would show that she'd never done it before. Little did she know the Russian General would have been thrilled if he'd known the extent of her innocence.

Ana was still wet from the shower. Shalakov always insisted the girls take a shower as soon as they entered the apartment. So now she wore a robe of white towelling, and her dark hair was wet. She was sipping a Bacardi and coke. She'd already refused Shalakov's offer of a line of marching powder.

'I have been in London almost two weeks, Mr Shalakov.'

'I am Comrade-General Shalakov.'

'Yes, Comrade-General.'

She spoke in the low, submissive way that, as she'd been told, he particularly liked.

'You're a pretty girl. That's good. You're young. That's good too. You have chosen a very simple and childish drink. That amuses me. So where do you come from back home?'

'Kazakhstan, Comrade-General. I mean, originally. We moved to Moscow when I was fourteen. We are a Russian family, of course.'

Shalakov wasn't really interested in all this. He was impatient to get on to spelling out the scenario he had in mind for this evening. But these preliminary civilities had to be observed for at least five more minutes, purely to satisfy his own personal superstition. He had formed the belief that, if he didn't make some token effort to 'get to know' the girls whom Harrison fired at him, then their evenings together would go badly. He might even – banish the thought – be impotent with them. There was no excitement or pleasure in dominating someone you didn't know – at least a bit.

'Oh yes?' he said idly. 'So, did you like the move?'

'No, Comrade-General.'

Ana bowed her head, studying the pattern on the Persian rug that lay under the coffee table between them.

'Why not?'

'I had to leave my horses. In Kazakhstan my uncle had a livery stable and I spent all my spare time there. Horses were my main interest in life, Comrade-General, my passion actually. But I was not able to ride in Moscow.'

Listening to this speech, Shalakov perked up.

'A horse lover!' he crowed. 'Good, very good. I like horses too.'

He started boasting to Ana about his activities with horses: the Moscow racing and equestrian centre, his running horses with the trainer David Sinclair, and the stud farm near Newmarket.

'It's not doing as well as it can, or should. This is disappointing. It's taking longer than necessary to come to fruition, because Stanislav Shalakov is a man with much else to think about. But one day I personally will rule the world of horses. Just wait and see.'

He lit a smoke from the gold cigarette case, which lay before him on the coffee table, and looked at his watch.

'But enough of that, we must get on.'

He stood up and began pacing around.

'I shall explain what I have in mind for this evening –'

Shalakov's personal phone, which lay on the table beside the cigarette case, suddenly emitted an electronic melody. The number was known to just a handful of his closest associates, and the phone chirped only when something important had to be discussed. Impatiently he snatched it up and growled a greeting.

'Daddy, it's Nadia.'

Shalakov cursed inwardly, but the tetchiness drained from his voice. Nadia was his daughter. She was fifteen, and the only human being in the world he was truly afraid of.

'My darling one, can't we talk later? I'm busy at the moment.'

He found his voice acquiring an almost servile whine when speaking with Nadia. He hated anyone hearing that, but he couldn't stop himself.

'So?' Nadia queried. 'I need money and I'm on my way over. Be there in about fifteen minutes. And you can give me some dinner while I'm there.'

Unlike her well-trained mother, lodged at a safe distance in Shalakov's Queen Anne country house in the Kentish Weald ('my *dacha*', he called it), Nadia would not be told what to do, and if she really wanted something could never be placated or put off. Shalakov sometimes wondered if this ruthlessness was part of the genetic inheritance he had passed on, or a result of an expensive English education that he'd paid for. Not that it mattered, since it was his own fault either way. But, if Nadia was coming over, Ana the pretty little horse-lover, for whom Shalakov had devised such complicated short-term plans, would have to be paid off and turfed out without delay. There would be nowhere to hide from Nadia once she got here. His evening of pleasure was over before it had begun.

Shalakov disconnected the call and sighed deeply.

'Get your clothes on. Get out of here.'

'Yes, Comrade-General,' Ana said deferentially.

Harrison paid Ana's minder who was waiting downstairs. She wouldn't see a penny of it. She hadn't done any work.

14

Tipper's arrival at Sinclair's yard had attracted some notice in the racing press. He had also attracted another kind of interest, from an unexpected direction. Early in December, coming back from the gallops, Alison Sinclair rode up beside him.

'How are you enjoying the Newmarket nightlife, young Tipper?' she asked breezily.

'I don't go out much, Mrs Sinclair,' Tipper said guardedly. 'Got to get up so early in the morning, you see.'

'Surely your girlfriend won't put up with that.'

'No problem there, Mrs Sinclair. I haven't got one.'

'No girlfriend? I find it hard to believe in such a good-looking boy as yourself. It must be rather a – well, a deprivation.'

Tipper concentrated on his mount, not looking at Alison and just wishing she would go away.

'I'm all right, really,' he said. 'Although I

thought I might have ridden a few of the runners recently that Mr Sinclair used other jockeys for.'

'We'll have to see about that,' she told him, in a voice loaded with insinuation. 'He doesn't make all of the decisions on the jockey front you know. I'm closely involved in that.' Then she edged her mount a fraction closer and swung out her knee so that their legs touched.

Tipper was fly enough to see that he had to be careful about Mrs Sinclair. It hadn't been her words exactly, but her tone of voice and the way she touched his knee as they rode upsides each other. But he'd have to keep her on side.

In the next few weeks Alison Sinclair was in Tipper's space a fair bit. It made him feel uneasy. She was always asking him about horses, alright. No other stuff. And he always told her everything he could about the horses. But he wasn't used to the attention. Nobody had really talked to him at Doyle's.

'That kid O'Reilly, he's a rude little shit,' Alison said to Sinclair.

'Fancy him do you?' mocked her husband. 'I expect the idea's too much for him, and he's running a mile.'

'Don't sneer, David. I'd like a modicum of respect from the staff, that's all. O'Reilly has the manners of a sewer rat. Tell him to get his act together.'

Sinclair knew precisely what this was all about. But it was, after all, her credit card that bought the feed and paid the blacksmith; her finger on the internet banking clicker; her name on the cheques. He'd have to speak to Tipper.

Shelley was all over Tipper whenever he and Sam went to the Partridge. But Tipper showed no interest whatsoever. The whole scenario was winding up Sam and Shelley something rotten. Sam was desperate to have a crack at Shelley himself, but he had no chance while she practically threw herself at Tipper. Shelley too was getting agitated. The Duke had told her to get Tipper into the Covey Club sooner rather than later. He wanted to know why she wasn't using all of her assets to snare him.

'He's not bloody interested,' she told the Duke.

'Of course he is, for God's sake. He's a jockey. They'll bloody well ride anything if it stays still for long enough.'

'His bloody cousin. Christ. I can hardly keep the sod off me,' Shelley complained. The Duke thought about that.

'I tell you what. Let's try this. Put the cousin on a promise. Tell him he can have his way with you if he delivers O'Reilly into the club. And Shelley. Don't let him have his way till he's delivered. All right?'

'Who d'you think I am?' she protested.

Unless there'd been a hard frost, every trainer wanted to be first out onto the gallops, to get the best ground for their horses. The competition was so fierce that some of them would be on the Heath even before dawn.

Sinclair wasn't as sharp out as some, but on misty winter mornings Tipper could barely see where he was going. It felt like they were galloping into a cloud. And that suited the trainers. Because getting the freshest ground wasn't the only reason to be early out. It also avoided prying eyes of the scouts and the touts. In Newmarket, everyone likes to know everyone else's business. And it's no good having a good horse if the whole town knows it can go a bit before it sets foot on the racecourse.

Not that Tipper was put off. He loved the spooky atmosphere of the Heath around dawn. And he loved the adrenaline rush of galloping upsides two or three other horses. Most of the work riders would play the game of hiding how well their horses were going. They wouldn't even be straight with Sinclair, because this kind of knowledge, if they kept it to themselves, was valuable. When the horses ran, it gave the lad an edge. He could use the knowledge to assist his own betting or, for a price, someone else's.

But they couldn't hide anything from Tipper. He had all the time he needed to concentrate on his own horse, as well as take a good look at his galloping companions. Not only was he a better judge than the others, he was guileless with Sinclair too.

Sinclair wasn't a bad judge of horses, either, but he was always some distance from the action. On a couple of occasions he'd heard Tipper's opinions after working a horse and later, when the horse ran, found the boy had been spot-on. So now, every work morning, he got into the habit of riding back to the yard on his hack upsides Tipper, probing him for his opinions on this horse and that. On one morning, however, early in the new year, it was Tipper that had a question that he wanted answering.

He waited until Sinclair had picked his brains on all of the horses they'd had out that morning. He fidgeted with his reins and his girth-strap, and took a deep breath.

'Guvnor, do you mind if I ask you something?'

He was looking straight ahead over his horse's pricked ears.

'Fire away, if you must,' Sinclair replied, making no effort to make eye contact. He didn't particularly like the way Tipper sounded.

'Well, Guvnor, I'm wondering why it is that I'm good enough to ride all the best horses in their work, but not on the racecourse, like. Why don't you give me any rides on the all-weather?'

'I do. I've given you quite a few rides, haven't I?'

'Just one or two early on, and then since December nothing.'

'You've ridden a few. And I do have to think of the owners, actually. Some of them are difficult, when it comes to younger jockeys.'

Tipper knew it was bullshit. Owners rarely interfered in the choice of a jockey, and they usually rather liked it when a useful claimer was up, because it meant their horse carried a lighter weight.

'So tell me an owner who's objected to me,' Tipper challenged.

'Err. Well you know, none specifically. But racing is a team game Tipper. You have to fit in with everyone. My wife for example. You haven't gone out of your way to get on with her, have you? And she talks a lot to the owners. Yes, she has quite a lot of influence with them in a funny way.'

Tipper didn't know what to say. He'd been totally professional with Sinclair's wife. And she'd been weird with him. But he couldn't tell Sinclair that. How the hell could he? No, he would do himself no favours going down that route.

'I thought I got on fine with your wife, Guvnor,' Tipper protested.

'That doesn't seem to be the way she sees it. Says you're not very respectful. You know trainers' wives are very important in this business, Tipper. I can think of countless top jockeys who wouldn't have made it if they hadn't looked after business in the yard as well as being able to ride. Take Wally Perks, for instance. He'd never have made it if he hadn't had the support of Cunningham's wife. See?'

Tipper couldn't believe Sinclair was putting

up Wally Perks as a role model. Everyone in Newmarket knew he was shagging Slip Cunningham's wife. Surely Sinclair must know that too.

'Well I suppose I get on better with horses than humans, Guvnor. Isn't that what matters?'

'Well it's easy for you to say that. How do you think I'd get on if I took that attitude? Wouldn't have many horses for me to train or you to ride, would I? Grow up Tipper. If you want to get better rides then I suggest that you get along with Mrs Sinclair.'

With that Sinclair gave his hack a kick in the ribs and he trotted off before Tipper could reply.

Tipper wasn't one to make a big entrance. So he was pleased to see there was only Johnny the Fish, Shelley and Sam in the bar at the Partridge.

'Okay lads?' Tipper nodded.

'Ah, young Tipper,' Johnny beamed. 'We were wondering where you'd got to. Drink?'

'Jesus, Johnny I'd love one, but I'm struggling with my weight.'

'Have a little scotch. That won't put any weight on you.'

Tipper thought for a second and blew some air through his teeth.

'Go on then.'

'Scotch for our friend Tipper, Shelley.'

Shelley didn't bother to try and engage Tipper with eye contact. Sam neither. She didn't much like the way Sam was smiling at her since their little chat. He wasn't cute.

'Thanks. Jesus, I feel like I could do with a drink,' Tipper confessed.

Sam could see that Tipper was looking a bit edgy, so he moved towards the table in the corner under the television and beckoned Tipper towards it.

Apart from the fire crackling away behind them, all was peaceful in the bar. But it sure as hell wasn't in Tipper's head.

'So what's on your mind, my man?' Sam coaxed.

'Jesus, I'm not sure Sam. I'm just not sure. But I think Sinclair's wife fancies me.'

Sam burst into laughter.

Tipper took no notice and told about his conversations with Sinclair and Mrs Sinclair coming down off the gallops. A sly lecherous smile crept across Sam's face as he listened.

'Now Tipper, are you sure you've got this straight. She gave you the come-on, and the husband said go?'

'I swear, Sam. I just thought Mrs Sinclair was being a bit over-friendly. I've never had a bad word out of her over anything else.'

Sam was still chuckling.

'This is deadly! I've seen that woman and I wouldn't mind a spin on her myself. She'd win a little race somewhere.'

'She's not my type,' whispered Tipper desperately.

'Maybe not. But what must be done, must be done.'

'Jesus, Sam, me and *her*? Are you off your fockin' head or what?'

'No. Think about it. All you've bloody done for the last few weeks is fockin' whinge about not getting any rides. Well now we know why, don't we? You told me before she wore the trousers. So now *you've* got to pull them down, son.'

'Ah no.'

Sam thought he'd said something very funny. His shoulders were shaking as he took a fresh mouthful of Guinness. Tipper stared forlornly into his scotch.

'Look I'm not joking,' Sam went on when he'd swallowed. 'It's got to be done. And anyway, you're not exactly doing a lot of riding elsewhere. Now there's something else I need you to do for me.'

'Sure Sam, ask away.' Tipper was only too happy to change the subject.

'Well, boy. You know this Covey Club, where the lads get together for a bit of a craic. Well I think you should join it. I know you've got your doubts but quite a few of the top work riders are in it. You never know. They could put a good word in with their guvnors; maybe get you a few spare rides.'

Tipper had already given the club some thought. He shook his head.

'No way, Sam. Don't you remember what Delaney told us?'

'Jesus Tipper. These guys are work riders. Not gamblers. It's fine. Look you need to meet a few more people to get on.'

'So where do you think the information goes then?'

Sam paused. This wasn't going to plan. He hadn't thought that Tipper would be bothered at all. Then he thought of Shelley pulling her T-shirt off and unbuttoning his shirt.

'Look Tipper,' he snapped. 'I've fockin well given up a lot for you, I left a good job at home. I'm sitting on some stud farm in Newmarket to help you out. At least I might get to back the odd winner if you just join the Covey Club. All of the top work riders are in it for focks sake. No-one's giving them any grief.'

Tipper was quite taken aback by the urgency and abruptness of Sam's annoyance. He'd never seen his cousin so wound up, and he was also stung by Sam's talk of compromising his life for Tipper. Sam had been there for him when his mother died. Tipper had never forgotten that. And Sam was the only real friend he had in the world. He couldn't deny his cousin. He didn't want to upset his mate.

'Jesus Sam. Consider it done. You're right,' Tipper said quickly, embarrassed that he'd caused his cousin so much annoyance. Maybe Sam was right. It was no big deal. And he might make some good contacts.

15

In the normal course of events, Shalakov would have completely forgotten the existence of the pretty little hooker he'd bundled so hastily out of his penthouse. But, as it turned out, he had cause to remember her a few months later.

Shalakov had described his racehorse operation to Ana as disappointing. In fact, things had been going well enough in Moscow, where the rebuilt Hippodrome was complete and fully operational. And other facilities on the Russian side were on target. The problems lay in England, so Shalakov called a meeting to sort things out.

Sinclair and Shaunsheys were both summoned to the Shalakov penthouse, as well as Nico who, with his perfect command of English, had been drafted in to conduct the meeting. The General sat in on it, though, silently smoking, drinking coffee and listening. A disconcerting presence for the two Englishmen, who could never determine how much of the dialogue he was actually able to follow.

Taking his cue from notes he'd made during a prior briefing with Shalakov, Nico spoke first to Sinclair.

'Mr Sinclair. General Shalakov has asked you here because he is wondering why he should not dispense with your services.'

Sinclair took this like a sharp blow to the solar plexus. He had to force his face not to crumple.

'Well, I haven't had much of a chance,' he said. 'Perhaps I can explain –'

Nico flipped the palm of his hand towards Sinclair to shut him up.

'The General has had a total of nine horses with you this season,' he went on, his voice turning pleasurably steely, his glasses glinting. 'One of them, Salammbo, won a Group One before she broke down and had to be destroyed. Two others, Inquirer and Mr Thatcher, were placed in no less than five Group races between them, but they didn't win any. Of the others, none were Group class, although two, Colorado Lode and Jedediah, were supplemented for classic races after you reported they showed exceptional speed on your gallops.'

Nico had a few silent misgivings of his own about grilling Sinclair, since he'd personally done pretty well out of the information that he'd received from him over the past year. But this was what Shalakov had specifically told him to convey to the trainer. And now he was rather enjoying himself.

'Now, naturally, the General is very disappointed with these results. You assured him that his English racing operation would be self-financing through prize money, sales of successful horses and eventually stud fees. This would not seem to be where things are heading at the moment. So can you please explain why General Shalakov should not move to another, more successful trainer?'

Sinclair cleared his throat. Failure in racing is not necessarily open to rational explanation, but owners rarely accept this. So trainers become expert in manufacturing plausible excuses. The horse scoped dirty after the race; the mare was coming into season; there was a filly in season in the race that put our fellow off; the colt ran into traffic on the final bend and was barged out of it; the overnight rain; the *lack* of overnight rain; the bloody handicapper; the jockey disobeying my orders.

But something told him that, in this case, off-the-peg mitigations like this would hardly wash. He smiled at Nico and turned directly to Shalakov. He had decided on a bold strategy – with him, an almost unheard of one. He would risk telling the honest truth.

'General, the fact is we've had a desperately unlucky season. Salammbo was a very good horse indeed; her accident could not have been fore-seen. If she'd lived I have every reason to believe she would have been one of the race-mares of the decade. Inquirer and Mr Thatcher each had a good season. Not winning a single Group One race between them was pure bad luck. As you know in some cases they were touched off by only a few inches. If the dice had fallen even very slightly in our favour these three horses would have fulfilled all your requirements. We would have had real success at the top level, with no less than a quarter of the string. Anyone will tell you that would have been sensational. So I ask you to continue to be patient. On the other hand, General, if you want to *ensure* success I would urge you to do more.'

He took a deep gulp of coffee and an even deeper breath. What he was about to say would make him or break him. He didn't hold a particularly good hand, but he was going all in. He put down his cup.

'You must increase your investment,' he said. 'In the end, the way to win top races is to spend big money buying only the very best-bred stock. That's what the Maktoums did. It's what John Magnier did and what O'Callaghan's in the process of doing. I am absolutely confident, if you commit enough funds to this project, we can make you the most successful owner in the country, within the *next* four years. If not in Europe.'

He realized he'd been trembling, but he felt better now. He kept his eyes fixed on Shalakov, though the General seemed absorbed in the view of the sky through the window. His only response was to grunt when Nico said something to him in

Russian, after which Nico smiled emolliently and thanked Sinclair. Then he turned to Shaunsheys, who had the look of a Victorian schoolboy waiting outside the headmaster's study.

'Now, Mr Shaunsheys. You have been given the opportunity to buy a mare for General Shalakov, but you keep suggesting unsuitable animals.

Shaunsheys opened his fishlike mouth to speak but Nico got in first.

'I am going to tell you for the last time. General Shalakov considers any markings on a horse to be a weakness. So he doesn't care how much you like a mare. Unless it has no markings on it, no white legs, no stars on its forehead, he is not interested. Do I make myself clear? It must be just one colour. Chestnut, bay, brown, black. He doesn't mind as long as it is the best. Price no problem.'

Shaunsheys nodded quickly. He felt his system flooding with the champagne of relief, when he'd expected to be given a stomach full of vinegar. Price no problem! Perhaps God was not a delusion after all.

'Thank you, Nico,' he said nodding his head vigorously. 'You're a gentleman. Thank you, General. I won't let you down. I promise.'

After the two Englishmen had left the General and Nico discussed the state of Sinclair's business, and whether it was worth persisting with.

'I won't make an immediate decision about it,' said Shalakov. 'And in the meantime we shall update the dossier on Sinclair. If I do decide to stay with him, I have to know what's going on inside that stable.'

'Why not put someone in there?' suggested Nico. 'Someone who can report back to you, without Sinclair knowing.'

Shalakov stroked his chin. Suddenly the image of the little prostitute that he'd been denied came back to him. What had she said? *Horses were my main interest in life, Comrade-General, my passion actually.* He didn't think she'd need much persuasion, then. He knew there were plenty of East Europeans in Newmarket. She would probably feel perfectly at home.

'Yes, that's a good idea,' he said. 'And you know? I think I have someone who'll fit our requirements very well indeed. Get me Harrison.'

16

Tipper usually looked after the horses in the isolation yard if he wasn't racing in the afternoons. It was a couple of hundred yards from the main yard and always quiet and semi-deserted. Alison Sinclair also kept her own horse there. She knew he was the only person in the isolation yard when she brought her horse back to its stable.

'Tipper!' she called out. 'Give me a hand here, will you?'

He jogged over to hold the horse's head as Alison slid from the saddle. She removed her hard hat and shook out her tangled hair.

He led her horse into the stable and assumed that she'd be gone by the time he'd untacked him. But when he emerged ten minutes later he found that she was still in the yard, standing just inside the open door of an empty stable. It had been made ready with fresh straw for a horse expected to arrive the next day. She crooked her finger at Tipper.

'Come here. There's something in here I want you to look at.'

She then retreated to the back of the box as he approached warily. The electric light was off and the air in the shadowy interior was heavy with the sweetish smell of straw dust. Alison was over by the manger with her back turned and her head slightly bowed. Tipper couldn't make out what she was doing. He took a step towards her and, as if on a signal, she spun round to face him. It was then that he realized she had been undoing her buttons, for she slid her shirt from her shoulders and let it fall on the straw. She wasn't wearing a bra.

'Well?' she asked as she ran her fingers over her nipples. 'What do you think? Do you like them?'

Some men would have found Alison Sinclair very sexy all right, at least in appearance. But Tipper didn't. She wasn't actually fat, but everything about her struck him as being alarmingly, even overwhelmingly large: the mass of brown hair, the greedy mouth, the prominent nose and the broad horsewoman's arse and thighs. Now, with a mixture of incredulity and abject terror, he found himself being invited to evaluate her naked, swaying breasts.

Alison took a step towards him.

'Haven't you anything to say? Try looking more closely.'

Her eyes were wide, intense like a bird's, but

also green and witchy. She reached out and grabbed him by the back of the neck, pulling his face into her cleavage. Then she lowered her face into his hair. She was a good six inches taller than he was.

'That's it. I like the smell of your sweat,' she purred.

He couldn't smell her in return because his nose was flattened against her breast-bone. Nor could he breathe. He struggled in her grip.

'Why are you struggling? Don't be so shy. You'll never be a top jockey if you're shy, you know.'

Tipper let his knees sag, so that by the force of gravity his face began to slide down from Alison's thorax towards her belly. For a moment Tipper's mouth met her puckered navel before it slithered on. She clutched him as his nose snagged painfully on the waistband of her jodhpurs. Tipper dropped down into the straw. Alison took this as a positive sign. The next moment she was on top of him.

'No! No! Mrs Sinclair!' he protested.

'Don't be bloody stupid,' she grunted, breathing heavily as she tried to get her hands on the zip of his jeans. 'You know you want it, Tipper, as much as I do.'

'This isn't right, Mrs Sinclair. I mean, what if Mr Sinclair –?'

'You know what? He doesn't care, Tipper. He's at it too, believe me. Keep *still*.'

But pound for pound Tipper was considerably

stronger than Alison. He grabbed her by her arms and threw her onto her back. Alison lay in the straw, mistakenly thinking that Tipper was going to jump on top of her. But nothing was further from his mind.

'You ungrateful little pikey,' she snarled when she realized Tipper was planning a rapid exit. 'I offer you a good time and you behave like this.'

Tipper could sense her eyes glaring at him, but he fixed his own on the straw. She was utterly humiliated as she scrambled to her feet. Her face was red with anger and exertion. She was breathing heavily.

'All right,' she virtually spat out. 'Have it your way. But let one thing be understood. You won't be riding any good horses for this yard – *never*. Now fuck off out of here!'

Tipper emerged from the stable into the dull late afternoon light. He was trying to brush the straw off him when he looked up. David Sinclair was standing at the yard gate, watching him.

Tipper called Sam as he left the yard, but there was no response. His phone was turned off for a good reason. It was pay-back time for Shelley. But when Sam walked into the Partridge he had a big smile on his face for more than one reason, and it was the other reason he was bursting to tell Tipper about.

'You're not going to believe this, my man. But guess which mare came to board at the stud today for a few weeks before she goes through the sale ring?' Tipper wasn't in the mood for games. And Sam had a stupid look on his face anyway, he was probably taking the piss.

'No idea.'

'Go on. Think. Which horse would you most like to see in the world?'

'No way.' Tipper smiled, instantly forgetting his problems. 'No way.'

'Oh yes. Red's out at the stud alright. She looks great.'

'Come on. Let's go and see her. Jesus. She's being sold here?'

'Can I have a pint please?' Sam gesticulated.

Tipper calmed. 'Okay. But tell me, why's she with you?'

'Oh some long story. The guy who leases the stud to O'Callaghan knows the owner. I think he thinks if O'Callaghan sees the mare before she goes through the sale ring he'll buy her. I'd say he will too.'

'Jesus that's wicked. Then she'll always be here. Come on hurry up.'

Sam had a good gulp of his beer. He didn't want to leave. Shelley would be appearing in a minute. He wanted to have another look at her to remind himself. She was late.

'Hey. How was your first meeting with the Covey Club?' Sam asked. Tipper didn't immediately reply and looked at the pattern of the stone floor.

'It was okay,' he eventually admitted. 'There was Spud, Jimmy, Chuck, Dobbo, Arthur, Rodney and Ray. Good lads.'

'God, they sound like the seven dwarves, so they do,' said Sam.

'We're all in different yards. And we all have a contact that we got to give our phone numbers to. The contacts phone us for the latest news, like.'

'What sort of news is that?'

'Things like do any of the yards have shy eaters, and how much is left in the mangers. Also they want to know how well the horses work, and what weights they carry on the gallops. Things like that.'

'So who's your contact?'

'He's a guy called the Duke. He rang during the meeting. Nice guy. Says if there's anything I need any time to give him a ring. Wants me to drop in for a drink next time I'm in London.'

'That sounds okay, boy. There's no harm in that.'

Tipper wasn't so sure. Nobody had ever given him something for nothing, so why would this guy? But he hoped Sam was right.

17

Shaunsheys had been waiting for a long time to land a proper touch. He'd been planning to retire to a little place in the Philippines, or maybe Thailand. He went for his holidays to one or the other every year. What he needed was one final deal to help him on his way.

When the Russians had initially approached him to find the best mare money could buy, he reckoned his moment had come. The promised two per cent commission was handy. But it wasn't enough to keep him in little boys for the rest of his days. Now, however, he sensed his moment had come. He wasn't going to muck about with two per cents now.

Over the years Shaunsheys had developed a sideline helping casinos round up bad debts – nothing physical, more along the lines of 'I'm sure you wouldn't want this to be known about on the racetrack, *sir*'. One of those with whom he'd had such conversations was the Honourable Rupert

Robinson. Rupert was in a bad financial corner. His father had been too raddled with drink to consider accountants or financial planning, and anyway he hadn't been intending to die. And there wasn't just inheritance tax. Young Robinson's appetite for Brazilians was fairly voracious, particularly after he'd downed a few bottles of bubbly and shoved half a gram of coke up his rapidly disintegrating nose. And for someone who could hardly use a calculator he was a little too keen on blackjack.

So Shug Shaunsheys's face, while hardly welcome, wasn't completely strange when, around noon three days after the meeting with Shalakov, he knocked on Robinson's door in Sloane Avenue.

Robinson wasn't unattractive. In fact the women in Virginia, where he hunted every year, fell over each other to dance with him. He was tall, athletically built and had rather soulful eyes. He also had a sloping forehead and straight swept-back hair. But today, as he opened the door of his sister's house wearing a silk dressing gown, the bloodshot eyeballs, greasy hair and three-day stubble told a different story. The Honourable Rupert had been on yet another bender.

'Shaunsheys. What the fuck do you want?'

'I think it may be in your interest if we have a little chat.'

Robinson closed his eyes wearily.

'Look, you bloody know I'm broke. I'm doing

my best to get that money together, but it's incredibly difficult. The Revenue have got their claws into my back.'

'Then today's your birthday, Rupert. I may be able to offer you a lot of money. Shall I come in?'

Robinson frowned. Shaunsheys's visits had always *cost* him money in the past.

'Oh,' he said warily, 'come on in then.'

Shaunsheys trailed his personal aroma, a combination of stale sweat and cigarette smoke, past Robinson. He stopped in the narrow hallway to admire a matching pair of paintings.

'Ferneley. Very nice.'

Robinson ignored him and pointed towards an open door that led into a sitting room. Shaunsheys went through and sank into a deep, green leather armchair. Next to the chair was a mahogany table with a bronze of a horse and jockey. Must be worth a few quid, he thought, as must the big landscape over the fireplace, which he suspected of being a Munnings. A startling modern semi-abstract canvas dominated the opposite wall. So why didn't Robinson just sell some of this stuff, if he needed money? Or, come to think of it, flog the whole house?

Robinson knew what he was thinking. He gestured at the art and furniture.

'All my sister's. So's the house. She's in New York at the moment. So don't get any ideas that your grubby casino is going to get their hands on any of it.'

'Mr Robinson, I'm not here on casino business. I want to talk to you about Stella Maris. As I understand it you retired her from the track?'

'Something like that.'

'So you've entered her in the sales, right?'

Robinson winced. For the past year Stella Maris had been his only useful asset, and very useful she had been – the difference between concealed penury and very public bankruptcy. The mare's victory in the Irish Oaks had been tax-free earnings that kept her owner well topped up with vintage Krug and Class A drugs, as well as staving off his creditors for a while. But now the prize money had all gone. Robinson had no choice but to kill the Golden Goose.

'As a matter of fact I have. But I don't need the likes of you running her up, if that's why you're here. There's plenty of interest already, let me tell you.'

'You misunderstand me. I'd like to buy her. What are you hoping she'll make?'

Robinson was astounded. Shaunsheys's collars were always grubby, his suits were unpressed, his hair greasily unkempt. Where was he going to find the money?

'How do I know what she'll make, for God's sake?' he asked testily. Hangover pains were stabbing into his cerebellum. 'She'll make what she makes.'

'Come, come. You must have an idea what she'll make. Half a million, perhaps?'

'More like two. You haven't got that kind of money.'

'Now Rupert.' Shaunsheys chuckled patronizingly. 'You're hardly in a position to judge what I'm worth. But I shouldn't be too confident of selling her for two million. We both know how volatile the market is at the moment.'

Robinson's head began throbbing like the business end of road-mender's hammer. He really was not up to this.

'Well one and a half, minimum,' he managed. 'You realize what her breeding is?'

'Yes I do, though one and a half mill's still a lot . . .'

Shaunsheys made a show of considering, cocking his head towards the ceiling.

'I tell you what, though,' he went on. 'I'll give you a million for her right now. No risk. You can have the money tomorrow, in any account you like.'

Robinson shook his head in disbelief.

'But you can't – I can't do that. She's entered in the sale.'

'So? She'll stay in the sale. No one will ever know you sold her to me. She'll go through the ring and what she makes will no longer be your worry, it'll be mine.'

'But what if she makes more than that?'

'Then I'm laughing. But if she makes less, it's you rolling in the aisles. There aren't many buyers for a filly like her at the top end, and if those jokers happen not to turn up, she'll go for a few hundred thou. This offer guarantees you a return which, in my opinion, you can't turn down. My *professional* opinion, Rupert.'

Now it was Robinson's turn to consider. Or to try to think, at least. Christ, if only a some bastard hadn't infiltrated his skull with a pair of pliers.

'One and a half,' he said, 'and we split anything on top fifty-fifty.'

'You can't have your cake and eat it, Rupert,' sneered Shaunsheys. 'Sell the horse to me now for a million. It's terrible what accidents horses can have just before they go to the sales.'

'That is bloody extortion.'

'Really? I would say I'm making you a very generous offer. Yes or no?'

Rupert Robinson looked out of the window. An old lady was struggling with her shopping over the zebra crossing. Suddenly a car hurtled past, narrowly missing her. He winced. He couldn't afford anything to go wrong with Stella Maris before the sale. He needed a million pounds. He just had to get it. And Shaunsheys was right, he might not if the horse went through the ring.

'I'll take one and a quarter,' he muttered, trying to sound cool, though he felt as if he had a raging fever.

'The offer is one million, Rupert. Yes or no.'

Robinson turned from the window, his fists clenched.

'Damn you, Shaunsheys! Where will you get

the money? It's not really you, is it? You're acting for someone.'

Shaunsheys stood up, a satisfied smile playing over his lips.

'Good, so it's a deal. If you just tell me where you want the money, it will be with you tomorrow. I was sure you'd see sense, so I took the liberty of printing off a little contract. Just so you don't forget.'

Shaunsheys pulled an envelope out of his jacket pocket and took out two pages, both with the same agreement printed on them. It was that Stella Maris was sold to Shug Shaunsheys by Rupert Robinson for one million pounds. With the bookie's biro that Shaunsheys fished from his trousers, Robinson reluctantly signed both copies. Shaunsheys took back one of them, carefully folded it and slipped it into his jacket pocket.

'There you are,' he said, in the voice of a dentist to a child. 'That didn't hurt. There are just a couple of small points in addition. You're never to tell anyone that we've done this. It would be most distressing for your uncle if it ever got out. He might even have to resign from the Jockey Club. Where would he go for lunch then? As far as everyone's concerned you are still the seller, and you will of course be at Newmarket for the sale. You will *even* remember to buy us a drink if we buy her, won't you Rupert? I don't want you forgetting those nice manners you learnt at Eton.'

'Us? Who is us?'

'You'll see.'

Slowly his befuddled brain had pieced together Shaunsheys's scam. It was the middleman's revenge, playing both ends. He must be certain his client would go over the million, so the difference would be clear profit for Shaunsheys. Rupert knew that, if the fraud squad got to hear about it, they'd all be in the shit, including himself now that he'd signed Shaunsheys's contract.

The bloodstock agent held out his hand and clicked his pudgy fingers.

'Now, your bank details.'

Wearily Robinson walked over to his desk and took out his cheque book from the top right hand drawer. On a post-it note he copied the account name and number from a blank cheque.

'If it's not there by close of play tomorrow, the deal's off,' Robinson hissed as he marched sulkily into the hall and yanked open the front door. He stood leaning on the doorframe with his eyes closed, holding out the post-it note. It wasn't that he was all that disappointed with the amount he was getting for Stella Maris. What really tweaked his wick was the fact that a slug like Shaunsheys was driving the deal, and making himself rich in the process.

Shaunsheys picked the bank details from Robinson's fingers as he walked through the door. His face wore a smug smile.

'Nice doing business, Rupert,' he smirked.

But the door had already slammed behind him.

Shaunsheys didn't mind. He had twenty-four hours to find someone who'd lend him the million. It wouldn't exactly be at bank rate, of course, but Shaunsheys wasn't worried about that.

18

Newmarket after dark in December can feel like the coldest place on earth. And it's not just the people. The wind that comes whipping in off the North Sea was originally refrigerated in Siberia.

Stanislav Shalakov swept into the Newmarket thoroughbred sales in a convoy of blacked-out Mercedes. A detail of bodyguards in bulky overcoats spilled out of the first of these, as the rest of them pulled up. The entrance to the sales was weakly lit, and it was surrounded by pitch darkness.

Shalakov had plenty of enemies, but he had no intention of suffering a demise similar to Alexander Litvenenko. If anyone wanted to get at him with Polonium they'd have to get past Martin Harrison and Alexei first. Harrison, with his army training, had swept the ground around the entrance. Now he stepped out of the shadows and approached the stocky, thickset bodyguard standing by the door of the third car. He gave him a nod. Alexei looked around suspiciously. He was out of his territory. Bodyguards don't much like the unknown. After a third and final check he knocked twice on the door. A couple of seconds later he pulled it open.

Shalakov got out of the car stiffly in his long black leather coat. Years of severe Siberian winters had left their legacy with the General. If he sat in a car for too long his back seized up, which did nothing for his mood. Neither had the journey from London on the traffic-clogged M11.

'This had better be worth my while,' he barked at Nico, who was hovering by the door of the third car, clutching his sales catalogue and trying to smile. His credibility as a bloodstock fix-it was on thin ice tonight.

Shalakov and his entourage had barely walked through the gate when Shaunsheys, wearing a New York Yankees baseball cap, sidled up like a crab. Shalakov looked him up and down. There was nothing remotely trustworthy about the man, and Shalakov knew it.

'Why can't you English do something with your roads?' Shalakov growled. 'Do you understand how much time I have wasted? When will this horse go through the ring?'

'Oh, not long, General,' Shaunsheys said humbly. 'She's in the ring in a couple of lots time.'

'So, we are nearly late? Show me the way.'

Shalakov may not have liked Shaunsheys and certainly didn't trust him, but he didn't need to.

Shalakov was used to working with people he despised. And, as long as the bloodstock agent had seized this last chance and found him the best mare that money could buy, he was satisfied.

Tipper and Sam had already found their spot from which to watch Red go through the ring. Tipper pointed out Shalakov and his hangers-on to Sam as they made their late entry.

'Here's Sinclair's guy, Sam. The Russian. I'd say he'll have a serious crack at her.'

'Well he'll need to. O'Callaghan was talking an awful lot about her in the office this morning. He says she's got three of the four aces in the pack – that's the words he used. One, she's bred from the best stock. Two, she was great stuff herself.'

'She was a fighter in a race all right,' agreed Tipper.

'But the best bit, O'Callaghan says, is that, three, she's feminine. He wouldn't give you shite for one of those fillies that look so big and butch but breed fock all. This one's a lady, so he says.'

'So what's the fourth ace then?'

'Luck of course. And you can't buy that, can you?'

'What'll she make, then?'

'Ah, a million plus, easy. She's worth that. You don't get many like her coming on the market. She's the future. If she throws a filly, you can breed from it. If it's a colt, it'll have a stallion's pedigree. O'Callaghan loves this sire line, too. You can't beat the Northern Dancer line. It's the best that ever came out of America. Jesus, look what it did for John Magnier.'

'It seems like a fockin' lifetime since I was riding her,' Tipper muttered mournfully. 'Winning the fockin' Irish Oaks. And will you look at me now? I'm lucky if I ride a shite winner on the sand somewhere.'

Sam laughed.

'You should've shagged Mrs S., didn't I tell you?'

'Pipe down!' Tipper hissed. 'There's people can hear you. Anyway, I hope O'Callaghan buys her. At least she'll stay close by.'

Sam rested his elbows on the guard rail and looked around.

'All right. So who else is going to be in for this mare? Those lads I suppose.'

He nodded towards a section of the crowd in which sat a group of a dozen or so Chinese.

Sam leaned over and saw Shalakov and his men shuffling into their seats. Shalakov, with his pock-marked, vodka-raddled complexion looked oddly out of place in the packed, Barbour-coated or tweed-jacketed audience. And, while there's never a shortage of heavy drinkers in any racing crowd, Shalakov looked like he could out-drink the lot of them and then twist the cap on a fresh bottle just for himself.

'Jesus, Tipper, he looks like the second cousin of Tyrannosaurus Rex,' Sam chuckled.

'They say he was a commando in Afghanistan,

or somewhere; it was only that he's deadly accurate with his throwing knife that kept him alive.'

Sam whistled. 'Okay. Let's see what he's made of in the sales ring.'

19

'Now we come to lot number seventy-three, Stella Maris,' announced the auctioneer Jimmy Giles. 'Twice a Group One winning mare. By Giant's Causeway out of Star Dust. An absolutely first-class prospect, ladies and gentlemen.'

It may have been a freezing, black February night, but inside the ring the atmosphere was red hot. The likes of Stella Maris are not seen in the ring very often. If it hadn't been for Robinson's dire lack of funds, she wouldn't have been there at all. She swaggered around the ring taking everything in. The sales ring is a claustrophobic place when it's packed and she was beginning to feel it coming in on top of her.

'God, I hope she behaves herself,' whispered Tipper.

Jimmy also looked a trifle anxious. This was by far the most valuable horse he'd ever auctioned. If the truth be known, he was not the world's greatest hammer man, but he did play a bit of golf at the Royal Worlingham with Rupert Robinson, and Robinson liked him. Even more, he liked Jimmy Giles's daughter Cassandra, who he'd run into in a couple of clubs in London. So Robinson had insisted to the sale company that Cassandra's old man should be on the rostrum when his mare went through the ring.

Robinson might not have allowed his lust for Cassandra to sway his judgement, had he known the man's woeful reputation. The problem was that Jimmy was nervous and tended to get muddled as the bids came in. He found it difficult to look for bids, and to remember what the last one was. So selling Stella Maris would test him to the limit.

He adjusted the earpiece, through which a company spotter would alert him to any bids he might miss – a vital resource in Jimmy's case. Then he checked his Global Positioning Satellite screen to see where the big hitters were sitting. High up on the left he could see Dermot O'Callaghan and his Irish advisers. Jimmy liked the Irish. They were good customers and very generous with the vintage Leoville-Barton.

To his right he could see the gaggle of oriental faces. In recent years they'd become numerically the largest owners of racehorses in training in England. But they were an auctioneer's night- mare. They took it in turns to bid and, as there always seemed to be at least ten of them, this made life very confusing. They were also cunning.

Jimmy never quite knew whether they were really gunning for one of the lots, or merely bluffing. If he were a seller, he'd hate to run these guys up on the bidding.

Then there were the Russians. There was no doubt that they had money. Jimmy had seen their bank guarantee that morning. Amazing who the so-called smart private banks would act for, he'd remarked to his boss in the office. He'd shrugged his shoulders as if to say 'money's money, what do we care?'

Jimmy looked carefully at Shalakov. As far as Jimmy was concerned he was a charmless bully, who employed an even more revolting bloodstock agent. Shaunsheys, most people knew, had slept with plenty of dogs, and caught plenty of fleas. His shenanigans polluted the sale ring, but no one had ever been able to nail him. You couldn't risk blowing the whistle without cast-iron proof.

Jimmy cleared his throat, took a final sip of water and turned back to his mike. He looked down towards the arena where the lights made Stella Maris's deep browny-red coat gleam like polished mahogany.

'So ladies and gentlemen,' he announced, 'who'll start me away at two hundred and fifty thousand guineas for this beautiful bay mare? No? two hundred thousand, then . . .'

Jimmy wasn't surprised that there was no rush to start bidding. Buying a racehorse can be a bit like a game of poker. It doesn't always pay to show too much enthusiasm at the start. So he took a few bids 'off the wall' and advanced her smoothly up, in steps of fifty thousand, to her reserve of five hundred thousand guineas. The next bid, though, would have to be for real.

'Who will give me five hundred and fifty thousand?' Jimmy asked, fighting his nerves. Surely she had to sell. As he cast his eyes around the ring there was nothing. Then, after an agonizing pause, Jimmy got a bleep on his GPS monitor. He glanced at the screen. Dermot O'Callaghan was in.

O'Callaghan didn't always like people knowing when he was bidding. He bought many expensive horses, so he was an easy target to bid up. Anyone selling a horse knew, if O'Callaghan wanted a horse, he wouldn't readily stop. So he liked to bid primarily through the GPS system. By pushing a button his bid would come up on the auctioneer's GPS screen, which showed a plan of the arena. In this way the man with the hammer knew where the bid had come from, but no one else did. Then, just occasionally and to confuse everyone, O'Callaghan would also bid by publicly raising his finger.

'Five hundred and fifty thousand I have,' Jimmy boomed. Thank God for that. He looked down towards the Russians. Shaunsheys was standing right beside Shalakov, who nodded.

'Six hundred thousand guineas.' Jimmy barked the figure in a staccato voice. O'Callaghan immediately responded, and Shalakov came straight back again. Jimmy looked sharply at O'Callaghan, who now raised his finger to let the ring see he was bidding.

'Seven hundred and fifty thousand guineas,' Jimmy announced. Then he cast his eyes up at the Chinese. Nothing from there. He looked down towards the Russians and Shalakov obliged by raising his catalogue. Eight hundred.

Jimmy's GPS system bleeped. O'Callaghan was in a hurry. He jumped a bid and bounced it to nine hundred thousand. Jimmy started to relax. This was good money. He would continue with steps of a hundred thou. So concentrate. He mustn't forget where he'd got to. He looked down at the Russians. Shalakov and Shaunsheys were in conference.

'Do I hear one million?' Jimmy chivvied. 'You'll never have another chance like this gentlemen.'

He was beginning to feel cocky. After another moment, Shalakov raised his catalogue again.

'One million! Thank you sir!' crowed Jimmy, with the triumphant voice of a darts commentator calling a three-dart treble top. He looked around for the next bid, but the whole thing seemed to have suddenly ground to a halt. What had happened to O'Callaghan?

Standing beside Shalakov, Shaunsheys was acting the professional agent, urgently consulting with his client, offering sage advice. He pulled off his baseball cap and wiped his sweaty brow, flicking a glance across to the other side of the ring. He could just see the skinny, red-headed man he'd brought in as his very private associate. His instructions to this man had been simple. Watch me all the time. If the cap's on, don't bid. If it's off, bid. If it's on again, stop bidding.

'I have one million guineas,' Jimmy Giles repeated, desperate for another bidder. 'One million guineas, one million, and I'm going to have to sell, ladies and gentleman.'

Out of the corner of Jimmy's eye, a hand was raised in the dense crowd. The auctioneer hesiated. It was definitely a bid, but he'd never seen the guy before in his life. Jimmy glanced across at one of the senior auctioneers standing to one side of him. He inclined his head quizzically in the direction of the new bidder, as if to ask whether he should take a bid of one million one hundred thousand from a complete stranger. The senior auctioneer looked back at him with a totally blank face. Pissed off that he wasn't on the rostrum, he wasn't going to help out. Jimmy took the bid.

'One-one. Fresh bidder,' he called. But fuck, who was he? Jimmy could feel the sweat running down the inside of his arm. Suddenly there was a voice in his earpiece. *On your right!* Jimmy looked up at the Chinese. One of them was wafting his catalogue.

'One two, *another* fresh bidder. *Thank* you, sir.'
And he really meant it. This was going off now.

Jimmy pulled round to look at O'Callaghan. After a fractional hesitation the Irishman made a gesture, rolling his hands over each other three times. Jimmy knew what it meant – a three-bid jump.

'One and a half million, sir? Yes! I have one a half million ladies and gentlemen!'

This was getting interesting. O'Callaghan knew the Russians and Chinese were for real. He was trying to blow them out of the water. The murmur in the crowd turned into a buzz. The mare herself started to jink uneasily in the ring, jerking the hand of the lad who held her. The Chinese consulted together but kept their hands and catalogues down. It looked as if their go was over, so Jimmy turned his attention back to Shalakov. Surely the Russian was finished. Shalakov raised his chin and gave O'Callaghan a long defiant stare. Then he smiled and deliberately jerked his catalogue up once, twice and then a third time – another three-step bid, tit-for-tat.

'One million eight hundred thousand,' called Jimmy. He glanced back at O'Callaghan, who now looked as if the wind had been knocked right out of him.

'Go on sir, one more could do it,' Jimmy almost pleaded. But O'Callaghan was shaking his head and shutting his catalogue. The Irishman was out, and the Russians would surely get her now. Jimmy looked towards the Chinese, in case they were changing their minds, but they looked back at him with blank expressions. Finally Jimmy glanced up at the ginger-haired stranger. He saw the man raise his hand.

Sam nudged Tipper. 'Who the fock is that?' he asked.

'Not a clue. Jesus it looks like O'Callaghan's out,' Tipper replied dejectedly.

Jimmy hesitated before he spoke, his voice suddenly growing squeaky. 'Ah, I'm bid one million nine hundred thousand.'

Jesus, he hoped this guy was for real. If not, he was going to be the laughing-stock of Newmarket. He glanced back down towards the Russian camp. Suddenly, he desperately wanted them to buy her. At least he knew they had the money and his commission would be safe.

Shalakov's body language had completely changed. This time there was no showboating smile. He couldn't see the other bidder from where he was standing and appeared to be in frantic, angry conversation with Shaunsheys.

While they were speaking Shaunsheys hurriedly rammed his cap back on his head, as if to free his hand for a rapid consultation of the catalogue. Jimmy paused, then said, with as much bravado as he could muster,

'I'm going to have to hurry you, gentlemen.'

As he said it he glanced in the direction of his mystery bidder. The red-head had vanished. Oh God! Where the hell was he? He couldn't have gone. He shouldn't. But he had. The stranger had melted completely away.

Shalakov turned away from his agent and looked straight at Jimmy. His expression was unreadable.

'She's a collector's item,' Jimmy fatuously told the audience, more to fill the silence than anything. He was now willing that Russian bastard to bid, or he was finished.

At last, his face grim, Shalakov nodded.

'Two million guineas, I have two million guineas!' The pitch of Jimmy's voice had gone up another octave. He was conscious of being desperate to empty his bladder but tried to stay composed. He was off the hook, that was the main thing.

'Anyone else, ladies and gentleman?' he enquired. He didn't really mean it. He wanted this nightmare over. 'All right, I'm selling at two million, once . . . twice . . .'

He banged his hammer down as hard as he could on the wooden block, and nodded towards Shalakov.

'Thank you very much sir,' he said.

And Christ, did he mean it.

133

20

'Rupert my man, you look like you've seen a ghost.'

The seventh Viscount Linbury, Fearless Phil to his friends, came up and patted Rupert Robinson on the back as they emerged from the sale ring.

'Do I?'

'You're two million quid richer than you were ten minutes ago. You can afford to buy a drink for once.'

'Yes, yes, absolutely,' stammered Robinson. 'It's a bit of a shock, if you want to know. But I need a bloody drink. I'd better offer those Russian blokes one first. It's the done thing.'

'All right,' said Phil accommodatingly. 'See you in the bar. Don't hang around.'

Rupert had no intention of hanging around. He felt like he'd just put a million quid on black and red had come up for the tenth spin in succession. Sick as a pig. Shaunsheys had just cleared exactly one million profit out of Stella Maris. He'd been comprehensively rogered, and there was nothing he could do about it.

As the Russian entourage spilled out of the sales ring into the December night, he could see the smugness on Shaunsheys's face as he trotted along behind the striding billionaire. 'Such a great horse, I thought she was very reasonable at the price,' he was babbling. The Russian didn't appear to be paying the agent any attention. Rupert approached and extended a hand.

'You have just bought my mare Mr Shalakov,' he said with spurious bonhomie. He still felt nauseous. 'So, er, congratulations. May I buy you a drink for luck?'

Shalakov stopped; and his court halted around him. He hadn't got to the top of the Russian army without being able to smell a rat. Shalakov's instincts told him that he'd been run up in the ring. There was nothing that he could do right then and there; but he'd get even with whomever had picked his pocket. Starting with the idiot now standing in front of him trying to look innocent. The billionaire made no attempt to shake hands, but merely looked Rupert up and down with distaste. He turned to a man upsides him who wore an earpiece, murmured a few words that Rupert couldn't hear, then strode off without warning towards his waiting motorcade.

Rupert looked after him. The man's rudeness was extreme but Robinson was relieved at not having to drink with him.

'Have it your own way,' he muttered. But he was slightly puzzled and perturbed by the Russian's reaction.

Robinson spent the night after the sale at Keeper's cottage with Phil Linbury. The cottage was part of a large property which had been bought by an eighteenth-century Linbury for a residence during race meetings and bloodstock sales at Newmarket. It had been used in that capacity by his linear descendents ever since, but the current Lord Linbury's personal circumstances were much reduced compared to those of his ancestors, and he had been forced to let the main house and stud on a long lease to Dermot O'Callaghan. He had kept for his own use only Keeper's Cottage, a charming but small-scale dwelling standing in one acre on the edge of the estate. Over the years the lanky viscount had got used to wounding his head on the low oak beams whenever he got drunk.

O'Callaghan meanwhile had turned the estate into one of the best stud farms in the country; and it was here that Sam had found work. So it didn't take him long to find out some of the details of how the two friends had celebrated the successful sale of Rupert's mare.

'They were at it most of the night, is what I heard,' he told Tipper in the pub at lunchtime. 'They got some girls in. They were singing and playing stupid games in and out of the garden until four in the morning. Jesus, they're some piss heads. Linbury was got up in a kaftan, so he was

– that's a long dress type of thing. He must have been on the disco biscuits.'

'A dress?' queried Tipper. 'That's warped.'

Rupert had slept until noon, then extricated himself from a bed where some girl lay prostrate. 'I didn't did I?' Rupert thought to himself as he dressed quietly. He didn't want to wake her up or she'd want paying again. His hangover was for some reason not as savage as usual. Instead of feeling gutted about the sale, and Shug Shaunsheys's devious role in it, he found himself looking on the brighter side. He was, for the moment, solvent. Of course some of his creditors would have to be paid, but he fancied a horse that was running in a few days' time and, if he put his online account back into credit, he might be able to land a nice touch and even clear some of his liabilities with the Revenue.

It was in this relatively sunny mood that he turned the key of his house in Sloane Avenue and slipped inside. But as soon as he closed his front door behind him, he knew something was wrong. In the narrow hallway was the lingering smell of some alien aftershave, mixed with smoke from a foreign cigarette, as acrid as burning bracken. The sitting-room door was half-open. He listened.

'Who's there?' he called through.

There was no reply to this quavering enquiry, so he edged nervously into the room.

'What the *fuck*?'

The words came out as a squawk of alarm. There

were two men sprawled in his armchairs. A thin balding one was leafing through a Christie's catalogue that he'd picked up from the coffee table, while his companion, muscles splitting the seams of his suit, was smoking the cigarette. It was, Rupert now realized, a Russian brand. Half of it was filled with tobacco and the rest was a cardboard tube.

As the first shock wore off, he realized he'd seen the men with Shalakov the night before. The thinner guy was the one who'd worn the ear piece.

'What are you doing here? How'd you get in?'

The thin man tossed the catalogue back onto the table and slowly rose to his feet. He spoke in the slightly nasal tones of London's suburbs.

'My name's Harrison, Martin Harrison. Mr Shalakov asked me to call.'

Harrison's tone was clipped.

'Shalakov? Why? And how d'you get into my house?'

Harrison didn't bother to answer.

'Mr Shalakov had a few supplementary questions for you, arising from last evening's transaction. Alexei?'

He half turned towards the other intruder, who now stubbed out his cigarette, planted his hands on the arms of the chair and pushed himself to his feet. He advanced towards Rupert. Alexei experienced close-to was impressive. He was built like an alpha-male gorilla, a block of hard muscle so square and solid that Rupert couldn't see where the head ended and the neck began, except for the rolls of fat above the collar of his black leather jacket. His shaven head had marginally less stubble than his face. And his thighs were so massive that he walked like a duck, moving his feet in a circular movement, rather than backwards and forwards.

Rupert hadn't been born during the Chinese year of the rabbit for nothing. As soon as Alexei's huge hand grabbed and enclosed the back of his neck he wet himself. His ancestors might have fought in the Crimea, but their subsequent inbreeding rendered Rupert a long second favourite in any skirmish with Russians.

'I suggest you make this easy for yourself,' said Harrison. 'How much did you promise Shaunsheys? Ten per cent? More?'

'Shaunsheys?' Rupert squeaked. 'Look, I didn't give him anything. I promise . . . I *swear*.'

'Why should we believe you? Do we look stupid? I'll ask you one more time and then Alexei will take over. What have you given Shaunsheys?'

'Please don't hurt me.' Rupert was pig-squealing now, writhing in Alexei's grip. 'I mean, it wasn't like that. It was *him*. He came here last week and threatened me. He told me something would happen to her, to the horse, if I didn't do a deal with him. It wasn't my fault. I needed the money. He made me sell the mare to him.'

'Sell? For how much? What did you get for her?'

Not waiting for an answer, Harrison made a

finger signal and Alexei swung his arm, smacking Rupert across the face. The blow snapped Rupert's head to the side and back, painfully jarring his neck and instantly depriving him of any further desire to resist.

'All right, all right, I'll tell you.' He was virtually sobbing now. 'Just let me go, and I'll tell you.'

Harrison nodded at Alexei, who released Rupert and took a step back into an attentive at-ease position. Rupert staggered backwards until he bumped into the wall. Alexei looked disappointed. Robinson was relieved.

'Shaunsheys more or less stole the horse from me,' he went on, pressing a hand against the side of his head where Alexei had made contact. 'He paid me a million. It was extortion. Shaunsheys has got the rest.'

Harrison listened intently.

'I don't get it,' he said after a moment's thought. 'Why did you sell? It doesn't look like a very good bargain to me.'

'I needed the money, as I said, and I was also, well, I was concerned – for myself, and for the horse. He threatened her, see? I'm sorry, I'm really sorry. I didn't know Mr Shalakov was interested in buying her . . . I would have told him, I would! I *promise* you.'

Harrison had heard enough of Rupert's whining. And he'd got what he wanted. He made another impatient motion towards Alexei, who smiled and stepped towards Rupert again, grabbed him by the throat and pulled him into the hall. Harrison followed, pointed at the sitting-room door, which was slowly swinging.

He indicated where the door hung from the frame, and the V-shaped opening between the frame and the hinged edge of the door.

'It's the leverage, you see. Archimedes's principle. The pressure exerted is incredible.'

Rupert looked at him in disbelief.

'But I've *told* you. I've told you everything!'

'Yes, very possibly. But this is to make sure you warn your friends that it is unacceptable for anyone to rip off Mr Shalakov.'

He nodded to Alexei who smiled again like a child about to delve into his Christmas stocking. He shoved Rupert nearer to the door.

'No, no,' pleaded Rupert desperately. 'I've told you everything. I didn't know you were going to buy the mare. I swear on my LIFE!'

Alexei took no notice. He simply kneed Rupert hard in the testicles, making him double over. Then the big Russian grabbed Rupert's hand, jammed its fingers into the gap between the door and the frame, seized the door handle and pulled the door inwards. Desperately winded though he was, Rupert let out a hideous agonized scream as his fingers squashed and splintered.

'Fine,' said Harrison briskly as Alexei allowed the door to swing open again.

'Oh yeah, almost forgot!'

Harrison slipped quickly back into the sitting

room and a moment later came back with the little abstract painting tucked under his arm.

'Nice Kandinsky,' Harrison said to Rupert, who'd sunk to the floor. He was in such agony he couldn't have cared less. 'It will fit nicely into Mr Shalakov's collection of modern Russians. I see no reason why you and Mr Shalakov should ever see one another again.' He motioned his head towards the door. Alexei stepped over Robinson who was writhing on the floor.

21

'Cuh. Get a load of this!'

It was mid-morning and the Partridge's bar was empty. Apart from Shelley, who was cleaning the pipes, and Johnny the Fish, who was reading the *Sun*.

'What is it?' she asked distractedly.

'Our old mate Shug, no less. He's made the *Sun*. It says here he went to Thailand and he's been found dead!' declared the Fish.

'Had it coming, I'd say,' Shelley said without any sympathy or even interest. As if it was a daily occurrence.

The Fish began to read out the article.

MURDER IN PARADISE – ENGLISHMAN
TORTURED AND KILLED.
English tourist Shug Shaunsheys' Thailand holiday
ended violently this week. Thai police said in a state-
ment today that his body was found on Tuesday,
hanging by the neck at his luxury beach house in

Phuket. Shaunsheys, forty-two from Newmarket, Suffolk, is thought to have travelled alone to Bangkok three weeks ago, before renting the holiday house in the upmarket resort. Police have ruled out suicide, saying Mr Shaunsheys's body showed signs of having been tortured before he was killed. They point out that the death follows a pattern seen before in the country, when alleged Western sex-tourists have been singled out and executed by local vigilantes intent on ridding the country of the sex-trade. Witnesses claim they saw a large, muscular man in dark glasses – described by one as being a 'giant' – leaving Shaunsheys's house with another man around the time of the murder. These individuals have not been identified and no arrests have been made.

The Fish looked up over the rim of his spectacles at his barmaid.

'What had he gone and got himself into?' the Fish wondered out loud.

'Something he's never going to get out of. Not now,' she smiled vindictively. 'He was a bloody paedo for god's sake.'

The Fish was genuinely amazed.

'Was he? I had no idea.'

'No Johnny. There's a few things you don't have no idea about,' she remarked cryptically.

'Cuh. What d'you mean by that?'

Nico's Jensen nosed through the gates of the Sinclair yard, accelerated smoothly along the short drive, and stopped on the half-circle of parking area in front of the house. It was late in the afternoon and Alison was looking out of the sitting room window, while swirling the gin and tonic in her hand to make the ice cubes clink. She observed their visitor easing himself from the driver's seat, tucking a leather document case under his arm, walking briskly to the front door, and giving the bell a sharp press. He then stood combing the fingers of his free hand through his long swept-back hair. Momentarily Alison's eyes closed as she listened to the sounds from the hall: David welcoming the Russian, the two men crossing the hall and disappearing into the office, the door closing behind them.

'Creep,' she murmured.

But her mind couldn't help dwelling on the way the Russian's long fingers had Welsh-combed his luxuriant hair.

Inside the office, Sinclair and Nico sat on opposite sides of the trainer's dark mahogany desk. The desk somehow empowered Sinclair.

'This young boy from Ireland – O'Reilly,' Nico was saying.

'Yes?'

'We haven't seen him ride for you yet.'

'We've not had him very long and –'

'Mr Shalakov thinks he has great, great potential. So do I. We must see him in action.'

At that moment there was a tap on the door and Alison walked in.

'Nico! How lovely to see you,' she said with all

the jollity she could muster. 'Drink? What can I get you?'

Nico stood and shook her hand.

'Nothing thank you Mrs Sinclair.'

'Call me Alison please. Are you sure? Well, to what do we owe this visit? What are you two scheming?' she added playfully.

'We're discussing Tipper O'Reilly, actually,' said Nico.

Alison kept a straight face. She was a pro.

'O'Reilly? Yes. Very promising. Hope he doesn't get too heavy though. So difficult for the young boys who are growing,' she reflected sympathetically as she left the room.

Sinclair smiled nervously.

'General Shalakov has asked me to show you something,' Nico said as soon as the door was shut. He drew a laptop computer from his document case, laid it on the desk and turned it on. While it started up, he asked, 'You remember Shug Shaunsheys, the bloodstock agent?'

'How could I forget? Terrible the way he died the other day. You wouldn't wish that on your worst enemy. Mind you, I'm not sure what he was up to out there.'

'Yes, his body was found in Thailand. He disappointed Mr Shalakov. He was supposed to be his trusted agent but he cheated over the mare we purchased in December. This is between us, you understand?'

'Of course,' Sinclair agreed, but he was

146

frowning. 'You're not trying to tell me there's some . . . well, connection? Shaunsheys's death and his . . . *disappointing* Mr Shalakov?'

'Yes, of course there is. Look.'

Nico clicked an icon on the computer screen, and a window opened. He clicked again making a picture appear, a moving picture, close-focussed on a man's head. The definition was slightly fuzzy and the image jittered and swayed. It had obviously been taken using a mobile phone.

The head was Shaunsheys's and he appeared to be standing in a barely furnished room. His face was contorted and sweating, the eyes blinking compulsively, the lips drawn back to show his uneven teeth. He was not speaking but only moaning piteously as large hands looped a cord about the thickness of a finger around his neck.

A command came from somewhere off-screen and Shaunsheys started to speak, the words coming in effortful grunts. But it was impossible to make out what he was trying to say.

The effort petered out and the eyeballs rotated from side to side, as if searching futilely for some salvation. The gruff prompting voice was heard again and the victim garbled something.

Then he fell silent as the hands tied the end of the rope around his neck to some place above his head. Nothing more was said. After a pause, while Shaunsheys mouth gaped and his eyes revolved madly, there was a sudden sharp cracking sound. His face contorted in a moment of supreme agony, his tongue came out and his head dropped several inches, cinching the rope tightly around his neck. His eyes bulged, and his mouth snapped shut around his tongue. Finally the head canted sharply to the side, the tightened rope preventing any further sound from him beyond a few last gurgles.

The person holding the camera-phone now backed slowly away and a full-length view of Shaunsheys was revealed. He was hanging by the neck from some fixture in the ceiling, twitching and turning as his life dribbled away. His feet touched the floor but the legs were unnaturally crooked. They had been smashed deliberately so that, unable to support his weight, the bloodstock agent would inevitably choke himself to death.

Nico watched Sinclair watching the execution of Shaunsheys. The trainer's face was chalk-white, his mouth slack. Sinclair could taste vomit welling up in his throat.

'Oh my God. That's just . . . well, it's. . . . what the fuck . . . no one deserves to die like that.'

'He did.'

'But what the hell did he do?'

'He took a million out of the Stella Maris sale,' Nico said calmly. 'Not smart.'

'I suppose he got someone to bid her up. It wouldn't be the first time he'd done it; he'd have done anything to get more commission.'

'It was not just for the commission. It was an elaborate fraud.'

'Well, I won't ask about the details. But to kill him, like that! I mean, it's sickening.'

'What Shaunsheys did was sickening, to Mr Shalakov.'

'Well, I wish you hadn't shown it to me. Why did you? Jesus.'

Nico shut down the laptop, closed the lid and tucked it back in his case.

'Like I said, Mr Shalakov thought you might be interested. He asked me to show you.'

Sinclair looked away, thoroughly shaken.

'Are you threatening me?'

'David. Mr Shalakov insists on the very highest standards of loyalty. Now . . .'

He slapped his hands down onto his knees and got up.

'I have a dinner appointment in Cambridge. High table. I'm talking to the Master about the proposed Shalakov Professorship of Russian Studies. Better not be late.'

Sinclair didn't tell Alison about the video of Shaunsheys's death. When she asked about the visit he tried to persuade her Nico was merely en route for his meeting in Cambridge, and he'd dropped by for a casual briefing on the Shalakov horses. Alison didn't buy the story.

'If he'd come for that, you'd have taken him down to the yard. You always do. What did the creep really come for? I don't like him. He's always turning up unannounced. And what was all that about Tipper O'Reilly?'

She was relentless and Sinclair was so badly shaken after seeing the Shaunsheys video that his defences were down and he blurted out the truth.

'It's just that Shalakov wants Tipper to ride his horses. He's insisting. I'll have to agree.'

'Don't be a bloody wimp, David. What do they know about what riders to use, or about anything that goes on round here? Tell them you're the trainer. They wouldn't eat you.'

Sinclair shook his head.

'I wouldn't bet on that, Alison.'

22

'Sam, I was wondering about Red,' Tipper said. 'Will she soon be off to Russia, then?'

They were in the Partridge at lunchtime. It was Covey Club day and Tipper's fellow members would be turning up over the next half an hour.

'Yeah, one of the blokes was talking about it yesterday. Everybody thinks it's weird. She's still here, like, but they've got her in isolation. It's an old disused stud, a small one over Burrough Green way; but it's been done up with CCTV, electric fences, the lot. Security's as tight as my arse. There's a huge great security guard from Russia. Apart from a girl who looks after the mare, only the vet goes in there.'

'Why'd Shalakov not take her back to Russia? He's got a bloody great stud over there, so they say.'

'He wants her to be covered by a top class English or Irish stallion. No point in sending her over there in the winter only to bring her back in the spring to be covered. It's bloody cold in Russia.'

'Jesus I wish I could go and see her.'

'Forget it boy. No chance.'

Sam drained his pint and went to the bar. Shelley poured him two more of the same. When he brought them back to the table, Tipper looked doubtfully at his.

'I need to watch my weight.'

'Drink up for Christ's sake! You're not getting any rides anyway, to watch your weight for. Talking of which, has Mrs Sinclair had those lovely tits of hers out again? You were a bloody fool about that, you know? If it was me –'

'It wasn't you. I just couldn't have done it with her. I don't even like her.'

'Anyway it's time you had a girlfriend. You've not had a shag since you were at Doyle's. You'll have a nervous breakdown, so you will.'

Tipper leaned closer to his cousin and lowered his voice.

'As a matter of fact, there is somebody. There's a new girl in the yard.'

'Oh yeah? Who's that, then?'

'She's a Russian called Ana. I walked into the tack room, like, and there she was. It was her first day. She's awful pretty and she looked at me like . . . I don't know, like we could talk.'

'Talk?' Sam scoffed. 'Talk's not what this is about, me boy. A roll in the hay, that's what you need.'

'I think maybe I've fallen in love, Sam. Don't fockin' laugh. I *do*!'

But Sam did laugh, a little. On the other hand, a part of him was envious. Sam was a danger to the virtue of any girl who crossed his sights, but he'd never been in love. He wondered what it felt like. 'What she look like then?' he asked Tipper.

'She's only about my height. She's got lovely hair down to her shoulders and very white skin except when she comes in from the gallops. Then she gets bright red cheeks. She's a great rider. And she has these big green eyes, like they're maybe too big for her face, you know? And she wrinkles her nose, in a way that really turns me on. She looks kind of surprised about everything.'

'I bet she's surprised when you go mooning around telling her you love her.'

'I don't! I haven't! Jesus. I wouldn't know how.'

'Nice bum?'

'Yeah, real nice, and even nicer when she's wearing her tight jeans for riding.'

Sam had no trouble visualizing it.

'What's her tits like?' he asked.

'Jesus, shut up, Sam. They're great, okay? Really great. Sinclair thinks they are, too. I seen him staring at them like he wants to eat them. He's a right lech, but I'm not worried. She's not going to let him near. She's too good for him.'

'Just like you're too good for his missis, is it?'

Looking round, Tipper had noticed the Covey

Club assembling in the snug. He picked up his pint.

'Exactly. You got it. Now, I better go in. See you later.'

Tipper's acuteness and instinctive appreciation of racehorses made his information as valuable to the Covey Club as to Sinclair. Had the trainer found out about these titbits of stable talk and gallops intelligence, Tipper would have been out on his ear and warned off before he knew it – even Shalakov would not have been able to save him. But what protected him from any suspicion was the openness of his personality. It seemed impossible to believe that he actually *was* doing anything wrong. Combined with his brown eyes wide-set in that pale, bony face, made Tipper appear to everyone on the yard utterly straightforward and trustworthy.

To everyone, that is, except Alison Sinclair. No yard is without its bully, as Tipper had found at Doyle's when he'd inadvertently crossed Dermot Quigley. But this time he'd crossed the governor's wife and life was even worse. She constantly gave Tipper dirty, demeaning jobs. She screamed curses at him on the Limekilns, and ridiculed him afterwards as the string walked back to the yard. She set out to get rid of him and her plan was beginning to succeed.

None of Shalakov's horses were due to race until three or four weeks into the flat season, so there was no question of Tipper doing any immediate race-riding for the Sinclairs; though he kicked a few winners in here and there for other trainers. Sinclair kept him in the dark about being chosen as Shalakov's principal rider. So he might simply have cut his losses and quit the job. But he stayed on, telling himself Alison would soon lose interest in persecuting him, or find another victim, and then his chance would come.

In the meantime his weight began to creep up. He adopted the strategy of eating less, and drinking more, especially whisky, with unfortunate results in someone who, even on a full stomach, found it difficult to hold his drink. Tipper got legless in public a few too many times which, in a place like Newmarket, gets noticed and talked about. Tipper had an ally in Delaney who did his best to cover for him. He kept him away from the Sinclairs if he thought he looked a bit ropey in the morning.

But there was no helping Tipper the day he got stuck in at the Partridge after a Covey Club meeting. Tipper was filing out of the pub with the rest of the club as Johnny the Fish arrived back from a golfing weekend, wearing tweed plus-fours in a loud check, and carrying his golf bag. He stood on the threshold for a moment, peering around.

'Glad to see the place is still standing. What's your poison?'

'Jesus, Johnny. I'm just on my way.'

'Go on. Have a quick one with me. How's life at Sinclair's? Chinless sort of bird but he might go the right way eventually. His missis is a tough enough pullet, though. Cuh . . . her father's a mate of mine. We shoot together. Books and covers. Books and covers.'

Tipper sank the scotch that Johnny had thrust into his hand and made as if to leave. But the Fish nudged Tipper's glass towards Shelley, who filled it this time with a triple from the optic.

'That's more like it,' the Fish approved. 'He might be able to taste that one.'

As Tipper sank the drink he could feel it hitting the mark.

'Stay and have some lunch, old boy,' the Fish suggested.

'Well, I've got to watch my weight, Johnny. Maybe just a salad.'

A salad was about all that could be found and it didn't do a lot to cushion the effect of half a bottle of scotch. By the time he got to Sinclair's yard for evening stables he was legless. The first person who found him slumped in a chair in the tack room was Sinclair.

'Oh, O'Reilly! How was Fighting Talk this morning after his bit of work?'

Tipper looked up sidelong, his eyes out of focus.

'Brilliant, man, 'solutely fucking brilliant.'

'What? O'Reilly, are you drunk?'

'Course I am. Haven't you ever been drunk? If I had a missis like yours I would be.' Sinclair was totally taken aback.

'Okay. That's enough. You're talking rubbish.

I'll speak to you in the morning. Make sure you're bloody well sober.'

Shaking his head, Sinclair left before he could get involved in an argument. Tipper staggered to his feet and spewed up in a corner, then slumped back into the chair. He didn't wake up until Delaney threw a bucket of water over him several hours later.

23

Tipper's problem ran deeper than simply drinking scotch instead of eating solid food. There was Ana. He was getting himself into a state about her, but he couldn't begin to think how to chat her up. If he faced up to how unapproachable she was it scared him, so he drank. And then he felt lonely and depressed – so he drank a bit more. Every morning the pounding of hooves under him on the gallops were matched throb for throb by his own pounding head.

Sam never tired of giving Tipper the benefit of his superior knowledge of women and how to handle them. He instructed him to find out which bunch of horses Ana was scheduled to ride out with, and make sure Delaney put him in there too. Delaney was a sympathetic old skin, so he didn't mind. And that way Tipper got the chance to let her know he liked her. That was first base. Second base was to ask her out. Tipper shrank from the very thought, but said he'd try.

But in the end he didn't need to. One morning, in the very early spring, all the pieces simply fell into place. Tipper found himself upsides Ana on the horsewalk going back to the yard. She asked him a simple question about where he came from, and it all started tumbling out – about his dead mother and disappeared father, his brother, and the estate where he grew up. Then he talked about Himself, the first horse he ever fell in love with, and the Golden Vale, where the best horses in the world came from. And then the miracle happened. Ana responded. She began to open up to him about herself. Not, of course, about her life in London prior to coming to Newmarket, or how she'd ended up in Newmarket. All that she kept absolutely to herself. But she realized that Tipper could be a useful source of information to feed back to Shalakov, so she decided to let him get a bit closer to her. Then before she knew it, she was enjoying his company. She told him about being a child in Kazakhstan, of her uncle's horses, and of her teenage years in Moscow where she missed the horses so desperately.

'So why'd you come to London?'

'A change. Also to learn English. And I still wanted to work with horses.'

'Jesus. Your English is amazing. So why London if you like horses?'

'Everyone starts in London, of course. But now I am here in Newmarket, doing what I like to do! Is it okay?'

'You're good at it. I think so.'

'I am glad, because I heard them talking about you, Tipper. They said you are a very, very good horseman.'

'Bollocks! They didn't!'

'They did!'

'Anyway I don't only want to be a horseman. I want to be a jockey, but they won't give me any race-rides.'

'You will get a chance, soon. You need – what is it? – patience. We have a saying: the last to reach the samovar gets the strongest tea. You know what a samovar is?'

'No.'

'A teapot, with a tap. It is a Russian tradition always to make tea in a samovar.'

'What if the last one gets to this samovar thing and just finds it empty?'

She laughed, enjoying his show of stubborn pessimism.

'You don't know,' she said. 'A samovar is a very *big* teapot.'

It was like starting a cold engine of a big old classic car. It might take an age to spark, but once it did, it was roaring. Tipper now found himself talking to Ana every day, like a long-established friend: about their lives, the horses, the other stable staff, or local bits of news.

But being 'just friends' was not what he wanted and, after a few days, as Sam firmly informed Tipper, it was time to run for second base.

'Take her to the movies, me boy. Only choose a film about love, not a war film or a martial arts film.'

'I like war and martial arts films.'

'She won't, I promise you. I tell you what, see if there's a horror film on, that would be deadly, because she'll be so scared she'll jump into your arms.'

'In the flicks?'

'Well, she'll grab your hand, anyway.'

That night Tipper took Ana to the local multiplex and she did indeed grab his hand at one shock moment, then held on to it for the rest of the film. That was as far as she would go, but next day Sam told Tipper what it meant.

'She's got the screaming hots for you, me boy. Sure as hard-boiled eggs she has. Another night like that and you go for the home run.'

The next week they went to the cinema again, and held hands again. But again it ended there. Ana never seemed to drink alcohol, and refused to let Tipper take her to the pub afterwards. She would not even kiss him, let alone go home with him or invite him to her own place, a one-room flat in a new housing development off Exning Road. So something more adventurous had to be cooked up.

Even Sam had no ideas. So, leaning on the Partridge bar one night, he thought he'd tap Johnny the Fish for some.

'Where do you take a girl when you're bored

with the flicks, and she doesn't like going to the pub? For a special occasion, like.'

'London, old boy,' said the Fish. 'It's the only thing. See a West End show. Something musical, in period costume. Most women like that kind of thing.'

'What shows would you recommend, Johnny?'

'Me? Now you're asking. I've not seen one since my last divorce. We did see that *Phantom of the Opera*, I remember. Total load of tosh I thought, but my then-wife, she liked it. As a matter of fact in bed that night she kept calling me Michael. The woman was thinking of bloody Michael Crawford all the time.'

'Who's he?'

'Star of the show. Cuh! It was the beginning of the end for us, I can tell you.'

Sam later reported what he saw as the gist of this to Tipper.

'The Fish says his wife was dead turned on by *The Phantom of the Opera* when they saw it. She couldn't get him into bed quick enough, after. And guess what, me boy! It's still going in the West End. So I reckon that's the one.'

Nervously negotiating the credit card booking line, Tipper bought two tickets for what seemed to him an enormous amount of money. When he showed them to Ana she was taken by surprise.

'But you didn't ask me yet! Maybe I say no.'

Tipper shook his head.

'These tickets cost a mind-blowing amount of money. You *can't* say no.'

'We come back here on the same night?'

It was a disappointing question. Tipper had been fantasizing about London hotels with emperor-sized beds – Ana walking into the bedroom from the bathroom in a negligee – standing at the end of the bed and letting it fall onto the floor. But he said,

'If you want.'

'All right, then,' she said. 'I'll go. But we *have* to come back that night.'

A few days later they went to Cambridge and caught the train to King's Cross, arriving in London in plenty of time for the theatre.

'We might as well have a drink while we wait,' Tipper suggested.

Ana was feeling relaxed and, as the pub across the road from the theatre wouldn't be full of ogling stable lads, she agreed. Feeling distinctly nervous Tipper had a couple of large scotches while she drank a Bacardi and coke. Then he knocked back another when she went to the Ladies.

'Jesus, Ana, you look great in that dress,' he told her when she came back to the bar. He tried to put his arm around her waist but she wriggled away.

'Come on Tipper. We're going to be late.'

The next hour and a half were agony for Tipper. Whatever was going on up there on stage, Tipper didn't understand it. Some nutter in a mask, a lot of opera singing, a girl that the nutter was in love with, clouds of dry-ice wafting across the stage. To lessen his boredom he kept looking sideways at Ana. In profile, lit by the stage lighting, she was more desirable than he'd ever seen her. He soon forgot about the play and lapsed into thinking only about her.

By the time they got to the interval Tipper's feelings were ready to burst. Most of the people in their row went out, but he and Ana still sat in their seats. Suddenly Tipper made a grab for her hand, locking it inside his own.

'Jesus, Ana,' he blurted out. The Scotch had wiped away his inhibitions. He was squeezing and pawing her hand a good deal too hard. 'You know what? I'm just like that bloke in the mask. You're so sexy . . . I'm desperate to get in the sack with you.'

He knew it was a mistake as soon as he said it. Ana froze, then told him icily, 'Let go of me, Tipper,' before yanking her hand away. Then she sat stonily, staring straight ahead. Tipper didn't know what to do or say to get her out of the sulk.

'I'm going to the bog, okay?'

He stood up and shuffled clumsily along the row until he was out. It took him a long time to shoulder his way through the throng of theatre-goers, locate the toilets, shoulder his way out and up to the bar, order another double Scotch, sink it, and then get back to the auditorium.

By this time, he hoped he'd have worked out

some way of apologizing to her. He hadn't, but it didn't matter anyway. Ana was no longer there. For ten minutes after the show re-started Tipper assumed she was in the Ladies. Then it dawned on him: Ana had done a runner, and he was alone.

24

Tipper felt sick. His stomach was knotted tight and he could feel the sweat under his armpits.

Out on the street he rang her mobile but there was no answer. As he fished in his pockets for his phone he remembered that Ana had their train tickets; and he didn't have much money on him. He began running up Haymarket and into Piccadilly Circus, shouting her name and looking around him. There was no sign of her. He stopped and sent her a text begging her to ring him. Nothing. He sent another one saying he was sorry. Still nothing. He stood in front of the Eros fountain, surrounded by a mob of tourists. He felt almost as wretched as the day he learned his Ma was dead. He stood alone by the fountain for what felt like hours.

There was only one person in the world he knew would be in London. He didn't want to ring him. But what else was he going to do? 'If you need anything give me a ring; come and have a drink when you're in London,' was what the Duke had told him. And the information from the Covey Club that he'd been giving the Duke had been good. What else could he do? He tried Ana again. Still no answer. So he scrolled through the contacts list in his phone.

'How are you Duke?' Tipper shouted above the traffic. 'It's Tipper. Tipper O'Reilly. Are you around for a drink?'

'Young Tipper, is it? Course I am, mate. Where are you?'

'Jesus, I'm in fockin' Piccadilly next to this great fountain thing.'

'Great! You're five minutes away. We're the Pirhana Club on Berwick Street. Yes, Berwick Street. Ask anyone. All the boys are here.'

Tipper first tried Ana again. No answer. He sent her another text message telling her where he was going. Then he set off into Soho, asking directions from just about anyone, until he found the Piranha Club. On the door there were two bruisers, who ushered Tipper to the desk inside.

'I'm here to meet the Duke,' Tipper informed a friendly looking woman in her mid-fifties.

'That's fine. Can I just have a name and address? And then I'll ask you to smile at the camera on the wall.'

'You want my picture?'

'Yes. It's just the gambling regulations. You won't need to do it next time. This gentleman will show you downstairs.'

The gentleman turned out to be another hunk of meat that had appeared from a lower area of the building, like a bad-tempered badger nosing out of his sett. He waited impatiently while Tipper completed the formalities, and then took him down into the lower depths.

Tipper had never seen a place quite like it, except maybe in the films. There were waiters scuttling around in black and white uniforms, foreign looking men crouched over different shaped tables with dice and cards flying around, and groups of women in elegant *couture* standing around looking bored. Tipper's escort beckoned towards the bar, but Tipper hesitated. His natural shyness didn't equip him for situations like this. He had no idea what the 'Duke' looked like. Then a friendly looking man broke from the group, threw an arm up in an expansive gesture and boomed out.

'Well now, is this him? Is this the Man Himself? Is it the one and only Tipper O'Reilly?'

Tipper recognized his voice from the phone: a rich, loud, wheezy East London croak.

'What are you having son? I know! Irish whiskey for an Irishman, am I right? Course I am.'

Before Tipper could assure him that a glass of Scotch would be quite in order, the Duke had ordered up a bottle of Bushmill's.

'These jockeys know how to drink. Come and sit down here, young Tipper. Oi, Tony, come and meet Tipper O'Reilly.'

Tony had on a blue, short-sleeved shirt, which might have fitted him at some point in the past. But it wasn't Tony's biceps that Tipper was looking at. It was his knuckles. He had 'Dad' tattooed on one set, and 'Mum' on the other.

'Alright?' Tony enquired, in what passed for a kindly tone.

'Grand, thanks,' Tipper smiled before taking a good slug of whiskey.

He checked his phone. Ana hadn't rung.

'The Duke says you know what's going on,' said Tony

'How d'you mean?'

'With the horses, like.'

'Oh! Yeah! Well, I'm out there on the gallops every morning. Should know something.'

The Duke appeared at Tony's shoulder.

'He's the best, Tone – the best. Tone likes a bet, don't you Tone?'

'As long as it's not from that dozy bastard that used to give you the information.'

'Who was that? Bullet?' said Tipper.

'I'll give him a fucking bullet and all if he comes up with any more crap tips,' Tony growled.

The Duke turned to Tipper.

'Anything good coming up, then?'

'Jesus, yeah, there's plenty. There's lots of eyes and ears in Newmarket.'

The Duke smiled.

'That's what we like, isn't it Tone? Plenty of eyes and ears. Tone's in that game, ain't you Tone?'

'I cut their fucking ears off, if I have to.'

The Duke loved that. He roared with laughter. Tipper forced a smile.

'Tone is very special to us, Tipper,' the Duke explained. 'He finds people for us. People what owes us money. He's in personal finance, he is. I've got another one for you over here. Oi, Ladders, get over here!'

He grabbed hold of the bottle on the bar and filled Tipper up. Tipper had one last woozy look at his phone and fumbled it into his pocket.

'This is Ladders, Tipper. Tipper's our man with the gee-gees.'

'Good to meet you Ladders,' said Tipper. 'What's your game then?'

'Burglar mate. I'm a burglar. But only high class stuff. No televisions or any of that crap. I'm top end. Do the odd car as well, if it's nice. Any thing good coming up?'

Despite the company, Tipper was beginning to relax. He'd come across petty criminals during his childhood, and this lot seemed like more of the same. At this stage of a disastrous evening, they were as good drinking partners as any. The whiskey was kicking in and Ana had done a vanishing act, so he might as well stay and enjoy himself.

By the end of the evening Tipper had given everybody his telephone number. Under the rules of racing he wasn't meant to pass on information, but he told himself there was no harm in breaking petty rules. He might have been more worried about breaking the rules of the Covey Club, under which he was only meant to pass information to the Duke. But these were all mates of the Duke and all mates of each other. So what harm was there?

Tipper had a memorable evening, or would have had, if he'd been able to remember it afterwards. The Duke's friends were all lovely people and they all loved their racing. By the time he was half way down his bottle of Bushmill's they were all going to look after him. They were lovely blokes.

'We'll always have plenty on for you son,' said the Duke. 'We've all got to live haven't we?'

Before long Tipper was completely relaxed – in particular his legs, which weren't working too well. Later someone helped him to a car and, the next thing he knew, the driver was shaking him awake in Newmarket High Street.

25

As if to prove that the bloodstock industry has a sense of humour, the first day of the covering season – when mares and stallions start their unromantic liaisons – is the fourteenth of February, St Valentine's Day. Breeders like to have their foals on the ground as early in the year as possible, and some will risk having their mares covered before that. The theory is, the sooner the foal is walking, the quicker it'll strengthen up and learn to gallop. Mistakes, however, can happen, and that's where the risk lies. It's all right for a foal to appear a few days prematurely. But if it pops out before the first of January it's an unmitigated disaster; because New Year's Day is the official birthday of all thoroughbreds, and any foal born before then is classified as a one-year-old. Even though it's only a few days old. For the first years of their lives, horses run against their own age, so a December foal has to race other two-year-olds when it is actually only one; an impossible task. Of course it's far from unknown for premature foals to be hidden with their mothers in a back barn until the new year. But in the racing world, secrets like that are hard to keep. One groom knowing the truth is one too many.

Accordingly Stella Maris was scheduled to lose her virginity on the eighteenth of February. The equine gentleman on whom she would be calling was Border Dispute, a blue-blooded son of Rock of Gibraltar. Stella Maris had been as carefully prepared for the appointment as a Mughal emperor's daughter for her wedding day – but much more scientifically. The vet had visited every day for a month to inject her with a hormone to suppress her reproductive cycle. This would ensure that, as soon as she was taken off the hormone, the cycle would be immediately kick-started. Then her ovulation became calculable to within a few hours.

Once a week another, much older visitor also appeared. His shock of grey, curly hair and studious half-rimmed glasses made him instantly recognizable. He conferred with the vet, read the data on the latter's computer, and gave the mare a careful examination of his own. His name was Jameson, and Alexei looked forward to his visits. Jameson always had a present for him – Russian comic books, bars of his favourite Korkunov chocolate, pots of *tvorog* cheese or cans of the weak beer Russians make from fermented rye bread, called *kvass*. Alexei devoured these simple gifts with a desperate, homesick voraciousness.

First thing in the morning on Stella Maris's big day, the vet came over and took her temperature, entering it on his laptop computer. Jameson was there too, to make sure everything was correct. Satisfied that she was ovulating, he told the stable girl Mandy to get the mare ready to travel.

The horse-transporter arrived. Mandy, who'd been specially chosen for her precocious skill with difficult horses, loaded the mare, then got into the passenger seat beside the driver. With Jameson following in his car, Alexei by his side, Stella Maris was driven through the Suffolk country lanes. It only took them twenty minutes to reach the stud farm where Border Dispute plied his trade at £100,000 a pop.

Ten minutes later, with Stella Maris unloaded and installed in her preparation stable, Jameson returned to his car and withdrew a black attaché case from the boot.

Alexei followed Jameson back into the building, with the attaché case tucked under his coat. He felt very ill at ease. This wasn't his scene and though he knew in outline what was going to happen, he had little idea of the details. Nor could he trust himself, in this environment, to intuit where trouble might come from. The bodyguard had no way of knowing if the usual covering-shed routines were being followed, though, in fact, they were. His education had been extremely controlled, and had not included the sex life of animals.

But Alexei's instructions were to stay close at all times. So, despite feeling useless, he ducked into the shed immediately behind Jameson. He noticed that there was a CCTV camera mounted high in the wall, where it had a wide-angle view of the entire proceedings.

'We give you blue movie to take home,' one of the stallion men joked when he saw Alexei peering at the camera. Alexei hadn't got a clue what he was on about, but he understood when he and Jameson were warned to stand well out of the way.

Border Dispute – as muscled, arrogant and stroppy as a heavyweight boxer at a title-fight weigh-in – pawed the ground in the covering shed. While Jameson admired the stallion's mono-toned, black shining coat, gleaming with good health, next door the teaser stallion was introduced to Stella Maris. Living a life of permanent sexual frustration, his sole job was foreplay, exciting the mare so that she would be receptive to the advances of her main suitor.

When she was altogether ready, Stella Maris was led in to the covering shed.

'Blimey, she's a big mare this one,' one of the handlers laughed. 'We'd better get our lad the ramp.'

The business in the covering shed never has much to do with romance. Jameson and Alexei watched as a wooden ramp was fetched and placed behind the mare. This was for Border Dispute to stand on – before he mounted her. Her hind feet were then placed in big padded boots, to protect the stallion in case she failed to appreciate his efforts and lashed out. In addition she had one of her front legs pulled up in a sling, to make it almost impossible for her to kick him as he approached her. And just to make sure she didn't feel like using her teeth, or dodging out of the way, one of the handlers slipped a loop of thin rope over her nose and twisted it tight. Stella Maris would be biting nothing, and going nowhere.

She did at least have a padded rug laid over her neck and withers. This was for her own safety, as stallions often express their passion by biting a mare while mounting her. As Border Dispute snorted with excitement and clambered aboard from the rear, her front leg was let out of the sling so she could take his weight. Thirty seconds later, with a guiding hand from the stallion men here and there, Border Dispute shuddered a few times, then shuffled back until he stood on all fours again. It was over. Alexei felt quite embarrassed.

As the mare was led out of the covering shed, the senior stallion man beckoned Jameson to follow him through the door into an untidy office off to one side of the barn. There, Jameson took his attaché case from Alexei, opened it – it had unusually secure combination locks – and took out a big brown envelope with £10,000 in cash inside. The case had its own freezing unit built in, and from this Jameson removed a large bottle of iced vodka which he presented to the stallion man along with the envelope.

'Enjoy the vodka,' Jameson smiled.

'Nice to do business with you,' the stallion man beamed. Jameson checked his watch. If there were no problems with the plane they'd be in Xanadu in five hours.

26

What had he done that was so very wrong? Ana had overreacted. She'd left him in the lurch in the middle of a very expensive date. She was a moody cow. It was worse than being stood up.

In his more self-defensive moments, these were the thoughts that ran through Tipper's mind. But the problem would not go away. He still wanted her. He still loved her. So how could he blame her? If anyone was to blame, it was himself. He was clumsy, klutzy, and tactless. He always said and did the wrong things. How could he get it right?

Ana completely froze Tipper out after London. So a few days later, when he saw her going into the tack-room, he followed. He stopped in the doorway and spoke her name. Her back was to him but she flinched visibly. Then she just stood, staring straight ahead.

'Ana,' he said plaintively. 'What happened to you? How'd you get back home? I was worried.'

She didn't turn around, and didn't answer.

'Let me make it up to you,' he stumbled on. 'Look. There's this hare-coursing meet over at Balsham. It's illegal but they never get busted. Some of the boys bring their lurchers – you know, dogs, for chasing the hares. It's great craic. Why don't you come?'

Ana stiffened her back slightly, then began hanging the various pieces of tack she had with her in their places. When she had finished she turned and, with her nose and chin defiantly raised, but without so much as a word, she pushed past Tipper and flounced away.

'Ah, come on, now!' he called after her.

Sam gave Tipper a piece of his mind over a sandwich in the Partridge at lunchtime.

'The girl's a fockin' vegetarian, for Christ's sake! Use your head, boy! Instead of inviting her to blood-sports, have you tried saying sorry yet?'

Tipper shook his head.

'What about?'

Sam looked pained.

'About what you said to her in the theatre, you fockin' eejit?'

'Okay, I said the wrong thing maybe. But it was a small thing compared to what she did. She fucked off and left me.' He tapped himself on the chest. 'She should say sorry to me.'

Sam sighed. 'You got a lot to learn, boy. Look, it's like this. You always have to say sorry. That's a rule between men and women. The guy's always in the wrong and the price he pays is he says sorry and maybe gets her a bunch of flowers. Tell you what. Why don't you write to her? Then we can be sure you say the right thing.'

'Well maybe. But you're not bloody well reading it, that's for sure.'

It took Tipper about half an hour of indecision in W.H. Smith before he settled on the right card. He almost chose a cartoon one. But the jokes were mostly one way or another sexual and even the ones that weren't she might not understand. So he settled for a simple card with a red rose on it. It took him even longer to write:

Ana – Look I'm really sorry, I drank too much and I shouldn't have. Please give me another chance. I have to be with you. I'll even give up the drink for you. Just say the word. Tipper.

There was a lot more he would like to have written, but fluency with a pen was not his strength, and besides, his promise to give up drink was going in a bit deep. He sealed the envelope, wrote her name on it and asked one of the other girls in the yard to give it to her.

The card had the effect Sam predicted. When they were riding out the next morning Ana came up beside him and smiled tentatively.

'Ana, look, I haven't touched a drop for days. Can we try again?'

'I don't know, Tipper.'

He loved hearing her say his name. *Teeper.*

'We could just do something together, go out for the day.'

'I don't want to watch dogs killing hares.'

'No, but I thought we could go to a place called Woburn. It's got a Safari Park. There are elephants and monkeys and stuff.'

The smile that spread across her face was a good sign. There was a definite thaw, he reckoned.

Tipper borrowed Sam's car, a banger he'd bought through the local paper. It looked terrible but it got them to Woburn. Driving around the park in the spring sunshine seemed perfect to Tipper. They could talk freely, with no pressure, and no one to interrupt.

Ana loved the elephants. 'They're so soulful,' she said.

'Don't they look a bit sad, though?'

'I don't think so. I think it is just their way. They are calm and thoughtful and do everything in their own time.'

'Some people say they shouldn't be kept in captivity.'

'I don't think it worries them. They know the routine. They're like horses. They don't worry when they have a routine.'

'What do you worry about, Ana?'

Like most people in the first flush of love, Tipper quickly got bored talking about anything except Ana. She paused for a while before she answered.

'Me? I worry about the future. What will happen to me. Whether I will have a sad life or a happy life. In my country there are too many have sad lives. There used to be a lot of killing and cruelty. Now there is a lot of very rich people but even more very poor people. I just hope it will get better.' Then she paused again. 'So what do you worry about Tipper?'

Tipper hadn't reckoned on the guns being turned on him.

'Er, I suppose I worry about my future. Being without a family around me, and dying a complete failure.'

'But you do have family! Your brother.'

'I used to. He's gone.'

'What about Sam?'

'Sam's my cousin but he's really my mate. It was my Ma who made us a family. Once she'd gone, the family went west.'

'What do you regret in your life, Tipper? Is there anything you wish you'd never done?'

He felt it was a loaded question, but couldn't tell exactly where the load lay.

'I regret being such an eejit in London,' he muttered out of the corner of his mouth.

Ana laughed and punched him lightly on the arm.

'Be serious, Tipper. I mean it.'

Tipper slowed the car to walking pace as they approached a pair of giraffes, walking along as if in slow-motion. Ana looked at Tipper. Her original plan had been to string him along and suck information out of him. But, even though he'd got a bit over-excited in London, it was dawning on her that she had feelings for Tipper stirring in her. He was cute. He was actually very gentle. He was different.

'Well it's true,' he decided finally. 'I've no regrets at all. I'm glad I work with horses, because I'm good at it. And I'm glad I came to England because I met you. What about your regrets, then?'

'I can't say.'

'Yes you can. I did.'

'You regret nothing but I regret much. Very much.'

'So, what is it?'

She fell silent, gnawing her lower lip. She seemed about to speak again when suddenly there was an almighty metallic bang and a family of baboons landed on the car bonnet. They began trying to tear off Sam's windscreen wipers, so Tipper turned the wipers on to discourage them. When that didn't work he got the car moving again, accelerating fast, and then slowing down to allow the now frightened animals to jump off. Then he picked up his speed again. The moment in which Ana might have confided in him had passed.

All in all the day had been a greater success than Tipper had dared to hope for. He and Ana had talked properly about things that mattered to them both. They had laughed and joked and she seemed to have forgiven him. So after dropping Ana off at her flat (he wasn't invited in) Tipper took himself round to the Partridge for a celebratory drink.

'You're looking very chipper, Tipper, if you'll excuse the rhyme,' the Fish remarked, as he pressed the glass to the whisky optic.

'Been to Woburn with my girl, Johnny. Had a great day too. Great day.'

'"With my girl", is it now? I don't think we've had the pleasure . . .'

'She doesn't like pubs.'

'Doesn't she? Oh dear. That doesn't sound too promising to me.'

'No but really, she's the business, Johnny. She's magic!'

'Get your tin hats out. Here we go! Tipper's in love.'

Tipper didn't deny it. He gave Johnny a big grin, sank his whisky and banged the glass down.

'Well, that's my lot for tonight. Early start tomorrow.'

'You're not going home already?' Johnny looked shocked. 'You wouldn't even fail the breathalyser yet!'

But Tipper was already on his way out.

27

The pilot had instructions to taxi straight to the hangar as soon as he touched down at Xanadu. His cargo was to be unloaded out of the biting wind. If Newmarket was chilly, this place, two hours from Moscow, was bloody freezing.

As the plane circled above the airstrip, Alexei looked down through his porthole window. Below him, set in a swathe of thick pine forest, was a vast compound with a heavily electrified perimeter fence that would take all day to walk around. The complex's main features were a dozen identical buildings, low, huge and windowless like gigantic warehouses. It also contained the airstrip, with its hanger and control tower, a power generating station and an oval dirt-track, beside which stood a small viewing stand. The whole compound was subdivided by razor-wire fencing into different zones, to be entered and left through check-points. It was a highly secure facility.

Whilst most people's hearts would have sunk

at the sight of Shalakov's experimental Xanadu complex, in all its brutal functionality, Alexei buckled his seatbelt feeling very happy to be home. His three-month exile was over.

Shalakov himself was waiting as the horse-plane's ramp was lowered.

'Be careful with her,' he barked at the nervous groom who ran up the ramp to bring the mare down. She came hesitantly, scenting the unfamiliar air and the strangers who handled her. She had just one more leg of her journey, which had started as soon as she left Border Dispute's covering shed, to complete: a short horsebox ride to the warmth of the stabling block. She was now a very different animal from the bundle of nerves Tipper had coaxed so painstakingly into the starting stalls on the Curragh. She had grown up, and blossomed in courage and confidence. And she was going to be a mother.

Jameson greeted Shalakov warmly. Like Alexei, the elderly Englishman was in high spirits. Virtually his whole adult life had passed in obscurity. After decades of scientific planning and hundreds of laboratory experiments, Jameson was looking forward to a success within the next year that would make him world famous.

As a child Jameson had been considered rather a freak of nature. His mother Susan had been a cleaner at the Atomic Research Laboratory near Oxford, and his father had driven a refuse lorry in Abingdon for the local council – a *refusenik*, as

Jameson used to tell Russian friends, a joke few of them understood. When his third son appeared, Reg Jameson naturally called him William Jameson after the finest footballer he'd ever seen: William Dixie Dean.

Young Billy had sprouted a thick mop of curly hair, which slightly surprised the neighbours given that Nobby and Alf, his elder brothers, had very thin, straight greasy hair just like their dad. Nobby and Alf had both played up front for the Abingdon Boys Football Club in their time and Reg assumed that young Billy would be another chip off the old block.

The trouble was, from a very early age Billy didn't really like getting his knees dirty and generally fell over when he tried to kick the ball back to his dad. Reg had him out in the garden night after night, summer and winter, but to no avail.

'I've only gone and bred a bloody malco,' he finally conceded to his crew doing the bins one morning. 'I'd take my belt to him, but it would make no bloody difference.'

Billy was his mother's little miracle – sensitive, bright as a button and gentle, unlike his father. Reg regularly gave his wife a slap when he got back from the pub on Saturday nights. She would have got a lot more than a slap if Reg had been aware of a certain physical resemblance between young Billy and the curly-headed chief nuclear physicist at the research laboratory.

But Reg soon ceased to care. His son was a

bitter disappointment to him and that was that. Not only did Billy stay on at school when he was fourteen, he moved to a better one. His brilliance frightened the life out of his teachers, who wrote in their reports of his 'exceptional ability'.

'Never mind that,' grumbled his father. 'He should be doing a job of bloody work and paying for his grub, not poncing around with those books.'

By the time Billy was sixteen he'd won a scholarship in Natural Sciences to Oxford University, amazing the dons with his ability to solve mathematical equations. By his second year as a student he was being spoken of as potentially one of the best scientific brains in the country.

The last time Billy went home to see his family it was Cup Final day. He walked up to the front door wearing a new, bright tangerine corduroy suit. He was very pleased with it. His father, on the other hand, wasn't.

'What the hell do you look like?' he snapped. Then left his son standing at the door whilst he went back to the TV. Billy tentatively stepped into the cramped, narrow hall and went straight through to the kitchen. His mother was busying herself nervously, pretending she hadn't heard Billy arrive. She didn't want to get into a row with Reg.

'How are you Billy?' she said in a hushed voice trying to disguise the fact that she was keeping her voice down. Billy didn't want to put his mum at odds with his father. So he kept his voice down too.

'Good mum. I'm good,' he smiled. He didn't know how his mother could keep on living the way she did.

'Mum, don't worry about him,' Billy said. 'We can always see each other when he's not around. Anyway, how are Nobby and Alf?'

'Oh . . . they're fine,' his mum replied guardedly. 'Don't see much of them now.' Billy knew that wasn't true, but he understood why she said it. She felt guilty.

Billy's mum chatted nervously as she made him a cup of tea. Billy drank it as fast as he could without scalding his tongue. Then he made his excuses, kissed his mother and slipped quietly out of the door.

He never went back to Abingdon again. Susan would catch the bus into Oxford once a fortnight when Reg was at away matches, always taking her son his favourite cake: chocolate sponge.

Had Jameson had his own way, he'd have mixed only with people on his wavelength. He was blissfully happy locked inside laboratories with senior professors for hours at a time. Poring over experimental data all night was the only thing he wanted to do. But Oxford didn't allow him to have it his way. He had to eat and sleep in college with his peer group, predominantly ex-public school boys from a very different background. Jameson's absorption in theoretical abstractions, combined with the poverty of his family, his proletarian accent and his peculiar

189

dress-sense, made him an obvious target for their sneers and their relentless bullying.

When not in the lab Jameson took refuge in the University Communist Club. This was the only place he knew where being working class was regarded as praiseworthy, and it transformed his life. He soon embraced the ideology and aims of the Club without question. From the perspective of the late 1950s the same public school twats who tormented him in college were the future rulers of the country. It would be they who set his boundaries, his research budgets, his time-tables. But what could such numbskulls ever know of the subtlety and the power of science? To them, science was something done by the Lower Orders, while they cricketed, raced horses, did a bit of stock-broking and stood for Parliament. It gradually dawned on Jameson that he wasn't prepared to let these people control his destiny. Nor, he ultimately decided, was he prepared to wait for the Revolution to overturn them.

Susan Jameson arrived from Abingdon at her usual time one Saturday, with Billy's chocolate sponge. He was always in his room on Saturday afternoons. The labs were closed and he could count on some peace and quiet with the Neanderthals running around on the playing fields. There was silence when Susan knocked on his door. She tried the handle and it opened. As soon as she walked in she had an impression of emptiness. His pink sheepskin chair covers were still there but there were no David Hemmings 'Blow Up' film posters. Susan suddenly felt alarmed. She looked around and saw an envelope on his desk with her name on it. The letter inside was brief and to the point.

Dear Mum I've gone to work abroad. Can't say anything about it but it will be nice and better than this place. Sorry I couldn't say good-bye. I'll send you a post card. Thanks for everything.

Billy hadn't signed it, but it was his writing all right. She lowered herself into one of his sheepskin-covered chairs and sat there staring at the empty wall as if hypnotized. After about three minutes tears were trickling down her cheeks. She knew she'd never see her little miracle again.

The defector, however, took easily to life in Moscow, a place where many people had left their mothers behind. True some of the scientific work, especially in biology, was close to primitive by comparison with what he'd been doing at Oxford. But he, Jameson, was there to do something about that.

Now, half a century later, he was stroking Stella Maris's neck, and feeling the firm layers of muscle under her silky coat. As far as he was concerned, she and the embryonic cargo she carried were the only good things to have come out of England for a long time. With them Jameson was going to change the world.

28

Tipper was making a real effort on the whisky front. The Duke and his mates had been urging him up to London, to thank him for the winners he'd put them onto and the losers he'd told them to lay. But he'd given London a wide berth. He didn't want to mess things up with Ana.

A crazy new idea had begun to form in his head. He and Ana . . . Ana and he . . . should make a family! As the weeks passed the idea grew, and he hadn't even slept with her yet. Which was why he hadn't shared his plans. It was too much too soon. But apart from his mother, she was the only person in the world that he'd ever loved. Having Ana round to watch television with in the evenings was the nicest thing. The sense of calm and security that she gave him reminded him of how he used to feel at home with his mum, curled up on the sofa drinking her cups of tea.

A few days after their trip to Woburn, Tipper

very nonchalantly slipped his hand up the back of Ana's loose shirt. He waited for her to move his hand but she didn't. He'd never felt such soft skin in his life. But he didn't want to tell her in case she made him take his hand away.

Ana turned to look at him without saying a word. He rubbed the end of her nose with the end of his. He could just focus on her unblinking eyes. Her face looked very pensive.

'Tipper, how can you really want me when you know nothing about my past?'

'It doesn't matter. It makes me love you more. You're a mystery.'

Tipper kissed her on the cheek – the only kind of kiss she'd so far permitted. Suddenly she looked abysmally sad.

'Hey! Try a smile,' he said, and put a finger on her lips.

She tried to, but it wasn't much of a smile.

'I don't care about anything but what's going on right now, Ana. To me you're perfect. Can I kiss you properly? Don't stop me.'

Ana didn't stop him, but it was a hesitant first kiss. Tipper didn't push it. He thought of how you break in a young horse. Go very gently, very slowly. Then back away. That's what he had to do with Ana. Rather than go to her, he had to persuade her to come to him.

Ana formed the habit of coming round to Tipper's place to watch television on certain nights of the week. Sundays were favourite, but

Wednesdays and Fridays were regular too. She prepared healthy food for Tipper and Sam; which was good for Tipper's weight problems. Tipper began to feel, both mentally and physically, in better shape than he had for a long time. He was still sexually frustrated, but he could bear that as long as he could believe the situation was going to change.

Ana was compulsive about improving her English, and insisted on spending an hour each night practising phrases from her *Better English Language* text-book.

'Could you tell me the way to the benefit office please? I'm trying to find the benefit office. Do you want to know the name of my lawyer? My lawyer's called Mr Wilson. Where is the housing office? I wish to see the housing officer . . .'

She could do this for up to an hour, walking around the room holding these one-way conversations. Tipper found it distracting as he tried to watch TV. But nothing Ana did could annoy him for long.

One evening, when Sam was out – probably hovering around Shelley in the Partridge – she put her books away unexpectedly early and came and sat by Tipper on the sofa, slightly closer to him than normal.

'What are you watching?' she whispered, as if there were other people listening. Then she moved closer.

'Celebrity Marriage,' Tipper replied casually. 'Just some game show.'

She didn't much like reality game shows, but tonight she seemed to be interested.

'How is that working?'

'How does that work,' he corrected.

'Yes, how does that work?'

'Well famous people get married, and the audience votes on which ones will stay together.'

'No! Seriously? That is so terrible.'

'Yes, it is terrible. It's a terrible programme. But I'm waiting for the football to come on.'

Ana liked football even less than game shows. He braced himself for a mocking tirade against the Beautiful Game, but instead she slid her hand onto his leg. Suddenly every light in Tipper's brain was flashing red alert. Jesus, he thought, what should he do now?

It was Ana, though, who led the way by putting her mouth close to his ear and whispering.

'I feel cold. Maybe you could put your arm around my shoulder, Tipper?'

And then, quite unexpectedly, with a delicious jolt of excitement, he felt her tongue touch his earlobe. Tipper felt paralysed and just sat there like an idiot while Ana took her hand from his leg and tucked it round behind him, into the small of his back. Then she put her button nose very close to his face, kissed him momentarily on the lips, and pulled her face away. She was looking him square in the eyes. He didn't know whether he should respond, or leave the moves to her. For a few minutes they went on staring into each other's eyes, without speaking. Then instinct took over and Tipper leaned forward and kissed her mouth. This time there was no unease, no nervousness, no holding back.

Ana had wanted to be sure of Tipper before she slept with him. She didn't want to be just another in the long string of his conquests – not knowing, of course, that there was never much of a string at all. Tipper had been, and would continue to be, too wary and shy to tell her of his scant experiences in bed, in case she thought there was something wrong with him. But in fact Ana was learning the contrary. There was nothing wrong with him. Tipper was totally different from any other man in her experience, and it was all good. He had such a soft touch. And he seemed more interested in what gave pleasure to her than to himself.

All this she began to discover that night. They kissed for half an hour on the sofa and stroked each other. Then he got up, took her by the hand and led her into the bedroom.

Once the dam had burst it didn't take long for the valley to flood. Tipper just couldn't be in the same room without touching Ana. Cooking was fraught with problems because he wouldn't let go of her. He hid her language books and made her cuddle up on the sofa to watch TV with him – not that they did much watching.

Tipper told Ana all about the three best things

in his life. His wonderful mother who did everything for him. The heavenliness of the stud with the big white barn. And of course Red. How she'd been as a foal. Her accident. Her reappearance. And their finest hour. He just wished he could take Ana to meet her.

Then one night in bed, quite unexpectedly, Ana opened a new chapter in their relationship.

'Tipper,' she said softly as she lay in his arms. 'Can I ask you something?'

'Ask away.'

'Can I stay with you?'

'No problem. Of course you can. We've got all night.'

'No, no! I mean I want to be with you *every* night.'

Tipper propped himself up on his elbow and looked down at her, frowning incredulously.

'Say that again.'

'I want to live with you, Tipper O'Reilly,' she whispered, reaching to stroke his face. 'Would you like that?'

Would he like it? Tipper could hardly grasp what she had suggested.

'You mean – the two of us, together?' he gasped, stupidly.

'Yes here, in your flat, together.'

'Your flat's much better than this one.'

But she was adamant.

'No, Tipper. I want to be in your flat. I don't care which is nicer. I want us to be in yours.'

He didn't care. He'd happily agree to live with her in the hay-barn, just so long as he could wake up in the middle of the night and know she was lying next to him.

29

Sir Godfrey Thomson had been perfectly right in his cagey assessment of his son-in-law's character and motives. David Sinclair had fancied Alison Thomson's money, and her family's influence, a good deal more than he'd fancied her oversized breasts and an arse that was built for comfort. The problem for Sinclair was that that he was hamstrung by Sir Godfrey Thomson's pre-nuptial agreement, which left the financial reins solely in his daughter's hands.

He had been twenty-four, and she twenty-one, when they'd first met. Alison had projected a simpering sweetness, which had led him fatally to assume, despite her father's strictures, that he would be able to control her with his manly authority. But the girliness had been nothing but a pose, put on purely to attract marriageable men. Her guise swiftly evaporated after they got married.

She patrolled the petty cash box with all the zeal of a Zurich bank. Everything had to be accounted for so that Sinclair couldn't help himself for poker in the Partridge, spoofing at the golf club or blackjack in London. The only way he could indulge himself with cash was if he backed a few winners on the racecourse. That meant listening to his jockeys, guys like Tipper O'Reilly, who galloped the horses in the mornings and knew best which ones were fit enough to have the money down on.

More seriously, Alison insisted on controlling the bank accounts, writing the cheques, and dealing personally with the accountants and the bank. Then deciding how much pocket money her husband could have.

To make sure he looked the part she cast him in, she ring-fenced some of his money for a clothing allowance, hand-picking the garments herself.

'Just let me look after the pounds, darling,' she told him slightly too firmly. 'You mind the horses. That's what you do best.'

Nine years into the marriage, the couple's discussions about money had become considerably more aggressive.

'The Partridge,' she grumbled, scanning Johnny the Fish's invoice with a basilisk eye. 'Almost five grand. How the hell can you spend five grand in the local *pub*?'

'It's a gastro-pub, actually. And I entertain a lot of owners there. If you'd be prepared to cook for them here I wouldn't have to.'

'Don't start. Don't you dare start!'

Angrily, she picked up another letter from the pile.

'Aspinalls.'

She studied the crisp, classy piece of notepaper that detailed her husband's gambling disasters.

'Ten grand in one night. Ten *grand*? What did you do in there? Set fire to the place?'

Sinclair managed his most cheerful smile.

'A hellish unlucky session. But I'll get it back, no fear. I just don't have the money at the moment.'

'So you expect me to pay these exorbitant roulette losses of yours, do you?'

The simple answer to the question was 'Yes'. However, when she countered with 'And why should I?' he knew he wouldn't have much of an answer. Instead, he turned his back and wandered across to the window, waving his hand nonchalantly.

'Oh, we'll make a profit this year, a good one. Just take it out of that.'

That wasn't what Alison wanted to hear. She wanted degradation. It gave her the most delicious sensation to demean her husband by facing him with evidence of his pathetic addiction, and for him to beg her to pay for it. It was even better than naked jockeys kneeling at her feet for the favour of rides.

She picked up a third invoice in the pile, a mobile phone bill, and glanced at it, pursing her lips.

'What's she like, then?' she murmured casually. 'Good in bed?'

Sinclair spun round.

'What are you talking about?'

'This, oh! This floozy of yours. I expect that's what she is. The one who owns the mysterious number that keeps coming up in your list of calls.'

She wafted the bill to and fro in the air. He grabbed for it but she jerked it out of the way.

'Look, if that's my phone bill –'

'It *is* your phone bill, David. And there's this *one* number on it you seem especially fond of.'

'Probably the vet. Let me see it.'

'I know the vet's number.'

'He changed his phone, didn't he? I think he did.'

'Oh, well, if you insist,' Alison sighed. She didn't much care, anyway, and if she pushed him too far now, she'd be missing out on more fun further down the line.

What was doubly frustrating about the cash flow restrictions was that things were going rather well at the yard. Sinclair was getting plenty of winners and getting flattering write ups in the press. The number of enquiries the yard was receiving from prospective owners was increasing; exciting people like a Chinese mineral trader and an Indian car manufacturer. But more often from men like Mike Champion. He was a self-made printer from the Thames Valley who rang Sinclair one evening to say he was thinking of getting some horses; and could he come over for a tour of the yard?

'Classy place this, Dave,' said Champion on a windy spring morning a few days later. 'I know class when I see it, and I like what I see here.'

They were walking into the main stable block and, much as it pained Sinclair to be called Dave, he waved his arm in an enthusiastic gesture that embraced the entire building.

'I'm very pleased with it, Mr Champion. It's always been state-of-the-art and we intend to keep it that way.'

This was perfectly true. The yard was a beautiful one, a grand nineteenth century construction with a great archway leading into a main square yard of fifty stables. The original Victorian builder had spared no expense. The stables were lined with seasoned wood panelling, with strips of brass between to stop the horses chewing the panels. The ceilings were high and a discreet ventilation shaft ensured a flow of fresh air. The old brick floors were lined with rubber – a modern adaptation – to protect the horses. David Sinclair had thought he'd woken up in heaven when he first looked over the yard – the establishment where he would lord it as a trainer, or so he'd thought. It didn't take him long to realize that this was not quite the deal.

'Ah, here comes my wife Alison,' he said in a voice that struck just the right note of pleasant surprise. 'I must introduce you.'

Alison was dressed in hard hat, jodhpurs, riding boots and a T-shirt under which her bosom swung and bobbed in counter-rhythm to her stride. Watching her approach, Champion didn't mince his words.

'Blimey,' he said in low but admiring tones. 'She's got a fair old superstructure on her, Dave, and no mistake.'

Coming nearer, Alison held out her hand in greeting.

'Hello,' she said shaking hands and wearing her sincerest smile. 'You must be Mr Champion. I'm Alison Sinclair. I hear you may be going to have a horse with us.'

'Nice to meet you Alison, very nice indeed.'

Champion could not stop himself from giving her a leering up-and-down look.

'Ye-es,' he went on. 'I was just telling Dave here that I do like his yard. So I won't have *a* horse, I'll have a couple or three with him for definite.'

The smile nearly slipped from Alison's face. *'I was just telling Dave here that I like his yard?'*

'Yes,' she continued to smile. 'It's lovely. Do stay for lunch,' she managed to add before she went to find her horse. Two minutes later Sinclair's text message alert vibrated in his pocket. It was from Alison. *'Your yard is it Dave? Suggest U take that jerk to your pub for lunch. Seeing as U clearly bought it recently.'*

'Right Mr Champion,' Sinclair smiled falsely. 'I think we're done here. To be honest with you I think you'll find lunch in the Partridge a bit more entertaining. They always have a table for me.'

'Right,' said Champion. 'Nice idea. Unless, of course, Mrs Sinclair's spent all morning doing the eats.'

'Oh, no. Don't worry about her.'

'The public house it is, then. Will Alison be joining us? And call me Mike, will you? Only the taxman calls me Mr Champion.'

At about the same time that Mike Champion followed Sinclair towards the Partridge, Ana was arriving at the Bedford Lodge hotel in the middle of Newmarket for one of her regular meetings with Shalakov.

She despised the sneering receptionists. Not that they gave her any bother. They were paid not to. In fact they got paid for doing nothing, Ana thought, as she ran the gauntlet of their contemptuous looks. She knew what they thought she was, and she would have loved to put them straight. But revealing that she was a spy, not a hooker, would have been extremely unwise in a town as small as Newmarket.

Ana knew it was highly unlikely that any of the receptionists would ever meet Tipper. But she was still petrified at the prospect of him finding out about her meetings. How would she explain them?

As she stood at the door of Suite One she tried to put Tipper out of her mind. It opened quickly after she knocked. Harrison, Shalakov's head of security, gave Ana a thin, sly smile and nodded his head sideways at her without bothering to say a word. He made her feel like she wasn't worth even bothering to talk to.

Ana could hear voices in the bedroom. She was relieved one of them was female. Her mind darted back to the first time she'd met Shalakov in London. How sick she'd felt. And what a result she'd had. Being paid to spy on a racehorse trainer in Newmarket was like winning the lottery to her. She just prayed every time that there'd be another girl there.

After half an hour of being blanked by Harrison, the bedroom door finally opened and a tall dark girl came out. Ana didn't like her expensive looking clothes which were totally out of place in Newmarket. The girl ignored Ana (who was wearing jeans) as she waited for Harrison to get up out of his chair. He deliberately hesitated so she had to wait for him. Then he put his hand into his pocket and pulled out a brown envelope.

Shalakov, in his dressing gown, was on the phone when Harrison ushered Ana into his bedroom. The Russian looked at her without showing a flicker of recognition. His expression was completely blank as he carried on with his conversation. Ana sat uncomfortably on the end of his bed. After five minutes, which felt like an hour to Ana, he slammed the phone down and took a swig from his glass of vodka.

'Idiots,' he said vaguely in Ana's direction. 'Why am I always working with idiots?'

Ana forced a smile and shrugged her shoulders.

'So, Ana. What have you got to tell me this week?'

'Nothing important Comrade General. I still don't think Sinclair's horses are healthy. He's trying to be patient, I think.'

'What is the matter with them?'

'It's difficult to say. They give a few coughs after they've worked, and that is about it.'

'My colt by Mastercraftsman. How is he?'

'He looks good Comrade General. Tipper O'Reilly says he has the feel of a good horse. But Sinclair is bringing him along slowly.'

'This Tipper. Does he know what he's talking about? Is he any good with horses?'

'He is amazing Comrade General,' Ana said with too much passion. She immediately regretted it.

'Is he? Is he amazing at any thing else, too?' Shalakov laughed. He took another swig of his vodka and continued to chuckle to himself. Ana felt nervous.

'The information that I get from him is very important, Comrade General. I do what I have to do to make sure that I get you the best information.'

Shalakov liked the sound of that. A soldier who would go beyond the call of duty.

'You are doing well Ana. Just make sure you continue to do so. And Ana. Make sure you remember who you work for.'

'Of course Comrade General.'

'Go now.'

Ana gave Harrison a triumphant smile as she took her envelope from him on her way out. She positively bounced down the corridor past a glum looking maid pushing a room service trolley. Ana thought about Tipper as her own words came back to her. 'I do what I have to do to make sure that I get you the best information.'

'Sorry about that,' she said to an imaginary Tipper and then giggled. 'Business is business. Which is good for both of us.'

30

Sometime after midday Johnny the Fish had the *Sun* spread out in front of him. He was studying the card for Brighton races. He'd been having a bad morning. His book-keeper had phoned in to say she'd got a toothache, so there was no one to do the banking. Then the bank itself had phoned to say he'd gone over his overdraft limit yet again. And finally he'd wandered into the kitchen to check that his butcher and fish man had got their orders right, to find the chef sitting on the floor. He'd looped a tie around his upper arm and was pulling it tight with his teeth as he prepared to shoot something from a syringe into his arm.

Johnny had politely enquired if the chef was a diabetic. The chef said no, he wasn't, and then argued that Johnny had invaded his privacy. The Fish had begged to differ and summarily fired the chef. Now the teenage sous-chef was preparing lunch and Shelley was nowhere to be seen. The Fish had spent most of the morning on the phone scouring the employment agencies for a replacement chef. At the same time he had to man the bar on his own.

Amidst the frustration and stress, a single ray of light shone out from the one-thirty race at Brighton. For all his slipshod ways and shortcomings as a businessman, Johnny was, on the quiet, one of Newmarket's more successful punters. Playing genial host to the town's trainers and headlads, he frequently got to hear when a horse would be running with the hand-brake on, and when it wouldn't. Better still, a tiny microphone, linked wirelessly to a recording device in his office, ensured the work-riders of the Covey Club unwittingly shared all their insights with him. Johnny had made himself one of the best-informed gamblers in town.

Having played back the most recent get-together in the snug, he had formed a better than shrewd idea of who was going to win the first race on Brighton's card. The horse was called Armband and he'd lumped the money on: it was his only chance of balancing the till for the week. Now, as if to make sure nothing could go wrong, he was running his finger down the list of runners and riders. At this moment Sinclair and his new owner breezed in.

'Looking for a steer on the mile handicap, are you?' boomed Sinclair, when he saw what the Fish was doing. 'Look no further. Mine should win it. Cardew Castle. He's been working exceptionally well. I've already invested – got a monkey on him.'

'A monkey?' said Shelley who'd finally pitched up for work. 'Wouldn't some kind of jockey be preferable?'

'A monkey's five-hundred –' began Sinclair, before he looked across at Shelley who was smiling sarcastically. She liked winding up Sinclair.

Sinclair ignored her.

'Actually I've got my stable jockey on this one,' he told Champion. 'He's a very dependable chap.'

Then he ordered a bottle of claret and the two wandered off to occupy a table.

Almost an hour later Johnny was tuning in the television to Racing UK when Sinclair and Champion, now half way through their second bottle, returned to the bar area to get a better view of the Brighton race.

'Mr Champion fancies a bet in this, Johnny,' Sinclair said. 'See if you can get him fifteen hundred to five on Cardew Castle to win, will you?'

As the commentator was going through the runners in race-card order, the Fish disappeared into his office where he made a fictional phone call. He was happy to take this bet on himself, confident that, come one-forty, Champion's five hundred pounds would be clear profit to the pub. He knew, of course, that Sinclair's horse had been working well at home. Very well. But not as well as Armband who, as the Fish knew, had gone a second quicker, with the same amount of lead in the weight cloth, and on exactly the same stretch of the Heath. It meant that, over today's mile, wherever Cardew Castle finished Armband would be up to three lengths in front. After a suitable time had elapsed Johnny came back out again.

'No problem, sir,' he said to Champion. 'The money's on for you, at three to one.'

'Cheers. You're a geezer,' Champion told him.

The race started and soon Mike Champion was bobbing up and down with excitement as the wall of horses charged line abreast down the course.

'I see him, Dave!' he shouted. 'He's going well. Come on Cardew!'

'Yes,' said Sinclair, more quietly. 'He's in the ideal position, travelling nicely.'

Until they'd passed the halfway point in the race, this was quite true. But about two furlongs out Sinclair's jockey began to bend his knees and crouch lower in the saddle. He was niggling at his mount, and then he gave him a crack with the whip. The horse immediately picked up and, with the early leaders tiring, hit the front.

'Brilliant!' yelled Champion. 'Come on my son! Come on Cardew!'

But Sinclair could see the danger behind and already knew his horse was no longer favourite to win. For in the blink of an eye, while Champion was crowing and stamping his feet, the race had changed. Armband had moved easily into second, and had now found a new gear. He ghosted upsides

Cardew Castle at the furlong pole and went effort-
lessly past him to win by two and a half lengths.
Sinclair's horse had not been stopping, and had
trounced the rest of the field. And yet he was a
loser.

Mike Champion had gone uncharacteristically
quiet.

'Fucking jockey hit the front too soon, didn't
he Dave?' he muttered.

Sinclair nodded. He knew full well that, once
they'd passed the halfway mark, no other strategy
bar foul play would have stopped Armband from
winning. On the other hand he had little choice
but to go along with Champion's ignorant assessment, or lose face with his new owner.

'Exactly Mike. They've got brains in proportion
to their bodies, most of them. I do everything right
at home and send them out in perfect nick, and
look what happens? Bloody idiot on board loses
the plot. If only I could find a jockey with a brain
I could get probably twenty more winners a
season.'

Champion could well afford his loss of five
hundred pounds. But he didn't forget what Sinclair
had said about jockeys and, a few weeks later,
coming down to see his useful new prospect, a
colt called Fighting Talk, he asked for a word with
the work-rider who usually galloped him.

It was Tipper who appeared.

'You ride Fighting Talk every day. What d'you

213

think of him? Have I bought myself a winner would you say?'

Tipper gave a wide grin.

'He's a winner, all right, sir. Big and strong, as anyone can see, and he enjoys galloping all right. But the point is he wants to get his head in front. I'm always feeling him get a hold of the bit when he gets alongside another horse. That's a sign he's competitive, like. Doesn't mind a fight. Wants to win.'

'Sounds like we've given him the right name. Any weaknesses?'

'Well, every horse has weaknesses, you know. This one runs out of petrol after a mile and a furlong. He'd never get a mile and a quarter, not with a booster rocket on him. A mile's his best distance. Also you wouldn't want him to cut out his own pace. He doesn't fancy being out on his own. He idles and another fast finishing horse would pass him before he woke up. He needs to be mixing it with the other horses all the time. Because that's what turns him on, makes him run. And he's pretty fast. I doubt he's Group One class, now, but he could be Group Three.'

Champion was impressed by Tipper and, as soon as he got the chance, he said as much to Sinclair.

'O'Reilly talks a lot of sense. Why can't he ride Fighting Talk in his races? I've heard he was pretty useful in Ireland as a kid. Won the Irish Oaks, didn't he?'

'Yes, that's so,' Sinclair replied cautiously.

'So why not use him? He couldn't do a worse job than your man did on Cardew's Castle the other day, remember? You said most of them are thick as camel shit. But in my book O'Reilly isn't. He's got his head screwed on.'

'Where horses are concerned, yes, I agree. But in other directions, I have to say, Tipper's a tad wobbly. Actually he's not done that much race riding over here. We have one owner who likes us to use him, and we do whenever we can. But he's had weight problems and, um, confidence problems too. But he's talented.'

'I don't care about his personal problems, Dave. Let me spell it out. I want to see O'Reilly riding my horse. You will arrange that for me, won't you?'

31

A couple of months after she moved in with Tipper, Ana missed a period, and a Boot's home pregnancy test confirmed her fears. At a rational level she was both horrified and terrified. She'd fallen in love with Tipper and was in little doubt he loved her. But they'd only been together a short time, they didn't know each other, not really, not in the way people who were going to become parents should. And they were so young. Were they ready for this, either of them? Would their love last? And if Tipper found out that she hadn't been straight with him how would he react? He might feel that she'd used him.

'Tipper,' she whispered that night, snuggling up to him under the bed-covers. 'I have something to tell you. Something very, very serious.'

'Go on then.'

'It's difficult. You will be angry.'

'No, I won't. Tell me.'

'I'm pregnant, Tipper. I'm sorry. I didn't mean it to happen. I'm so sorry.'

Tipper rolled onto his back and stared at the ceiling while he took this in. He was amazed at how calm he felt, though his heart was undoubtedly beating faster.

'That's amazing,' he said, in a measured way.

But tears were welling up in Ana's eyes.

'I don't know how it happened. I was not careful enough, I think. It is my fault.'

But for Tipper the whole thing had already completely resolved itself. Ana being pregnant seemed nothing but a natural consequence of their love for each other.

'Fault?' he said. 'I don't think it's your fault. I don't think it's a fault at all.'

'Then you will help me with it?'

'How do you mean, help?' He dug her playfully in the side. 'Haven't I done my bit already?'

'I mean, I haven't got enough money saved . . .'

'What're you talking about? We can get by, the two of us – well, three of us I suppose it'll be. We got a flat, we got jobs. We'll make a grand little family.'

'No, no, Tipper! I mean I can't have it. I can't, really I can't.'

'Jesus. Why not?'

'Why not? Because there's no one to help me. I have no family here. It will be no good for my life.'

'Hey, you mustn't be afraid. I'm here, amn't I? I'll be all the help you need. It'll be absolutely fockin' brilliant.'

But Ana turned away from him and hugged the pillow tightly. Tipper rolled back towards her again and spoke to the nape of her neck.

'Is it not being married that's bugging you?' he murmured. 'Look, it's not a problem! We can get married. We *will* get married.'

'No, Tipper, no. It's nothing to do with not being married. It's all too quick.'

Tipper felt a sudden surge of panic. She couldn't mean getting rid of it!

'It's not too quick. It's all I want, Ana. Please marry me. Please, please have our baby.'

'I am so frightened that you will leave me. Then I will be on my own with the baby.'

Tipper's hand stole around her side and he touched her stomach.

'Never. No way. This is what I've been dreaming of. I'm going to be with you for ever, Ana. For ever and ever.'

He slid his arm under her and tried to rock her gently, reassuringly, and at the same time imploringly.

She touched the hand that he'd placed on her stomach.

'Please, Tipper, you mustn't go so fast.'

'Well we got to talk about this properly,' he said firmly, rolling out of bed. 'But first I'm going to make us tea.'

They talked almost all night, going round and round the central point. Ana was afraid, unsure of Tipper. Look what Tipper's father had done! Gone off and left his family. Tipper might do the same. And he would drink, like almost all the men she knew in racing. And most of the men back in Moscow. Men that drank were never any good as husbands and fathers. Her own father had been the same. She had to know, really know, that Tipper was not going to turn out like her father, or his.

This line of argument shut Tipper up for a bit, and made him thoughtful. Although he'd been trying for her sake not to drink he was still sneaking off to the Partridge with Sam, who'd now moved out to live at the stud. He didn't get legless but he'd not exactly kissed good-bye to the bottle. Would he be able to do so, if Ana demanded it?

Sam had started to be a bit funny about Ana. He felt she was getting between them. She didn't like Tipper going to the pub to meet him and he thought Tipper should stand up to her.

Finally Tipper made up his mind.

'Jesus, Ana, I'll never touch it again. Not a drop. Look, I barely do already. But from now on it's Red Bull and stuff like that all the time. I've got you – sure, what do I need take a drink for?'

Ana looked at him and put her finger on his lips. 'You must not promise unless you really mean it.'

'I do, Jesus. I really mean it! Give me a chance to be a father. Let me be your husband. I have nothing without you. Have the baby. What'll you do otherwise? What'll you do?'

The horrifying idea of abortion came before his mind again. It should be unthinkable, but she was thinking about it.

'Tipper it's too much, too quick.'

'Well promise you'll think about it. Don't do anything about the baby just yet, because there's plenty of time, isn't there? Just think about it. Think about what I said.'

Suddenly she smiled and kissed him gently and it was like the sun coming out.

'You are a sweet boy, Tipper,' she said. 'All right. I will think about it.' As Tipper drifted off to sleep she lay awake thinking about a lot of things. She knew she should come clean with Tipper about her life, about why she came to Newmarket, about – so many things. If she didn't, and he found out, what then?

32

The Agroscience Complex known as Xanadu, a couple of hours' drive from Moscow, had been created by the Red Army in the early 1970s to ensure that the biggest threat to Mother Russia could never materialize. That was not America. It was hunger.

In the previous generation Josef Stalin, like all dictators, had loved to patronize clever people, believing some of the angel-dust of genius would settle on his own head in the process. But, like all dictators, his judgement of genius was erratic, with the result that Soviet think tanks and research institutes were as often as not stuffed with men and women whose only genius lay in massaging the autocrat's tastes and prejudices. One of the most influential of these charlatans was the self-styled biologist Trofim Lysenko.

Lysenko had peddled the idea of applying socialist theory to agricultural science. Social engineering, he preached, could influence and accelerate evolution. If a collectivised peasant learned to be more proficient with the plough, his children would directly inherit the knowledge. He also 'collectivized' plants by sowing the seeds impossibly close together. Never mind that the plants died. For Lysenko this was the way forward. Genetics was bunk.

The result was crop failure after crop failure. No matter. Under Stalin, famine could always be airbrushed away by the state propaganda machine. But by the 1960s the Soviet Praesidium realized how much the world was changing. New technologies, and instant communications, meant agricultural mistakes could neither be easily excused nor concealed. And the rest of the world was increasing its production at an alarming rate: in some regions farm yields had doubled, and doubled again, thanks to advances in fertility, genetics and other bio-sciences. The Soviet Union with no advanced genetics programme, had fallen far behind.

It wasn't until 1965 that they finally dismissed Lysenko, and the rush to catch up began. Previously disgraced geneticists were recalled from the Gulag, many skeletal and consumptive and quite a few senile or mad. Nevertheless institutes were set up, laboratories equipped and, most important of all, foreign experts recruited. One who arrived directly from Oxford was Jameson. He was the ideal candidate, brilliant, up-to-the-minute and completely committed to the cause.

For fifteen years Jameson laboured, clawing his way up the promotion ladder until full recognition came with his appointment as the Chief Scientist at Xanadu. The ambitious young General Shalakov had recognized the Englishman's potential, and given him complete authority over the establishment's research programmes.

Jameson's activities were daring in the extreme. Fungus-tolerant wheat and drought-proof maize were produced, as were sheep the size of small cows, and cows the size of small elephants. The most dramatic advances were in pharmacology. Fertilizers laced with laboratory chemicals produced gigantic results. Cocktails of drugs forced the growth of livestock at previously unattainable rates.

Following privatization, with Shalakov as Chief Executive and majority shareholder, Xanadu continued on the same path. With no legal or moral limits to worry about, the majority of experiments produced results that would have been greeted with public revulsion. Deer were put on treadmills to gallop until their hearts burst. Dogs received head transplants. Pigs, loaded with three or four times the normal hormone-levels, were sacrificed in their thousands. Growth hormone was injected into foetuses causing them to grow so big that they killed their mothers at birth. Transgenic monsters of all kinds were created. Some were even born. But the public were unaware of Xanadu's existence and Jameson's kingdom remained unpenetrated.

It was not until Putin decided to revitalize horse racing in Moscow, developing the run-down Hippodrome as a modern leisure facility to which the capital's new rich would flock in their tens of thousands, that Shalakov realized he could use Xanadu in a new way. As levels of prize money increased, Russian breeders began importing western stock to improve their existing bloodlines. But – as experience had shown in other countries – everyone assumed it would take decades to become competitive with existing breeders from England, Ireland and the United States. Everyone, that is, except Shalakov. He was confident that, as always before, Jameson and Xanadu could lead the world, and do it before anyone could stop them. He began a new programme at Xanadu. By the turn of the millennium, another complex of buildings had appeared on the site, and before long horses from the six studs that Shalakov owned around the country began to arrive there. It was a few more years before they were ready to take in their first western inmate. But now she, too, was ensconced at Xanadu.

Throughout the spring, summer and autumn Jameson zealously watched over Stella Maris. She had plenty of veterinarians, farriers and grooms to see to her needs in the high-tech stable that had been specially built for her comfort. But Jameson never let a day go by without paying a personal visit. For him the appeal of this project was that its results would be there for the world to see. Soon champions would come out of Russia to conquer the horseracing world, as testaments to the brilliance of his concepts and his unequalled scientific courage. His role could not of course be acknowledged – not yet – but he would see his work proved in action, and know his legacy. That would be enough for him.

Jameson got very wound up during the days leading up to Stella Maris's foaling date. He pestered the vets over and over again to be extra vigilant. Then she finally showed signs that she might be ready. Her teats started to wax up and she looked restless in her box. At one in the morning she was sweating. A moisture detector on her neck triggered an alarm that roused Jameson and he hurried down to the foaling barn. At their quarters nearby he found the two night-duty vets stretched out on sofas, drinking glasses of tea and watching the mare on closed circuit.

'Look at you!' he shouted. 'Shouldn't you be doing something? She's sweating up.'

The vets looked at each other impassively. They'd had about enough. She wasn't the only mare foaling. The two of them had been up every night for the past ten days pulling out foal after foal. They would do the same for this mare when she needed help. In the meantime they needed their tea and a rest.

Jameson didn't care any more about the other mares. He left them and pressed his face to the glass panel in the stable door. Stella Maris was standing in a deep bed of straw, looking dejected. But then it seemed to him horses on their own always looked like that. He paced up and down outside the stable like an expectant father, smoking and looking in again and again. After what felt like an eternity, he saw her sniffing the straw. After a few minutes, as if making up her mind to it, she gently lay down. A couple of minutes later her waters broke.

'Here comes another one,' said one of the vets, heaving himself to his feet.

'Great. Can't wait,' grunted the other.

As they made their way to the barn Jameson was dancing around them.

'Quick, quick. Get him out. Get him out,' he gibbered.

'Might be a filly,' the most knackered vet sniped, wondering why everyone wanted a colt.

'No, no, it's a colt,' returned Jameson, rising to the bait. 'I've been scanning him. I'm not a complete idiot you know.'

Kneeling down, one of the vets shoved his hand inside her to make sure that the foal was lying in the right position.

'All feels pretty normal. So far so good.'

He patted the expectant mother on the rump.

'Come on old girl, let's have a push.'

A few minutes later Jameson saw something poking out of her – small feet. The vets leapt into action. In an almost mechanical way they grabbed one front leg each and started pulling. They looked to Jameson like deckhands on Shalakov's yacht, the time he'd cruised on her in the Black Sea.

'It's another big motherfucker,' one of them grunted as the foal came sliding out.

'Quick! Is he all right?' Jameson demanded.

'He's fine. Mother's fine too,' the chief vet confirmed, after a quick examination. 'Next time suggest General Shalakov picks a smaller stallion. We were lucky there wasn't trouble.'

The foal was lying in a heap on the straw. His mother had stretched around and was licking the mucus off his nose, so he could breathe. She was going to be a good mother. Half an hour later the little one scrambled to his feet and tottered towards her.

Jameson just stood there and marvelled. He'd looked at the foal through his three dimensional scanner a million times but now he was looking at the real thing. He looked so gangly, so delicate. It was hard to believe this spindly-legged colt might be the horse that was going to change the balance of power in the world of thoroughbreds. And maybe change the face of racing and breeding forever. But that was going to be his destiny, at least if Jameson had anything to do with it.

33

A stream of the foulest verbal filth was issuing from Ana's throat and echoing round the birthing room. Usually so demure in her speech, today she was swearing like a St Petersburg docker.

'What's the matter? Why doesn't it come?' asked Tipper, sitting beside her, stroking her hand and occasionally wiping the sweat from her face with a damp cloth.

'Shhh. It will come,' the midwife reassured him. 'This is normal.'

'You mean hurting as much as this?'

'A lot of the time, yes.'

'Jesus. I knew it hurt but not like this.'

Ana's resolute determination not to have the baby was based on her mother's advice. As a teenager she'd had it drummed into her that men couldn't be trusted. And nothing subsequently had persuaded Ana that her mother was wrong. Ana knew that Tipper's father had abandoned his mother. She knew the same had happened to her mother. So why should she make the same mistake and have a baby with someone she'd known for less than a year?

Tipper and Ana had been riding back from the gallops together, leading the first lot home. Half a mile from the yard Tipper was watching the grass beside the horsewalk. He'd seen a black cat scratching around in the grass. Probably hunting a mouse. Then, as they approached, the cat was spooked by them and ran between the legs of Ana's mount.

'Jesus, a black cat ran clean under you,' Tipper laughed. 'Did you see?'

'Where's it gone?' asked Ana, scanning the ground for a glimpse of the cat. 'Was it really black?'

'Of course it was. Didn't you see?'

'I saw something. But I mean was it black all over? No white at all?'

'It was as black as the Ace of Spades.'

Ana put her hand to her mouth.

'Oh my God!'

'In Ireland, we'd say that was a sign of something.'

'Yes. In Russia too.'

'But what's it a sign of, Ana?'

She didn't reply, but later that night, she admitted she'd been thinking about the baby when they were walking along the horsewalk. Her mind was now finally made up. She'd have the baby.

'Jesus, Mary and Joseph, that's brilliant!'

He took her in his arms and bear-hugged her, swaying her this way and that. Tears were prickling his eyes.

'I don't know what to say,' he told her after he'd put her down. 'What made your mind up?'

'It was the cat.'

Tipper had forgotten the cat.

'Don't you remember?' she said. 'The black cat that ran under my horse this morning? It was a sign, like you said. I know what it meant. I've got to have this baby. Otherwise the horse would have shied, I'd have fallen off and the baby would not have survived. So, I'm going to have it. I am sure it is the right thing to do, now. You're going to be a Dad, Tipper.'

Ana's labour some months later was very short, but when it was over, and their baby daughter had been safely delivered, Tipper felt completely drained.

'Jesus that was desperate,' he said to the midwife.

'It was as easy as shelling peas, compared with a lot of births.'

'It may have been easy for you, but I'm more knackered than I was after I won the Oaks.'

They'd finished washing and weighing the baby and now she lay in her mother's arms. The obstetrics team had gone. Tipper lay down on the bed beside them.

'Tipper she has your shape eyes. They will turn brown, you can tell,' said Ana.

Tipper looked.

'I don't know. Maybe. She has your nose, for definite.'

'All babies have noses like that.'

'What's it going to be then?'

They'd agreed to make it his call if the baby was a boy, and hers in the case of a girl.

'Lara Carmen O'Reilly,' Ana smiled.

'Nice. I was going to go for Frankie Lester if it had been my shout. But I like Lara Carmen.'

'Thank God it's a girl then,' she laughed. Then the door swung open and Sam walked in carrying a large teddy bear.

'Congratulations, me boy. And Ana, you look great. Let me take a look at the little darling. What's it called?'

Ana looked proud as Tipper told him.

Tipper was so excited by the baby's arrival he let Sam drive him to the Partridge for a celebration. Tipper felt it was a good way of dealing with the tension that had been between them recently. Without hesitating, Johnny the Fish reached into his cool cabinet and brought out a bottle of vintage champagne.

'Johnny, I shouldn't,' said Tipper. 'I'm off the drink at the moment.'

'Nonsense, boy. I got pissed for a week when I had my first. You need something to ease you through the transition.'

He put three flutes on the counter, popped the

cork and carefully poured. Then he hoisted his into the air and cleared his throat.

'Cuh! As I was saying, forget wetting the baby's head, Tipper. It's you who needs this, because your life's never going to be the same again. Cheers.'

'Jesus,' said Tipper reaching for his own drink. 'It's a big occasion all right, so one glass won't do any harm. You don't have a baby every day.'

'Amen to that,' said the Fish, with an elaborate shudder. He emptied his glass and poured himself another.

'So how long were you pacing up and down outside the room?' he asked.

'I didn't, Johnny. I was in there all the time, so I was. I saw everything.'

The Fish's eyes widened in astonishment.

'Are you mad? I shot a seventy-three at Sunningdale the day my first ankle-biter appeared. Best round of golf I ever played. When I got to the nineteenth hole, there was a message waiting for me. I didn't know whether to laugh or cry at the time.'

'Ah, come on, now,' called Sam. 'Don't be a misery. This is a celebration. Here's to Lara!'

'Lara is it? Didn't know you were a cricket fan, Tipper,' the Fish said as he drained his glass.

34

Shalakov liked the harbour in Monaco. It felt safe.
The cabin of his yacht served as his communications centre. A bottle of vodka and a shot glass
stood on the desk in front of him; beside two
reports, printed and wire-bound in perspex covers.
Shalakov was old-fashioned like that.

He picked one of them up. It was headed
'Economic Prospects for Horse Racing in Russia'.
It had been commissioned by the Russian government from a London business consultancy. Their
task had been to sketch the way in which the new
go-getting, gambling-crazy, free-market Russia was
falling in love with racing.

'Since the three-phase modernization of the old
Soviet Hippodrome in Moscow was completed, this
has been only a matter of time,' the report stated.
'The Hippodrome's re-launch two years ago
gave the industry an immediate and substantial
boost. The course is now completely redeveloped,
using a mixture of private investment and public

money. Under Phase One, the site of the old stable blocks became a complex of advanced office and residential developments. These generated sufficient profits to trigger Phase Two, in which excavation of the middle of the course allowed for the construction of a sunken shopping mall, providing a concourse of cafés and luxury franchises under a glass roof – which lies at ground level in order not to impede the view of the racing. The mall is within easy reach of the race viewing areas and has proved immensely popular with shoppers and racegoers alike.

'These projects raised half a billion dollars, which were ploughed back into Phase Three. This involved building a multi-storey stable block, laying a new track and constructing three new grandstands. The brief for this scheme called for a suite of ultra-modern stands, containing a range of leisure facilities calculated to appeal to the rising class of wealthy business people and professionals who live in and around the capital city. These operate before, during and after racing, and even on days when there is no racing at all. The facilities include a casino, two night clubs, a health hydro and several restaurants, of which the most fashionable is currently run by Marco Pierre White.'

Shalakov yawned. He knew most of this already, but then the report was not intended for him. It was a briefing paper for Western journalists and business interests. He turned to another section headed 'A Rejuvenated Gambling Industry'.

'Gambling on horses,' he read, 'is good business in Russia today. The government's off-track betting monopoly turns over on average a million roubles a race, twenty per cent of which goes to the government, while the rest is distributed in prize money. State security has opened a special department to crack down on illegal bookmaking, and a number of individuals have been successfully prosecuted and jailed. Meanwhile policy has concentrated on making gambling as easy for the public as possible, with every bar and café being equipped with the most up-to-date American pool betting terminals.

'As betting revenues have risen, so has the prize-money. This in turn has created a powerful incentive to own horses for racing and, further along the supply-chain, for breeding. In the past, racing in Russia had been an occasional activity, restricted to weekends and popular holidays. Now, with new courses opening in different parts of the country, the sport is open for business every day of the week.'

Shalakov licked his finger and turned the page. The next section of the report was headed 'Prospects for Breeders'. Shalakov, with his canny business eye, had seen all along that breeding was the area that promised the greatest future profits.

'As the Maktoums of Dubai, the Coolmore operation in Ireland and more recently Dermot O'Callaghan have all shown, if you own the best stallions you can make substantial returns at the top end of the market. We estimate that in Western Europe covering fees of the top five studs today generate £500 million a year. A Russian breeder who has a supreme stallion standing in his stud, a horse bred from the best available sources in the world – England, Ireland and America – might be on his way to dominance over the bloodstock market of Russia. His offspring could create a cadre of stallions who might go on to dominate the world.'

Shalakov smiled and closed the report. In Xanadu he and Jameson both believed they were on the way to achieving this already. Their belief was centred on Stella Maris's one-year-old colt that Shalakov had named Citizen. He was the subject of the other report, which Shalakov turned to.

Written by Jameson, it was a progress report on this very special yearling. Jameson gave a detailed, even loving description of Citizen's exceptionally rapid development.

'The dam's temperament, previously reported as wayward, appears much calmed by motherhood and she has been a highly attentive mother, producing good milk yields. Her voracious offspring has, however, regularly drained her of milk. Novel formula supplements (see confidential annexe) have been administered with very good results.'

There were also a series of tables and graphs detailing the youngster's progress in weight, height, lung capacity and other indicators. The first annexe consisted of a number of chemical formulae, together with detailed day-by-day feeding charts. A second annexe showed a series of colour photographs of the foal at various stages of growth. Shalakov cast a fond yet expert eye over them: it was obvious even in his biased assessment that this was an exceptionally sturdy young horse.

Shalakov closed the report and tossed it back on the table. He smiled as he poured himself a brimming glass of Stolichnaya. Xanadu was working as it should. Nothing was being left to chance.

35

Three months later, and a couple of thousand miles away, Tipper was enjoying what he did best. Working good horses on the gallops. Mike Champion had high expectations of the four-year-old Fighting Talk, who had some pretty decent form as a three-year-old. He was powerful, responsive and very fast like a Ferrari.

The early morning sun made the dew sparkle on the grass. There were a dozen or more rival strings, with around twenty thoroughbreds in each, all cantering in single file in various directions across the wide Heath. Tipper and Fighting Talk were down to do a sharp piece of work to set him up for a crack at the Ormonde Stakes at Chester the next day. Just a six furlong 'blow out' with two other horses up the all-weather gallop, a strip of ground three metres wide with a surface made of sand mixed with shredded plastic and grease to bind it together.

Tipper was cruising along behind his two work

companions, so smoothly it felt like floating. He waited until three furlongs from the top of the gallop, when he gave the horse a gentle squeeze with his legs. The colt responded, lengthening his stride and taking closer order. Then, two furlongs from the top, Tipper woke him up. He gave a firm slap to the shoulder with his stick; the signal for Fighting Talk to go upsides and then pass the leading pair.

There was no response. Tipper gave him a harder slap. Still nothing. In fact, Fighting Talk's stride shortened. Suddenly the Ferrari's engine was missing a stroke, the tyres were spongy and the fuel gauge was on empty. Instead of grabbing the ground, he was faltering. They ended the gallop two lengths behind and Fighting Talk pulled up blowing hard. Tipper lowered his head and listened. There was much more blowing than was usual and then, after another ten seconds, the horse coughed twice.

Tipper knew what it might mean if a horse coughed immediately after work. At best, the lungs would be full of mucus, which had been blown up into the upper airways by the lungs under pressure. That causes a tickling sensation, and the cough. At worst, though, it meant the horse's lungs had haemorrhaged to some degree. Either way the cause is the same – one of several respiratory infections that are more or less endemic in Newmarket. Monitoring those infections is part of every trainer's job, and means having the vet over after fast work, when the horse is at rest.

An endoscope is slid into the nostril and the mucus is extracted from the upper airway. If it's thick and green, or has blood in it, that horse should be going nowhere near a racecourse.

'What the fuck happened there?' demanded Sinclair as they walked down from the top of the gallop, where he'd been watching them work.

'He couldn't quicken when I asked him, Guvnor,' said Tipper. 'He was just sort of lifeless. And he coughed a couple of times when we pulled up. He must have something on him.'

'That's bollocks, he's fine!' said Sinclair, jabbing his finger towards the horse. 'That horse is going to Chester tomorrow as planned. The owner's entertaining a party of his chums in a private box, and he wants to see his horse run. He's just having an off-day today. Be fine tomorrow.'

He wheeled his hack round and cantered away, with Tipper looking after him in disbelief.

Tipper didn't give much thought to Fighting Talk for the rest of the day. He was sure he wouldn't run the next day. Sinclair would see sense when he'd cooled down. Trainers tend to get a bit het up on the gallops when things don't go according to plan. But Tipper had more important things on his mind.

This was a special day. He'd rather have died than tell the lads and girls in the tack-room why. But on this day two years ago he and Ana had first gone to bed together. It still amazed Tipper that she wanted him at all; but he wanted her more and more.

He planned a celebration because she was in desperate need of cheering up. After the euphoria of childbirth had worn off, she had lost all her enthusiasm, and seemed drained of energy. Tipper would leave her in the morning in her pyjamas on the sofa with the TV on, and come back in the evening to find her in exactly the same spot. Post-natal depression is what the doctors called it. They said she'd get better in time. But giving it a name wasn't enough. At times Tipper was desperately sorry for her, at others he just wanted her to snap out of it, for his and Lara's sake.

Walking along the High Street, he called in at a shop called The Home Design Studio and bought four big candles; two fat ones and two smaller ones.

When Ana was working in the kitchen after supper, he slipped into the bedroom, drew the curtains and pulled a table up to the foot of the bed. He placed the two larger lights in the middle of the table, flanked them with the smaller ones, then lit all four. The large ones were scented, a rosy, spicy smell.

Then he went through, past Lara's cot, to the kitchen and took Ana's hands in his.

'Shut your eyes and come with me,' he said.

'Tipper, I have to check Lara,' she protested.

'I've done that. She's sleeping. Just keep your eyes shut.'

Tipper led her into the bedroom and shut the door.

'What's that smell?' she asked.

'Okay, you can look now.'

Ana opened her eyes to see her bedroom dancing with shadows, as the candles flickered.

'You see these lights?' he went on. 'That's you and my Ma in the middle. You are the two lights of my life, see? That's Lara on one end, she's only small yet. And the candle at the other end is for our next one.'

'Our next one?' Ana said, doubtfully.

'Yes, and by the way, don't you think it's time we got started on it?'

He put his finger against Ana's lips, to stop her speaking, and then took her loosely in is arms. His face was just inches from Ana's. They stared into each others eyes, and then Tipper rubbed his nose gently against hers, first on one side, and then on the other.

'I love it when you do that,' Ana whispered. 'Don't stop. Don't ever stop.'

Tipper twitched his nose from side to side like a rabbit. Ana laughed.

36

The next morning Fighting Talk was not down to be ridden out, because he was running at Chester. Tipper couldn't believe it. He'd expected Sinclair to get a vet's report and scratch him from the race, but the vet had never gone near the horse.

'Jesus!' Tipper fumed to Delaney in the tack room. 'It's fockin' madness. He worked like a dog yesterday. Why's the Guvnor doing this? I told him he's wrong.'

Delaney shrugged and spat through the door and into the yard.

'Don't ask me, son. Just be pleased you've got a decent horse to ride in a Group race. You're not exactly in the same sort of demand as Frankie Dettori at the moment, are you?'

'But he won't be a decent horse today. He's not right, I'm telling you.'

'You're not the trainer, nor am I. See this?'

That morning's *Sun* was lying on the tack-room

table. Delaney tapped the headline. FIGHTING TALK TO HAVE HIS SAY.

'He'll start favourite, and he deserves it. He's got a stone in hand over the others. Even if he's not quite right, he can still win.'

'It's not that he's "not quite right". He's focked. I'm telling you! He'd not win a match with a Jersey cow today.'

Delaney gave a sigh.

'You just give him the best ride you can, Tipper. And don't be telling anyone else in the yard about this. Stable walls have ears, remember!'

Tipper decided to drive himself across country to Chester in Sam's car. He didn't feel at ease sharing long journeys with other jocks. As he joined the M6 south of Birmingham his phone's ringtone sounded. He pressed the green button.

'Morning, son. How are things?'

Tipper recognized the gravely tone of voice.

'Morning Duke. Things are not great. I'm knackered. Haven't had a proper night's sleep for months. I love her to bits, our Lara, but she's got a hell of a strong pair of lungs.'

'Bless her,' said the Duke. 'They grow up sooner or later. Got a bit in hand today in the Group 3, wouldn't you say?'

'Oh, yes, of course. But to tell you the truth, we're going to get lapped. He was stone dead on the gallops yesterday and he coughed after. I wouldn't have money on him if it was stolen.'

This was beautiful music to the Duke's ears.

'You don't say. No chance of a place, even?'

'He's got no chance.'

'I see. In that case, thanks a lot, son. We'll look after you. Go steady.'

And he was gone. Tipper chewed his lower lip, thoughtfully. He was getting increasingly uneasy about his friendship with the Duke. He knew he wasn't supposed to pass information, but then again everyone was doing it; the rule was generally regarded as a bit of a joke. You only had to look at the adverts in papers: PHONE AFTER MIDDAY FOR THE LATEST RACING INFORMATION. Where was this information leaking from? The yards, where else? Jockeys were arrested from time to time; even Kieren Fallon hadn't been immune from police investigations in the past. But breaking the speed limit on the motorway was illegal too, and he was doing it right now. Half the cars on the road with him were doing it. No one expected to get caught. And anyway choice is a luxury of the rich. He now had two more mouths to feed. The Duke 'looking after him' would be handy.

He imagined what the Duke was up to now. Probably getting onto the betting exchanges and laying Fighting Talk. Offering bigger odds on him than anyone else. Maybe he'd back something else in the race as well if he had any other info. Tipper's phoned sounded again. It was Tattoo Tony.

'All right, Tipper? You got a steering job at Chester today, right? . . . Oh! That's a shame . . . Thanks, mate . . . We'll look after you. Bye.'

Then in quick succession there were calls from more of the Duke's Pirhana Club pals. Tipper thought maybe he should have kept quiet, or lied, but in the position he was in that was just as dangerous as spilling the beans. The Duke's associates, as he well knew, were capable of doing anything if he didn't play ball.

Tipper told himself it would be okay. But as he pulled into the jockeys' car park at the course, one question was still niggling him. Why was Sinclair so insistent on running the horse? He didn't know the answer.

He went straight to the jockeys' room to drop his bag with the valet who'd be preparing his riding kit. He jumped on the scales and saw with approval that he weighed fifty-eight kilos in his street clothes; the same as he was due to carry in the race. He would strip down to fifty-five kilos and since his breeches, silks, boots and underwear weighed a kilo and a half, he would be able to use the medium-weight 1500 gram saddle.

He was about to go through for a cup of coffee in the jockeys' relaxation room when the tannoy crackled.

'Mr Tipper O'Reilly to the trainers' area, please. Mr Tipper O'Reilly.'

The trainer's area is the only part of the weighing room complex where trainers have access. Tipper found Sinclair waiting there for him.

'The TV people want to interview you before your race, Tipper. I told them you'd do it.'

'Me, Guvnor? Jesus! I'm crap at interviews.'

'Course you're not. You're Irish, aren't you? Just talk about the horse in general. Don't say a word about yesterday's work. I don't want the owners getting upset with us. They want a day out and only time will tell how he runs.'

'I think I know how he'll run.'

'Well don't go there in the interview, son, okay? Or I promise you will regret it.'

Tipper loathed being interviewed at the best of times. Today he'd be on a hiding to nothing.

'Yes, John, I'm joined by Tipper O'Reilly, who rides Fighting Talk in the big one. Tipper this horse was clear favourite overnight but now his price is drifting faster than a piece of wood. Is there something up with him?'

'No, no, he's fine—'

'But in the market he's out for a walk with Captain Oates. Why does no one seem to want to back him?'

'The market's been wrong before,' said Tipper guardedly. 'It's all speculation, like, isn't it? We'll see how he runs.'

'How are you going to ride him?'

Tipper shrugged.

'Oh I'll wait till I see how the race turns out, see what the others do . . .'

'But you like your chances?'

'Yes, I like the horse. On his day he's a great ride.'

'So is this going to be his day? Are you going to win, Tipper?'

Tipper's brain was furiously churning.

'We'll do our best,' was all he said.

The interviewer seemed non-plussed by Tipper's stonewalling. Something was said in his ear and he cut the uninformative interview short. Tipper was let go. He hated dealing with the media, but he felt quite good about the interview overall. The one problem was the 'yes' that had slipped out. It might be understood to imply that he expected to win. But perhaps no one had noticed.

37

Fighting Talk was drawn in stall one, on the rail. He'd be scraping the paint, as they call it down under, which could be a very favourable draw provided the horse jumped out smartly because it gave the jockey options. Tipper would be able to choose a position in running, and adjust his tactics according to how the race unravelled. If on the other hand they missed the kick or came out sluggishly, the rest of the field would swamp the inside berth ahead, leaving Tipper with no choice but to lob along behind, hoping for a break.

Tipper was one of the first to take his horse into the gate. He stood up in his irons and sat on the frame of the stalls, easing the weight on the Fighting Talk's back. Then he pulled down his goggles and adjusted the small audio transmitter that fitted under the rim of his helmet beside his left ear. This was the 'Jockeycom', whereby trainers could contact their jockeys in running, giving instructions as events unfolded. As had already happened in motor sport, this device could be accessed by the public address system and the broadcasters, with the idea of involving the crowd and the television viewers more closely in race tactics. The audio could also be produced later for the Stewards, should there be any enquiry. Needless to say it was unpopular with jockeys, who thought they had plenty to think about in a race without having orders barked into their ears by someone half a mile away. Many trainers also disliked it, but Sinclair was not one of them.

'I'm leaving tactics to you, Tipper,' said Sinclair's voice now. 'Just get a good position from the gate and make sure he's up with the pace.'

This was for public consumption and a little different from what Sinclair had whispered into Tipper's ear in the paddock, when he was preparing to mount.

'Don't give him a hard race. If he doesn't feel right, look after him.'

When the bell rang and the stalls flew open, Fighting Talk dwelled. Tipper thought he'd fallen asleep. He gave him a slap with the stick and the horse half-heartedly lumbered out to find himself chasing the majority of the field, with three other back markers leaning in on him. So much for keeping up with the pace.

'For fock's sake, give us some room, boys!' Tipper shouted.

The jockeys on his outside took no notice. They never did. Tipper knew he couldn't let the horse immediately next to him get ahead, or he might cut in and take his ground. So Fighting Talk had to be kept to his work, though he was all the time hating it. Maybe the problem was Chester's endless left-handed turn, but having to run fractionally less far than his rivals at least helped the horse hold his position. Suddenly Sinclair's clipped tones were again ringing in Tipper's left ear.

'Move up! What are you doing? Get closer to the leaders.'

This was impossible. Tipper had a solid block of horses in front of him and, being hemmed in, couldn't pull to the outside.

Fighting Talk still wasn't travelling well and, to Tipper's ears, his breathing sounded louder than usual. But his class kept him just about in touch and, at the three-furlong pole, the horse immediately in front rolled slightly off the rail to open a hint of a gap for Fighting Talk to move into.

'Grrrrr!' growled Tipper, giving the horse another slap with his stick.

In an instinctive response the horse quickened for a moment, but the gap closed again before he could take advantage, and now the whips were raised across the whole field. They were approaching the end of the long turn into the straight, where, Chester's inside rail is displaced eight or nine feet further to the inside, to spread the field out and give horses in Fighting Talk's position a chance of challenging for the lead. Tipper grabbed hold of the horse by shortening his reins and gave him another slap with the stick. Nothing happened. As the rail cut-in flashed past, Fighting Talk was going backwards relative to the rest of the field, and being squeezed as horses swerved in towards the adjusted rail.

Fighting Talk's ears were lying flat now, and he sounded as if he might be choking. With all possible chance in the race gone, Tipper could only accept the situation. He eased the horse down and they crossed the line last, twenty-five lengths adrift of the winner.

There was no comment from Sinclair via the Jockeycom, but there were plenty of catcalls from the crowd.

'You're a bent bastard!' shouted one aggrieved racegoer. 'You didn't try. You want hanging.'

Next thing, Tipper heard the public address announce a Stewards' Enquiry into the race. But, said the voice, this did not affect the winner or the placings.

Tipper had been involved in a few Stewards' Enquiries, but these had been simple questions of one horse bumping another, or swerving into its path. The penalty might be nothing more severe than the jockey suffering a few days' suspension from riding. But now, as Tipper stood before the stewards matters were rather more serious.

'Mr O'Reilly, thank you for attending,' said the senior steward. He was peering severely at Tipper over the rim of his reading glasses. 'Take a seat, please.'

Tipper sat in the vacant chair next to the one already occupied by Sinclair.

'Mr O'Reilly, are you aware that Fighting Talk drifted alarmingly in the betting?'

'I heard something,' Tipper truthfully replied.

'Do you know of any reason why the horse should have drifted in such an unusual manner?'

'No.'

'We have reviewed the Ormonde Stakes on video,' the steward continued, 'and listened to the recording of the jockeycom. In this race you finished tailed off, despite being on one of the most fancied horses. Can you explain your poor showing?'

Tipper shot a glance at Sinclair, who was sitting hunched forward, while staring intently at his interlaced fingers.

'My horse didn't feel right, sir,' said Tipper. 'It was his breathing. He seemed to choke.'

'Just after the seven furlong marker Mr Sinclair instructed you to take closer order. You appeared to make no effort to do so.'

'I couldn't. I didn't have the room at the time. You must have been able to see that for yourself, on the video. A small gap opened later and I did try to put him through it.'

'You didn't try very hard, did you?'

'Something was wrong with the horse. I didn't see any point in punishing him. I'm sure Mr Sinclair will agree—'

'Thank you. Mr O'Reilly! We are capable of

asking Mr Sinclair ourselves. Mr Sinclair? What do you think?'

Sinclair cleared his throat.

'It's a bit of a mystery, sir,' he said, his brow furrowed. 'I just can't explain it at all.'

'Do you have any reason to suppose the horse is other than perfectly fit?'

'No, no, I haven't.'

Tipper gave Sinclair a long hard stare, but said nothing.

'And that is all you have to say, Mr Sinclair?'

'Yes, it is.'

'Anything to add, Mr O'Reilly?'

Tipper's brain was working furiously. He could give the lie to Sinclair by telling the stewards about what he'd told Sinclair the previous day. He could also pass on Sinclair's pre-race instruction – that he should go easy on the horse if he didn't seem right – or even how Sinclair told him not to mention the horse's work in his TV interview. He could, that is, if he wanted to lose his job. So instead he just shook his head and mumbled, 'No, sir.'

'In that case, will you kindly wait outside, Mr O'Reilly? And, Mr Sinclair, thank you for your attendance.'

In the ante-room outside the Stewards' Room, Tipper angrily faced his employer.

'Jesus, Guvnor, how could you drop me in it like that?' he challenged in a savage whisper. 'Didn't I *tell* you the horse was wrong yesterday?'

'I know, Tipper,' said Sinclair out of the side of his mouth. 'But I had to pretend not. If I lose my training license for knowingly running a sick horse, everyone suffers, don't you see? A lot of people depend on me. I can't let it happen.'

'Oh, well, excuse me for complaining. It's *my* job I'm worried about!'

'Of course you are,' murmured Sinclair emolliently. 'But they've got nothing on you. You'll be fine.'

He looked at his watch.

'Now look, I've got to go down and face Champion. He's not happy. I'll see you later.'

Tipper was not a happy man either, but there was nothing he could do. Sinclair had deliberately dropped him in the shit to save his own skin. In frustration Tipper walked up and down banging the fist of one hand into the palm of the other.

There were ten minutes to go before the Stewards would be needed at the start of the next race. A quick decision was required and the stewards' secretary was soon putting his head around the door and inviting Tipper back inside.

'Mr O'Reilly,' the senior steward said, 'we find you in breach of Rule 43a, preventing your horse from achieving its best possible placing. This as I am sure you know is a very serious offence, because it undermines the credibility of the sport. Therefore we order that your licence to ride under the rules of racing be revoked with immediate effect.'

Tipper's mouth fell open in astonishment and he rocked back in his chair. Suspended? Jesus!

'But, but . . .' he stammered. 'I done nothing wrong.'

'That isn't how we see it. And there is more.'

The steward adjusted his spectacles, consulted a sheet of handwritten notes before him, and looked back at Tipper.

'We intend to ask the authorities to look into betting patterns before the race. We give you fair warning here and now, Mr O'Reilly, that we consider you may also have been in breach of Rule 83, passing information to one or more improper persons. That will be investigated at a later date but I am telling you now not to expect an early return to the saddle. That is all. You may go.'

38

Over the next ten days Sinclair talked Tipper out of lodging an appeal. He said it was pointless at this stage, with the question of passing information still hanging over Tipper's head. All he could do for the time being was sweat it out.

And so he did. Week succeeded week without the slightest clue about how 'the authorities' were progressing with their investigations. Meanwhile Tipper's future hung in the balance. True, as Sinclair has said, he still had his job at the stable, but that wasn't much consolation. He asked himself, would he ever ride as a jockey again, even if the formal ban was lifted? Alison Sinclair's hostility had not abated. Mike Champion, he supposed, would not want to use him again. And most important of all was the attitude of his other patron. What would General Shalakov make of it all?

A suspended and warned off jockey is a miserable creature. He's a pariah with whom people in the industry are wary of associating.

Ana did her best to sympathise with him but she wanted a harmonious family life and hated Tipper's depressive moods.

But there was one place where he could relax: the Partridge. Tipper began dropping in there more and more and, with no racing weight to watch, he began drinking again. Nothing excessive, though, he kept telling himself.

Tipper and Sam were not getting on too well. Tipper blamed Sam for getting him involved with the Covey Club and told him as much.

'You did it with your eyes wide open,' Sam told him.

'Jesus, thanks, pal,' was Tipper's reply. 'I thought you said it was the least I could do for you? If it hadn't been for that fockin' club and the Duke and his mates I might not be in this mess.'

Ana was not happy about him going to the pub, but he had an excuse one night. Or a reason, as he put it to her. This was business. Johnny the Fish had been on with the news that Nico, Shalakov's man, had suggested that they meet up. Ana wasn't impressed by this and, for good measure, they had a row before he went out.

It was a miserable, drizzly autumn evening. Tipper had to pull his jacket over his head to hurry into the pub without getting drenched. Johnny the Fish was at his table by the TV reading the evening paper.

'Tipper my son, you look a bit holed below the waterline tonight,' he observed.

'Had a bit of a barney with Ana,' Tipper confessed.

'You'll be needing a bracer, then. What'll it be? A little of my amber Scottish wine?'

'Thanks, Johnny. Jesus this disciplinary case is doing my head in. All I want is my licence back.'

'Naturally. Anything new on that front?'

Johnny placed a large Scotch in front of Tipper, who shook his head as he took a deep swallow.

'I'm as far away from riding again as ever.'

Johnny the Fish glanced furtively around the pub for prying ears.

'I think we'd better retire to the snug, old boy. Walls have ears. Some of my customers haven't even heard of Chatham House, let alone know the rules.' Tipper hadn't a clue what he was talking about. The war-time intelligence centre at Chatham House hadn't come onto his radar screen. But he was happy to be led through the narrow door into the bolt hole he knew well to get the world off his shoulders.

They sat round the familiar table on the bench seats and Johnny asked Shelley to bring the bottle of scotch and a jug of water. Tipper emptied his glass and reached for the bottle. He didn't bother to add any water.

'Jesus, the missis is a nightmare at the moment, Johnny. I've hardly had a drop in the last month. You'd think she'd understand wouldn't you?

She's been on desperate form recently. Always bloody complaining if I go out.'

'That's how it goes, old boy,' the Fish mused. 'They just don't understand us. Never have. Never will. They're all the same. At least all my wives have been. My first wife hid a kipper under the driver's seat of my car. Cuh. The smell was awful – couldn't get anyone in the back of the car after that. Then there was Mrs Fish number two.' The Fish took a large gulp of scotch and water and collected his thoughts. 'One evening she said shall we swap positions tonight. I thought, Cuh, this sounds alright. Then she said "You stay at home and do the ironing and I'll go to the pub and get shit faced."'

Before The Fish could add any further wisdom to the proceedings their peace in the snug was interrupted by the door opening.

'Evening gentlemen,' Nico said smoothly.

'Ah. Monsieur Nico,' Johnny said expansively. 'Welcome.'

'Tipper. Good to see you. You're looking well.'

'Well?' Tipper replied sarcastically. 'Well focked, more like, Nico.'

Nico sat down next to Tipper and helped himself to the scotch.

'Tipper. I can't believe how they've treated you. Terrible. I've already talked to General Shalakov and you have our total support. Total. You'll be riding all of ours when this is over.'

Tipper was happy to hear it. Any support was

welcome right now. Especially from one of Sinclair's big owners.

Johnny, Tipper and Nico quietly worked their way through the whisky bottle, until Johnny emptied it into their glasses and got to his feet.

'Bird never flew on one wing, you know,' he informed them. 'Better get the other half.'

'Won't be a minute, Nico. Need the jax,' Tipper said apologetically as he followed Johnny out to the bar.

Nico couldn't believe his luck. He fished into his pocket and pulled out a small brown glass bottle of white pills. He carefully unscrewed the lid, shook a couple of the pills into the palm of his hand, and flipped one into Tipper's drink and the other into Johnny's. They made a brief fizz then disappeared. Nico then slid a small amount of white powder wrapped in an elaborately folded piece of shiny, non-absorbent magazine paper into the pocket of Tipper's coat, which was lying on the seat. Job half done, he thought to himself. Then he sat back and checked his Blackberry. A satisfied smile crept across his face when he saw his latest message. Ekatarina and Kristabel were on their way.

If Johnny the Fish and Tipper hadn't been so pissed they might have wondered how two fairly pretty girls ended up drinking with them and Nico in the snug after hours. But the thought never crossed their minds. And who cared anyway?

The most remarkable attribute of Johnny the Fish, and one not commonly appreciated, was that in spite of his alcohol intake, he had no intention of dying quoting the poet laureate John Betjeman's greatest regret, 'Not enough sex.'

So he wasn't sorry when Nico said he had to be off back to London. 'Four's company, five's a crowd,' he kept saying. But in spite of his interest, particularly in Kristabel, he was beginning to feel inexplicably tired.

Ekatarina followed Nico out into the car park.

'There you go,' Nico smiled as he handed over the readies. Make sure you text me the photos straight away. 'Make it look messy. And here's a bonus.'

Nico gave her a similar package to the one he'd slid into Tipper's pocket.

'You're a gentleman,' she smiled. 'Nice doing business with you.'

'Don't forget to take his jacket to the bedroom with you,' Nico added.

Ekatarina and Kristabel waited for the sedative pills to kick in. Tipper was out cold first.

'You're a rather sweet little thing,' Johnny told Kristabel before he finally gave up the unequal struggle to stay awake and let his head fall onto the table. The girls then hauled Tipper up to the bedroom.

'Get his jacket,' Ekatarina told her mate, as she steadied Tipper. He was mumbling away to them as they dragged him up the stairs. But he hadn't got a clue what was going on.

Kristabel stripped Tipper while Ekatarina got her phone out. Nico's instructions were clear. If his eyes were closed keep them out of shot. But make sure it was obvious it was him. Which was why they left his green and white Celtic Y-fronts on.

Kristabel did a passable simulation of oral sex. Nothing was happening but it wasn't going to look pretty. God help this bloke, she thought. And wondered what he'd done to be shafted.

And shafted he was. As soon as Nico got the images of Tipper from Ekatarina he anonymously forwarded them to Ana's mobile phone number. Which Sinclair had given to him.

39

The Fish was an early riser by habit, even with the best part of Nico's pill inside him. So he heard the hammering on the front door as he pottered around the bar surveying last night's debris and wondering why he'd fallen asleep in the snug.

'We're closed,' he shouted out of instinct. 'Anyway we don't take football coaches. Buzz off.'

'It's the police. We'd like to come in please,' the voice outside the door said firmly.

The Fish knew the form. The police came in for a drink from time to time and then left him and his customers alone.

'Okay hang on,' he gasped as he pulled the fag out of his mouth and unbolted the door. 'Bloody hell. You're a bit early aren't you, Slade?'

Inspector Slade gave Johnny the Fish a withering look as he stepped into the Partridge.

'You got a Tipper O'Reilly on the premises?'

'What's this about?' Johnny knew Slade vaguely

and had never liked him. He had always humoured him, obviously, for the sake of his clients.

'Where is he, Mr Ferrett?'

'Well. He's . . . have you got a warrant? You can't just come barging in here shouting the odds.'

'Can't I?' Slade said snidely. 'Well let's see how many customers you keep if we were to park a car up the road from here every night for the next three months.'

It didn't take the Fish long to figure that one out. 'Cup of coffee?'

'Is he here or not, Mr Ferrett. You're pushing your luck.'

The Fish's instincts told him to lie but his brain said the stakes were too high. 'Cuh . . . you better look upstairs,' he reluctantly suggested.

Tipper was still out cold when they found him in the Galileo Suite.

'Christ it smells in here. Open the window,' Slade barked as he picked up Tipper's jacket which was in a heap on the floor. He found what he was looking for in the first pocket. The small folded package. He carefully opened it on the cheap table by the window. It was full of white powder. Slade dampened his index finger with his tongue then lightly dabbed it into the cocaine. Then he rubbed his finger across his top gum.

'Hmm. Usual stuff they sell in Cambridge,' he said appreciatively to his sergeant. 'Pity there's not more. Still, nice to get a jockey.'

The sergeant shook Tipper, who tried to roll over.

'Come on you. Wake up,' he said sympathetically. His tone irritated Slade, who shook Tipper more abruptly.

Tipper opened his eyes and focused on the fat man in the cheap suit who was standing over him.

'Jesus, who are you?'

Tipper's mouth tasted of scotch. It was dry as a bone. His head felt like it was splitting in two. He could feel the throb of blood pumping through his temples.

'Are you Tipper O'Reilly?'

'Of course I am.'

'You're under arrest on suspicion of possessing illegal substances.'

'What? What the fock's going on?'

'You're coming with us. That's what's going on.'

By the time Tipper arrived at Cambridge police station he was feeling very rough. He still hadn't drunk any water and he reeked of whisky. He didn't have the sort of body weight required to absorb the cocktail of whisky and Nico's pill that he'd unwittingly downed. He was a mess and operating on auto-pilot as he was taken through the back door and down a long flight of stairs to the basement. A large swing door led into the reception area where a couple of glum looking women were standing behind a substantial counter.

'Empty your pockets and take off your watch,'

one of them requested, without bothering to look at Tipper. He rummaged through them; loose change, wallet, phone, key ring.

'Any shoelaces or necklaces?' the robot demanded. Tipper shook his head and then remembered his lucky necklace. Reluctantly he undid his shirt and pulled it over his head. He looked at the tiny picture of Lara as he put it on the counter.

Behind him there was one hell of a row as two policemen bundled a very agitated woman in a white papery looking suit through the reception down a corridor. She was putting up a good fight and screaming obscenities at them. They didn't look too fussed. Tipper was then taken into the ID room.

'Right we want a swab from inside your cheek and your finger prints,' a new automaton demanded.

Tipper picked up the wooden stick and scraped around the inside of his mouth. This only happened on TV, he thought to himself. He'd be locked up in a bloody cell with ten smack-heads at this rate.

Even though he was mighty relieved to see the cell was empty when the door was swung open, it smelt horrible. Disinfectant mixed with something else.

'I'm not going in that cell, okay,' he protested. 'You're not going to treat me like a bloody criminal. I want to see a lawyer right now.'

'Either you go in there or we charge you with obstruction. Just do yourself a favour.' Tipper gave up. He felt too knackered to put up any fight. There was a bench at the end of the room with a mattress on it and a seatless loo in the right hand corner. Everything was painted shiny off-yellow. Tipper lay on the bench and looked at the cell door. What the fuck was he doing there? How the hell had the police found drugs in his pocket? Who put them onto him anyway? None of it made sense.

Tipper drank some water but it wasn't helping. He now had a serious headache right behind his eyes. He felt isolated, angry and apprehensive. He needed reassurance, protection from the storm raging around him. And what about Ana? She was going to need someone with her. She'd never cope on her own.

He wanted a big mug of tea, just like his mother used to make it. He wanted Ana cuddled up next to him. And then for no reason at all, completely out of the blue, he wanted to be in the big white barn in Tipperary, sitting on a deep bed of straw listening to the rain lashing down outside.

Tipper curled up on the bed and fell into an uncomfortable, fretful half-sleep.

A couple of hours later he was taken into a small plain room, where a small plain man was waiting for him. 'Mr O'Reilly, this is Mr Cunningham,' the policewoman said to him. 'He's here to represent you.'

Tipper sat down without saying anything.

'Mr O'Reilly, the police allege you were in possession of cocaine when you were arrested.'

'It's not mine. I've never touched the stuff.'

Cunningham sighed and picked up a copy of the charge sheet.

'Well, it's a fairly serious offence, so I advise you to be careful what you say – all right?'

But Tipper had stopped listening. He was looking at the wall thinking about Ana and Lara. Jesus what a mess.

When Slade finally arrived he went off at a tangent that Cunningham hadn't anticipated.

'You were on the phone a lot on your way Chester races recently, weren't you?'

'You don't have to answer that,' Cunningham cut in.

'Thank you Mr Cunningham,' Slade said sarcastically. Then, one by one, he ran through the calls. Most of the surnames he mentioned were genuinely unknown to Tipper, but he knew who they belonged to.

'So, Mr O'Reilly, it would seem that you have a lot of friends who just happened to ring you up on a day when you have a good chance in a race. They all bet against the horse and you make no effort to win the race. What a coincidence.'

Again Cunningham told Tipper not to answer. But images of the Duke, Tattoo Tony and Ladders started flashing through Tipper's head. Cold sweat glistened on his forehead.

'Which one of them supplies you with the drugs? We're not interested in you taking drugs; as long as you tell us who gave them to you. Payment, isn't it? For information. Make this easy for yourself young man.'

'That is speculation,' Cunningham blurted out animatedly. 'My client is not here to speculate.' Tipper was surprised. He had assumed that the lawyer was just there to make sure he wasn't roughed up.

'So Mr O'Reilly, why did you stop Fighting Talk?' Slade persisted.

'That is of no relevance,' Cunningham cut in. 'I want this interview suspended.'

'He stopped himself,' Tipper retorted. 'Talk to a vet. That isn't speculation.'

Slade ignored Cunningham's repeated request and kept at it for half an hour, but finally he knew he wasn't getting anywhere.

'You're a lucky boy,' Slade finally informed him as he switched off the tape recorder. 'You didn't have enough coke on you to take this any further. You're free to go.'

Slade then suggested Tipper left by the back exit, to avoid the journalists outside the front doors. Tipper didn't really understand, but he accepted the offer.

It was already dark when he stepped out into the street. He immediately switched his phone on to check his messages, hoping there would be one from Ana.

'You have one new message,' his phone told him. 'Tipper, David Sinclair here. Are you okay? I guess you're in the police station at the moment. Sorry to hear about that – outrageous. The bloody police have no idea. Ring me as soon as you get this message?' Tipper's heart sank. What about Ana? He couldn't believe she hadn't rung him. He'd got drunk, but he'd had a bad experience. Surely she could understand that? Tipper tried her mobile but only got her answering service. 'Ana, sweetheart,' he said. 'I'm sorry about last night. I know I shouldn't have had a drink. It won't happen again. I was upset. Please ring me.'

40

Tipper felt like seventeen kinds of shit by the time he was at last standing at his front door, and turning the key to let himself in. He'd been phoning Ana every five minutes since the police turfed him out of the police station. She hadn't picked up.

He'd had visions all the way home of Ana being there when he got back, herself and Lara curled up on the sofa, with something like a shepherd's pie warming in the oven. It would be such a relief. But when he went inside and called out, there was no reply. The house was deserted, the lights were off. Where were they?

Standing in the hallway he keyed in Johnny the Fish's number.

'It's Tipper.'

'How are you, my boy? I sincerely hope the rozzers treated you with respect. Where did they take you?'

'Cambridge. But I'm not phoning for a chat.

It's Ana. I just got home and she's not here. She's not picking up my calls. Did she phone or come looking for me at the pub today? Does she know that I got pissed last night? And that I got arrested?'

'I don't know, Tipper. I've not seen her at all.'

Tipper disconnected and climbed the stairs to the living area. The place had been tidied. It seemed too tidy. What was going on?

It wasn't until he entered the kitchen that he found out. There was a note on the table.

I don't know how to start. You bastard. You have destroyed my life AND Lara's life.

Tipper was aghast. What was this?

How could you do this to us? You are disgusting like most men. I trusted you but you lied. How could you do that thing which you did? You said you loved us. Liar. We have gone and we never want to see you again ever. Don't look for us. Leave me and Lara alone. Don't upset her. God help you Tipper.

The note was not signed. Tipper stared at the words in disbelief. He sank into one of the chairs at the kitchen table, where he had sat so often to eat with Ana, where he had spooned food into his daughter's mouth. He read the note again, and then a third time. What did she mean, that he was disgusting? That he lied about loving them? That he'd ruined Lara's life? All he'd done was have a bit of a row, get pissed and stay out all night. He admitted such a thing was bad, but not *that* bad.

He tried her number again, with the same result. Ana had gone. But where? And how in the name of Jesus was he going to find her?

41

Tipper woke at six thirty in the morning. He was curled up on the sofa, fully dressed, his face buried in the upholstery. The previous day had completely bottomed him. Even the shock of Ana's inexplicable disappearance couldn't overcome his exhaustion. He'd fallen into a deep, dreamless, anaesthetized sleep. He was awoken by noises from the street; mainly the clatter of horses returning from their exercise. They reminded him that he hadn't turned up for work for the last two mornings.

He dialled Delaney's mobile phone number.

'Jim. It's Tipper. Have you seen Ana? Has she been down at the yard?' His voice sounded rough.

'Two coppers were here yesterday morning, son,' Delaney said, ignoring the question. 'They were looking for you.'

'Jim. Have you seen her?' Tipper persisted.

'No sign of her. What –?'

But Tipper had cut him off. He didn't need some

long lecture. What he needed was some water. His lips were practically stuck together. He poured himself a glass of water from the tap and found an aspirin in the drawer. He had a splitting headache. Then for a moment he stopped thinking about Ana and Lara and remembered his 'drug problem'. He rang Johnny the Fish.

'Hello,' Johnny grunted.

'Johnny. It's Tipper. What the fock happened? How did those drugs get in my pocket. I've never touched that stuff . . .'

'You've been stitched up, mate. Can only be four people. Nico, the girls or that policeman. Any idea why?'

'Jesus, Johnny, none. It doesn't make sense . . .'

'Drop in later, old boy . . . look, I can't talk now.' Johnny the Fish obviously couldn't work it out either.

Tipper put the kettle on and sat and blankly watched it as it boiled. He really didn't know what to do. He'd rung Johnny the Fish. He'd rung Delaney. Sam, as far as he knew, was travelling mares in Ireland. Who the hell could help him? Then he remembered. *If you ever have a problem give me a bell.'* The Duke.

'You're all over the paper,' the Duke said without Tipper needing to identify himself. 'Helping the police with their enquiries, is the word. Not being *too* helpful, I hope.'

'Jesus, Duke, I told them nothing.'

'Good boy. Stay solid.'

'Jesus it's a mess. And now, my girlfriend, she's –'

'So what did the Old Bill actually want?' the Duke cut in. 'What's their exact line of enquiry, if I might ask?'

'I had some coke planted on me. And they're saying I made the horse choke in the Ormonde, deliberately. And they asked about a load of phone calls I had in the morning. But the thing is I'm looking for my girl –'

'*Phone calls*? The saucy bastards! But you said nothing?'

'Jesus, of course not.'

'Good. They're only having a laugh.'

'Duke, it's not looking too funny from my side. You see Ana, my bird, and our little girl, they've gone.'

'What do you mean, gone?'

'They've gone! She left a note saying she was leaving, but she didn't say why. I'm desperate to find them, so I am. It's a nightmare.'

There was a pause while the Duke thought about this. None of this was welcome news.

'I see,' he said. 'What can I do to help, son?'

'That's why I'm ringing. Can't you and the boys help me find her? I don't know who else to ask and there's no one in London you guys don't know.'

'What makes you sure she's here?'

'I'm not. I'm just guessing. It's where she was before she came to Newmarket.'

'That's reasonable. D'you have an address for her?'

'No. And her phone's not answering. You're a legend if you can help.'

'Course I will, Tipper. You're one of us, mate. I'll ring round. Tattoo Tony. He'll do anything for you.'

Tipper felt a little better after putting the phone down. There was a glimmer of hope.

The Duke's conversation with Tattoo Tony was brief. 'You seen about Tipper in the papers?'

'Yer, I seen it.'

'It's gone beyond the Stewards now. It's the Law we're dealing with. That concerns me.'

'Me too, Duke.'

'And Tipper says his bird's done a runner. He's asked me if I can find her.'

'Can you?'

'You joking? She's Russian. Probably gone back to bloody Moscow for all I know. Anyway he's soiled goods now. Wide berth job . . . So what's going on? Anything exciting?'

42

For weeks Tipper barely slept. His brain raced like a riderless horse. Always dwelling on the loss of Ana and Lara. The dark cloud that had lifted when things came together with Ana now blew back over his life with a vengeance.

Sam put their differences to one side and was sympathetic. Getting banned from riding was one thing. Losing Ana and Lara was something else. Sam floated the idea of hiring a private detective, which Tipper liked until he realized he'd have to shell out thousands of pounds that he hadn't got, with no guarantee of success.

Delaney also chipped in. He suggested he contact the police, and report Ana as a missing person. But after his experiences at Cambridge they were the last people Tipper would trust to help him out. Johnny the Fish, meanwhile, had heard nothing of the girls, and said Nico was nowhere to be found. Johnny recommended an almost Zen Buddhist line of positive passivity.

'Do nothing, Tipper, and something will transpire.'

'I don't get you, Johnny.'

'Listen, she'll come back to you. She'll turn up. I've found they always do. It hasn't necessarily been a welcome development in my own case, but you do seem –'

'What if they don't?'

'Believe me, son, they *will*.'

Tipper followed Johnny's advice. He did nothing . . . and nothing happened. The investigation into him by the Racing Board meandered on; they gave him no information, no timescale, they divulged nothing. He was in limbo. Summer dragged into autumn and still nothing happened. Then Tipper got a strange text message from Sinclair. *Come and meet me in London. Will explain why. Car can pick you up at 3 pm. Confirm ok.*

Tipper didn't know what to make of it. But he had nothing to lose so he confirmed.

The door man at Aspinalls was used to eccentric dressers. But he'd never let anyone in Tipper's attire over his threshold before. Tipper had made a bit of an effort but his crumpled suit made him look like a tramp.

'It's okay,' Sinclair reassured the old retainer in his sleek green coat and top hat. 'We're going to the private room.'

He hurried his guest up the back stairs to a room whose luxury struck Tipper dumb. Although of no great size, it was all gilded furniture, thick velvets and oriental rugs. The walls were hung with oil paintings of elephants and lions and a large antique bracket clock ticked importantly on the marble mantelpiece. Tipper felt nervous about sitting on one of the brocaded sofas and had to force himself to relax. The whole building groaned with sophistication far beyond his grasp.

Tipper hesitantly ordered a whisky and soda, which came on a silver tray. Sinclair plumped down opposite his jockey and took a pull at his own extra large tumbler of scotch.

'Tipper, something's come up which I want to tell you about. I've had a lucky break. General Shalakov has made me an offer. He wants me to become his private trainer.'

'Sounds good, Guvnor.'

'It is good. It's an amazing opportunity. The General's going to spend a fortune on horses. Anyway the thing is, he says he'd like you to come in with us as the retained jockey.'

'Me? But how can I? I haven't got my licence.'

Sinclair waved his hand airily.

'Oh! That'll be no problem. Everything can be fixed in Moscow.'

'Moscow? How do you mean, Moscow?'

'That's where I'm going, didn't I say? General Shalakov has a big training stable out in the country. But most of the racing's at the new Moscow Hippodrome. You'll love it there. It's an absolutely top-notch modern racecourse. And it seems to me the timing couldn't be better. It'll get you away from this atmosphere of suspicion in the UK.'

'What about the yard here? And Mrs Sinclair, won't she . . .'

Sinclair became less animated and looked at the fire.

'Well, things between us haven't been . . . I mean a little time apart will be good for both of us. So the plan is Mrs Sinclair will take over next season here as the licence holder. The place belongs to her anyway, so it's logical.'

Tipper glanced around at the African landscapes on the walls, but he hardly saw them. He was thinking furiously. Mrs Sinclair as the new guvnor? Even when he got his licence back, with her in charge, he was out of the Sinclair yard. He could sense the options running out on him.

'Go on, Tipper, come with me,' Sinclair pressed. 'You'd be riding the best horses in Europe in the best Group One races. Whereas if you stay here there's a good chance you're finished.'

'Are you sure about General Shalakov? I mean, is he for real?'

'Of course he is. He always thinks big, and he's got the kind if money to follow through. So, what do you say? Is it yes?'

'I think I'd have to clear my name here first, wouldn't I?'

Sinclair clicked his tongue and shook his head.

'Don't worry about that. The Russians don't much care and by the time you've earned a name for yourself in Russia, the people here'll be only too glad to welcome you back. You'll be a star.'

'And you're definitely going, are you?'

'Absolutely. Best offer I've ever had. I'd be a fool to turn it down, and so would you.'

'Maybe you're right,' said Tipper. 'But sure, I have to find Ana first. I can't even think about this until I do.'

Sinclair leaned forward and spoke in a more confidential voice.

'I don't know, Tipper. Think about this. Your Ana is probably back home in Moscow right now. I'd say your best hope of finding her is by being there yourself – in Moscow. Don't you agree?'

Tipper stared at the paintings again. His prospects were miserable. And Sinclair had a good point about Ana and Lara; if they really had gone back to Russia, he'd never find them without going there himself. And now he was being presented with the opportunity to do so for free. At the same time he had the chance to make a new start in his messed-up life. He raised his eyes to meet Sinclair's. His heart was thumping, but he suddenly found himself committing to Sinclair's package.

'Okay, Guvnor,' he said almost in a whisper, 'I suppose I've got nothing to lose, really, have I? So I'll do it. I'll go with you.'

Sinclair reached out and briefly gripped Tipper's upper arm. He gave it a momentary shake.

'Good man, Tipper. You won't regret it.'

A couple of days later Sam drove Tipper to

Farnborough private airfield in his rusty hatch-back. He was mighty relieved that an exit had been found for his cousin. He had become a wreck and Sam knew indirectly that he was partly to blame.

They were waved through a side gate onto the tarmac. Shalakov's G4 jet was painted with the logo of one of his companies; its engines were already whistling. A beautifully groomed female member of the flight crew stepped up to the car with a clip-board and confirmed Tipper's identity. She told him Sinclair was already on board.

'You'll tell me if you hear anything about Ana and Lara won't you?' Tipper demanded of Sam.

'I will. And you tell me if you find them in Russia. Good luck, so.'

'Yeah. Thanks. Make sure Johnny the Fish keeps looking for those two tarts, will you?'

Tipper got out of the car, heaved his one piece of luggage out of the back, and stumped up the plane's steps.

PART TWO

PART TWO

43

Tipper hadn't known what to expect, but the view from the window of the aircraft, as it lined up for landing, came as a shock. Having flown across countless miles of closely packed, snow-laden conifers, he now saw a gigantic clearing opening up below, with a complex of grey buildings in it. Xanadu. It looked like a secret military base in some James Bond film.

When the plane's door opened Tipper felt the blast of Russia's icy winter for the first time. Shalakov's car, with a uniformed driver, was waiting to carry them from the airstrip to the main complex. On the way Tipper saw smoke billowing from a chimney that rose above a bunker-like structure. It was a small-scale power-plant. Its generator gave Shalakov's research station complete self-sufficiency in electricity.

Sinclair and Tipper scurried from the car to a building that looked, on the outside, no different from all the other nondescript warehouses scattered around the place. But, inside, this was another world. The heat in the long marbled reception area was sub-tropical. Polished flooring stretched as far as the eye could see. Fountains and columns stood to attention. And plants and shrubs, like nothing Tipper had ever seen before, burst out of giant urns.

The reception area was bustling. Men and women in white coats rushed about purposefully with phones pressed to their ears.

The General was waiting to greet the arrivals in a large, minimally furnished room. It was neither an office nor a reception room. The black marble desk had enough square footage to flatter the vanity of a fascist dictator; and a series of eight very large and abstract paintings – each a dark smudgy square on a variety of coloured backgrounds – took the place of windows.

'Welcome to Xanadu,' he boomed theatrically, coming round from behind his desk and effusively pumping Sinclair and Tipper's hands. 'It is our name for this place, you know. It is fitting. I am told it was the palace of the great Kublai Khan. It was also what Charles Foster Kane called his house in *Citizen Kane*. So the name is perfect for me, don't you agree? Those are two kinds of strength: the Mongol fighter and the American capitalist. And now they meet together in one man – me.'

His simulated smile showed a fairly unattractive set of teeth. Tipper could smell a distinctive, cloying musk aftershave. It was a smell that permeated any room Shalakov was in. Tipper loathed it.

'This is where I run my bank from. The Haven Bank. We used it to mop up assets around the world back in 2009. They were cheap. I can have a conference in my virtual conference room around the clock. But it is not all hard work here.'

He gestured proudly at the paintings.

'Do you like my Rothkos?'

His guests looked around. They had no idea what a Rothko was.

'Yes. They're, er, very nice,' bluffed Sinclair.

'I am glad. They cost me more than two hundred million dollars.'

Shalakov turned to the desk and spoke into an intercom, then swung round again, rubbing his hands together.

'But why should you be interested in art? You are horsemen, yes? Come, I must show you the stables.'

He beckoned them to follow. They processed out of the room, back across the hallway and down some steps into a subway tunnel. It hummed with air-conditioning. The light came from beneath glass panels set into the floor. It soon became clear they were walking through a labyrinth of tunnels, with every junction sign-posted.

'Through these tunnels I have access to all the buildings on the site without going outside. For longer distances we use golf carts, but for this visit it is better to walk.'

They passed a security guard who admitted them to a chamber like an air-lock. The door behind them slid shut before the one ahead opened.

'We are in the zone of the stable barn now,' Shalakov explained, striding ahead. 'The air is heated to exactly thirty-eight degrees, the horse's body temperature. Come.'

A pair of swing doors led into a cavernous stable area, lined along all four walls with loose-boxes. Stable hands in shirt sleeves were criss-crossing the central space with brooms and buckets of feedstuff.

'The air is hotter in here. It is also thinner. Only ten per cent oxygen. Do not run, or you will lose your breath. It is the same as living high in the mountains. So, you see, my horses live at high altitude, but they exercise at the sea-level. It is very good for their lung capacity. So now, I show you. Let us go down to the sea-level.'

Passing through another air lock they entered a covered building of astonishing size. It housed an oval indoor gallop on which a variety of horses were being put through their paces. Tipper had used Newmarket's covered gallops a few times, but they were on nothing like this scale. Shalakov told them his circuit measured a statute mile.

'And our power station heats everything under the floor. It means we can work the horses even in the cold Russian winter.'

He gestured towards a large screen, which

showed a couple of horses cantering along the back straight. 'And we can see what they are doing at the other side of the building.' Then he called out to a small man of about forty who was riding around on a hack nearby.

'I introduce you to my trainer Vassily Vassilovich. From this day he will of course act under your instructions, Mr Sinclair.'

'David, please,' said Sinclair with an ingratiating smile, as he watched the Russian horseman approaching.

Vassily did not speak a word of English and, having seen all the signs in Cyrillic script, and heard everyone around them jabbering away in a language neither of them understood, Tipper and Sinclair had both begun to worry how they were going to leap over the language barrier. Then, while Shalakov fired a series of questions at his trainer, who replied with palpable nervousness, Tipper noticed a strange-looking elderly man. He was wearing an orange corduroy suit and a purple shirt. He broke away from whatever he'd been doing with one of the horses and began limping in their direction. Shalakov greeted him with considerable enthusiasm.

'Ah! Look, this is Jameson, our chief scientist!'

Jameson was evidently on intimate and easy terms with Shalakov. He greeted the General warmly in Russian, with none of the hesitant sycophancy of Vassilovich. He was holding in his hand a small electronic device.

'Two hundred and sixty beats per minute,' he said wheezily in English, then turned to the two newcomers. 'You must be David Sinclair, and you . . .'

He bowed to Tipper.

'. . . are, I presume, the young genius who will be riding our best horses. Welcome to Russia.'

He returned to the matter in hand, waving at the horse he had just left and repeated to Shalakov.

'Yes, as I was saying, two hundred and sixty beats per minute. It won't do. The horse is no good, I'm afraid. No good at all. We shall have to dispense with him.'

Sinclair noted that Shalakov seemed very relaxed about one of his horses being dismissed so summarily.

A few more words were exchanged in Russian and then Shalakov turned back to Sinclair and Tipper.

'I have some business, so I will leave you with Mr Jameson, who will show you everything.'

After Shalakov had left Tipper pointed to the box in Jameson's hand.

'What you got there, pal?'

'This?' replied Jameson. 'My equine heart monitor. Very effective device, and enormously useful.'

Tipper had a good look at Jameson's face. It was criss-crossed with a network of lines and wrinkles. His skin was dry and thin as paper, his fingers heavily nicotine-stained. He was reaching for his breath with a certain amount of effort, raising his shoulders with each inhalation.

'Now, let's see,' Jameson went on. 'Did he show you the chamber? No? Then you must follow me. This will impress you.'

44

The section they now entered was very much smaller and dominated by what looked like a stainless steel tank with glass portholes in its side.

'I don't suppose you've got one of these babies in Newmarket – not yet, anyway. One day everyone will have one! When they find out about them.'

'What on earth is it?' asked Sinclair.

'The key to our future success, if you want to know. With this chamber we'll produce champions, world-beaters, starting of course with Citizen.'

'Citizen?' asked Sinclair.

'You'll be meeting him soon. He's our pride and joy. But first the chamber.'

He made a proud sweeping gesture with his arm.

'I'd be dead with out it – it keeps my poor lungs going. It's the kriotherapy chamber. The temperature in there is minus 135 degrees centigrade.'

'Minus 135 degrees centigrade?' said Sinclair. 'You don't mean you actually take this horse Citizen in there?'

'Yes we do, but briefly. We've never found out how long a horse could survive at that temperature. We probably should do I suppose,' he said quietly, almost as a note to self. 'We only let him in there for four minutes. That's the maximum.'

Jameson nodded to the white-coated technician sitting in front of a bank of dials and monitors. She threw a switch and the door of the kriotherapy chamber slid open, revealing an interior swirling with icy vapour. Tipper had a flashback to the impenetrable mist that sometimes swirled across Newmarket Heath when dawn broke.

'Come inside,' invited Jameson. 'It's perfectly safe.'

Gingerly Tipper and Sinclair followed Jameson into the chamber. It took a moment to register, but then Tipper's cheeks became the first parts of his anatomy to feel it – the coldest air he'd ever experienced.

'Let me explain how it all works. After any horse has exercised he needs to recover before he can exercise again. Recovery is effected by the circulation of oxygen carried in the blood by haemoglobin into the areas where there might be small muscular strains, stresses, aches, that sort of thing. And it enables the muscles, after a time, to relax back into their normal resting condition. But when we put a horse in here, the process is greatly accelerated. The intense cold is right now making our blood retreat to the core of our bodies, taking the oxygen with it. When we come out to a normally warm environment, the oxygenated blood rushes back around the limbs in far greater amounts than it normally would: four times as much blood and oxygen go through the legs. But that's only the half of it. The extreme cold of the chamber also stimulates the endocrine system, which secretes much higher levels of hormones and endorphins than would be usual. So it's like legal doping.'

Jameson smiled knowingly.

'Believe me. I've done the blood tests. I've measured it. All those physical stresses I've mentioned are repaired much faster; any horse using this can exercise twice, three times as often as you would normally dare to do. Previously impossible levels of fitness can be achieved.'

It was too cold for Sinclair or Tipper to make conversation, unlike Jameson, who was used to it. Sinclair pointed urgently at the door.

'Couldn't we . . .?' he suggested, hugging himself for warmth and jiggling up and down.

'Jesus Christ!' Tipper swore as the chamber door opened. 'That is bloody cold all right.'

As they trooped out, Jameson laughed. And then Tipper and Sinclair started laughing too.

'You see?' Jameson said. 'You're both laughing now. Endorphins. The shock to the body makes you produce more endorphins. And they make you happy. Really. I'm not joking. I've done the measurements.'

As his grin faded, Sinclair was nodding.

'I see what you mean. It's a bit of a buzz. Do the horses like it?'

'Well, not to start with. Then they get into it. It's almost as if they know they'll get a high from it. Citizen, he loves it. Walks straight in with no bother now. You'll see. He can recover from any problem with miraculous speed. Not just soreness from hard exercise, but from any cuts or other injuries he might pick up. And he won't have bacterial or viral infections in the lungs to worry about. With this chamber, he'll never have any breathing problems, I guarantee.'

Tipper thought of Fighting Talk's cough. But irrespective of whether this kriotherapy might have saved him all that grief, he didn't much like the idea of it. It seemed unnatural and, in his opinion, if it wasn't quite natural, it wasn't quite right.

But Jameson was in no doubt. His enthusiasm was supercharged.

'When Citizen goes to the Hippodrome in Moscow to be trained, he'll come back to the chamber every Sunday. It'll be the making of him. It's an incredible machine.'

'Isn't it about time we actually met this horse Citizen?' Tipper asked bluntly. He wasn't feeling good about all this technology.

45

The rendezvous with Vassily Vassilovich and Citizen was in a large, circular barn-like area. The walls, four foot thick for insulation, were gleaming white and spotless. In the centre of the roof was a massive glass dome to let natural light in. The floor was covered with a thick layer of greasy sand, immaculately raked. And in the middle of the barn Vassilovich was superintending a groom, as he walked a horse in tight circles.

The horse was perfectly black with no markings whatsoever, and his silky coat gleamed luxuriantly.

'May I introduce Citizen,' Jameson said reverently. 'Unbroken and still a yearling. He's by Border Dispute, out of Stella Maris.'

He glanced sideways at Sinclair and Tipper to gauge their reactions to the breeding.

'Jesus! Red's foal!' said Tipper, immediately moving forward to get a closer look. 'I rode his mother.'

Citizen was restless, looking round, his eyes rolling, as Tipper and Sinclair circled him so they could look at him from every angle.

'Jesus, will you look at the arse on him?' marvelled Tipper. 'He looks like he's a three-year-old already.'

'Incredible,' Sinclair agreed. 'Never seen anything like it. He's well ahead in his development.'

'He's burly, so he is, like some sumo-wrestler. What the fock are they feeding him?'

'The feed's very good here, very scientific,' Jameson interjected, delighted with their reaction. 'So you like him?'

Tipper smiled. Suddenly all of the negative thoughts that had disturbed him after looking at the krio chamber disappeared.

'He's fabulous.'

Sinclair concurred.

'Too right. He's awesome.'

'Well, when do you start?' Jameson asked. 'He's all yours now.'

'No time like the present, so,' Tipper said chirpily. He took the reins from the groom and gave Citizen a pat as the others retreated. Tipper quietly started undoing the reins and ten seconds later he'd slipped them off the bridle and let Citizen loose. The horse stuck his head down and gave an almighty buck. Then he squealed and took off round the school kicking out his hind legs. He'd never been let loose before in the school. He was loving it.

Tipper stood laughing. Vassily looked worried. Jameson was horrified.

'I haven't got his heart monitor on him,' he yelled, waving his arm. 'Stop him! Stop him now! What are you doing?'

'My job,' Tipper reminded the scientist over his shoulder. 'And I need time on my own with him now. So can you lot piss off?'

Tipper jerked his thumb towards the huge steel doors. Obediently, Jameson, still fretting about his heart monitor, Sinclair and the Russians retreated and let themselves out. Tipper sighed with pleasure. It felt good to be back working with a horse – and what a horse!

Within five minutes Citizen had slowed to a trot, and then stopped altogether. He pawed the sand and elegantly, for a horse of his size, went down on his knees and had a roll. When he stood up, he launched another powerful buck.

He likes to show off, Tipper thought to himself. No bad thing. Didn't stop George Washington winning the 2000 Guineas in Newmarket. Tipper was liking what he was seeing. The horse could use himself. He was a real athlete.

Citizen spent a couple more minutes sniffing the sand and looking about, then he eyed Tipper warily. Tipper knew why. Citizen wanted company. And he was checking out the possibilities. Tipper stood still and met the horse's glance with all his powers of concentration.

After minutes of indecision Citizen got brave.

Holding his head high and pricking his ears, he advanced on Tipper, who waited until there were about five yards separating them. Then, still looking the horse in the eye, he drove him away with a wave of his arms. Startled, Citizen jinked and cantered to the far end of the barn.

Tipper knew what he was doing. Renowned horse-handlers like Monty Roberts had used this approach to great effect for years. Tipper himself had broken many young horses using the same method.

The idea was to replicate, as far as possible, what occurs in the wild. Tipper was playing the role of the herd matriarch who drives away cocky young colts that are being a pest to the rest of the herd.

Being excluded from the herd is dangerous for a young horse. Having played up and mucked about in his own time, back in the herd is the safest place to be – safe, at least, from passing lions and other predators. Citizen had enjoyed his freedom galloping around the school, but now his instinct was telling him to seek out that safety.

So he kept looking round at Tipper, snorting, tossing his head, then trying to approach him again. But Tipper was looking for signs that the colt would be tractable, that he was *asking* to be readmitted to the herd rather than expecting it. Tipper was looking for signs that Citizen sincerely desired to be his friend.

Not far away, unbeknownst to Tipper, Vassily

and his side-kick were watching his every move, with growing incomprehension, on the CCTV. They may have been able to see what Tipper was doing, but they didn't understand the logic of it at all.

It took two hours of continually rejecting Citizen, much longer than it normally takes, before Tipper saw the right signs. Jesus you're a strong-minded bastard, Tipper had thought after the first hour. But it was vital that he and the horse connected on the right terms. Otherwise there'd be trouble for ever.

Citizen finally came up to him with his head lowered and then, at a distance of a few feet, stood still, lowering his head even more while licking his lips and making chewing motions with his mouth. Tipper dropped his own head and let his arms hang loosely by the sides of his body. Citizen circled around and suddenly Tipper felt a nose prodding his back. It was Citizen's submission, almost like an oath of loyalty, and it meant he and Tipper were joined in a pact of trust that, if given a chance, would last a lifetime.

Tipper allowed Citizen a comfortable chew on his jacket then, keeping his back turned, began walking away. He was testing Citizen, and he wasn't disappointed. The colt began to walk after him, directly in his wake, in no mood now to be left outside the herd that Tipper represented to him. Tipper turned around and raised his hand to the horse's ears, and Citizen let himself be scratched.

Then he consented to having a rope put round his neck, and a small saddle placed on his back. He tensed noticeably, but he didn't pull away. He trusted Tipper and wanted to be with him.

Tipper let Citizen follow him around the barn with the small saddle on his back. It clearly irritated the colt to start with, but he soon got used to it. When Tipper sensed he was ready he laid half his body weight over the saddle. Citizen stayed still. Gradually Tipper slid over the saddle until Citizen was taking his entire weight. Citizen fidgeted a bit. So Tipper slid off and started again. After half an hour of progressing and retreating Tipper was quietly sitting in the saddle. He had no hold on Citizen's mouth, just a halter around his neck. But he didn't need one; the colt trusted him.

46

To the north of Euston Road, there's an urban jumble of Victorian terraces and twentieth-century housing estates between London's King's Cross and Euston stations. The people living there aren't wealthy. The single room in the boarding house that Ana found was cheap. And anonymous.

Ana had no idea how Shalakov would react to her deserting her job. She'd been so distraught when she'd seen the images of Tipper she hadn't stopped to think about that. Now it was too late to go back.

She had some money saved from the General's envelopes but she knew she had to be careful with it. In the mornings she tried to occupy Lara in their room. She fed her with formula baby food from jars. Mrs Phelps, the landlady, made much of her generosity in allowing Lara to be fed in the room. But she drew the line firmly at Ana feeding herself.

'We got a strict no-food policy in our rooms,' she declared. 'Seeing as she's only little, you can feed the kid here as a special favour; as long as there's no cooking mind. But you got to eat out, sorry. There's a McDonald's less than ten minutes' walk from here.'

There was also an unkempt bit of green space, hardly large enough to be called a park, and Ana went there most days to wheel Lara's buggy round and round its circling path. Then she went to the bookies nearby.

Ana was smart enough not to be a mug punter. Although she was quite canny at backing the odd winner, she knew she couldn't try and gamble her way out of her situation. But she could work out which trainers came into form when. And who would be riding their fancied runners.

There was usually a small group of old Irishmen in tweed caps in the betting shop, arguing amongst themselves about the state of the going or the merits of various jockeys. But the main clientele were Chinese, most of them playing the gaming machines in a state of high excitement.

'Another one bites the dust,' said the man with the athletic physique standing next to Ana one day. He crumpled a betting slip in his fist, tossed it in the air and headed it into a corner. 'The horse was called Having a Laugh – and he was.'

Ana looked at the losing punter. He was untypical for the place, a youngish man in a good business suit and a bright tie. He was tanned, and looked as if he worked out regularly.

'You are right,' she told him. 'You should not waste your money.'

He smiled with unaffected cheerfulness.

'That's easy to say now.'

'I knew he wouldn't win the race.'

'That's easy to say as well. But did you get the actual winner?'

'In that race, no, I didn't know. So I didn't have a bet. In the next one, maybe I do.'

'Aha! Now we're getting down to it. Let's have your tip then, since you know so much.'

Next up was a flat race on the all-weather track at Wolverhampton. Ana recognized a couple of the Newmarket trainers with runners in it. The yard that had the second favourite was in form at the moment. The horse was called Seesaw.

'All right,' she said. 'In this one I'd definitely go for Seesaw.'

'How much are you going to put on?' asked her new acquaintance.

'Me? Oh, I don't bet much. Horses have good days and bad.'

His eyes widened in a look of mock distress.

'Oh, now look, we can't possibly let this go to waste.'

He ripped a blank slip out of the dispenser and wrote briefly on it, then presented it at the window.

'A tenner win,' he said, returning to Ana's side. 'I hope you haven't let me down.'

She hadn't. Seesaw breezed past the winning post a length clear, and the man in the suit came back from the pay-out window thirty pounds richer.

'We must celebrate,' he said. 'There's a café next door. Will you join me? I'm Alan by the way. Alan Carter.'

'I can't,' she said, 'I haven't got any money to spare.'

'Don't worry about that. I owe you. My win, my treat. Don't say no.'

Ana realized she'd been enjoying herself in the last few minutes. So, she thought to herself, why not?

'That would be lovely. Thank you, Alan. I am Ana.'

The café was all steam, sizzling bacon and cracked formica. Alan spoke to the man at the counter then returned to Ana. Lara was out of her buggy now and being bounced on her mother's knee.

He appeared quite interested in Lara. He tickled her tummy and asked her name.

'So where are you from, Ana? How do you know so much about horses?'

Ana told him part of the truth.

'You mean you actually worked at a racing stable?' Alan asked.

'Yes. I loved the horses. I loved to ride.'

She told him about the horse-riding she had done as a child and how this stopped when her family moved to Moscow. By the time mugs of tea and two thick bacon sandwiches arrived, she'd forgotten that she hardly knew this man. It helped, too, that she was suddenly absolutely ravenous.

'So why did you leave Newmarket, if you liked it so much?'

'It got difficult. I had Lara. Her father, he . . . He left us. I had to get away so, you see, I am here.'

'It can't be easy. With the baby, I mean.'

He sounded sympathetic and understanding.

'It isn't.'

Ana took a huge bite out of her sandwich. Alan did the same and they chewed in time with each other until one after the other they swallowed and gulped down some tea.

'You know, I am vegetarian,' she said with a laugh.

Alan nodded at the sandwich between her now greasy fingers.

'You realize that's—'

'Yes,' she said. 'I know. Bacon. But it's so nice!'

They chatted for a while until Lara started grumbling.

'We have to go now. Thank you. It's been nice.'

With a show of reluctance, Alan let her go.

'See you in the bookies tomorrow, maybe?' he suggested. She ducked her head ambiguously.

On her way back to the room, she realized they'd talked a lot about her and Lara, and not at all about him. She hardly knew anything about this Alan Carter and she was curious.

Mr Phelps – 'Call me Vic' – was a postman, a sallow, slick-haired man in his fifties, with a loose mouth through which he seemed to do most of his breathing. Shift work meant he was often around the house in the afternoon and he was there now, coming up from the basement just as Ana pushed Lara's buggy into the hall.

He said hello in his usual creepily familiar way, and hovered where he was, watching while Ana undid Lara's straps and lifted the child up.

'Wanna hand?' he grunted.

He collapsed the buggy, hoisted it onto one shoulder and began following her up the stairs. On the landing she fiddled with her key while he stood behind her, breathing heavily. And then, as soon as the lock clicked, he reached past her shoulder to push the door open.

Without a glance, Ana said a clipped thank-you and bustled inside. She laid Lara on the plastic changing mat on the floor, then stood up and stretched her back, looking around for the nappies. This gave Vic Phelps his chance. He dumped the folded buggy, grabbed Ana around her middle from behind and rammed her up against the wall.

'Oh yeah,' he panted, 'you're a pretty little thing. You be nice to your uncle Vic, and I'll be nice to you, okay?'

He was trying to kiss her neck and she could smell the stench of beer on his breath. His pelvis was grinding against her bottom.

'No! Not okay! No! Don't!'

He pushed harder and she could feel his tongue sliding up and down her neck. She lashed out with her elbow, catching him in the rib cage. He doubled up with a grunt and stepped backwards onto the folded buggy, which tripped him up. He hit the deck with a crash.

Ana heard a door on the landing opening , and a voice. Vic Phelps heard the same. Quickly he got to his feet and brushed himself down. Then, muttering something abusive, he shambled out of the room.

Ana leant against the back of the door for what felt like minutes. She was just relieved that her mother couldn't see her now. She felt like she couldn't sink much lower.

47

For the first time since he'd been involved with racehorses Tipper had no mucking out or grooming to do. He'd been brought to Xanadu as a specialist to work one-on-one with Citizen; his work was strictly confined to the hours between six and twelve in the mornings. Then he went back to the accommodation block.

Xanadu's accommodation appeared to be modelled on a gentleman's club. In addition to the rather soulless service flats occupied by Tipper, Sinclair, Jameson and an assortment of other scientists, it had a well-stocked bar, dining room, large kitchen, games room and fully equipped gym. There was a chef, a housekeeper and a range of stewards and maids to look after them. So Tipper found himself living at a level of luxury he'd never known before.

The trouble was, he was unable to enjoy it. There was too much time to think about things – his riding ban, Ana and Lara. What wouldn't he give, he kept asking himself, to have them with him? During the nights he kept having the same dream. He was lying in bed with Ana and a little bundle tunnelled its way through the bottom of the sheets and snuggled up between him and Ana . . . then he'd wake up. But it was his mother who snapped him out of his malaise.

Tipper was riding Citizen one morning. It was the part of the day when he felt most positive. And he was thinking about his mother. Thinking about how she'd always made the best of things. How she'd never once complained about anything. Or blamed anyone. And then he thought about himself. He blamed his brother for being a prick. And yet he was the eejit who'd given him his motorbike. At the back of his mind he'd put the Covey Club and the Duke down as Sam's fault. But he was the twat who'd gone along with it. Ana had dumped him. Was she to blame for him getting legless and not going home? Did he have to go to the pub in the first place? No.

'Jesus I've been some jerk,' he told Citizen as they trotted around the school. 'I've been some focking loser. But not any more. I'm going to get out of this. And you're going to help me.'

Sinclair was not much company. He seemed to spend most of his spare time on the internet playing poker. Jameson was only around in the evenings. He lived in his laboratory during the day. But he wasn't a bad companion over dinner. Tipper regaled him with tales of the race track and stables in Ireland and England. And Jameson was fascinated to hear about Citizen's dam, Stella Maris, or Red to Tipper, and of the bond he'd formed with her back home. The old scientist ate hardly anything, but he was greedy for any information on Red's temperament and habits in her early days. Tipper asked Jameson if he could see her. Jameson shook his head vehemently.

'That won't be possible, I'm afraid, Tipper.'

'Why not?'

'This is not just a place for the preparation of racehorses, you know. It's a research station, a scientific enterprise. People can only go where they need to for work. Those are the rules. No exceptions.'

'That is complete bollocks,' Tipper objected, but Jameson had no more to say on the subject.

Citizen was their constant topic of conversation. Jameson questioned Tipper incessantly about every aspect of the young horse's educational progress – was he finding the work hard, was he happy, aggressive, tired, lazy? He told Tipper about the results obtained from the heart monitor, which was always attached under the horse's girth during exercise. But Tipper wasn't interested in that. He was more interested in the horse's personality.

'It's like he's different every day,' Tipper told Jameson, 'depending on his mood. He's changeable. One day I got him eating out of my hand, and the next he's trying to bite it off.'

'So he's a bit like you then,' Jameson joked drily.

'Jesus. I'm not that bad am I?' Tipper laughed. But he got the hint. He knew what the Doc was referring to.

'I just got to do something about finding Ana and Lara, Doc. It's doing my head in. I need to find her. She's Russian. Maybe she came back here. Couldn't Shalakov do something? He must be able to find anyone.'

'It's a possibility, I suppose.'

'Can you ask him for me?'

'Shalakov's a busy man, Tipper.'

'I know, I know, but he must have contacts. If she's back here in Russia, someone must be able to find her. I can't do much, stuck here not speaking the lingo. I need help. You couldn't have a word with him, could you?'

'All right. If I get the chance. No guarantees, mind.'

'Thanks a lot, Doc.'

What Tipper didn't know was that under normal circumstances Shalakov would have immediately punished Ana for deserting her post. No-one let him down without regretting it. But he'd put her punishment on hold. She did, after all, have Tipper's child. Which might turn out to be very useful leverage if Tipper failed to perform to expectation in Russia.

It hadn't taken Tipper and Sinclair long to realize that, at Xanadu, their every move was being watched, especially their dealings with Citizen.

CCTV cameras had been installed in every part of the complex. But that wasn't what bugged Tipper. His bête noire was the smallish guy who shadowed him the whole time he was working with Citizen. He just stood and watched. And never said a word or offered to help in any way. This was getting on Tipper's nerves and he complained about it to Sinclair.

'Don't worry about him,' Sinclair insisted. 'He's a student. He's learning from the master. You! It's like in the top racing stables in the old days, when the apprentices were expected to follow the Head Lad everywhere he went, bar the bog.'

'Well this boy's not going to learn much, just randomly watching. Why don't I teach him properly in the afternoons?'

'Oh no, you can't do that. Like I told you, the equine areas are closed in the afternoon on General Shalakov's orders. He thinks horses should rest in complete tranquillity every afternoon.'

Tipper let it go. Instead he used the idle afternoons to improve himself physically. He spent two hours in the gym, furiously working with light weights, to tone his muscles without putting on bulk, and cycling for his wind. Citizen was going to be his break. And he was going to be ready for it when it came.

48

Ana got to the betting shop the next day a bit earlier than usual. She was studying the first race when she heard a familiar voice.

'I hope you haven't got a killer tip for me in the next race – I've just had a bet.'

There was the smiling face of Alan Carter. Today he was wearing an expensive pair of designer jeans, cashmere jumper and black leather jacket. Ana was glad to see him.

'It's okay, I haven't,' she said. 'This is a steeple-chase. I don't know much about that kind of racing. There aren't many jumping stables in Newmarket.'

'So it all hangs on my own feeble judgement, does it?'

He told her about the bet he'd made, and they watched his selection slogging through the mud and falling at the second to last fence.

'Oh well,' said Alan. '*Another* one bites the dust.'

Ana laughed.

'It's not dust. It's mud, really.'

'Another one bites the mud, then. So, how are you?'

'Oh, worried, a little. I have to move to some place new. I'm having trouble with a man where I am now.'

'God, that sounds fairly grim. What sort of trouble?'

'Oh, don't worry. I can manage him. But I still want to leave, and I would do it today if everywhere was not so expensive.'

As before, Carter invited her and Lara to the café next door for a cup of tea. This time she agreed without hesitation. Once settled inside it was Ana who asked the questions, and Carter who, after he'd ordered the tea and a couple of dictionary-thick bacon sandwiches, told her something about himself.

'I've only just arrived in London. I've been working in Edinburgh for the past three years in a merchant bank. Now I've got a new job in the City. It'll be a big challenge. Commodity trading. But I haven't started yet, which is why I'm a layabout at the moment.'

'What commodity do you trade?' Ana asked.

Carter was slightly taken aback. He hadn't expected her to be so inquisitive. So his explanation went into a lot of technical detail, none of which Ana understood, though she pretended to be fascinated. For a few moments after he'd finished they ate their food in silence.

'I've been thinking,' said Alan, dropping the uneaten sandwich crusts onto his plate. 'I've just moved into a flat near here. I'm on my own and I've got two bedrooms. Why don't you and Lara have one of them? It's just going to waste otherwise.'

Ana's eyes narrowed. Warning signals pulsed in her brain.

'You must have a smart modern flat,' she said. 'Expensive.'

'Yes,' agreed Carter. 'Described by the agents as a luxury contemporary canalside development. It's quite groovy, actually.'

'Thank you. You are kind. But of course I can't. I haven't got the kind of money you need to live in a luxury flat.'

'So?'

'I mean I can't pay rent like that.'

'Well I had something else in mind. How about you do the cooking and the cleaning and we call it quits.'

He held up his hand to avert her coming back at him in indignation. He knew how she would interpret his offer.

'Look, I know you don't know me all that well. But it's all right, I'm not going to try anything.' Then he smiled and lowered his voice. 'I'm gay, you see. I would really enjoy having you and lovely Lara as flatmates, and that's all it would be. I'm quite lonely in this town too, if you want to know. You'd be doing me a favour.'

318

Ana considered for a moment. Yes, now that she thought about it, he probably was gay. She might know for sure if she saw his place.

'Can I come round and see the flat before I decide?' she asked cautiously.

'Course you can. Tomorrow afternoon all right?'

Taking a pen from his jacket, he wrote down the address for her on a paper napkin and included a crude sketch map of the location. She took and folded the napkin carefully and stored it in the pocket of Lara's buggy.

The flat was in a refurbished factory building that stood beside the Regent Canal, a few hundred yards from King's Cross station. A glass lift took Ana and the push-chair up to a timber-floored landing, leading directly into a corridor with four identical front doors. She wheeled Lara along to the one with Carter's number on it and knocked loudly.

He was wearing flips-flops, baggy cargo trousers and a T-shirt.

'Hi, Ana. I'm so glad! Come in. Let me show you round.'

After the gloom of living with the Phelps family, the airy light-filled apartment lifted her spirits. The floors were hardwood and the furniture was all glass and stainless steel. The kitchen and bathroom had modern white goods and gadgets, and the second bedroom – hers, if she chose – had its own shower. From the window there was a view of a canal basin, where brightly coloured narrow boats were moored. It was all spotless, apparently brand new. There was hardly a sign that anyone lived there.

'It's very clean,' Ana said almost nervously.

'Yes. Well as I said I've only just come down from Edinburgh. Haven't been here long as you can see. You're welcome to use the computer if you want to.'

Ana was struck by the emptiness of the apartment. It was fabulous but she wasn't sure. Then she saw the posters on the wall and started to relax. Alan clearly liked young guys in sweaty vests – from the youthful Brando and James Dean to Brad Pitt.

The glass table in the middle of the room had *The Gay Directory of London* on it. If she'd thought about it, she might have realized this was a bit obvious. But the thought of the Phelps's house compared to this was blurring her judgement. She decided right there to accept Alan's offer.

'Great! Really cool!' he smiled. It was not just words. He was visibly delighted.

'First I must say something,' Ana said. 'Like I told you I cannot pay rent.'

'And like I told you, hey, that's not a problem. I earn plenty. When will you move in?'

'Is right now okay?'

49

Tipper worked like a slave in the gym and was looking after his health in general. But one night, totally out of the blue, he got properly drunk in the accommodation block. And grew very maudlin about Ana and Lara. It panicked Jameson. He hadn't put the best part of a lifetime's work into a project for it to be ruined by a drunk jockey.

'Tipper's drinking could turn into a problem,' he told Sinclair. 'Why don't we just bring her here?'

'Are you bloody mad?' Sinclair broke in. 'Absolutely not. She'd be an appalling security risk. And she's trouble anyway. He's better off without her.'

Jameson didn't have much answer to that. Obviously Sinclair knew best. And Jameson knew that Ana was part of a web of deceit, that she'd been used to spy on Sinclair. Which Sinclair had never figured out.

'And don't worry about the drinking,' Sinclair continued. 'All jockeys drink. They can handle it.'

Luckily for Jameson, Sinclair was, for once, proved right.

Tipper got himself a Russian mobile phone and racked up huge charges with rambling late-night calls to Sam in Newmarket. He was careful what he said to him, but he missed Sam, he was happy talking to him about nothing much. And Sam was a tenuous link to Ana.

As Christmas approached, Jameson warned Sinclair and Tipper not to expect much of it.

'The Russians. They don't do Christmas,' he explained. 'They give each other presents on the sixth of January, Twelfth Night.'

Presents were the last thing on Tipper's mind. And no-one was going to be giving Sinclair any, though he didn't care. Unlike Tipper, he was so bloody happy he wouldn't be spending Christmas with his wife.

The housekeeper of the accommodation block had a baby tree brought in from the surrounding forest on Christmas Eve. It was stuck in a pot on the end of the bar and decorated with a few sorry-looking ornaments. Tipper viewed the result with disdain. Even at their poorest moments, his Ma would make sure their flat in Dublin was graced with a bushy tree groaning under the weight of baubles and tinsel. Even if few presents had lain under it, they always had that tree. By comparison with those days, Tipper was now rich. The account at the Haven Bank that Shalakov had opened for him was testament to that. But this Russian Christmas was the loneliest he'd ever spent in his life. It spurred him on all the more to work his way out.

Alan Carter turned out to be a strange person to share with. Not that share was quite the right word. He was always around at some point in the day but very rarely in the evenings. And he was usually away overnight. Ana assumed that he must be sleeping with other men. She didn't like to dwell on this much, but it was better than him trying to get into her bed.

The freedom of Carter's flat gave Ana breathing space. She used it by signing up for an internet Spanish course. Her time in London, then Newmarket, had taught her one thing. More people in the world were speaking Spanish than English. Learning Spanish could be very useful one day. Even if only to teach to Lara as she grew up.

Lara's speech was coming along slowly. What came out of her mouth was a jumble of noises. But one day she made a sound that caught Ana's attention. She dropped down on one knee.

'What was that, darling? What did you say?'

The child looked at her mother through big brown eyes.

'Jesus!' she said.

'Did you hear that?' Ana asked Alan, who was reading his paper and minding his own business.

'Hear what?' he asked without bothering to look up. That irritated Ana.

'Why do you not go to work yet?' she snapped.

'Is it bothering you, me being around?'

'Of course not. This is your place and you can do what you like. But I'm just wondering.'

'I'm on what's called "gardening leave",' Alan explained.

'But you haven't got a garden,' she replied stubbornly.

'No, but I've agreed with my old employers that I wouldn't start my new job until a certain amount of time has gone by.'

He tapped the side of his nose and grinned conspiratorially.

'You see, I'm joining a rival firm and I sort of know too much. I might leak.'

'So when will this new job start?'

'Don't say a word, but I've already started. A bit of work on the sly, from home.'

That was all he'd say. But if his phone rang when he was with her, he'd mutter into it and leave the room. Occasionally he put on a suit and went out carrying a briefcase, though rarely for more than a couple of hours. Every so often couriers turned up with packages to be signed for.

'Don't you be looking inside my packages,' Alan said sternly. Too sternly, for Ana's liking. His cheerful 'I'm your best mate' tone in the betting shop had changed to something noticeably harder.

But he never tried to lay a finger on her. After uncle Vic, that was a big improvement.

A month after starting the Spanish course Ana was struck by a sudden attack of nausea while sitting at Carter's computer. Her head swam and the screen went out of focus.

When she told him later, the 'concerned' Carter re-surfaced and he took her down to the doctor's surgery in his car. There she received the news straight.

'You're pregnant,' the doctor told her matter of factly, after completing an examination.

'No. I can't be!'

'There's no doubt. And you're quite advanced – about twenty-one weeks. Congratulations.'

Ana knew she'd missed several periods, but that had happened to her before, when she'd been under particular stress. And this wasn't a bit like her pregnancy with Lara. Then she'd put on weight steadily, while this time she'd actually lost weight – five or six kilos since she'd parted from Tipper. Lara was a handful as it was. And she might become worse if she had a baby brother or sister to compete with. How could she have been so stupid and careless? And what in God's name was she going to do?

After three weeks of dithering, she made her mind up. It would be best for Lara. She went back to the clinic and demanded an abortion. With hands thrust into the pockets of her white coat, the doctor looked at Ana with pursed lips and shook her head.

'Pity you didn't come back and say that last week, dear. You're too late now, I'm afraid. It's against the law for us to terminate a pregnancy that's gone beyond twenty-four weeks.'

'You mean . . . I got to have the baby?'

'Yes, I'm afraid you do.'

50

Tipper knew it was dangerous to get carried away over one horse. They're fragile animals, one step away from injury at any time. But under his care, distantly supervised by Sinclair and with Jameson dancing attendance, Citizen improved in leaps and bounds; and a few bucks and kicks. He was now ready to start working on the indoor circular gallop.

'Always keep note of the heart monitor,' Jameson repeatedly pestered Tipper. 'Never let the rate go above two hundred and forty beats per minute. Never. If it does, stop straight away.'

'You mean pull him up?'

'Yes, yes. Is that the correct term? Yes, pull him up.'

Tipper looked at Sinclair, expecting him to react to the scientist issuing orders over his head. But while Sinclair may have been irritated to distraction by Jameson's demands, he was totally impassive.

'Can we just get on with it, please?' was all he would say.

Tipper was amazed by Sinclair's passive acceptance of all this interference. At Newmarket the trainer may have privately listened to advice, but in public he always made sure he was seen to call the shots.

'Jesus, Guvnor, he's not a horseman,' Tipper said grumpily. 'Why do we have to do everything he says? Why are we constantly loading the colt into the Kriotherapy chamber? If you ask me, it's totally warped. If they know so much, what do they need us for?'

Sinclair didn't answer.

If Tipper was bemused by Jameson's idea of training a horse according to its heart-rate, he was delighted with the horse himself. Despite the colt's regular attacks of moodiness, Tipper felt something special whenever Citizen was allowed to stretch out. His fluent, devouring stride made it feel like they were floating across the ground.

There was, however, one strange thing. In accordance with Jameson's wishes Tipper would let Citizen breeze around the mile-long gallop in his own time. Citizen was always eager, until he came to some big double steel doors set in the side wall of the indoor gallop. Then sometimes, when he got to that point of the circuit, his stride would falter and he'd hesitate. Tipper had to grab hold of him to ride him past the doors. Then he'd be back to his normal self.

'I don't know what he does that for,' he told Sinclair. 'He loves bowling around there. Then sometimes he loses his rhythm when he gets to those big doors in the wall. That's strange, Guvnor, because he's never been out through those doors in his life. Come to think of it, what's behind them?'

'It's where they keep the tractors that work the gallop surface in the afternoons,' Sinclair said dismissively. 'He's just curious about everything.'

'Right. I suppose it's nothing,' Tipper agreed. It was no big deal so he let it go.

Shalakov appeared now and again to check on Citizen's progress. Vassily Vassilyvich trotted along behind him as if he were on a leash. Shalakov seemed pleased enough with what he saw of Citizen in his work. He made gruff remarks to Vassily in Russian and called out 'Good! Good!' as Tipper and Citizen tanked past him at a fast canter. Jameson hovered like a firefly, his eyes glued to the heart monitor readout.

'What you think about my horse?' Shalakov demanded one day, squinting up at Tipper, his voice full of pride. 'You like him? Professor Jameson tells me he is a machine. He is a strong one, yes?'

'Certainly,' said Tipper. 'He's a grand steed right enough.'

Tipper was usually struck dumb in Shalakov's

presence. But sitting on Citizen and looking down on the top of the Russian's head, he felt emboldened.

'He's not broken sweat yet,' Tipper advised, 'but he feels as strong as an elephant and as fast as a greyhound.'

Shalakov didn't know exactly what the Irishman meant by 'broken sweat', but he got the idea and repeated happily, 'Good! Good! Not broken sweat yet. Good!'

He swung around towards Vassily to make another comment. But Tipper interrupted.

'General Shalakov?'

Shalakov turned back with a momentary frown. Tipper pressed on.

'Has Dr Jameson spoken to you at all – about my family? I'm very worried about them.'

The General's face hardened a fraction.

'Yes?'

'I'm talking about my fiancée, General, and our little girl. I don't know where they are. I need to find them.'

Shalakov bared his teeth in a chilly smile. Several of them were filled with gold.

'This is natural,' he said.

'But, General, what I'm saying is, can't you help? She is Russian, you know. She might be back here in Russia . . . or still in England. You have so many contacts. If anyone can find them, I'm thinking you can.'

Tipper had never previously said such a mouthful

to Shalakov. As he was speaking the General came closer to him and Citizen. He patted Citizen's neck. Tipper noticed the big gold rings on his fingers. He could smell Shalakov's acrid scent. It wafted up to his nose and made him feel anxious. Shalakov seemed to reflect for a moment.

'Yes,' he said at last. 'I can help you find Ana. So if you work well with my horse and bring me results, I'm sure you will see your family again.'

'Doc did you tell Shalakov Ana's name when you had a word with him?' Tipper asked Jameson that night.

'No. Why?'

'Well it was something he said today. That's all. You definitely didn't tell him her name?'

'No. I definitely didn't. Because he didn't ask,' Jameson confirmed.

51

'Bring me the shortlist for the Hippodrome job,' Shalakov said impatiently to his assistant, after his jet had climbed into the sky above Xanadu.

A kilo tin of caviar and a bottle of vodka arrived first. Shalakov shovelled a big spoonful into his mouth, scrunched the tiny eggs with his teeth, then washed them down with a slug of ice-cold vodka. He loved the bite of the vodka on the back of his throat, mixed with the caviar's saltiness.

Racing was going to be big business. General Shalakov had been charged with giving the Russian President a short list of candidates to administrate racing in Russia. The decision was going to come from the top. But Shalakov would make sure he got his man.

The first name on the list was a man who'd run no less than three big-time race-tracks and was highly proficient. Shalakov drew a diagonal line across his picture. He was American, and therefore impossible. The second candidate had managed one of the largest stud farms in Australia, and then become general manager of a company owning several race tracks. But she was female, and also impossible. He crossed her out. The penultimate name was a French *vicomte* of impeccable breeding. His paper credentials were excellent. Too excellent, Shalakov decided. And the French were stubborn. The man might not toe the line.

This left only Captain Jolyon Maine, late of the Horse Guards, previously Eton and Sandhurst. A soldier. Good! Shalakov skimmed through the military career. Three tours in Northern Ireland and action on the Kuwait border during the first Gulf War. A DSO, with a citation that spoke of 'outstanding leadership'. Then, only two years after he'd voluntarily resigned his commission Maine had been head-hunted to run Ascot Race Course. Now his contract was up for renewal but he was apparently unlikely to sign. Maine even knew a little Russian, courtesy of a language course as a student at Sandhurst. Shalakov was impressed. He glanced at the photograph. Maine was a tall bull-elephant of a man – he looked to weigh well over a hundred kilos – who had adopted for the camera a lip-jutting Churchillian expression. He looked like a tough guy, but he might just be dominated by a tougher one. And having had an army career, Maine would probably be financially naïve. Shalakov gazed out of his window over the snowy peaks of the

Caucuses. Maine was the man who would get his recommendation.

A couple of months later Jolyon Maine disembarked from Aeroflot's London flight and set his foot for the first time on Russian tarmac. It hadn't been a difficult decision to give up Ascot. The job had looked ideal at first sight, but then he found out about the legion of bean-counters and marketing geeks who were ruling his life. For any man used to issuing orders to his juniors rather than dancing to the tune of their rattling calculators, this would have been difficult. For Maine, it was impossible. He was essentially a maverick character – which was probably the reason his army career, despite his decoration, had stalled at two pips – and too much of one to go on working at Ascot.

The Moscow job looked much more the thing. It was well-funded and had the feel of an enterprise starting from scratch. He had a free hand, so he was assured, to ride into town, apply the regulations strictly and create the best racecourse in the world. And why shouldn't he pull it off? He rather relished the wild-west tales that had been coming out of Russia. If he could cope with the IRA, the UDA and Saddam's Tank Corps trying to blow him up, a few Russian mafia hoods would be manageable.

Maine took up his post in good time to prepare for the new turf season in Moscow, scheduled to begin as the snow melted in mid-April. He had no responsibility for the ancillary activities of the site: the restaurants, bars, casinos, only for the racing side. But he blew in like a hurricane. In an unstoppable burst of energy he overhauled the weighing-room, jockeys' changing rooms, judge's room, stabling, veterinary services and the digital race-recording system. He re-arranged the betting sites and moved to a more rational ticketing system.

Finally, and most importantly, he found the drug-testing programme for horses was totally inadequate. It was, as far as the jockeys were concerned, non-existent.

He put in place protocols that would ensure no trainer or jockey could be sure of escaping testing. Maine's team were in awe of him.

The horses in Moscow lived and trained at the Hippodrome for months before they started racing. When the worst of the winter was over forty of Shalakov's horses were shipped from Xanadu. It was by far the biggest string of horses owned by any one man in the capital.

Tipper was much happier with the set-up at the Hippodrome. There was no krio chamber, no high-altitude air and no one watching his every move while he worked. Everything felt much more natural. Citizen had plenty of admirers. He impressed from the first day he went out, standing out from all the other horses, and floating across the turf with even more majesty than on the artificial surface at Xanadu. It looked like every other horse had to take two strides to match one of his.

Tipper was the pilot, but he had no say in Citizen's training regime. The majority of young colts would canter for a mile round the track to warm up, gallop over seven furlongs at half speed, then finish with a warm down over five furlongs. But, according to Sinclair, Citizen's sheer bulk and bottled-up energy called for something like twice as much training. He would follow the established routine but take only a four furlong warm-down, in which he idled in his own time. This was followed by a second seven furlong burst, now at three-quarter speed, rounded off with a final warm-down over a second four furlongs.

'He's doing the work of two horses,' Tipper told Sam on the phone. 'It should be all wrong. But I'll have to admit he's taking it fine at the moment.'

Citizen was in fact thriving. But Tipper did wonder about the handling of his easy-time. All of the horses rested on Sunday. Only Citizen didn't rest. Instead, he was picked up by a horse-transporter early in the morning and taken on a day trip back to Xanadu.

Tipper tackled Sinclair about this as they were saddling him one morning.

'The trip in the horsebox is madness, Guvnor. He needs a real rest on Sundays, you know, like the Good Lord did when he made the world.'

Sinclair grunted and shrugged his shoulders.

'Perhaps you'd like to be the trainer. Then you could argue with the Scientist about it. He says Citizen has to go back to the kriotherapy chamber every Sunday, so that's that.'

Sinclair's relationship with Jameson, which had never been very buoyant, had now reached rock bottom. He now referred to him only as 'the Scientist'.

'What good can it do though, for God's sake,' Tipper persisted.

'Look they say it re-charges his batteries. That's why he can take so much work. It's probably bollocks. But it doesn't seem to be doing him any harm.'

But Tipper wasn't letting up. 'So why don't the other horses do it then?'

Since arriving in Moscow Sinclair had found an actual rather than a virtual poker table. He'd had a bad night at it the night before and he didn't need his bloody jockey chirping away all morning.

'Because they're glorified donkeys. And Citizen, you might remember, is different. He's quite well bred and he's doing nicely on it.'

What Sinclair said was true. On his reappearance every Monday morning, Citizen really was brimming with freshness, and so strong that Tipper was barely able to hold him. But Tipper could think of another good reason why this might be so. It was the same reason why on some days he was calm and tractable, and on others smouldering,

337

even aggressive. He'd seen horses in Newmarket like that, and they were generally surrounded by dodgy vets pumping them full of steroids.

If that was what was going on, it made sense that they took Citizen back to Xanadu every weekend, to keep the needles away from the prying eyes of Captain Maine. Steroids would explain his strength as well as the mood swings, but if Tipper was right, Citizen would surely soon burn out. Racing him would be especially risky: Jameson would have to withdraw the drugs at some point before he raced and the horse might then fall to pieces.

52

Ana first saw 'the sad case next door', as Carter described him, out on the neighbouring balcony. This young guy watering his daffodils, in boxes lashed to the balcony rails, seemed perfectly normal – late twenties, tall and slim, round wire-rimmed glasses, T-shirt and jeans. The ponytail was questionable, but he wasn't a bad-looking guy and it turned out Lara was fascinated by him.

When Lara played she reminded Ana of Tipper. She had his sense of fun. And the outline of her nose was like his. The shape her mouth made when she was angry was totally Tipper too. Now, the way she'd started saying 'Jesus' had become another reminder.

Whenever Ana saw Tipper in Lara, tears would well up uncontrollably in her eyes. Then she'd shake her head and curse herself for being so weak. She was a survivor, wasn't she?

'I'll get us out of here,' she promised Lara.

Sometimes Ana would go out onto the balcony

for a smoke; and sometimes the interesting neighbour would be there too, tending his plants. They got chatting. Hesitantly at first, like two birds fluttering around each other. But as she got to know him, the 'sad case' turned out to be nothing of the sort. In fact, he was a rather gentle junior school teacher from Croydon. Before long he was giving Lara story books and pictures for colouring in.

'Where did you get those?' Carter asked Ana one evening, when Lara was proudly showing off her artistic creation.

'Tony next door gave them to her,' Ana smiled. 'He's really nice. He's a teacher.'

'Is he just?' Carter replied coldly. 'When did this all start?'

'This what?' Ana replied defensively. 'Nothing's started.'

'These pictures, and books. Have you been chatting him up, this Tony?'

'No. Of course not. He's a teacher. He's helping Lara. He's a nice man.'

'No, he's not. He's a weirdo, and probably a paedophile. So just drop him.'

Carter was almost spitting his words out. He had never spoken to her quite like this before. So Ana let it go and took Lara to their room. But she wasn't happy. What was his bloody problem?

Ana heard Carter leave the apartment. She heard a knock and Tony's door opening. Then the murmur of Alan's voice, too low to make out.

Tony's side of the exchange she heard clearly, though. His voice rising in indignation.

'What the fuck do you mean, stay away?'

Again Carter's voice said something indistinct. Then Tony spluttered. 'Like hell I will!'

Carter then went into an indistinct monologue. And Tony didn't say another word.

She heard the door slam. And then the lift.

When Ana was sure Carter had gone she went out onto the balcony and called Tony. She heard his door slide shut. She got no reply.

53

Shalakov came to the track every Friday, without fail. He had forty horses in training, but he barely looked at any of them, only at Citizen. He stood by the track in his black leather trenchcoat, clapping his be-ringed hands together as he watched Tipper work the horse.

Citizen was close to being ready for his first race. His black spring coat shone like wet seal-skin, his muscles rippled and his eye rolled, drinking in everything that happened around him. Tipper still hadn't been told what the jockey situation would be when Citizen raced. But he was terrified some super-slick riding star would be brought in from overseas to take the ride. Citizen had a monster personality. He would be too much for one of the local Russian riders. Tipper had seen them in action and hadn't been impressed. Their idea of horse-handling was so inflexible, always keeping too tight a hold of their horse's heads and resorting to the whip too readily. It was exactly the kind of treatment that made Citizen boil over. And, if that happened, would he ever see Ana and Lara again?

'Guvnor, what's the riding plans with this horse?' he asked Sinclair.

'I don't know Tipper, honestly. I've been told the General will decide.'

'I want to ride him.'

'Of course you do. And I want to put you up. But it's just not my decision. You're still under suspension, you know.'

'Yes, and for how much longer, I'd like to know.'

'Trust me, Tipper. Don't go badgering the General about this. He's easily pissed off and, believe me, he's not a man you want to piss off.'

So it was a question of waiting for Shalakov to pronounce. Apart from asking how the horse worked – to which he expected a concise answer – Shalakov never said a word to Tipper during his visits at morning exercise. He was no more voluble with Sinclair. Vassily Vassilyvich was normally at the General's elbow, and might have been a source of information had he not lacked even the slightest knowledge of English. Alexei, the bodyguard, was never more than five paces from his master, but it was no use asking him either. And Jameson acted vague and distracted when Tipper quizzed him.

So, when the news came, it was a shot out of the dark. Shalakov appeared at Tipper's side when he was unsaddling the horse one morning. Tipper smelt his aftershave before he heard him. Shalakov reached up and slapped the horse's neck fondly.

'Next week will be time for Citizen's first race, here in Moscow,' he grunted in Tipper's ear. 'You will ride him.'

Tipper froze. Had he heard right?

'That's all I need to know, General. That will do for me. But what about my riding licence?'

Shalakov shook his head, as if to dislodge a fly.

'No problem,' he grunted. 'You work for General Shalakov. As long as you do, you won't have problems. I have fixed it.'

He didn't go into details, such as the fact that he'd flown the Chairman of the British Racing Board to Nice in his private plane. He'd explained over a very hospitable weekend that good relations with Russian racing were in the best interests of the British bloodstock market. And that it was essential, in this regard, for Tipper O'Reilly to have his licence back. The Chairman luckily had seen it the same way.

'Thanks General, thanks a million,' Tipper gasped, his spirits soaring. 'I can't tell you what this means, like.'

Shalakov stopped him, jabbing his finger towards Tipper's chest.

'I tell you what it means. It means you win. Citizen wins. Always. There can be no failure. Understand?'

'Yes, General. Right. I'll do my best.'

'No! You will do more. I have something else to tell you.'

The Russian's considerable bulk seemed to swell for a moment as he drew deeply on a Cuban cigar.

'I have found your woman, and your child.'

Tipper almost dropped the saddle that was balanced on his arm.

'You have? Jesus, Mary and Joseph!'

For a moment Shalakov regarded Tipper with suspicion, puzzled by the oath.

'Where are they, General?' Tipper gabbled. 'Where did you find them? How are they?'

'They are safe,' growled Shalakov. 'So now you must do your job. Win. Then one day you will see them again.'

He turned on his heel and strode away, with Vassily and Alexei marching in stride behind him.

Tipper stood there with the saddle on his arm, feeling disorientated. A few moments ago he'd been worrying about whether he would get the ride on Citizen. Now he was barely giving it a thought. The General knew where Ana and Lara were. What the hell did that mean?

He didn't know whether to laugh or cry. General Shalakov was not the sort of man you wanted knowing where your family were. But one thing was for sure. The General and his horse were the key to his future happiness in more ways than one.

He felt uneasy looking at Citizen. His life was now well and truly hanging as if by one of the strands in the horse's tail. Citizen could get injured tomorrow. He might be full of drugs. Tipper knew this was not a good place to be. But it was where he was and he had to make it work.

Maine may not have sat on Citizen, but he'd seen him work. He'd also seen some impressive two-year-olds over the years – Giant's Causeway, Henrythenavigator – and was beginning to believe Citizen could be as good as them, if not better. On the face of it this would give Moscow racing the kind of boost that publicists only dream of, and at exactly the right time. But Maine had a problem nagging away in the back of his mind.

He wanted to discuss it with David Sinclair, so he took him to have a bite of lunch at the brasserie overlooking Red Square. It was a favourite spot of his. He enjoyed imagining the troops marching up and down the cobbles, and wondered what was happening behind the fir trees in the Kremlin.

'What the hell is that monstrosity?' Sinclair asked without a thought that he might be insulting anyone in ear shot who happened to understand English. 'It looks like a border post in Northern Ireland.'

'Lenin's tomb,' Maine replied matter of factly. He wondered whether Sinclair had ever actually seen a border post in Northern Ireland, as he himself had.

'It's great news that O'Reilly's got his licence

back,' Maine said warmly, changing the subject. 'He seems like he's buckled down out here. Deserves another chance.'

The sommelier poured the 1989 Pomerol that Maine had chosen.

'Yes,' agreed Sinclair. 'I need him to ride Citizen. Tipper can be an awful bloody prat at times, you know, but he gets on well with the horse.'

Maine pondered as he looked at the diagonal lines of the cobblestones again.

'Strange how London lifted his suspension, don't you think?'

Sinclair shrugged.

'General Shalakov has many contacts. A lot of influence.'

'Hmm. Suppose so.'

Maine took a sip of wine. Sinclair took a gulp. He liked Pomerol. If he drank it quick enough Maine would have to order another bottle.

'And, um, by the way, talking of Citizen,' Maine went on, 'you seem to be giving him one hell of a lot of work. Of course I'm not the trainer . . .'

'Exactly,' agreed Sinclair. 'And I am. Citizen can take the work, believe me.'

Maine said nothing and took another sip of his wine.

'Don't you believe me?' Sinclair asked, a shade truculently. 'Look, he thrives on it. You should be able to see that for yourself.'

'Well, yes, I can. But I can also see he goes back to base, as it were, every Sunday. That's a very strange procedure, isn't it? What's the idea, exactly?'

Sinclair stared at the label on the wine bottle.

'It's just part of our routine,' he said without making eye contact with Maine. 'Why do you ask?'

'Because it's not part of anyone else's routine, is it?'

'Not everyone else has the kind of equipment we have. I obviously can't tell you; but it's perfectly legal.'

'Well, I'm sorry, but that's just my worry, David. Your owner is a stop-at-nothing-man, in my estimate. Does he realize that I have equally high-tech detection systems in place here? It would be disastrous if Citizen tested positive for anything illegal.'

Sinclair smiled thinly. He looked into his now empty glass and helped himself to more as if it were Algerian plonk.

'Just don't worry, Captain,' he said. 'We won't fail any blood test. On race day Citizen will be clean as a baby's conscience. I promise you.'

'You mean on other days he might not be?'

Sinclair flushed.

'No, that's not what I'm saying. I'm saying there won't be a problem. Which is all you should be worried about.' Sinclair's mind then drifted back to Nico standing over his desk in Newmarket. Playing the vile footage of Shaunsheys' demise. He shuddered.

'Captain,' he said, fixing Maine with a cold stare. 'Let me give you some advice. Don't cross Shalakov. Don't even give him any reason for thinking that you might.'

Maine didn't like being threatened. At least, that's what he assumed Sinclair was doing.

'David, I'm here to do a job,' he replied firmly. 'And I'll do it. Shalakov doesn't frighten me. I can assure you of that.'

Sinclair laughed to himself and shook his head.

'You have no idea, do you? Well I suggest you tread very carefully. And you can relax. Citizen won't fail any dope test.'

54

Citizen was slated to make his debut in Russia's first two-year-old Group race of the season. On the Sunday beforehand he went back, as usual, to Xanadu. Tipper was expecting Sinclair to give Citizen a quiet week in the build-up to the race as he was hardly short of work. But Sinclair scheduled Citizen for a fast gallop on Monday morning. The horse went great but Tipper couldn't understand the need to work the horse so much that close to a race.

Citizen was, at least, in an easy mood all week. Sometimes it would take two people to get his bridle on in the morning. But not that week. He was calm and relaxed.

On race day, Shalakov turned up with his full entourage, every member of which was dressed like him in a full-length leather coat, despite it being a warm spring day. Even the Swiss-German hooker on his arm, all long-limbs and sculpted cheek-bones, was encased – rather more sexily than the others – in black leather. They assembled in the paddock before Citizen's race. Xanadu horses had cleaned up in the first two races on the card. The crowd were buzzing with the expectation of a treble for Shalakov.

Tipper had not been booked to ride the other Xanadu horses. The ride on Citizen was to be his first since the disaster at far-away Chester on Mike Champion's Fighting Talk. His mouth was dry and the adrenaline was flushing through his veins. He'd never ridden in a race with so much depending on the result. All he could think about in the weighing room were Ana and Lara. But as soon as he walked out into the paddock, other emotions came flooding in. He was wearing coloured silks once more. He was back where he belonged.

As Tipper stood with Sinclair and Shalakov on the paddock grass, Citizen was in one of his most cooperative moods and wowing them on the oval walkway. He was a swaggering presence, towing along a groom on either side of him, his coat gleaming in the sun and his head cocked to the left, taking in the admiration of the crowd. He knew he was special.

Jameson had been getting on Sinclair's nerves all afternoon. Dressed in one of his preposterous corduroy suits, he'd kept on and on at Sinclair to make sure the heart monitor was properly attached. Finally, in the saddling box, Sinclair lost his temper.

'Look, Jameson, if you say one more fucking

word about that monitor I'm going to shove it down your throat. Just piss off, will you, and leave us to do our job.'

Jameson's lip curled in distaste.

'You'd better hope this horse wins and comes to no harm, Sinclair,' he blurted. 'Don't expect any help from me if it goes pear-shaped.'

'I expect nothing from you. Anyway he'll win and I'll take the credit, thank you very much.'

Jameson came up to him and stretched his neck to get his mouth as close as possible to the taller man's ear.

'Just be careful what you do take. Remember what happened to another who took what wasn't his.'

He stood on his toes and whispered a reminder. '*Shaunsheys.*'

Before the start Sinclair kept half an eye on Citizen and half on Shalakov. He repeatedly straightened his tie, coughed to ease his sandpaper throat and licked his lips. Not for the first time he wondered how the hell he'd got himself mixed up with these Russians.

In contrast to Sinclair, Tipper's nerves evaporated as soon as the paddock bell was rung and he swung his leg over Citizen. This was his thing, what he was good at: race riding. He hadn't needed to talk to Sinclair about tactics, but that didn't stop the trainer trotting along beside them as they circled the paddock one last time, repeating what had already been discussed half a dozen times.

'Just sit in third or fourth position for the first five furlongs,' Sinclair babbled. 'Then ask for an effort inside the last. Use his acceleration to burn the rest of the field off.'

'Guvnor, I've got that, we'll be fine,' said Tipper. He sounded like a nursemaid calming a frightened child. He knew Sinclair's susceptibility to panic well enough. He also knew that even the best-laid pre-race plans often had to be scrapped within the first few strides out of the stalls. It all depended on the pace set at the front, and the how the dice fell in the jostling for position behind.

There were a few dazzlingly dressed women within the paddock, but the faces along the rails outside the paddock were grim and universally male. Chester races was wall to wall sex appeal compared to this lot, Tipper mused. Then Ana and Lara forced themselves back into Tipper's thoughts as he walked out onto the track. Finally he banished them from his mind and gave Citizen his full attention.

When the stalls opened Citizen crashed out like a lion leaping at the throat of its prey. For the first furlong Tipper tried desperately to settle him in a discreet position, as per Sinclair's instructions, but it was useless. Citizen didn't want to be anywhere but in front, and Tipper might have been an ant perched on the saddle for all the notice his horse took of him. So much for Plan A.

Tipper had little choice but to let him go, and hope he would relax in front. Normally it would be suicidal for a horse to burn this much energy in the early stages of a race, and Tipper was praying the horse would drop the bit and take a breather. No such luck. Every time Tipper took a tug at the reins the horse fought him. They were already five lengths clear of the field, and going further ahead with each stride.

It was a six furlong race, and at half way their lead was still extending. And then, as they turned the final bend, instead of keeping to the inside, Citizen got it into his head to run diagonally for the stand side rail. With two furlongs still to go Tipper realized the rest of the field, now on the other side of the track to them, had reduced the gap by not following their leader. Yet, Citizen was going so well that this didn't become a problem until, just before the furlong pole, everything changed again. Citizen suddenly realized what he was running into: a tunnel of people and a gauntlet of sound, human voices roaring him on from the stands. The Moscow crowd had thrown off its depressive shell and was screaming its approval of him.

Citizen had never seen or heard anything like it. Without warning he shied violently and Tipper, thrown off balance, very nearly parted company with him. He just managed to right himself, only to find that Citizen was now veering away from the stand side rails, travelling sideways almost as fast as he was going forward. Tipper hauled on the reins but Citizen was too headstrong. There was nothing he could do to stop their crab-wise progress back towards the opposite side of the course. The rest of the field, coming up in a straight line, were closing the gap stride by stride.

They reached the far rail still just ahead of the advancing pack, and half a furlong from the winning post. But by now their forward momentum was almost zero. Desperately Tipper shortened his reins, pushed on Citizen's neck, kicked with his heels and yelled at him to go on. Whether it was this, or the sound of the other horses coming perilously close behind him, Tipper didn't know. But some new fire was kindled in Citizen. He lengthened his stride and with a sudden explosion of energy, like a furnace igniting, he was galloping at full stretch once more. They got to the line two lengths clear of the second.

'Yes! Yes! YES!' shouted Tipper, waving his stick in the air as Citizen careered on, blithely unaware of what he'd done. By degrees he pulled himself up, but they were four furlongs into doing another circuit before he finally slowed to a walk. They wheeled and started walking back. Tipper was elated. To win on his public return to the saddle was the best of feelings; to win on a horse like this was ecstatic. He waved delightedly at the applauding crowd. They knew they'd seen something better than they normally witnessed.

And then Tipper felt it. There was a slight

irregularity in Citizen's gait. Tipper looked down. It was his off fore front leg. He was favouring it, limping. Bollocks, bollocks, bollocks, Tipper thought. Citizen was lame.

55

As Citizen walked into the winner's enclosure there was some cheering from the crowd, but as far as his connections were concerned it was not a hero's welcome.

'What the bloody hell happened?' demanded Sinclair as soon as Tipper was on the ground. 'You weren't meant to make the running. And what happened to your steering, you plonker? You did the bloody slalom.'

'Jesus, he was so free early on, I couldn't settle him. And then when he saw the crowd in the stands . . . he's seen them lots of times before in the morning, but never full of people shouting at him. That's why he swerved away from them.'

Tipper had the saddle off and they lined up by the horse's head for a photograph.

'Well it's your job to stop him doing things like that,' hissed Sinclair through falsely smiling teeth.

'He'll know better next time, Guvnor.'

'He'd better. You'd better.'

The photographer stood back and out of the corner of his eye Tipper saw Shalakov and his mob advancing on them. He quickly turned to Sinclair and murmured.

'Guvnor, take a look at his off fore. I think he's lame.'

With that he spun around and walked double-quick towards the weighing room, leaving Sinclair looking after him, his face horror-struck. Seconds later Shalakov rapped his trainer on the shoulder and Sinclair switched to an ingratiating smile as he attempted to explain how their superstar horse had nearly got himself beaten at his first attempt.

Tipper, meanwhile, didn't make it to the weighing room without being intercepted by Jameson. The scientist darted up and grabbed him by the arm.

'Tipper! Look at this.'

Tipper was expecting another bollocking.

'What?'

Jameson showed Tipper the box that picked up signals from Citizen's heart-monitor.

'His heart rate never went above two forty beats per minute.'

'And that means?'

Jameson's face lit up as he jammed the device back in his pocket. His pleasure was genuine.

'That means things went very well.'

'Oh yeah?' said Tipper, weary of Jameson's monitor. 'So what does being lame mean? Does it mean you've been galloping the shite out of the horse and now he's broken down? Is that what that means?'

Tipper was practically shouting over his shoulder at a very bemused scientist as he walked off to weigh in.

Captain Maine went to the winner's enclosure to congratulate Shalakov, but his timing wasn't the best. Sinclair had just been told that Citizen's presence was required in the dope box. 'So, Captain Maine,' barked Shalakov, 'you insult my horse by testing him for drugs.'

Maine stood his ground.

'Not at all, General. It is our policy to test the winner of every race.'

He raised his eyebrows meaningfully, and continued.

'It's in line with your President's policy of preventing scandal and fraud from damaging the Hippodrome.'

Shalakov could hardly have claimed that he was unaware of this policy. Instead he grunted and crooked his finger to summon Alexei.

'So,' Maine went on breezily, 'best if we get it over with straight away, don't you agree?'

'As long as my man goes with him,' conceded Shalakov grudgingly. 'And, by the way, you are wasting your time.'

He gave Alexei an instruction and then, seeing Jameson standing nearby, he snapped his fingers.

'You go too,' he told the scientist. 'Make sure nothing happens to the horse.'

On arrival at the testing station, the first thing was to verify the horse's identity. Under the skin on the left side of his neck was an identity plaque. As carried by every horse licensed to race internationally. As soon as a horse entered the testing room, it came within range of the wireless varispectrum identity system – a bank of remote sensors that picked up the plaque's location and illuminated it with ultra-violet light. A bleep was heard as the Citizen's identity plaque was picked up. It could now be seen under his skin and read by all, and it confirmed that he was *CITIZEN (RUS)*.

Maine, with a certain pride, looked around to see if the visitors were suitably impressed by this novel technology.

But as his glance swept over Alexei he noticed something very strange. Half hidden by the rolled collar of his jumper, Alexei's neck appeared to have stuck to it, or inside it, something similar to the plaque in Citizen's neck. When the bodyguard moved his head slightly, the whole thing became visible and Maine could see that it read *ALEXEI (C)* in Russian lettering. Then the WVSIS sensor clicked off and Alexei's neck looked as unadorned as before. As did Citizen's.

Maine glanced at the others to see if anyone else had noticed Alexei's neck. It seemed not. Perhaps it was some system adopted by the Russian military, he thought, to identify recruits or conscripts. Maybe the man had been in prison at some point. Either way, it wasn't Maine's business.

By the time Citizen left the dope box, the adrenaline and endorphins released during the race had worn off and the animal's discomfort in his off fore could be spotted even by an untrained eye. Shalakov conferred with Jameson and then Sinclair. It was decided the horse should return to Xanadu without delay. Maine followed Sinclair to watch him onto the horse-van.

'Oh dear, he really is very lame,' said Maine, stating the obvious.

'Not at all,' said Sinclair airily. 'It's a minor knock. He'll be fine after a couple of days. He'd better be – I'm planning to run him again tomorrow week. We'll pack his leg with ice on the way back.'

Maine was surprised not to see more dismay on the faces of Citizen's people. They all seemed to subscribe to the notion that the injury was 'just a knock' and he'd be racing again soon. But Maine had seen equine leg injuries of all sorts in his time, and this one looked more serious. It looked like weeks, not days.

As the grooms hoisted the ramp and closed the van doors, Tipper came running up, still wearing his breeches and silks.

'How is he, Guvnor?' he asked anxiously.

Sinclair told him curtly there'd be no problem with the horse.

'But he'll be hurting,' Tipper said. 'Maybe I should go in the van with him. Just to keep him calm.'

But Sinclair was having none of it.

'Just let the grooms look after him. That's their job. We're not on the farm out in the bog, you know. He's not a bloody family pet.'

Three days later, a Monday, Tipper wandered into the stable yard at the Hippodrome at six-thirty in the morning. He had a thick head. Over the weekend he'd hit the bottle. Why not? Citizen was quite possibly knackered for a long time, if not for good. And with the horse sidelined, his prospects of a reunion with Ana and Lara were knackered. Sam had borne the brunt of Tipper's maudlin, alcoholic feelings over the telephone.

There was a board beside the door of Team Shalakov's tack-room, with exercise details. Tipper cast his aching eyes over it and was astonished to see Citizen's name down to gallop that morning.

Rubbing his face with his hands, Tipper wandered along to Citizen's stall, and there the colt was, nonchalantly eating his breakfast. Tipper slid back the bolts and went in, rummaging through his pocket for a mint.

'Hello boy! Nice surprise to see you.'

But Citizen seemed keen to spring another surprise. He raised his head from the manger, laid his ears flat and lunged, trying to bite Tipper's fingers. He was in one of his moods. Tipper dropped the mint and gently reached to rub the colt's forehead. Citizen calmed down and Tipper bent down to have a look at the colt's off fore leg.

Carefully, wary of Citizen having another bite, he ran his hands down the tendons below the left knee. They felt perfectly normal, not a degree of heat in them. Then he felt the knee. No swelling. He picked up the foot and now squeezed the tendons gently between finger and thumb, trying this all the way down to the hoof. There was no reaction, no pain. He felt over and under the hoof. There was no sign of any heat there. A huge smile spread across Tipper's face. The leg felt perfect.

'So,' came a voice from the doorway behind him. 'What do you think of my chamber now?'

It was Jameson, leaning on the half-door of the stall.

'I can't believe it,' said Tipper. 'I thought he was hurt bad.'

'Oh no, it wasn't very serious in the end, but even so he's made a remarkable recovery, wouldn't you say?'

Twenty minutes later, his head feeling much clearer, Tipper was ready to give Citizen his morning gallop. But Citizen had other ideas. As soon as his foot touched the sand of the horse-walk he was ready to explode and when Tipper came up beside him to mount he gave a loud long whinny and stood up on his hind legs, yanking the arms of the groom holding his head. The groom gave him some rope and Citizen, sensing the extra freedom, immediately plunged down, dropped his head and bucked. The disorientated groom lost his footing and fell on his arse, before being dragged by Citizen a good ten yards along the walk towards the opening to the track. As if to make him let go of the rein, Citizen now lashed out with his near hind leg and caught the groom in the ribcage. The groom was no hero. Now with three broken ribs to clutch, he dropped the leading rein and Citizen took off, bursting through onto the track before galloping away loose, with the leading rein trailing along the ground beneath him and his tail streaming behind.

56

Everyone scattered like marbles in pursuit of Citizen, who had now set off around the track in the wrong direction and at full tilt. Jameson had whipped out his heart-monitor's receiving box and was staring at it, screaming that Citizen's heart rate was rising past 200 . . . 220 . . . 230. Sinclair was running across the middle of the track, dodging around the great glass skylights that lit the shopping mall below, waving his arms and shouting directions to all and sundry. Only Tipper kept his head.

He'd seen plenty of loose horses. On the open spaces of the Curragh and Newmarket Heath, the place to intercept them was on the way back to their stable, a route they invariably took sooner or later. Comparatively, Citizen was loose within a very confined space, and Tipper reckoned he would be looking for his exit and his manger very soon. So he strolled up the track to the gate through which horses returned from exercise, and stationed himself there.

A full circuit was enough to satisfy Citizen. When he came to the gate where Tipper awaited him, snorting and blowing, there was no difficulty in grabbing his reins. Tipper walked him round in a circle to help him get his breath.

Jameson was the first to reach them, wheezing heavily.

'You caught him!'

'He gave himself up, more like,' said Tipper.

Jameson tried to reply, but he was much more out of breath than Citizen. Finally, after pressing his heaving chest with his hand and swallowing, he said, 'Two fifty beats per minute. Two hundred and fifty! That's the most pressure his heart's ever been under. Is he all right?'

'Ah, he's just fine, Doc. Jesus, horses get loose. It happens all the time.'

'I wish it wouldn't.'

Then Jameson hurried away, tucking the electronic box into his pocket. Tipper wondered why he was so anxious about Citizen's heart rate. He could well understand that a heart monitor was a useful tool in training a horse. The lower the rate, the easier he was finding the work. And the quicker the rate came down towards normal, the fitter he was. The same yardstick was used by human athletes.

But the heart rate during a random, riderless cavort round the track was meaningless, surely.

Shalakov, who had silently watched the whole episode from a spot near the rails, walked over to the groom who had let Citizen go. He was still lying on the ground, holding his ribcage and groaning. Tipper, still walking Citizen in circles to calm him, saw with his peripheral vision Shalakov draw back his foot and deliver a vicious kick into the groom's injured side. Then he made towards Tipper, waving his fingers to indicate he wanted a word. Tipper stood still and waited for him.

'You have another chance now,' Shalakov said, stroking the horse's withers. 'After your mistake on Thursday, I was going to find another jockey; but now you have another chance.'

He held up his finger.

'Do not waste it, for your family's sake.'

Again Shalakov had not even bothered to veil his threat. But Tipper didn't protest. He was thankful that Citizen and he were still in the game.

Captain Maine had watched the morning's drama from his office window high up in the grandstand. He had very mixed feelings. Citizen was obviously an astonishing horse. His size and looks alone were capable of commanding idolatry. He was a potential superstar, and might make Maine's Hippodrome famous throughout the world. And yet, there was no backlash more savage than against a fallen idol, a compromised hero. Maine had just read Citizen's post-race dope report and it was perfectly clean. That would have been enough to satisfy the majority of sports administrators in the world, but it didn't satisfy Maine. He knew by now that the lab was a privatized operation, which had formerly been part of the Ministry of Agriculture, Shalakov's domain. In his eyes, it was compromised.

Maine put the report in a manila folder and opened his filing cabinet. The drop-file into which he posted it was labelled *Shalakov*. If the dope-testing he paid for was corrupt, he was going to know about it – and sooner rather than later.

Moscow loves a drama and Citizen's first race caused quite a stir, as did news of his solo flight around the track a few days later. He was big, he was black, he was rebellious and he looked like a supreme athlete: one sports columnist went so far as to call him an equine Ali in the making.

The Saturday of his next race came, and twice as many Muscovites turned up to see this talented bad boy do his stuff. Tipper went to post knowing he was still on sufferance as far as Shalakov was concerned and only a resounding victory would suffice. He wished he knew more about the strength of the opposition. Unable to read the local racing press, such as it was, he was reduced to asking around. He gained the impression that it was a stronger field than before.

He'd assured Shalakov that Citizen must have learned from experience and would settle better in his second race. How wrong can you be? From the moment the gates slammed open, Citizen was rocket-powered, hurling himself at the course so ferociously that within a few strides he'd taken a three-length lead. Tipper was basically being carted: and, as there's nothing much a man can do on a bolting horse but hold on, he tried at least to make it look good – knees flexing, body bent at ninety degrees and eyes fixed between the horse's ears. The worst thing he could have done, he knew, was fight Citizen.

At the first bend Tipper managed to do a bit of steering, making sure they stayed close to the inner rail and away from the grandstand crowd. He couldn't hear anything from the opposition, no pounding hooves or jockeys' shouts, but they were galloping too furiously to allow him the luxury of a look around. On the long final bend he flicked his head to the left and caught sight of what he thought were remnants of the field, a good twenty lengths or more behind them. In fact, this was the *whole* of the field bar the leader. By the time Citizen had scorched down the straight and passed the post, twenty lengths was as near as the second horse could get to him. The opposition had quite simply been obliterated.

Such had not been the plan. The idea going into this second race was for Citizen to get an education – to win right enough, but by conventional means. That meant dropping in behind, conserving his energy while other horses cut out the running, then using his superior acceleration to surge to the front and win with a furlong and a half to go.

Unsaddling, Sinclair was not too happy.

'I thought I told you not to cut out the running.'

'Jesus, Guvnor, that wasn't front-running, that was two different races. We were in one and the rest were in the other.'

'But I specifically told you to settle him.'

'I could have fought him, yeah, but Christ knows what he'd have done. He's got a mind of his own, and he's three classes better than those other horses. You can't expect him to settle in behind that lot. To him, they're donkeys on Blackpool beach.'

'Well, I hope he's not done anything to himself this time. How did he feel coming back?'

'Sure, he's sound. Feel his legs.'

As he walked off to the weighing room Tipper felt angry with Sinclair. What was the matter with him? He shouldn't be carping, he should be going mad with excitement after that performance.

Jameson once again appeared at his elbow as he walked through the crowd, holding the little black record box with its liquid crystal display. He, at least, was in a celebrating mood.

'Two forty again!' he said jubilantly. 'His rate never went higher. How did he feel? No leg problems?'

'Nothing at all,' said Tipper. 'He was just brilliant, as you could see. Nothing could touch him.'

A sly smile crept over Jameson's gaunt features.

'You see. The chamber. Have you ever seen such a quick recovery?'

Tipper had to admit he had not.

'It really can work miracles!' Jameson grinned triumphantly.

In the dope-testing unit, the vet stood by Citizen's withers with his big syringe. He was about to extract a blood sample from the artery in Citizen's neck, but was for the moment simply running his finger along it, and marvelling at its size and beauty.

'Excuse me, can I have a word?'

Captain Maine was just behind him. The vet turned, clipped his heels and saluted by raising the syringe in front of his face. Maine was vaguely reminded of a guardsman bringing his weapon to the 'present' position.

'I want two samples of this one, please,' he said quietly.

Hearing this the vet performed a rather obvious double-take, but Maine's Russian had been admirably clear and concise. He wanted two samples. In all his time working at the track, no one had ever asked him to take more than one sample.

But Maine was the boss. If he wanted two samples, no problem!

Carefully he inserted the needle into Citizen's bulging artery and without comment drew off double the usual quantity of blood; two hundred cc of it. He then took the sample into an inner room where he carefully divided the blood between two phials, which he individually sealed and labelled.

Maine was standing inside the door with his hand outstretched. The vet handed over one of the phials, before locking the other inside the secure fridge, alongside the samples from the rest of the day's winners. These would all be analysed the next day. Maine slipped Citizen's second sample into his pocket and quietly left.

57

When her pregnancy was established Ana was in pretty good shape. Physically, at least. But mentally she was a mess. She was overshadowed by worries. She had sudden moments of panic. She couldn't lead a normal life even with Lara. How the hell was she going to cope with another mouth to feed? But at the same time she knew in her heart she didn't want the pregnancy to fail. Something was telling her to go through with it.

Tony next door was giving her a wide berth since his warning. Alan was the only adult she spoke to, apart from the staff at the ante-natal clinic. He had become definitely more attentive towards her since the business with Tony. She inflicted her Spanish on him, in the same un-relenting manner that she'd perfected her English on Tipper, and he let her. He helped her do the shopping. She should have felt grateful to this stranger who had taken her in, without demanding any payment, either monetary or otherwise.

They even had a heated husband/wife debate about Ana's insistence that she have a home birth with a midwife. Ana's instinctive mistrust of any type of institution was intransigent.

'They'll take Lara away from me,' she insisted. 'They'll take the baby. They'll throw me out of the country.'

Her paranoia was absolute. She was having the baby at home and that was that.

When Carter wasn't around Ana occasionally googled Tipper. She was only curious, she told herself. And he always stimulated a confusion of feelings inside her. He'd betrayed her trust big time. He'd lied and cheated. He'd driven her into her desperate existence. But she'd survive. And one day things would be good. But what should she tell Lara when she was old enough to ask?

She'd been waiting for the search engine to tell her something new about Tipper. So when it threw up the *Racing Post* article reporting Citizen's first victory, she felt a surge of excitement.

Captain Maine had read the same article on the *Racing Post* web-site. He was quite pleased. It was the first time the Hippodrome had made the *Racing Post* international section. Personally he found Shalakov's post-race remarks crass and over-dramatic. But they would be good for business, no doubt about it. And they also reminded him to make a phone call.

Picking up the phone he keyed the international

code for the United Kingdom, followed by the number for the Horseracing Forensic Laboratory in Newmarket. When the switchboard answered he asked for Professor Felix Webb.

'Morning, Felix,' he said when the Professor came on the line. 'Just wondering if you have anything on that sample I sent you?'

'Morning Jol. You're up early. Yes, as a matter of fact we finished the tests last night. Perfect timing.'

'And?' asked Maine impatiently.

'Well, it's good news. My guys gave your sample the works. We tested for everything from hormones to arsenic. If that horse had sniffed a coke dealer's twenty pound note we'd know about it.'

'So what did you find?'

'That's the thing, Jol. Nothing. Nothing at all. The sample was cleaner than clean.'

'Really? You absolutely sure about that?'

Webb laughed at Maine's serious tone. They were old friends.

'We do like to think we are the best in the business, Jol. There was nothing there that you wouldn't expect to find in the blood of a fit young horse. Is there any reason to believe this animal was given something unauthorized?'

'A suspicion, nothing more. A suspicion. But a pretty bloody strong one.'

'Well if he was, either it's been eliminated from the bloodstream before the sample was taken, or someone's come up with something undetectable. That's all I can say. We'll email the report.'

'Thanks Felix.'

Maine put the phone down, slumped back in his chair and stared at the wall. He didn't know if it was good news or bad. The Moscow lab that tested the first sample was in the clear. That was good. But he couldn't rule out the possibility that Webb might be right. They might have indeed come up with some new substance for which there was no test. He'd been making some discreet enquiries about Xanadu and he knew how sophisticated they were. If anyone was technically capable of this, they were. The question was, how to find out, and how to prove it.

Maine put his head into the palms of his hands and rubbed his eyes. He was pondering the one move he could make. He could introduce random dope testing on non-race days, bringing Russia into line with most other countries. But not only was Citizen Russia's sole star racehorse, Shalakov was a powerful adversary. If he'd reacted badly to his horse being routinely tested, he'd go off like a sky-rocket over a random test. He would be certain to accuse Maine of changing the rules solely to target Citizen, and a lot of people in Russia would believe him.

Maine rubbed his tired eyes again. This was something he was going to have to mull over very carefully.

58

Shalakov always appeared at the Hippodrome for his inspection shadowed by the shaven headed, leather jacketed Alexei. But one morning early in the summer Tipper and Sinclair were surprised to see Nico also in attendance. Nico was rarely seen in the land of his fathers.

As usual, the visitors were only interested in Citizen. After admiring him in his paces, they heard a glowing report from Tipper. The horse was flying, he told them, improving every day. He never galloped with another horse, because none of the others could live with him.

'Good, very good!' grunted Shalakov. He jabbed his finger at Tipper. 'I hope also you are making improvement.'

'How do you mean, General?'

Shalakov said something to Nico, who interpreted for him.

'The General wonders, Tipper, if you've got any

strength in your arms yet. He thinks your physique needs attending to.'

'I keep myself fit,' Tipper said, looking from Nico to the General. 'There's a good gym here. Tell him I work out.'

After a further brief discussion between the two Russians, Nico spoke to Tipper again.

'The General says you do not go to the gym every day. This week, for example, you have only been twice. It is not what he calls professional. He wants you to understand this. You must work out with weights every single day, in order to strengthen your arms and your body.'

Tipper was taken aback. How the hell did Shalakov know he'd only been to the gym twice that week?

'Look, Nico, no one can hold Citizen if he takes it into his head to go off on one. Handling horses isn't just a matter of how strong you are, it's about persuasion and relaxing them. This horse'll learn to settle. I'll teach him.'

Nico knew better than to translate every detail of this defence for Shalakov. He just gave the gist.

'The General says you must do as he says,' he continued. 'You must get stronger.'

'All right, I'll try,' conceded Tipper. 'Now, can you ask him something for me, please?'

Nico nodded.

'I'm wondering, is there any news of my family?'

Shalakov's reply was loud, explosive, and punctuated by his finger jabbing the air. When he'd finished, Nico hesitated for a second while he found more diplomatic words in English.

'The General says you should not be thinking about them. You have to concentrate on Citizen. Your job has hardly started yet. And if you fuck up you will have to forget that woman because you won't ever see her again. So just think about the horse, not about her.'

Shalakov smiled his strikingly threatening smile.

'He is right. You just think about the horse,' he said.

Tipper heard the end of all his hopes in the gruff voice. He said bluntly to Nico, staring him down as he said it, 'I want to talk to you about the Partridge.'

Nico made no reply and said something to Shalakov in Russian. The General answered him abruptly.

'The General repeats, you are not concentrating enough on Citizen,' Nico said with a slight smile. 'I suggest you don't give him reason to worry.' Then he ambled off in formation behind Shalakov. Tipper looked after them helplessly. He felt like a puppet, strung up and dancing to Shalakov's tune.

The reason Nico had been flown in was to make absolutely sure that Shalakov's British workers – he didn't differentiate between Irish and English –understood exactly what that tune was. Next up was David Sinclair.

They saw him across the yard shouting at a gormless groom, who had no idea what he was being expected to do. Shalakov conferred briefly with Nico, then sent Alexei over to fetch the trainer.

'Citizen is in great form this morning, General,' Sinclair said, bouncing over to them full of himself. He didn't see the trouble looming. 'I've got him coming to the boil nicely. Hello, Nico. We don't often see you in these parts.'

'The General asked me to come along,' Nico said dryly, 'to clear up some misunderstandings.'

Even Sinclair now picked up the negative vibes.

'Misunderstandings?' Sinclair repeated. 'The General speaks excellent English. We haven't had any misunderstandings, none at all.'

'As I said, he wants there to be no possibility.' Nico paused, then went on. 'It seems there is trouble between you and Professor Jameson. You and he have failed to work cooperatively. He has spoken to the General about it.'

Sinclair flashed a sarcastic smile.

'Oh really? The Scientist's been telling tales out of school, has he? Well, if you must know, I'm fed up to the back teeth with him. I wish he'd keep out of my way.'

Nico was shaking his head. He held up his hand in warning.

'Just a moment, David. Bear in mind that Professor Jameson has been here many years, and has many times proved his worth to the General. All personnel employed at Xanadu are placed implicitly under Professor Jameson, and must – I repeat *must* – cooperate with him. Those who don't . . . well, let's say they don't work for the General any more.'

It was Nico's turn to smile. A minute ago Sinclair had been feeling untouchable. Now his cockiness evaporated. Shalakov stepped up to him, his face within a few inches of Sinclair's. The powerful smell of his Cologne was like a whiff of cordite.

'You are a fool, Sinclair,' he spat. 'You must do everything now which Jameson tells you. You understand?'

Sinclair glanced at Alexei, and cast his mind back to Shaunsheys' last moments. He gave an involuntary shudder, which Shalakov was sure to have noticed.

'Oh! Er, yes, no, no problem there at all, General – none!' he managed in a weak voice.

Citizen's programme continued full on. He was to run four more times in Moscow, culminating in a two-year-old race on the same card as the President's Cup, Moscow's most prestigious all-age race. Maine's team had worked hard to create an atmosphere to rival the Palio in Siena or the Derby on the Epsom Downs. Flags flew, bunting fluttered and marching bands hammered out patriotic classics. Before racing started, mounted Cossacks careered up and down the straight, lopping the heads off blazing dummies with their sabres. They jumped through hoops of fire and hung from their saddles, their heads inches from the ground. All the while yipping and yodelling with crazy abandon. In the crowd, the fashions were extreme. The ladies' hats and fascinators, their dresses and accessories, were as elaborate and extreme as anything seen at Royal Ascot. The President set the tone for the men by wearing striped trousers and tails, with a grey top hat and a red carnation in his buttonhole. Shalakov for once jettisoned his trade mark leather coat. He wore his General's uniform, the tunic weighed down with row upon row of gaudy medals.

The victor in the President's Cup was given a standing ovation in the unsaddling enclosure, but the roar of the day was Citizen's, as he came from last to first in his race to win as he liked. Tipper's cool deserted him as he passed the winning post. He swivelled his body towards the grandstand and yelled, punching the air.

'This is for you Ana!' he roared. 'Where is she, Shalakov? Where the fock is she?'

Tipper's words were lost in the noise of the crowd, which was perhaps lucky for him. Shalakov's foot soldiers didn't even think of speaking to their boss like that, not if they wanted to stay around. Let alone broadcast it to a grandstand full of people.

After running on his usual quarter-circuit after the finishing line, Tipper pulled Citizen up. He had time to settle down by the time he got back to unsaddle.

But as soon as they passed through the gate off the track, Tipper felt Citizen tense up. The crowd were pressing against the rails of the horsewalk that led to the unsaddling enclosure. It was noisier and more drunk than usual. Citizen suddenly freaked out. He whipped round in the walkway, in the process flattening the groom who led him. Then he plunged back towards the racetrack scattering everyone like ants. Tipper, though, had been on his guard, and managed to stay on board. The gate, which had been closed behind them, loomed up in front of them. Jesus, he's going to jump it, Tipper thought as he took a desperate pull on the reins, hard enough to pull Citizen up. Tipper had him back under control, but it had been a near thing.

Fifteen minutes later Shalakov received the President's personal congratulations, and the silver trophy from the First Lady. Cradling the trophy in his arms – it was a statuette of a winged horse – Shalakov addressed the crowd.

'As you have seen today, my horse flies like this one,' he said into the microphone. 'And now I have an announcement. Because the best horses in England and Ireland and France do not fly, they do not come here. So I will take my Citizen to them. He will race at Newmarket in their biggest race for two-year-olds. We are going to conquer the world!'

His crass jingoism went down well with the crowd.

*   *   *

Back in Citizen's stable, jubilation had turned to concern. The world-conqueror's foot was bleeding. During his fit of panic in the horsewalk, he'd struck out with one of his rear hooves against a rail post and given himself a deep gash. Sinclair and Tipper were crouched over it.

'He'll be fine,' Sinclair said.

'It looks bad, though,' Tipper said despairingly. 'It could easily get infected. It's a bollocks of a place to heal. Jesus, this could knacker the Dewhurst.'

'The Scientist says the kriotherapy will sort him out,' said Sinclair.

'This is an awful deep gash, Guvnor! How can it help to put him in a bloody fridge?'

'It worked pretty well the last time he got injured. Anyway, he's going back to the chamber either way.'

'Well, if you ask me, it's crazy.'

Sinclair stood up.

'If you've got all the bloody answers, Tipper, why don't you go and tell them to the Scientist? Better still, tell Shalakov. But don't expect to be around too long afterwards.'

384

59

As the full-term of Ana's pregnancy approached she grew moody and ever more suspicious. She mooched around the flat and felt the presence of Alan oppressively. Finally, half way through her eighth month, she snapped.

'When are you going to go to work, Alan?' she asked as she sat at the kitchen table pouring herself a strong mug of tea. 'When is this job going to start? When is the bloody gardening going to stop?'

Under normal circumstances Alan would have told her to mind her own bloody business. And reminded her that it was his apartment to do what he liked in. But he didn't. Because these weren't normal circumstances.

'Oh, soon,' he said lightly. 'Quite soon.'

'But *actually* when? It has been so many months already, I'm wondering about it.'

Frowning, Ana propped her feet up against another of the chairs and rubbed her belly.

'Sometimes it takes this long, Ana,' he said

calmly. 'Deals have to be completed, and things like that.'

'But you don't answer my question. When?'

'I don't know, not precisely—'

Ana interrupted with a staccato laugh.

'You know what? I don't believe you. I don't think there is such a job. I don't think there is such a bank. I think you are lying to me.'

Alan laughed lightly in return.

'Ana, of course I'm not lying to you. Look, I'll show you my letter of appointment, shall I? Let me go and get it.'

He went out and came back with a sheet of paper in his hand. It was headed by the Haven Bank logo.

He'd been out of the room no more than two minutes but when he came back into the kitchen, the atmosphere had changed and Ana no longer cared. Her face was creased with pain and she was drumming her heels on the chair on which her feet rested. There was a pool of clear liquid on the floor around her.

Alan stood and stared.

'Bloody hell!' was all he said.

'The midwife!' Ana whispered. 'We've got to call her straight away. This is too soon. She won't be expecting to come now.' Alan didn't need telling twice. He was in a flat panic. He didn't want the responsibility. He hadn't got a clue what to do.

'Hold on Ana,' he begged once he'd rung the

midwife. 'Hold on. She's coming. She isn't far away.'

Ana was now on the floor, lying on her back, intermittently groaning and taking long breaths in which she expelled in short staccato puffs. Lara wanted to know what was the matter with her mummy. Her mummy couldn't tell her. She couldn't speak.

Alan put a fatherly arm around Lara and led her back to Ana's bedroom. 'Why don't you have a little play in here for a bit? Mummy's fine. She might have a baby soon. So you stay in here for a minute?'

Lara was confused by such close interaction with Alan. Her big brown eyes looked at him suspiciously.

'Jesus,' she said, but she went into the bedroom like a good little girl.

Over the next hour, Alan did everything he could to make Ana comfortable; he covered her with a blanket to keep her warm and he kept her sipping water. He just didn't know what else to do, other than try and persuade her to go to hospital. But she was having none of that. Every minute he looked at his watch praying that the midwife would arrive.

'It's coming now,' Ana groaned. 'I need some towels. Please Alan get me some towels.'

'Of course, of course.'

'What else can I do?' he said helplessly when

he came back with the towels. He put a reassuring hand on Ana's shoulder. Ana reflexively grabbed his hand and squeezed it as another contraction started to force the baby out.

'You'll be fine,' he said soothingly. 'The midwife won't be long, Ana.'

'Don't go anywhere, Alan. Please look after Lara if any thing goes wrong?'

'Nothing's going to go wrong, Ana,' he assured her. 'I won't go anywhere.' But how the hell did he know? Ana gave a sustained sigh. Her eyes were screwed shut. Then the baby slid out into the bed of towels that Ana had made.

'Oh my God!' he jabbered. 'Oh my God. You've done it. Are you alright?'

Trying to get her breath, Ana didn't say anything. But she smiled at Alan.

Then, 'I'm fine. Please can you get us some warm water?'

Alan went to get the water. And the door bell rang.

'She's here,' he shouted excitedly. 'She's here.'

The midwife bowled through the door and immediately took over. There was a flurry of activity during which Alan made a strategic retreat into the bedroom, and broke the news to Lara.

'You've got a brother,' Alan told her cheerily.

A mystified stare was all he got for his trouble. To Alan's surprise Lara showed no signs of wanting to go and investigate.

'Aren't you pleased?' Alan asked her.

Lara just fixed him with a stare and said nothing. Not even 'Jesus'.

Once the midwife had sorted Ana and the baby out Alan ventured back into the sitting room.

'You were amazing, Alan,' Ana smiled. 'I just want to thank you.'

Alan gave her a satisfied smile. 'God, you were so brave,' he said shaking his head. This was the concerned Alan back again, the one she'd met in the betting shop. Not the control freak who'd scared off Tony. She wanted to hug him.

'I want to call him Alan. Do you mind?' Ana asked, looking up at him with a big smile.

Carter was stunned into silence. And very uncomfortable. But then Lara came out of the bedroom at last. She ran to her mother with a big smile of her own, and Carter was off the hook.

Ana had time to reflect over the next few days. She suddenly had an urge to make contact with Tipper. But the only point of contact she had was Sam. She had his number on her phone.

Sam was lounging in his flat watching Top Gear re-runs. When he answered the phone he heard a low, almost suppressed whisper, yet he recognized it at once.

'Ana,' he said. 'Ana! God, I can't believe this. I thought I'd never hear from you again.' He reached for the remote control device and silenced Jeremy Clarkson.

'Hi, Sam. It's good to hear your voice. Can you talk?'

'Yeah, I'm just watching old stuff on TV. How are you? Where are you?'

'I can't tell you where I am. But I'm with Lara and she's fine – we're both fine. Are you in touch with Tipper, Sam?'

'Tipper's in Russia.'

'Yes, I know. Do you speak to him?'

'Sure I do. He gets lonely out there, poor sod. He's missing you Ana. And Lara. Really bad, you know.'

'Is he?'

'Yes. I'll give you his number. Ring him.'

Ring him! Ana started to panic and had second thoughts. This was a bad idea.

Sam blundered on, 'You know he's coming to England, so he is. With this great horse they've got out there. Citizen. He's running in the Dewhurst at Newmarket next month. It's a big, big deal, Ana. You must come.'

'Sam, I'm not sure. It's all too painful. I'm not sure.'

'But Ana. He's Lara's father, for god's sake. He must see her.'

'Sam, I'm upset. Do you know what he did?'

Despite knowing none of the facts, Sam did his best to stick up for his cousin.

'No, I don't. He's not told me a thing, except that he hasn't done anything. And he's got a right to see his kid, you *know* that.'

'If you knew, you wouldn't say that,' Ana said defensively. 'You wouldn't. Anyway you can tell him next time you speak Lara is happy. She's very healthy and she's talking and walking – she never stops. Now I've got to go. Good-bye, Sam.'

When she'd rung off Sam tried to call her back. But she'd withheld her number. He phoned Tipper instead. It was the middle of the night in Moscow.

'Tipper. You won't *believe* who I've just been speaking to,' he told his sleepy cousin.

60

Shalakov's airborne horse-transporter was sooth-ingly quiet. Its rear-mounted engines hardly made more than a continuous sigh to the passengers inside as they ghosted along at 35,000 feet. Citizen's cut had, as predicted, healed in a few days, and his training schedule had been uninter-rupted. He was standing placidly in his own rear compartment at the back of the plane. In the forward passenger seats Sinclair had his ears plugged into the soundtrack of some DVD. Jameson was peppering Tipper with questions about Newmarket. They were on their way to contest the biggest two-year-old race in Europe.

Tipper had had a tightly-wound ball of tension in his stomach for weeks. Since the midnight conversation with Sam, there had been no more information about Ana, but at least she knew he was going to be in England for the race. Sometimes he hugged himself at the thought that she'd been thinking of him, and wanted to pass on news about

Lara. By dwelling on this Tipper had convinced himself she still loved him, and that she'd get in touch while he was in England. The thought had become more than a straw to clutch at. It was a bloody great life-raft.

'So, Tipper,' Jameson was wheezing. 'Will he win?'

It was probably the twentieth time in the last week that Jameson had asked Tipper this question. His answer was always more or less the same.

'Jesus, I don't know, Doc. We're talking another level, you know? The other horses in Moscow aren't up to much, really. In Newmarket there'll be half a dozen of the best two-year-olds in the world. It should be real competitive.'

'What about the crowd? Will they frighten him? His heart rate went up to two fifty when he got spooked at the hippodrome. I couldn't believe it. It had only been two forty in the race, for Christ's sake!'

'I don't think it'll be the same,' Tipper reassured him. 'A lot of the crowd don't bother to look at the horses. They're either in the betting ring or boozing in the bars. That's good for us.'

'But it's a big race.'

'It is. But it's an even bigger racecourse. Plenty of room. The crowd isn't on top of the horses like at Moscow.'

'Will the track suit him, though? What's it like?'

'Like a prairie, Doc. Vast. Flat open ground for miles and miles. There's this big long mound of earth that runs across it called the Devil's Dyke. It's ancient. Some kind of defence system, I think. In the longer races the horses have to run through a gap in it. But I reckon Citizen will love those big open spaces. He doesn't like to be cramped.'

Jameson shut his eyes tightly, trying to visuaize Citizen triumphing. He wanted a cigarette.

'The tension's killing me,' he muttered to himself.

Sam was waiting for Tipper at Stansted.

'You look good boy,' he smiled as Tipper got into the car.

'Never better, Sam. Fit as a butcher's dog. And I'm going to need to be.'

'So this horse. Is he the real deal? Or is this guy Shalakov messing with everyone?'

'Jesus he's good all right. He's very good. He hasn't been beating much at home, but he'll make them go a bit here, I'm telling you.'

'Thought we'd grab something to eat at the Partridge. That suit you?' Sam wasn't sure if Tipper would fancy it.

'As a matter of fact, it does,' he nodded.

Tipper got a big welcome from the landlord.

'Ah! The Prodigal returns!' boomed Johnny the Fish when Tipper walked in. 'Tell chef to kill the fatted calf.'

'How are we Johnny?' Tipper said.

They shook hands and Tipper looked about him,

hoping there would be no members of the Covey Club around. He saw none and began to smile and relax.

'Large Scottish water for the weary traveller,' Johnny boomed. But Tipper raised his hand.

'Just cranberry juice thanks. I'm in hard training right now.'

'Cuh!' complained Johnny with an upward jerk of his head. 'What've they been doing to you in Russia? Did they try the electric shock treatment on you? Knew a fellow who got that once. Nasty.'

'Johnny,' Tipper asked urgently. 'Those girls that came that night. They stitched me up, planting that coke on me. I got to find them. You know anything?'

'Never seen them since, old boy. They just appeared, and then disappeared.'

Tipper fell silent. Johnny hadn't answered his question. Was he hiding something? Did he know? It was Sam who broke the silence, clapping his cousin on the shoulder.

'He's going to win the Dewhurst, Johnny,' he said.

'Of that my boy I am aware. I've been reading fascinating things about this horse of his. So unless Tipper tells me otherwise the guide dogs for the blind box and I will be paying a visit to the races. Luckily, it hasn't been emptied since Christmas. And we have a lot of dog lovers in here, if you get the drift.'

* * *

The racing press in England were not used to welcoming Russian horses and, despite the exciting stories that had been coming out of Moscow, Citizen's arrival was largely greeted with patronizing jokes. But Shalakov and Citizen were good copy and the papers were splashing on them across the front and back pages.

Sinclair, it was true, was given a fair amount of respect, but Tipper was being sniped at from all directions. The Press room was full of indignation. No adequate reason or explanation had been given, they wrote, for the re-instatement of Tipper O'Reilly's licence.

But a few days before the Dewhurst meeting, the journalists' fire was a little dampened by their first glimpse of Citizen. He had a routine canter on the public gallops on Newmarket Heath and, even to the eyes of the most jaundiced pressmen, his size and strength were awe-inspiring.

'Has anyone checked if this beast isn't really a three-year-old?' asked one columnist, not entirely joking.

A few others took Citizen's claims seriously. His pedigree, for one, was impressive. But, for most, sanity prevailed. Few tipsters gave him a chance. Horses from Russia just didn't win the Dewhurst – did they?

Tipper was in no doubt what was at stake. If they won, Shalakov would surely have to re-unite him with Ana and Lara. And he also needed to win for himself. This race was going to be every bit as important as the Irish Oaks had been. He needed to re-build his life. This was his chance. And maybe Ana would think twice if he could show her he was back in the big time.

61

Ask any trainer or jockey of a fancied horse a week before a race and they'll tell you it's a good thing. A day before the race doubts will have started to creep in. And by race day they will be seeing demons laying tripwires between every furlong pole. Tipper was no different. As he stepped out of the cab at Newmarket racecourse, the cut grass stretching for miles and the white rails snaking across the Heath suddenly looked very intimidating. It couldn't have been more different from the gritty urban scene at the Moscow Hippodrome. The Fish had wanted to know if Russia had changed him. Perhaps it had. Newmarket, he reflected, had been his life at one time, but this didn't feel at all like coming home.

As he walked towards the jockeys' gate, a couple of his old colleagues sitting in an open-top car recognized him. They called him over.

'How are you, buddy? Good to see you back.'

He could tell they didn't particularly mean it. 'What are your chances in the big one?'

'Oh, I don't know,' Tipper said cautiously. 'We'll be trying our best.'

'Your horse looks great, anyway,' butted in the other jockey, who had been talking on his mobile phone. 'I saw him on the Limekilns. Oh, by the way, I've got an old mate of yours on the line. Have a word.'

He handed the mobile to Tipper.

'How are you, Tipper boy?'

The gravely tones were unmistakeable: the Duke. Tipper frowned and, without answering, handed the phone back to its owner. He hurried off towards the jockeys' gate. 'Fock the lot of you,' he muttered under his breath

Sinclair had been looking forward to the moment when he'd stroll nonchalantly into the weighing room to pick up Tipper's saddle. There would be other trainers hanging around there, none of them with a prospect like his in the Dewhurst. He'd day-dreamed how they'd look at him with envy. He was going to milk it.

Once he'd picked the saddle up he had to push his way through a bit of a bottle neck towards the saddling boxes. He became jammed up in the scrum behind a woman who seemed slightly familiar. When she turned round he had the fright of his life.

'Hello, David,' Alison said, acidly. 'You look pleased with yourself.'

He looked at her. Christ, what had she been eating? Who had she been eating? She'd put on at least a stone. Her breasts, previously ample enough, were now bursting gigantically out of the yellow trouser-suit jacket she'd somehow squeezed into. Her thighs were threatening to split her trousers.

'Alison!' he said weakly. 'You look different. You've, er, gone blonde.'

'Yes. You like it?' She pushed her fingers through her hair with grotesque coquettishness. 'Mike does.'

'Mike?'

'Oh, *yes*, David! Me and Mike Champion! We're an item now. Don't they have newspapers in Moscow?'

'An item?'

'Partners,' she added with a smug smile.

'You, and that low-life? I can't believe it.'

She gave a snort that would have done justice to any of her horses.

'Mike sold one of his companies for two hundred and fifty million quid last week,' she informed him loftily. 'We're going to have a hundred horses in the stable by next season. And we've got the best runner in the Dewhurst. I've heard yours is like a bloody shire-horse.'

Sinclair closed his eyes briefly, to rest them from the sight of her.

'Is that what they're saying? Well you're all in for a bit of a shock, in that case. Now, if you'll excuse me.'

He dodged around her and headed purposefully towards the saddling boxes.

Tipper couldn't wait to see how Citizen compared to the English and Irish horses in the paddock. As he came through with the other jockeys, most of their mounts were circling with their handlers. Then a murmur rippled round the paddock as Citizen swaggered through the gate to join them. As soon as he saw him alongside his rivals, Tipper felt a spasm of excitement. Citizen looked magnificent, taller and more muscled-up than any of the others.

He joined the group around Sinclair, touching his whip to his cap.

'Who's the danger, do you reckon?' he asked.

He meant this for Sinclair, but it was Shalakov who answered.

'There is no danger except you. Just look at these horses. We have the best one. You do your job, we win.'

Sinclair took a more judicious line.

'Dermot O'Callaghan's has the best form, on paper anyway,' he said. 'Won a good race in Ireland last time, and he's quite a nice sort. But not as nice as Citizen,' he quickly added, with a side glance at Shalakov.

On the other side of the paddock, O'Callaghan and his people were gawping at Citizen. They'd never seen a two-year-old of his size and development. What in God's name were those Russians feeding him?

O'Callaghan swivelled, following Shalakov's horse as it passed by.

'Why don't our horses look like that?' he asked matter of factly.

His trainer's eyes narrowed.

'You can't train a horse to look like that,' he said drily. 'And you can't feed one to look like that either. Only a bloody chemist can make a horse like that.'

As promised, Johnny the Fish graced the racecourse with his presence. Leaving the Partridge in the hands of the chef, he'd set off with his pockets stuffed with cash and Shelley 'to ride shotgun'.

The Fish was going for broke, which was exactly what he would be if Citizen got beaten. He'd raided his office safe containing the week's takings. He'd emptied the envelope in which the staff's tips were kept. And he'd taken a knife to the Guide-Dogs for the Blind collecting box. 'Just borrowing,' he'd whispered to the hollow model dog, as he replaced it on the bar.

Citizen's arrival from Moscow had prompted some initial interest from ante-post punters but his price had been drifting throughout the morning and ten to one against was now the general price. The Fish was gobbling this up, going from bookie to bookie along the rails. The pundits in that morning's papers had been dubious about the quality of bloodstock in Russia, and had talked up Dermot O'Callaghan's horse. Meanwhile a

402

particularly opinionated bookie on Channel 4's 'The Morning Line' had been braying about the merits of Mike Champion's colt, while Citizen, he said, was like the Titanic: very big, very beautiful, but on a date with an iceberg.

Nevertheless the Fish's money had begun to attract attention. Now the price against Citizen's name on the boards was being trimmed to nines, then eights. But it stopped at that. The crowd was chauvinist. They couldn't believe a horse trained in Russia could win big in Britain.

The bell rang for jockeys to mount and parade out onto the course. Tipper knew that if any horse cantered past him on the way to the start, he might not be able to pull him up until they were through the Devil's Dyke and in another county. So the plan was to make sure they were last out of the paddock and to go down quietly, and alone. They'd then try to be last into the stalls, to prevent a long frustrating wait if one or more of their opponents proved difficult to load.

Sinclair made an elaborate pretence of discovering something amiss with the tack. He fiddled with the girth-strap until all the other runners had gone. Then he legged Tipper up. A couple of jobsworths fretted around them, twittering that they were holding things up. Sinclair took no notice of them. Shalakov would pay any fine they incurred. They went to the start a clear furlong behind the rest.

Fortified by a large Scotch, the Fish was

watching on a TV monitor in the bar. Like all punters who bet more than they can afford, he was having last minute doubts.

'Cuh! This could be expensive, Shelley,' he muttered. Shelley wasn't listening. She didn't care.

The first part of the plan worked well. Tipper arrived at the start without mishap. But to his dismay the handlers were keen to load him early and he had a long, tense time in his stall while the rest were put in. There were sixteen runners and he was drawn close to the stands rails. As this was the first time they'd been up against top-notch opposition, he didn't want Citizen to race in his usual bullish way. The plan was to tuck him in on the rails behind the early leaders so that, being hemmed in, his competitive instincts would be thwarted for the first few furlongs. It was a good plan on paper. But Citizen hadn't read the script.

62

The finishing post was a tiny pin sticking up from the rails seven furlongs ahead of them. As the stalls opened, the entire field took off towards it like a volley of arrows – all of them, except Citizen, who missed the break, his mind apparently elsewhere, so that he found himself scratching along through the first furlong in last place. Sinclair was already panicking, shouting into the jockey-com telling Tipper to take closer order. But Tipper sensed that this whole experience was a culture-shock for Citizen and didn't want to rush him. He'd find his stride, Tipper was sure; the question was, with only six furlongs to go, would it be in time?

At the half-way stage they were still scrubbing along last but then Tipper's hands felt something different. Citizen was beginning to grab hold of the bit. His stride was beginning to flow and soon enough he'd picked off four or five other stragglers. He was smoothly ghosting up to the bunch of horses just behind the front-runners. Now Tipper had to make a crucial decision. The horses ahead of him were spreading out across the track, looking for a run. But there were no gaps. How was he going to give Citizen a chance? He could pull out even wider, and come round the whole field. But he'd be giving the others at least two lengths in the process. Or he could hold his nerve and hope a wide enough gap would open. Finally, he could try to thread, push or muscle his way through them; which might attract the wrath of the stewards. Whatever he decided, it would have to be soon.

'Oh Christ!' wailed Johnny the Fish, his face chalk-white, his eyes riveted on the screen, his fists clenched. 'Come on, Tipper! Get stuck in! Wallop him!'

'He can't win, not from there,' Shelley chipped in unsympathetically.

'Hang on a minute, he's not beat yet,' the Fish said defiantly. 'He's going okay.'

'Don't kid yourself. You're stuffed,' Shelley predicted triumphantly. It still irked her that Tipper had never responded to her blatant availability.

Two furlongs from home a fast finishing back-marker surged up on Citizen's outside and was now racing stride-for-stride beside him. At the same time a gap between two tiring horses opened immediately ahead of them. Tipper had never asked Citizen to compete for a gap before. Would he give way to the other horse, or fight for it?

Tipper crouched low, kicked Citizen's flanks and pushed on his neck. The response was immediate. Suddenly Citizen was clean through, passing spent horses and looking at clear daylight ahead.

But he was still adrift of the two runners hugging the rail. They had four or five lengths lead – surely too much. Sinclair's voice in Tipper's ear was yelling incoherent instructions, but Tipper shut it out. Shortening his reins he gave Citizen a slap down his neck with his stick. The response was electric. Citizen rammed his head forward and in a few liquid strides was upsides and past one of them. With half a furlong to go, they were closing on the leader. But he wasn't stopping. As Citizen drew level, Tipper realized the other jockey was wearing O'Callaghan's colours. In a flash Citizen jerked his head to the left. Incredibly, he was trying to bite the other horse's neck. Tipper snatched Citizen's head back, gave him another slap, and they picked up again. At the line, Citizen was going away. He'd won by a clear length.

Tipper didn't even think of celebrating as they crossed the line. He'd been staring catastrophe in the face, but Citizen had saved him. They'd done it. They'd won the Dewhurst. Tears welled up in his eyes. He pulled his goggles down and wiped the sleeves of his silks across his face. He only had one thought in his mind. Had Ana watched the race?

'Christ Almighty!' O'Callaghan's jockey shouted at Tipper as they walked back to the gate that led off the track. 'What the hell are you feeding that? Rocket fuel?' He was evidently too close for Citizen's liking and the horse let fly with one of his hind legs. His hoof glanced off the other horse's right shoulder and narrowly missed the jockey's knee.

'Bloody hell! Is he mad?'

Tipper said nothing, but privately he was wondering the same.

Shalakov and Citizen were met by a wall of silence as they entered the winner's enclosure. The knowledgeable Newmarket crowd were stunned. Certainly not many had backed him, so there would be no wild cheering. Shalakov was as irked by the silence as Tipper was relieved. The last thing he wanted was Citizen going nuts.

A few minutes later, as the press huddled round the winner's enclosure Shalakov, speaking through Nico, let the hacks know that this was just the beginning.

'General Shalakov is convinced Citizen is not just the fastest in the world, but the toughest,' said Nico smoothly. 'You go so easy on your horses, but the General believes a race horse is for racing, which is why he's going to send Citizen to contest the Group One contest in France, the Criterium International in ten days' time.

There was a murmur of surprise amongst the press boys. The Dewhurst/Criterium International double was unprecedented. No horse had ever done it. Shalakov immediately picked up on the scepticism of the press and stepped in front of his spokesman.

'He is not soft like yours,' Shalakov boasted. 'It is all very easy for him, because he is strong. Next year he will come back and win your Derby and the St James Palace Stakes at your Royal Ascot. Then he will be stallion.'

Now there was a ripple of derision. The St James's Palace Stakes was never contested, let alone won, by the Derby winner. The Ascot race was run over two-thirds of the Derby distance and was designed for a completely different type of horse.

When the press briefing was over Dermot O'Callaghan, in spite of being bitterly disappointed, went to shake Shalakov's hand.

'Congratulations, General. He's a tough horse all right. Nearly bit my fellow's head off on the way past.'

'He is the best,' said Shalakov gruffly. 'The others are nothing.'

'Well, we rather like ours too,' said O'Callaghan mildly. 'And there's always another day – maybe it'll be Derby Day.'

'Have as many days as you like,' was Shalakov's rejoinder. 'You won't beat this horse – ever.'

O'Callaghan smiled neutrally, and wondered why he'd bothered to be polite.

According to protocol, Citizen had left the winner's enclosure escorted by two course officials to go to the dope-testing box. They were surprised to meet Professor Webb there. The head of equine forensics was rarely seen on the racecourse.

'Just checking up on everything,' smiled the scientist.

In truth he had come racing for one reason only – to have a look at Citizen in the flesh. And what he'd seen had convinced him to run the samples through every test known to man.

Johnny the Fish was in the bar celebrating with Shelley.

'Not a bad day's work, young Shelley,' he chuckled, as he downed his scotch. 'Think I'd better make a donation to the Guide Dogs.'

'What you wanna do that for?' she asked.

'Because, my little chickadee,' said Johnny, 'if that's not the best horse I've ever seen, I'll be wanting a guide-dog myself. Which is why I'm sticking my winnings on him ante-post for next year's Derby.'

63

'You've cracked it, boy,' Sam was raving as they left Newmarket racecourse. 'Jesus, can I have a smile please?'

Tipper forced one for his cousin, but he was frustrated because he felt he'd delivered his half of the bargain, but Shalakov hadn't. The Russian had disappeared before Tipper could press his case. In all the excitement, had the billionaire forgotten about their deal?

But Shalakov, drinking vodka in his car as it crawled through the approaches to London, was in fact giving Tipper, Ana and Lara some considerable thought. Now that Tipper was a successful jockey Ana might want to get back together with him, Shalakov mused. But that he would not allow. She was only alive because she had Tipper's kids anyway. The leverage of their absence was proving to be a very motivational force for Tipper. It would stay that way.

Shalakov had a conference call with an ex-CIA

soybean consortium in five minutes. Later that night some girls were coming in for a party, and he would have to make sure Mrs Shalakov went safely home to Kent beforehand. But in spite of those distractions he knew he needed to act decisively. He was going to have to let Tipper see Ana. Which would be fine as long as she had a visit from Nico first.

Nico rang Carter as he entered the building.

'A friend's here to see you,' Carter told Ana. 'Sit down.'

The hair stood up on the back of Ana's neck. 'But I don't have any friends.'

'You'll see,' Carter smiled.

Ana understood what was going on as soon as Nico opened his mouth. She froze.

'Nice apartment,' Nico said matter of factly. 'Very generous of General Shalakov, given you deserted your job.'

'I . . .' Ana couldn't get any words out. Her mouth had gone dry.

'Do you know how lucky you are?'

Ana didn't try and say anything.

'Let me spell things out to you, Ana.' Nico gave her a creepy, insincere smile.

'You have only been tolerated because you have Tipper's children. If you continue to do as you're told you'll be okay. But don't think for one moment you're coming to Moscow. Do you understand that?'

Ana still couldn't say a word. She looked at Carter who was reading the newspaper.

'I'll ask you again. Do you understand that?'

Ana nodded.

'Good. Then your children will be safe.'

Nico looked at Carter. 'Any problems?' Carter shook his head.

'Oh by the way. Just in case you are worried about Tipper, don't be. He's fine. The Moscow girls love him. And he seems pretty keen on them. By the way, if he happens to contact you, you don't ever tell him you work for Shalakov . . . or that he's found you a nice flat. Shame if something happened to that pretty little girl of yours.'

Nico smiled at Carter as they walked out of the apartment. Nico flicked his phone open and rang Shalakov.

'General. All is fine,' he reported. 'Should be safe enough to let Tipper see her.' Nico then listened to his instructions.

Ana was in bits. It all made sense now. She'd been a prisoner all along. She should have realized it wouldn't have been that easy to walk away from Shalakov. But what was making her blood boil was the creepy, rat-faced jerk's last jibe. 'The Moscow girls love him. And he seems pretty keen on them.' She'd seen the pleasure he'd got from taunting her with that.

Moments later Tipper was euphoric when he read his text message from Nico; *good news my*

friend. the general has fixed for you to see ana. car will
pick you up tomorrow morning – nico

Tipper was sick with nerves as he got out of the black Merc – different from the nerves he'd felt before riding a race, and much worse. In a race he had some control over events, but now he felt like a sitting duck. He had no idea how Ana would respond to his arrival and because he didn't have a clue what to expect, he had no game plan. He wasn't much good at discussing his feelings at the best of times, let alone when he was in a state like this. He was terrified of buggering it all up with a stupid comment. And what about Lara? He dreaded not being recognized or remembered by his own daughter.

He tried taking deep breaths to clear his mind as he walked into the apartment block. There was no reason why he would have made anything of the figure of Alan Carter, leaning against the bus shelter on the opposite side of the road.

Ana was working at the computer. She heard the lift stop at their floor and the doors open. Then, after a moment, the doorbell sounded. Ana opened the door, thinking it must be Carter. It was too late to slam it when she saw her mistake. He had his foot in the door-jamb.

'Ana,' he pleaded. 'Please don't shut the door.'

'Go away, Tipper!' she hissed. She didn't want to frighten Lara. But Tipper took no notice. Firmly, but carefully he pushed his way inside.

'Ana, please,' he said softly.

She retreated backwards as Lara, clutching Mr Sponge Bob, her animatronic cat, appeared from the kitchen to see what was going on.

'Who are you?' Lara demanded.

'I'm a friend of your mummy,' Tipper said carefully, glancing up at Ana.

The child held up her toy.

'This is *my* friend, Mr Sponge Bob,' she said, then turned to the toy. 'Say hello.'

Ana was stuck. Now that Lara had met their visitor, she'd have to mask her anger.

'Lara, sweetheart,' she said, 'would you take Mr Sponge Bob back into the kitchen and give him his tea?'

Lara hesitated. There was the sort of insistence in her mother's voice that she knew was non-negotiable. So she did as she was told while Ana ushered Tipper into the sitting room.

'What are you doing here?' she asked guardedly. 'Why now?'

Tipper looked imploringly at her.

'Because I've been desperate to see you. You have no idea what I've had to do to track you down. And I don't even know why you left me.'

'Of course you do. Who do you think I am? Just another of your girls?'

'Ana, this is stupid. We need to talk. I thought we loved each other, and don't you think Lara needs us to be together? I'm sorry about what happened. I know I shouldn't have got drunk with Johnny the Fish. Please forgive me.'

Ana could feel herself being pulled in different directions. He looked so sincere – but then she reminded herself of the damage he'd done.

'I did that once before – before I had Lara. Remember that? I told you what would happen, and then it did, but worse. We don't need to talk now. There's nothing to say.'

'But what about Lara?'

'She's doing fine without you. She doesn't need you.'

'Please Ana. She does need me. She needs to know I'm her father. We should go and tell her, now.'

He made a move towards the door but Ana was quicker. She blocked his path to the hallway.

'No. Leave her out of it. You can hurt me as much as you like, but you're not hurting her.'

Lara appeared, leaning on the door-frame. Mr Sponge Bob had finished his tea.

'Me and my mummy have got a baby,' she said smiling innocently. 'It's my brother.'

Tipper was stunned.

'What?'

'Lara!' shouted Ana. 'Will you please go back into the kitchen for a minute? I need to talk to my friend.'

'What's this about a baby?' asked Tipper.

Ana was flustered.

'I'm looking after a baby,' she improvised.

'It's . . . for a friend of mine. She's been very sick since she had it.'

'But Lara said it was her brother.'

'She doesn't understand. She doesn't understand a lot of things, thanks to you.'

'Is it your baby or not, Ana?'

'No! I told you. And, Tipper, you should go now, really . . .'

'No. No way. How can you do this just because I got drunk once? This is ridiculous for God's sake. Is there someone else?'

'No. Of course not. How dare you say that after what you did?'

'So whose flat is this then? The baby's father?'

No. 'It's just a gay guy I met. He's putting me up.'

'A gay guy, is it? Excuse me if I don't believe you. Tell me about this baby – it *is* yours, isn't it?'

Anger was boiling up within Tipper but Ana looked at him with not a flicker of emotion.

'Look, all this is none of your business now, anyway. You and me, it's all history.'

Everything that Tipper had dreaded was coming to pass. He'd said all the wrong things. He was hopeless. He covered his face with his hands and rubbed his eyes in exasperation and confusion. Then he took a deep breath: he would give it one last try.

'Ana,' he said, 'I want us to be together more than anything else in the world. You and Lara are my life. You always will be. Nothing is more important. I got drunk. I had a bad day. It was a mistake.

417

But I've hardly had a drink since and things are going well now. I won the Dewhurst at Newmarket yesterday. My career's back on track.'

Ana was standing with her arms folded, staring at the floor, hearing him out.

'You promised before,' she murmured. It was almost a whisper.

'Ana, please can we start again?'

She looked at him. Those big brown eyes that she liked so much were imploring her, but she hardened her heart.

'What – so you can just go and get drunk and sleep with more girls?'

Tipper looked wildly from side to side, as if to show there were no girls.

'Girls?' he said. 'What girls?'

'You know.'

'Jesus, I don't! I don't have a clue what you're talking about.'

Briskly Ana crossed to a chair where her bag was lying. She pulled out her phone and scrolled through the menus until she got what she wanted. She held it up in front of Tipper's face.

64

Tipper took the phone from Ana's hand and looked at the image on the screen. Then he looked at Ana. His mind was racing. Jesus! What the fuck was this? It couldn't be right. When was it taken? Who took it?

'Scroll down,' ordered Ana. 'There's more.'

Moments later Tipper knew the depth and extent of his disgrace. But he had no recollection of a blonde girl doing that to him.

'Ana,' he said. 'I don't know anything about this. I swear! Where the hell did you get these pictures from?'

'They were sent through to my phone – that phone. The night you got drunk. Do you think I'm stupid? You are not saying that this is not you?'

'Well, obviously it is, but I don't know anything about it. It must have been done when I was asleep. I passed out, Ana.'

'Just look at what you're doing with her.'

'But, Jesus, don't you see? I was legless. I can't remember anything like this happening. I must have been set up. I was stitched up with drugs, I do know that.'

He handed the phone back to Ana and covered his face with his hands. When he took them away, Lara had wandered back into the room with Mr Sponge Bob. At the same time the baby started bawling from a room down the hall. Ana stooped and picked Lara up.

'Tipper, please leave now,' she said. 'This isn't getting us anywhere. I don't want a scene. It's not fair.'

The screaming baby – the baby Ana wouldn't explain – was too much for Tipper. The whole thing was too complicated for him.

'Jesus, I'll go,' he said. 'But I'm coming back, with whoever it was that took these pictures. They're bullshit, you know. Total bullshit.'

He wanted to say something to Lara but instead it was the child who spoke.

'Our baby's crying,' she said simply. 'You woke him up.'

Our baby! It was the final knife into Tipper.

Tipper stormed out of the apartment. Ana's head was spinning. She left Lara to her own devices and went to comfort the baby. But they really were finished now. She'd done the right thing, she kept telling herself, not telling him the truth about their baby.

Carter was still lurking in the bus shelter when

Tipper came out. Tipper didn't see him; he wasn't seeing anything much as he slumped into the back of the car.

Tipper felt stricken. The last time he'd known such total desolation was when Mr Power had told him that his mother was dead. He felt like his insides had been ripped out. Ana had found herself another man. And she'd already had a baby with him. Tipper ground his teeth and made fists of his hands. He pounded his thigh. Only the presence of the driver stopped him screaming.

'Could you take me to Newmarket?' he asked, his voice shaking.

Tipper was not wearing the face of a man who'd won the Dewhurst the day before when he walked into the pub.

Johnny the Fish was no-one's fool. 'Cuh! Here comes trouble,' he whispered to Shelley, who didn't bother to catch Tipper's eye.

'So! The conquering hero returns,' the Fish blustered. 'Well done old chap. What will it be?'

'It'll be a word in the office, Johnny,' Tipper replied coldly. The Fish had never seen his favourite Irishman like this before.

'What seems to be on your mind, young Tipper?' Johnny enquired, when he had closed the office door behind them.

'Photographs. That's what's on my focking mind. Photographs that Ana's just shown me. They're of me on a bed with those two girls that were here that night – the night I spent here, before the police came busting in. What the fock's been going on Johnny? Who's behind this?'

Johnny the Fish scratched his forehead.

'What do you mean, Tipper? What photos?'

'Photos of me. Passed out on the bed. With fock all on.'

'Tipper I was out cold myself. I don't know anything about this.'

'Well where did those girls come from? I bloody well need to find them. And fast.'

'I swear Tipper on my spaniel's life that I'd never seen those bints before and never since. I thought you knew them.'

'Me? I never saw them in my life.'

Johnny the Fish swirled the whisky around in his glass and looked Tipper straight in the face.

'I think I may know who's at the bottom of this,' he said slowly. 'But you're going to have to promise me that what I'm about to say didn't come from me.'

'Of course Johnny,' Tipper promised.

'Well I always did wonder why Nico happened to drop in that night. The drugs? The girls? That's all I'm going to say.'

Johnny got up from his chair and shuffled towards the door.

'I think this calls for a family-sized,' he announced.

422

65

Tipper was still at boiling point when he got back into his chauffer-driven Merc. Nico, he thought to himself. The man that knows everyone. Tipper flipped opened his mobile and found his number.

'Ah! The great jockey,' Nico oozed sycophantically. 'Everything go well today I trust?'

'No Nico. You trust wrong. And you can cut the bullshit. What do you know about those two girls that were at the Partridge the night before I got arrested?'

'Sorry Tipper. I don't know what you are talking about.'

'You sure you don't?'

Nico went on the offensive fast. 'Of course I'm sure,' he lied. 'Tipper I should be very careful if I were you. Just remember who we work for. I can either choose to help you or not. I can be your friend or your enemy. But don't think you can blame me if you go around getting drunk and messing up your life.'

There was a cold threat in Nico's words that stopped Tipper in his tracks. He didn't need reminding who he worked for, and he had no proof.

'So I take it the meeting with Ana didn't go well?' Nico asked.

'Too focking right it didn't,' Tipper confirmed. 'I've been stitched up. I'm going to have to stay here and sort it out.'

'What d'you mean, stay here?'

'I'll go over to France to ride Citizen. But I'm not going back to Moscow without Ana.'

'Well I don't think General Shalakov will be happy about that, Tipper.'

'Well Nico,' Tipper said firmly. 'That's where I am. What'll he do? Kidnap me?'

'Look Tipper,' Nico said smoothly. 'Don't say anything rash. Let's see what I can do.'

'Well, apart from finding those girls and getting them to come clean I don't—'

Nico cut him short. 'Tipper, I will deal with this. I've got to go now. I'll get back to you.'

66

Under cover of darkness, Dermot O'Callaghan slipped into the mansion at the top of Warren Hill, Newmarket, that Wang Chung had bought from the Maktoums.

O'Callaghan liked to keep himself to himself. He spent half the year in America, mostly on the golf course, and half in Ireland or London. When he'd hit the jackpot with his software translating business, the first property that he'd bought had been a stud farm in Ireland, the land of his birth. He let his horses do the talking on the track and quite often never even got to see them run. But that didn't mean his finger wasn't on the pulse. He was happy to throw plenty of money at blood-stock, but he was a businessman first and a lover of horses second. A love that came from his Irish blood. But, if he was going to continue to invest in racehorses, he wanted to see there was, in theory at least, a chance of some return on his capital.

Wang Chung had sold off a sizeable percentage of his cargo fleet to Sheikh Maktoum in exchange for the Sheikh's bloodstock empire. The deal had suited the long-term aims of both parties. For the Sheikh it guaranteed business for the deep-water port he was developing in Dubai. Meanwhile Wang Chung had seen the potential of gambling in China, but had long been frustrated that horse racing there was restricted to his own home base of Hong Kong. He was working on the problem politically, and this exchange ensured he would be ready to flood mainland China with quality bloodstock as soon as his political allies thought the time right to make gambling on horses legal across the country.

So although Chung and O'Callaghan had different perspectives on the same market, they had the same objective at heart: to protect the value of their investments. And they recognized there was one prime threat to the interests of them both, who went by the name of Stanislav Shalakov.

It was clear from his public rantings that Shalakov's game would be to produce world-beating colts, and that these would then enable him to corner the stallion market. That was no surprise. Annual earnings from stallions mating with the twenty thousand mares in Western Europe were roughly three hundred million pounds, and Chung and O'Callaghan's stallions were covering sixty per cent of the mares!

In 1981 a little horse in Kentucky called

Northern Dancer had been able to earn his owners a million dollars every time he mated with a mare, which he did forty times a year. Chung and O'Callaghan didn't have a stallion that could command such a fee – those days were long gone – but the gap was made up by modern science and the aeroplane. The scientists could maintain the stallions' potency and at the same time predict practically to the nearest hour when a mating would be most likely to result in pregnancy. Air travel allowed their stallions to cover successfully more than a hundred mares in the covering seasons of both the northern and the southern hemispheres.

Wang Chung and O'Callaghan were well aware of the potential threat of Citizen. If he won the Derby and the St James's Palace stakes as a three-year-old, the asset columns on their balance sheets were going to take a big hit. But Citizen was only one extraordinary individual and, under normal circumstances, Chung and O'Callaghan might have been relaxed about the appearance of such a freak and taken the hit. But these were not normal circumstances. The real danger was that a critical mass of Russian winners would appear in the wake of Citizen's overwhelming success on the track. If O'Callaghan's and Chung's colts went on being trashed by the Russians on the course, they would be worth nothing like their former value when they retired to stud. Something had to be done.

* * *

O'Callaghan took his shoes off on the mat by the door and chose the most elaborate slippers that were lined up beside it. The butler nodded approvingly.

'Very good choice sir,' he observed, and led O'Callaghan into an enormous open plan room that was divided up by long, low leather sofas.

Wang Chung stood up when O'Callaghan came through the door and walked towards him. For a Chinese to invite a foreigner into his home was a significant honour. Since the Cultural Revolution in China, Westerners were not invited to visit Chinese homes, lest the hosts be suspected of plotting against communism and of being imperialist running-dogs. Restaurants were where one entertained and met such strangers and, even though Chung was now in England, he was old-school and old-school habits die hard. But now the gravity of the situation required Wang Chung to display his trust in O'Callaghan – a gesture O'Callaghan was worldly enough to appreciate. The Irishman bowed from the neck.

'Mr Wang, I'm honoured to be received by you in your home. I thank you.'

Chung returned the bow.

'It is my privilege, Mr O'Callaghan. I am grateful to you for coming. We have a matter of great importance to discuss. First though, will you have some tea with me?'

O'Callaghan admired the elaborate Chinese teapot and miniature cups laid out on the low ornate table. He wasn't a social tea drinker, but then this wasn't a party.

'That would be very nice. Thank you.'

They sat for a minute in contemplative silence sipping tea. Then, with careful precision, Wang Chung replaced his cup on the table and got down to business.

'So we have a difficulty?'

O'Callaghan drained his own tea.

'I'm afraid so,' he said. 'I've talked to my technical people, Mr Wang, and they think this is undoubtedly a serious problem. It concerns the whole industry.'

'Please, call me Chung. May I call you Der-mot? We have been bidding against each other for long enough, I think, and you are right. Now we should stand together. But how big is this problem?'

'Well, at the moment the main thing is that the testers can't detect what Shalakov's people are using. Either it's invisible to all known tests, or he's getting it out of the horse's system before samples are taken. Whichever is the case, if he goes on doing it, we won't produce a single really commercial stallion between us. We have to expose him.'

'Are you sure he will succeed?'

'Sure we're sure. Did you see the colt at Newmarket? Even his tail had muscles. I've never seen anything like it. And he tried to savage my runner-up. Whatever the jungle juice is that they're using, it works.'

'Then we must have tests that can reveal whatever substance is being used.'

'We're working on it. The trouble is there's more money in cheating than there is in catching. I just don't know how far behind them the testing guys are. Some of them have a dangerous habit of thinking they are little gods who can see anything. So, if they can't see something, there must be nothing there.'

'So what can we do, Der-mot?'

'Well, Chung, it seems to me we've got to get inside their camp.'

'I think that will be difficult with the Russians.'

'It's worse than difficult. It's impossible, with the Russians. But not necessarily with the Irish. We just may have a way in. Let me explain . . .'

67

Citizen went to France a week later to complete the highly unusual Group One double at St Cloud racecourse, easily beating the best of the French two-year-olds. By ten lengths. Shalakov told the post-race press conference that his champion colt's next run would be in the Derby at Epsom the following June, after his winter break in Russia.

Nico had been in the General's party at the races; but Tipper hadn't spoken to him since the bad-tempered phone call he'd made from the Partridge car park. Tipper now deeply distrusted Nico. He knew he was no ally of his. But a note came into the weighing room inviting him to join Nico that night for dinner at a fashionable restaurant on the Île St Louis.

After a long consultation with the waiter, Nico ordered food for them both, before turning to business. He didn't mince his words.

'General Shalakov says you must return with

Citizen to Russia, Tipper. No more of this absurd idea of staying in England.'

Tipper frowned.

'But I need to know who set me up and destroyed my relationship with Ana. I want some answers.'

'You'll get them. But it's not General Shalakov's fault that Ana doesn't want to come to Moscow. Why should his interests suffer because of that? You work for him, you must do your job. He can look for the two scrubbers that framed you, but only on condition that you come back to work.'

'How do I know he'll find them?'

'You don't. He'll try. And he'll keep an eye on Ana for you too; and make sure little Lara's all right. When you win the Derby on Citizen; well, that might bring Ana back. Women love winners, Tipper. They *don't* like losers.'

Nico was right. If he destroyed his career now, he'd never get Ana back.

'All right,' he said, 'I'll go back.'

Tipper had been back in Moscow for a couple of weeks when Sam rang him.

'I've some really great news for you, boy,' Sam announced. 'I'm coming out to see you. Thought I'd treat myself to a weekend city-break in Moscow.'

It was not Tipper's idea of 'really great news'. That would have been Ana contacting him. The suspicion that she had another man had grown into a near-certainty now. But there was still space in his head for the tiny possibility that he was wrong. But all the same Tipper was delighted that Sam was coming over.

'When are you coming, my man?'

'This weekend, boy. I've got a bit of time off so I thought I'd come and chase some of those Russian girls.'

He told Tipper the name of his hotel.

'I saw on the Internet there's a club called Night Vision next door. We can meet there.'

'I know it. Jesus, it's a terrible place. Full of whores.'

'Bring 'em on, boy! And we can see the Celtic game there, right?'

Tipper had winced when Sam suggested meeting at Night Vision. But it was the best place to watch a game, and Celtic were on a roll.

Night Vision was everything Sam had hoped it would be. The bar stools were soft, padded leather. The carpets were a deep crimson. The walls were covered in velvet. And the girls were sexy and available.

'Jesus. This is my sort of place,' he told Tipper with a big, sly grin on his face. 'Some mares in here, alright.'

A couple of the mares were making their way past the table. They looked as expensive as the club.

'That blonde one's eyeing me up, Tipper. I reckon she fancies me.'

'Sam, for fock's sake grow up. None of them fancy you. They just want your money! They're a desperate carry-on. Keep clear of them if you've got any sense. They'll take the shirt off your back.'

'Yeah, well, that was sort of what I had in mind, you know? D'you think these girls have any of those disco biscuits on them?'

'Don't even think about it Sam,' Tipper snapped. 'They probably put weed killer in those things over here.'

Sam had been planning to get a few drinks into Tipper, and was disappointed to find him ordering coke.

'Let me get you a proper drink,' he suggested.

'Given up, thanks. I know what I'm like. If I only start, I won't stop.'

Tipper being sober would make Sam's task that much more difficult, but he had to try.

'How's Citizen?' he asked. 'Will he make a three year old?'

'With a bit of luck. I'd say we've got your lot worried shitless by now.'

Sam had been given the link he needed. He took the plunge.

'Tipper, they reckon he must be on something. He looks so strong, and he behaved like a nutter at Newmarket.'

Tipper shook his head.

'He's clean. They've never found anything in him.'

Sam leaned forward, light from the TV monitor fixed to the table flickering on side of his face.

'Well, look, I've been asked to make you an offer.'

'*You* have?'

'I have. O'Callaghan's jockey is retiring at the end of the season. The boss says the job's yours if you can find out what they're using on Citizen.'

Tipper shook his head as he glanced at the screen.

'Impossible,' he said. 'The horse can't be on anything. They keep testing him – no result. Jesus, will you look at that? Celtic have scored.'

Sam ignored the screen at the end of the table.

'Tipper, they only test after racing. The horse isn't going to race until the spring. Now look at these.'

He reached a slim plastic case from his pocket and pushed it across the table. Tipper opened it and saw a pair of plastic hypodermic syringes wrapped in polythene.

'Jesus, Sam, what's the fock's these?'

'They're for you to take blood samples out of Citizen during the winter. Surely you could manage that? They're fitted with very fine needles, so they don't leave a trace.'

Tipper looked anxiously around the garish room, filled with its cacophonous noises and flickering with lights from its scores of screens.

'Jesus, are you on something, or what?' he

435

whispered urgently. 'For fock's sake put them away. This guy Shalakov would string me up if he found me with them. You remember that blood-stock agent that got it in Thailand?'

Sam covered the needles with his hand.

'Nobody knows for sure who did that. The guy was a pervert. He was involved in a paeodophile ring. Look, we can fly you out of here any time, only get us a sample of blood, or find out what the hell is going on. O'Callaghan will guarantee you'll be safe.'

'Forget it. Even the stuff I do know, I can't tell you about. I'd never be safe from a guy like Shalakov. If he couldn't find me, he'd hurt Ana and Lara.'

Tipper didn't tell Sam about the second baby, or the other man in Ana's life.

'Tipper,' Sam persisted, 'O'Callaghan is one hell of a good guy to work for. You'll never get another offer like this in your life. All you need do is just find out what they're giving him.'

Tipper stared into his glass of coke for a minute while Sam watched the Celtic game.

'Look Sam,' he finally said, looking up. 'It's tempting, the O'Callaghan job. So I'll think about it.'

Sam pushed the syringes under his hand towards Tipper.

'Take these, then.'

'All right. But I can't promise. It might not be possible.'

Tipper slid the syringes off the table and slipped them into his pocket.

'Can we watch the game now?'

Lying in bed that night, Tipper thought deeply about the conversation. O'Callaghan's offer of a job was a hell of a good one. If he accepted he could be back near Ana and Lara. Maybe even with them, because perhaps – just perhaps – she didn't have another man.

On top of that, working for O'Callaghan could potentially make him the most famous jockey in England. It would make him rich, and free of bloody Moscow. Maybe it wouldn't be all that difficult to find out what they were giving Citizen at Xanadu. Perhaps, when no one was looking, he would be able to sneak some blood out of the horse for O'Callaghan's scientists to test.

Then he remembered the CCTV, and the security goons everywhere. He pictured Shalakov kicking the shit out of the groom with broken ribs. And he thought about Shaunsheys. Perhaps it was all moonshine and Jameson wasn't using drugs at all. It could all be down to the chamber and the atmosphere-controlled stabling. Maybe he should just tell Sam about that, and get the hell out. But if he did that, there was still the chance that Shalakov would hunt him down and Ana and Lara too. He'd be able to run, but not hide – not if he was working for O'Callaghan. Tipper didn't sleep too well that night.

68

Captain Maine rather enjoyed the British Racing Board's annual awards, held in the Savoy hotel that year. A certain amount of reflected glory came his way through Citizen, who was International Two-Year-Old of the Year. An appreciable number of guests nodded in his direction when the winner was announced.

After what he saw as the Newmarket crowd's indifference to him, Shalakov stayed away. So big, so tough, so ugly and yet so vain, reflected Maine. In his absence Sinclair gave a cringe-inducing acceptance speech.

'My lords, ladies and gentleman. It's nice to be back. In triumph.' He paused for the applause, but there wasn't any. 'It's not only Newmarket trainers that win these awards. Back in the spring I had every confidence that I'd be standing here tonight and I'm sure that I will do so this time next year. It is time for the world to realize that racing doesn't revolve solely around one little town.'

Most of the tables were occupied by groups of Newmarket people, who hadn't come along to hear their town insulted. Soon background whispering had swollen to something like an approaching storm. But Sinclair was oblivious and took the ironic cheering that came when he at last sat down as a sign of his popularity.

Maine stayed at the Turf Club and had a lazy morning in the Reading Room. He'd always felt at peace with the world when slumped in one of the deep leather armchairs, surrounded by plenty to read and the room's deep hush, underscored by the distant booming of the hall porter as he greeted arrivals, and the gentle drone of traffic along the Mall.

Maine had invited Barry Phillips to lunch. He didn't know Phillips, but the retired scientist had been recommended for his bottomless knowledge of veterinary pharmacology. Sipping his Bloody Mary in the bar Maine winced a bit when Breakwell, the junior hall porter, ushered Phillips in. It was those brown shoes. But at least he had a tie on, and a suit too, albeit cheap and brownish in colour. They shook hands.

'Mr Phillips, how nice. What can I get you to drink?'

'One of those tomato juices that you're drinking, thank you.'

'It isn't *exactly* tomato juice. There's Tabasco, Worcester sauce, lemon juice and horseradish. Oh, yes, and plenty of vodka and sherry.'

'Christ, no, I'll be pissed,' Phillips said loudly enough for Brian the barman to cough.

Phillips was going to stand out like a particularly sore thumb. Maine knew he should have taken him to Whites.

'Just straight tomato juice, please Brian,' Maine requested with a nervous smile.

They exchanged small-talk as they drank. The bar had begun to fill up with members. After five minutes Maine suggested they go up to the dining room.

'By the way, Barry,' he added, 'we're not really allowed to talk shop in the club, so we'll have to keep our voices down, if that's alright. I'm fascinated to hear what you've got to tell me.'

Phillips, on the other hand, was interested in the décor.

'What a very nice collection of portraits.'

'Yes. All departed members. Half of them died for their country, and the other half were dead broke. Cleaned out by their bookmakers.'

'I don't have much success myself. I'm buggered if I can back a winner. Got any tips?'

'Good lord no. No betting for me, given my job. But Grace, the head porter is happy to divulge that Alfie Bradstock will ride the winner in the last at Leicester today.'

'That's very nice of him,' Phillips smiled, beginning to feel more at home.

Maine led the way briskly across the marble hallway and up the wide staircase. At the dining room door they met the club secretary, who raised an eyebrow at Phillips's attire. Maine's rubicund complexion darkened a bit and he headed for a remote table by the kitchen door, where few liked sitting.

They settled down and ordered. Phillips had soup and white fish; Maine devilled kidneys and grouse.

'Been looking forward to one of these,' he told his guest. 'Never got to December before without having a grouse, but believe it or not they're completely unobtainable in Russia. Staggering, isn't it? Now, a drop of Chablis before we crack into the claret?'

'That'd be very nice.'

Barry Phillips was quite enjoying himself. Everything was very nice.

'So Barry,' said Maine in a subdued voice, when the wine was poured. 'What can you tell me?'

Phillips's voice was a shade louder, but within the boundaries of confidentiality.

'Well, I've had an ask-around, and the general feeling is that they may be using a variety of things. And it's probably things that work in such a way that makes them especially hard to detect.'

'How d'you mean?'

'In the old days drug cheats would administer anabolic steroids, equine growth hormone or EPO Cera, say. And those drugs would create a change in the body: steroids make a horse put on more muscle; growth hormone allows it to

441

regenerate tissue more quickly, which meant it could be trained harder; and EPO Cera stimulates the production of red blood cells. Now, those drugs are quite easy to test for. But the new drugs work in a different way. They change the way the horse's own systems work. Put another way, they get the horse to dope itself.'

'I'm with you so far. Just.'

'I can't talk about Russia, but most commonly used in the UK right now is stuff that works on the horse's joints – specifically the knees and ankles. It antagonizes the joints' pain receptors, and the horse will push itself harder because it doesn't feel any soreness.'

'Running through the pain barrier, eh?'

'Well, not really. There is no pain, so the barrier goes.'

'Hmm. I see what you mean. The horse I'm thinking of, which shall be nameless, certainly doesn't *appear* to feel any pain. What else is around?'

'The Anti-Inhibitor. Clever, this one. In a healthy body the release of growth hormone is naturally restricted to what is needed – it is inhibited. The substance I'm talking about – we don't know exactly what it is – blocks this process. The animal then produces much more growth hormone, speeding up its metabolism and bulking up the body. As this is the horse's *own* growth hormone, it can't fail an artificial drugs test.'

'Can't they test for this substance that makes it happen – the Anti-Inhibitor?'

'Not without knowing what it is. That's the problem.'

Maine's grouse arrived sitting on a throne of fried bread that had soaked up the juice from the bird as it was flashed in and out of the oven. Maine cut into the breast and peered expertly at the evidence.

'Look at that. Marvellous. How's your cod?'

'Very nice, thank you. And I'm glad to say cod stocks have recovered pretty well, now that the Spanish aren't hoovering the bloody lot out of the sea.'

'Exactly. Never had a problem like that with grouse. It's probably the most carefully conserved wild bird on the planet.'

Maine waited while the claret was poured and, as the sommelier moved off to another table, dragged his guest back to the matter in hand.

'Anything else?'

'Oh yes. Stem cells.'

'What's wrong with stem cells? Marvellous things, so I've read. They're using them to mend people's spinal cords and horse's tendons and what-not. What's wrong with them?'

Phillips held up his fork for emphasis.

'It depends where you put them. Think about this. Just suppose they've taken some bone marrow out of this horse of yours.'

'Who shall be nameless.'

'Of course. So they've taken some bone marrow out of him and harvested the stem cells and treated

443

them in a test tube with growth factors and hormones. They could then inject those cells into certain tissue so that they grow as that tissue. If they inject them into the horse's heart, he ends up with a bigger, stronger heart. Or they could inject it into the spleen which would get bigger and make more red blood cells. But I'm not so sure about that one, because red blood cells are already in plentiful supply. But you get my drift.'

'Yes, but my God, how are we going to test for that?'

'You can't. Clever isn't it?'

After lunch, Maine walked Barry Phillips up to Knightsbridge tube station. He'd overdone the stilton and needed to stretch his legs. He should have pulled up stumps after the treacle pudding and double cream, but it wasn't every day that he got a chance to drink Taylor's 1963 port, and what was better than a slice or two of stilton to wash it down with?

'I'll have tea in the reading room,' he told Grace, after his stroll. 'Give me a shake at five if I've nodded off, will you?'

Fifteen minutes later he let the newspaper fall to his knees as his eyelids drooped. But then, as sometimes happens on the edge of sleep, something sparked in his brain and he was wide awake again. David Sinclair! Tipper O'Reilly! Fighting Talk! The three names were chasing themselves around in his head. If he couldn't get much further with the pharmacology of the problem, he could attack it from another angle – through the men recruited by Shalakov to train and ride Citizen. How honest were they? Had they previously been corrupt? The key to both these questions was, of course, the Fighting Talk case.

Suddenly full of energy, Maine sprang from his chair, went directly to the phone booth in the hall, where mobile phone calls were permitted, and keyed in the number of the English Racing Board. He urgently needed to speak to an old friend.

Jim Jones had served as a senior NCO under Maine in the Guards. They'd been together in more than a few dodgy situations in Iraq, but now Jones had done his twelve years and, with Maine's help, had been appointed an investigator with the Racing Board's Disciplinary Unit. The morning after his lunch at the Turf Club with Barry Phillips, Maine went along to see his former Sergeant.

'You're looking well, Jones. How's it going?'

'Good, sir. Not quite the Regiment, but we get by.'

They exchanged some regimental gossip and then Maine glanced around the open-plan office to make sure he would not be overheard. He lowered his voice.

'Tell me, Jones. The Tipper O'Reilly/Fighting Talk inquiry. What was the score there?'

Jones hesitated then tipped his head towards an empty corner office, which had glass walls but also, crucially, a door. They went inside and Jones shut the door.

'It was very strange,' he said. 'We had a pretty solid tip-off and, on the day, the jockey O'Reilly was bang to rights. Everyone he phoned that morning had laid the horse, and made quite a few quid. But then a few months ago upstairs told us the case was closed.'

'What was the original tip-off?'

'Phone call. Before the race. We recorded it as a matter of routine. The unidentified male caller told us O'Reilly was going to stop Fighting Talk.'

'Hmmm. Really. I don't suppose you have a copy of the recording to hand do you?'

'Well sir. The regulations are very tight here, but . . .'

Captain Maine was probably the only man in the world Jones would have trusted with the recording of that phone call. And the case was closed anyway. So Maine walked out with a CD in his pocket.

69

Ana replayed in her head again and again the shock that had been in Tipper's eyes when he'd seen the images of him and the girl on the bed. His shock had been for real. And she didn't think it was just because she was confronting him with them. She was now almost certain that he really didn't know anything about what the girl had been doing to him. He could have been unconscious.

Ana now had to think how she'd play Carter. She wanted to put him at ease so his watchfulness would lapse.

'Alan, I really don't blame you,' she told him. 'You are just doing your job. And you were amazing when the baby came. Don't worry, I won't be any trouble. After all I couldn't go far with two kids.'

Carter seemed to accept that Ana wasn't about to do a bunk. But she needed to make one, quick trip. She wanted to see Johnny the Fish in person. It would be important to see his reaction when she confronted him with the evidence. And that couldn't be done on the phone.

The next day she had the baby and Lara ready and, as soon as Carter had gone out, she hurried round to the local mini cab office. It was going to cost her, but this was more important than money and she couldn't face the train with the kids.

'Newmarket please,' she told the surprised driver.

Walking into the Partridge with a babe in arms and a toddler was daunting for Ana. Luckily the place was virtually empty when she got there, at eleven thirty in the morning.

The Fish was having a nip of sherry at his table in the corner, while he worked out his selections for the racing that afternoon.

'Cuh, here comes trouble,' he whispered to himself, as he saw Ana walking into the bar. But he put on his most charming smile.

'Hello my dear. Ana, isn't it? What a lovely surprise.'

The Fish had the odd fault here and there, but his manners were impeccable. Ana had rarely been in the Partridge, but she knew exactly who Johnny the Fish was. He had a face that one would recognize in a crowd, and he was looking particularly reptilian that morning.

'Could I have a word in private, please?' Ana asked, as she approached him.

'Of course, my dear. Come into the snug. Coffee?'

'No thank you. I'm not thirsty.'

Lara wandered across to the snug window and looked out as Johnny the Fish closed the door.

'So, what can I do for you?'

'It's about those girls that were here with Tipper.'

'Girls? Now you know that was all very unfair. I can vouch for Tipper. He was an innocent victim. Pure as newly fallen snow.'

'How do you know that?'

'Yes, well, you see . . . one of the girls told me. Yes. That's right. One of them confessed. It was what we call a stitch-up. They were paid to do it. I don't know who paid them, or indeed why, but one of them confessed all to yours truly. Tipper was drugged. Your man is innocent. That is all I know – maybe you know more.'

Ana considered. The Fish sounded deeply sincere, but could she trust him?

'So where are these girls? I need to speak to them.'

'A lot of people want to find them. It's not been possible I'm afraid. No one has the slightest idea where they've gone.'

Ana looked at him without expression. She felt he was telling the truth.

'And you really have no idea who did it? Who paid them?'

The Fish showed her the palms of his hands.

'No, as I said, I haven't a notion. And given who's employing him now, I don't want to have one either.'

The conversation went round in circles for a while, until Ana looked anxiously at her watch. The mini-cab driver was counting the minutes.

'I've come all this way and that's all you can tell me. Oh well, now we have to go.'

Within a minute she and the children were gone. The Fish topped up his sherry and went back to the runners in the 4.20 at Ripon. She's rather a sweet little thing when her dander's up, he thought to himself.

On the way back to London Ana felt a very strange mixture of emotions. She was no closer to finding the girl photographed with Tipper. But she didn't need to now. It was a set up. And Tipper was innocent of doing anything. She believed Johnny on that. But she was still at her wits' end. If Tipper knew that Ana had never come clean as to why she'd been in Newmarket in the first place, he'd probably never trust her. The boot was now on the other foot.

She bitterly regretted now not telling Tipper the baby was his. She'd really messed things up on all fronts. Her life had been destroyed, mainly by Shalakov, but she'd contributed by being over-hasty and stupid not trusting Tipper. She wanted to scream. She wanted to cry. But she didn't. She had to put a brave face on for Lara.

It wasn't until he'd flown back to Moscow that Maine learned of the English Racing Board's new rule. It stated: 'any horse that is intended to race in the United Kingdom, in whatever country or

450

jurisdiction, should be available at all times to be tested by English Racing Board officials'. This was an unprecedented move. Never before had any authority claimed the right to test horses trained outside its domain. The rule was blatantly aimed at Citizen.

Captain Maine was not best pleased at what he felt was a slight on his own administration. To make matters worse, he was summoned to a meeting in the Kremlin with the Russian Minister of Agriculture. The message, delivered with a charming smile, was that Maine would now be held personally responsible for anything that threatened Citizen's career. The horse had become the nation's standard-bearer, to be protected at all costs from outside forces.

Maine had visions of himself trapped in No Man's Land, being shot at from both sides. Only a year or so before, he'd been told to keep all racehorses in Moscow clean. Now he was charged with protecting one potentially dirty horse from any testing – a complete reversal of policy. Of course while Citizen was at Xanadu he would be anything but available to the English testers and, as such, would have to be scratched from all races in the United Kingdom. If that happened, there would be no Derby for him, and no Royal Ascot. In which case Shalakov would certainly see to it that Maine's career as a racing administrator came to an abrupt end.

Maine called Felix Webb to say he'd consider

it a favour if he were given prior warning of a visit by British testers to Russia. In the meantime, he was determined to pursue his own enquiries into the men surrounding Citizen. In particular, he intended to follow up a hunch he had about the anonymous tip-off the Racing Board received prior to Fighting Talk's debacle at Chester.

First he rang Sinclair as a courtesy – so he said – to alert him to the new testing rule. He failed to mention he was recording the conversation. Afterwards he played it back, complete with Sinclair's expostulations about the outrageousness of the rule. Then he contacted a man he had met casually at the races a few months earlier, a former KGB operative with interesting contacts. Did Ivan know of any voice-recognition experts, Maine asked? Specifically ones who could analyse voices speaking in English. The Cold War had produced several such specialists, Ivan told him. For a small fee, he would be happy to act as courier for any material that required analysis. There would be no questions asked.

It took a few days for the report to come back. It said that a naïve effort had been made by the informant on Jones's recording to disguise his voice, but Maine's hunch had nevertheless been right. It was Sinclair's.

Confronted with the unequivocal evidence, Maine thought for the first time about the implications. Sinclair had known Fighting Talk was going to lose at Chester, despite being a hot favourite. His call to the Racing Board could not have been because he really thought Tipper O'Reilly was going to stop the horse. If that had worried him, he would have simply got another jockey. He must have got Tipper to ride the horse and then made his call to the Disciplinary Unit specifically to land him in trouble. And now they were colleagues together in Russia. Maine couldn't see the sense in it.

Sam was constantly texting Tipper, begging him to get a sample of Citizen's blood, but Tipper hesitated. He had too much to lose if he was caught. And his mind hardened against the plan anyway, when he received another text message from a phone whose identity was withheld. It removed the point of his going back. In fact, it ripped the guts out of him.

tipper . . . leave us alone . . . ana.

A few minutes later, in London, Ana opened a text-message of her own. Again, the number of the sender was not given. She glanced through the message, then shut her eyes tight. But it was as if the words were printed on the inside of her eyelids –

ana . . . you used me . . . good riddance to you . . . tipper

70

Over the winter that followed, Tipper tried to forget Ana by focusing his energies on Citizen. From time to time he wondered whether the horse was just a precocious two-year-old who, by the time the Derby came round in June, would be caught up by other, later-maturing types. But, after he rode him in his first major gallop at the training track that spring, his fears evaporated. Citizen had simply flown, shredding his own time trial records from the year before. Citizen was back, and he was faster and tougher than ever.

Following the Racing Board's decision about international testing, the question of when to bring the horse to Moscow from Xanadu had become urgent.

'He's registered as being Moscow-trained,' Maine told Sinclair. 'If he's at Xanadu when the testers arrive looking for him here, they'll throw him out of the Derby, and any other race in England.'

'They can't do that,' Sinclair protested. 'They'd be behaving like communists.'

'Probably best if you don't go around saying that, David.'

'Bloody cheek. Anyway, they wouldn't find anything.'

Maine didn't comment on the ambiguity of the remark.

'In that case,' he said, 'you have nothing to fear. Bring him back to Moscow.'

'The snow hasn't melted yet. In Xanadu we have facilities—'

'I have an excellent all-weather gallop, David.'

Given the large number of weekend race meetings in the UK, Sinclair reckoned it was unlikely that English testers could be spared for a foray to Moscow on Saturday or Sunday. So, as long as Citizen's weekdays were spent in Moscow, it would be safe to return him to Xanadu on Sundays.

Shalakov meanwhile was making double sure. He had Webb's name, and that of all his known colleagues, placed on a red alert warning system at Passport Control. None of them would be able to step off an aeroplane on a Saturday or Sunday without immigration officials immediately embarking on a minute scrutiny of their visas – a process guaranteed to last until Monday morning. The only element of risk lay in the arrival of a previously unknown tester. But Shalakov had other means at his disposal for dealing with such surprises.

*　　*　　*

455

Sinclair started the spring, as he had ended the autumn, by galloping Citizen beyond all known limits. Tipper just couldn't believe what he was doing with the horse. He well knew that the St James's Palace Stakes, over the distance of a mile, requires a high cruising speed through the whole race. So the training work should be in short, very sharp bursts. The Derby, run over a mile and a half, needed more than sustained speed. It was won by horses with a rare combination of agility to stay out of trouble in a rough race, acceleration to get into and hold a decent running position and, finally, stamina to see out the longer trip. Derby horses are probably born with the first two qualities, but they have to be worked in the right way to build their stamina.

Sinclair, however, seemed to be training Citizen for the Royal Ascot race and the Derby at the same time – one week like a miler and the next back to longer, steadier work. When Tipper questioned this, Sinclair said blandly.

'Well, of course I'm training him for both races. He's going to run in both races. And don't worry about over-work. The kriotherapy chamber lets his muscles recover so quickly there's no harm done.'

Tipper couldn't see any way of finding out if there was any test-tube assistance to all this. Sticking one of Sam's syringes into Citizen to extract some blood was just too risky. The needles Sam gave him may have been extra-fine, but they would surely still leave a mark for all to see. And it wasn't that easy for an untrained person to do, especially with an unpredictable character like Citizen.

So while Sam kept texting and calling, Tipper kept stalling. He thought, perhaps, he'd spill some of the beans after the Derby – tell them about the cold chamber and the simulated altitude air. Just revealing that much, however, could make him a marked man. He'd just have to disappear. Maybe in County Cork. Shalakov wouldn't know where to look for him in Cork, and being on his own would help. Tipper had given up all ideas of Ana joining him.

Tipper had decided to keep a lid on the secrets he knew of Xanadu until after the Derby. But that didn't stop him checking every Monday for needle marks when Citizen got back from Xanadu. Two weeks ahead of the Derby, he was nearly caught.

'What are you doing?' boomed Sinclair's voice.

It was just before exercise. Citizen was still rugged up, and Tipper was running a finger along his jugular vein when Sinclair appeared. Tipper snatched his hand away.

'Jesus, Guvnor! I thought he'd a spot there. I was worried it might be ringworm. It'd be a disaster if he got that now.'

'He hasn't got bloody ringworm. Now come on, pull him out. Let's get on with some work.'

The incident underlined for Tipper the riskiness of attempting to get a blood sample. Sinclair, for

457

his part, had noted the way Tipper snatched his hand away from the place he'd been feeling on the horse's neck. It looked like a guilty movement. But surely Tipper wasn't fool enough to jeopardise the run in the Derby, was he? He wanted to win it, didn't he?

Sinclair was almost sure of it. But he was glad to know, nevertheless, that Shalakov still had tabs on Tipper's child. Whatever the jockey now thought of the woman, the little girl was still his weak spot. It was insurance, of a kind.

71

Derby Day had been moved that year back to its traditional spot, on the first Wednesday in June. The press coverage on Saturdays had been increasingly swamped by other sports. Now it was hoped to re-establish the event as a unique British occasion, a day so special that, in the past, even Parliament had suspended its sitting so that members could be there on Epsom Downs.

The race couldn't come quickly enough for Tipper. He knew Citizen was now twice the horse that had blown away the opposition in the Dewhurst. Bar a disaster, he would win again. But Tipper had one concern. Epsom is a hell of a noisy place on Derby Day: the fairground at the top of the home straight, the open-top buses full of screaming drunks, and the pop concert in the middle of the track, all roaring away even before the massive crowd had collectively opened its lungs. The biggest threat to Citizen winning the Derby was from himself. He might just get panicked by noise and excitement. He might boil over.

For two hundred years the Derby had been a day out for Londoners, nobles and commoners alike. But several years into the twenty-first century it looked and sounded more like a binge for the common men and women of Europe. The Eastern European girls had raised the bar considerably in the beauty stakes, and more and more of them were in the owners' enclosure, minimally clothed and fawning over their top-hatted escorts. These girls were not only beautiful, they were smart and ambitious. They loved to marry titles, as long as these came with money and real estate.

Compared to the purist Newmarket crowd, the euro-kids in the enclosures had a very different attitude to Citizen and Shalakov. The horse was one of their own. Like them, he was here to conquer, and they would not entertain the thought of his defeat. Accordingly they had loaded his broad back with their wagers.

Johnny the Fish, too, was there to cheer Citizen home. Clutching his betting slips from last autumn, he wandered from bar to bar, drinking heavily. After the Dewhurst Stakes he'd got ten to one for a horse that was now trading at six to four. His mind was empty and numb, unable to think about the enormity of his liabilities, or the scale of his possible winnings, should Citizen win.

* * *

It was a gloriously hot day. Sinclair wiped the sweat off his forehead as he came out of the weighing room with Tipper's saddle under his arm. Alison was hovering near the steps towards the saddling enclosure.

'Hello David,' she said, with a high, artificial giggle. 'I hope you realize, your horse will never get a mile and a half round Epsom. He wouldn't get the trip in a horse box.'

She was half cut, and reminded him of an over-packed bag of French onions. Her hair had become a strange shade of orange. Sinclair squinted at her.

'Alison. You seem somehow different . . .'

'God, David, you're looking awfully seedy these days,' she cut in, in a tone of mock concern.

Sinclair tried to think of a quick retort, but he wasn't very good at those. And at that particular moment he was more concerned about getting Citizen saddled up. So, without replying, he allowed himself to be separated from his ex-wife and carried off in the tidal-race of the moving crowd.

Tipper had alerted Sinclair to his fears about the noise and mayhem at Epsom, and proposed a simple solution. Ear plugs. Put some cotton wool in his ears, right?

Much as he hated the idea – not having thought of it himself – Sinclair agreed, and the ploy was working a treat. Citizen ambled round the paddock without a care in the world. The baying of the overheated multitude was nothing but a vague mumbling in his ears.

It would be even quieter down at the start – a haven of peace on the other side of Epsom Downs, half a mile from the stands. So Tipper did the opposite of his plan at Newmarket, and was first out of the paddock. Citizen's eyes were rolling around, taking in the vast partying crowd on the inside of the track. A revival concert by Atomic Kitten was thumping its mush out, but Citizen stayed calm. He seemed too busy checking out the rows-upon-rows of open-top buses parked tight up against the running rail to get stroppy.

Still, Tipper was a relieved man when they got safely to the start. Citizen agreed to be walked around in the shade of the trees and, even as his keyed-up rivals started to gather around him, he remained as meek as a child's pony. So far so good thought Tipper. The hardest part might be over.

Ana had not been able to stop herself from watching the race on television. Her heart was pounding almost at fast as Tipper's. She was gripping the sofa and tensing her legs, as if riding Citizen herself.

Eighteen runners had gone to post. Wang Chung had the third favourite, Shanghai, winner of the Chester Derby Trial. Dermot O'Callaghan had three runners in the race. His best chance looked to be Translation, winner of the first classic of the season, Newmarket's 2,000 Guineas. Translation had been favourite in the build-up to the race, but had now drifted to three-to-one second favourite behind

Citizen, who'd been backed on course by his fellow compatriots, as if defeat was impossible.

Citizen was in stall eighteen so that, when the gate sprang open, he would be on the extreme outside. Tipper was happy with that. He only had horses on his left to start with, meaning fewer traffic problems, and no opportunities for the other jockeys to box him in, or nail him up against the rails.

The first, furious half mile of the Derby is straight up a stiff climb. Then the track curves gently right-handed. Tipper had secured a position near the front of the field. So Citizen was able to go the shortest way round the first bend. But this meant, by the same token, he would be very wide out on the track as it snaked left handed towards Tattenham corner. Tipper used Citizen's size and speed to lean in on smaller, slower horses, pushing them towards the rails. He could hear aggrieved shouting as the other jockeys were squeezed concertina-like, bumping each other. But there was sod all they could do about it. Big horses often get unbalanced by the steep downhill bend round Tattenham Corner. Not Citizen. Sitting just behind a leading trio of runners, one of whom was Shanghai, he handled it as if on tramlines.

Keeping up a smooth rhythmical gallop, Tipper let his horse roll slightly wide as he swung round Tattenham Corner and into the straight. He hadn't forgotten their first race, and didn't want to hit the front too soon. Giving away a bit of ground was all right if it kept their momentum going. After entering the straight Tipper restrained Citizen and sat in fourth place. There was nothing upsides him on his left, so he took the opportunity of edging closer to the inside rail.

As Tipper concentrated on a smooth tempo, a couple of horses came past him, but he didn't panic. The second of them was Translation, his biggest threat. So he went to pull out in order to get in the O'Callaghan star's slipstream. But one of Translation's stable mates ranged up alongside to box him in behind the front horses. Suddenly Citizen was trapped.

For a furlong Tipper could do nothing. He was happy, to the extent that having horses around him distracted Citizen from the crowd. But the longer it went on the more urgent became the need to get out. With two furlongs to go Tipper was still boxed in. Translation's stable mate was now deliberately bumping and boring them.

'You're not going anywhere, pal,' the jockey upsides him shouted derisively. 'You're staying just where you are.'

'Come on Tipper. Come on,' Ana was pleading through gritted teeth shaking the sofa. She could see the race was slipping away from him.

'Get out of there, get out of there.'

Up ahead Translation had taken the lead and kicked for home. There was no way Tipper could risk barging his way out to the right. Any such rough riding would lose him the race in the

Stewards' Room. He just had to pray that one of the horses in front would tire and drop back in time to give him a run. At last one of the horses in front faltered, leaving a slight gap. Tipper urged Citizen to go through it. He only had to ask once. Enjoying the scrap, Citizen burst through into daylight, and the view of Translation's rump three lengths ahead.

A furlong out Citizen was devouring the deficit. But he still needed to find a length to get to Translation. Then Translation made a common Derby mistake. The track in the straight has a marked camber sloping into the left-hand rail. O'Callaghan's horse began to drift down it towards the rail. That suited Tipper perfectly. Running ruler-straight towards the middle of the course, away from the crowd on the rails, he gained ground. But he needed one last effort from Citizen. Doing something he'd never done before, Tipper shortened his reins, smoothly transferred them into his right hand and gave Citizen a crack round the arse with his stick in his left. The effect was like a rocket-launch. Citizen exploded past Translation as if he were standing still. They were two lengths clear at the line.

In the last furlong Ana had been on her feet screaming and, as they flashed past the post, she punched the air with her right hand. Lara came running in from the bedroom. She hated missing anything.

'Why are you so shouting?' she demanded.

'That man that came here once – see him there in the screen? He's just won the Derby!'

'What's the Derby?' asked Lara.

'It's only the most wonderful thing to win in the whole world,' her mother replied.

'Then why are you crying, Mummy?'

72

As Tipper tried to ease Citizen down after the winning post – what had once been described as 'the most important piece of wood in the world' – he could hardly see. Like Ana, he too had tears in his eyes. He pulled his goggles down as he passed the Rubbing House pub and held his face with his left hand for a second. Then he concentrated on keeping Citizen balanced as he pulled him up – or tried to. The pull up area at Epsom was horrible. Down hill and round left hand bend. But Tipper didn't care. He'd won the Derby. Citizen came to a shuddering halt as he ran out of track. As the other horses pulled up around him Tipper shouted a warning to them.

'Watch this fellow, lads. He'll kick you.'

'Well done mate!' shouted one of the jockeys on an unfancied long shot. 'You deserved that.'

It was a spontaneous congratulation from a weighing room colleague who knew Tipper had been through the mill. But he was hardly listening.

He was concentrating on his horse, and on the moment.

When Shalakov marched into the famous circular winner's enclosure to await his triumphant horse, he received a hero's reception. There were more Russians around that space than there had been in Moscow: bricklayers, bankers, hookers, plumbers, billionaires, thieves, drug-dealers. They were all there. Just like the old days. Except, before, they were British.

The Brits retreated and watched with mixed feelings. Their natural instinct for sportsmanship was being stretched – in those who had that instinct, that is. Mike Champion and Alison looked on with sour faces.

'Look at them, cavorting! We shouldn't let them into the country,' said Champion. 'At least the Arabs bother to learn English. This lot don't care. We've gone soft. We should kick the lot of them out. Disgusting.'

Tipper was prepared for trouble as he rode Citizen towards the claustrophobic space where he'd be unsaddled. Citizen was jig-jogging, he was unsure. Then he stopped. There was a heaving mass of people pushing and shoving to get close to the horse. He snorted. It looked like a very threatening place to be.

Tipper gave him a reassuring pat on the neck.

'You'll be all right in there, boy. Come on, in you go.'

This was technically a waste of breath since

Citizen still had cotton wool in his ears. But the horse sensed Tipper's wishes and cautiously stepped into the winner's enclosure. Tipper understood what his horse was saying: 'If you want me to go in there, then I'll go in there.' It was the operation of that implicit trust that Tipper had instilled in him from the day they first met.

High up the stands, O'Callaghan and his team sat ruefully in their executive box. They'd just seen the stud-value of their 2,000 Guineas winner cut in half. If this went on, O'Callaghan would have to start concentrating on his golf swing. Three boxes along Wang Chung had snapped his chop sticks. He wasn't too bothered about his runner Shanghai, who'd finished down the field. He was thinking about his top miler, the winner of the Irish Guineas, who was aiming to cap that with victory in the St James's Palace Stakes at Royal Ascot. That race would make or break his horse's reputation, and his value, and Wang knew that Citizen was going to oppose him. This wasn't a question of gambling. Hundreds of millions of pounds in stud fees were at stake.

Tipper got a great reception in the weighing-room. Most of the jockeys were prepared to cut him a lot of slack, knowing that his problems might easily have been visited on any of them. He'd been unfairly accused of stopping a horse, there had been brushes with alcohol and cocaine, his woman had fucked off with his child, and his professional life had seemed for a while to be on indefinite hold. Sure, he was lucky to be back, and on a horse like this one, but everybody needed a bit of luck. Luck, as somebody once said, is juice – the fuel of the racing game.

The press, though, were a different matter. They were sharpening their pencils in the press-room, ready to fire a lot of awkward questions at Tipper in the post-race press conference. Their treatment of Jim Bolger after New Approach's 2008 Derby victory was going to be a picnic compared to the grilling they had in store for Tipper. They'd want to talk about the Fighting Talk affair, and know just how Tipper had wangled his licence back.

So, as soon as he'd changed, Tipper slipped out of the fire door and into the jockeys' car park. He had some questions of his own he wanted answering, such as who had hired the girls who'd framed him?

Tipper rang Johnny the Fish, not knowing that the Fish had just landed the biggest touch of his life. He was, in fact, now a flying fish.

'Hi there Johnny. It's Tipper. Just wondering, have you had any luck tracking either of those girls down?'

The Fish's voice was heavily slurred.

'Tipper? Is that you? I'm so happy. So happy. You're my hero, you know that? You. Are. My. Hero. Where are you? Come and have a drink with the Fish.'

'I'm on my way to the airport, Johnny. Have you had any luck finding those girls?'

'Look, don't worry about that. It's not necessary. I've sorted it all out. Come and have a drink.'

'How do you mean you've sorted it out, Johnny?'

'How do you mean, how do I mean? I've talked to your missis is how I mean. Sweet little thing, really. Told her you had nothing to do with it. Fuck, I've just dropped my hat. Hang on a minute.'

But bending over to recover his top hat, the Fish lost his balance and pitched head first towards the Epsom car park turf. His head connected with the bumper of a 1945 Bentley and knocked him out cold.

73

Tipper flew back to Xanadu on the horse-transporter with Citizen a couple of hours after the Derby. It was slower and considerably less comfortable than Shalakov's jet. But Citizen travelled better with Tipper on board. He'd wanted to know what Johnny the Fish had meant about Ana. But Johnny had stopped answering his phone.

Jameson was waiting when they touched down at Xanadu. He wanted to be the first to admire his Derby winner. And make sure he had his session in the kriotherapy chamber. Citizen hoovered mints off his hand like a child's pony.

'Jesus Doc, you wouldn't think he could behave like such a lunatic sometimes, looking at him now!'

'Guess he's tired,' Jameson smiled. 'Come on, we're going to Moscow to celebrate.'

His father's favourite sport had never done much for Jameson, but he knew Tipper enjoyed watching football. Tonight Liverpool were playing Manchester United in a top of the table clash, so they dropped into Night Vision to catch the second half. And Jameson and Tipper were ready to let rip.

'We'll have a bottle of Johnny Walker Black label,' Jameson told the barman. Tipper smiled as Jameson poured the scotch into two glasses.

'I suppose if you can't get legless after you win the Derby, you never can?'

'You get as drunk as you like, son,' Jameson chuckled.

In the end they both did. The first round of toasts were to Citizen. 'He's the best horse in the world, Doc,' Tipper told Jameson four times. Jameson didn't mind. This was the night he'd been waiting for, for a long time. The night his one niggling fear could be laid to rest.

'We couldn't have done it without you, Doc,' Tipper told him five times.

'No, you're right,' Jameson replied quietly. 'You couldn't.'

But Tipper didn't take in his subtle assertion. He was now in transmitting mode, and not listening to much.

'We'll win the St James's Palace Stakes at Ascot, you know. I'm telling you there's nothing to beat this horse over any trip.'

Jameson wanted to talk about Ascot.

'How will Citizen cope with Ascot? Is it as noisy as Epsom?'

'Is lovely track Ascot,' Tipper slurred. 'Lovely track.' The scotch was beginning to get the better of him.

'Yes. I'm not worried about the track. It's the noise and atmosphere that worries me. Sometimes that can be a problem for Citizen.'

'Don't worry about that Doc. I'll use the cotton wool again. And this horse. He really trusts me.'

Jameson smiled and called the barman.

'We'll just have two glasses of your Thistle Dew Export please . . . and a small jug of water.'

'Doc. There's something I've been meaning to ask you. What exactly does Shalakov mean when he says he's got someone keeping an eye on Ana? Like, how closely would that be?'

The last person Jameson wanted to talk about was Ana. If only, he thought to himself, he'd told Tipper the truth about Ana from the minute Tipper had arrived in Russia the whole bloody Ana thing could have been dead and buried. He hadn't wanted to hurt the young Irishman. But Jameson now conceded to himself that his silence had been a mistake. A mistake which, however painful it would be for Tipper, should be rectified.

'Tipper, I think for your own happiness you should move on from Ana.'

'Doc. I can't. I love her,' Tipper replied, shaking his head. 'I don't care if she's had a kid with someone else, I love her.'

'She's misled you badly Tipper. It's time you knew that,' Jameson said looking Tipper square in the eyes.

'What d'you mean?'

'Ana used you to get information on Sinclair's horses to give to Shalakov.'

'No she didn't,' Tipper replied indignantly.

'I'm afraid she did. In fact the only reason that you met Ana was because Shalakov paid her to be in Newmarket.'

Tipper took a few seconds to take this in. 'Don't care,' he pronounced taking a slurp of his scotch. 'I love her.'

Jameson wished he hadn't started the conversation now. Tipper wasn't going to think straight. But he kept going. 'How do you think Ana met Shalakov, then?'

'Don't know. Don't care.'

'Shall I tell you?'

'Go on then.'

'Ana met Shalakov because she was a prostitute.'

Tipper took a few more seconds to mull it over. And empty his glass.

'Bollocks,' he finally said. 'How the fock would you know Doc?'

Tipper lay spread eagled on his bed after Jameson dropped him home. By rights he should have passed out cold. But he didn't. He just lay there thinking through a drunken haze. He fantasized about what he'd do to Shalakov. He'd get him in the indoor school and horsewhip him until he was covered in blood from head to foot. Then lasso him with the end of the whip, like he used to lasso buckets as a kid; and drag the bastard around the school on his knees. Tipper imagined Shalakov's pleading, blood splattered face. Then passed out.

Tipper appeared to be in remarkably good shape to Jameson when he rocked up at the track the next morning. Probably because he was still pissed. But having the Derby winner to sit on was as good a way as any of getting a hungover jockey out of bed.

Citizen was awake and raring to go when Tipper walked into his stable. He offered him one of his mints, but the colt wasn't interested. He tugged his ears playfully and the colt tried to bite him. Tipper sighed. Citizen was in one of those moods. Tipper felt Citizen's legs. They were 'as cold as ice'. Citizen had come out of the Derby in tip top condition. When he straightened up he felt giddy and his head throbbed.

'Those legs feel good,' Tipper told Jameson as he sipped a cup of coffee. Jameson took an exaggerated draw on his cigarette and blew a big smoke ring.

'You wouldn't believe me to start with, would you? That chamber is the business. Come on. I'll stick his heart monitor on and we can get going.'

'Jesus. You and your heart monitor. Where's Sinclair?'

'Still in England with Shalakov. He sent a message telling us to get on with the horses.'

'Doc. I want to talk to you about what you said last night. About Ana.'

'Fine,' Jameson replied. 'Over breakfast. Lets get these horses out.'

Citizen was led out of the barn by the usual groom, his ribs now fully recovered. It seemed as if he was hanging onto the lead rein as if his life depended on it.

Tipper prepared to get his usual leg up onto Citizen from the groom, who put his right hand under Tipper's raised ankle and flicked him up into the saddle; as he did every morning. Except that this morning Tipper's timing and balance were all over the place. He nearly went straight over the saddle and off the other side. He *was* still pissed.

He steadied himself. Must take things quietly, he thought, but Citizen was thinking something different. As the groom let him off his lead, he gave a snort and plunged forward. Tipper instinctively let the reins slip through his fingers, so he wouldn't be pulled over Citizen's head. Citizen, feeling sudden freedom, gave a squeal of joy and spun round throwing his head back. As Citizen's head came up Tipper was pitched forward. The top of Citizen's head crashed directly into Tipper's face.

Tipper was thrown off the back of the colt like a rag doll. Then, in a fit of exuberance, Citizen let fly with his back legs, and caught Tipper on the head as he hit the deck. Tipper lay motionless and broken on the ground, unconscious. Standing just a few yards away Jameson was convinced he was dead.

* * *

A week later Ana was listening to the news on television while she made Lara and the baby some lunch. Her ears caught the words 'Irish jockey Tipper O'Reilly'. By the time she'd got from the kitchen to the sitting room the news anchor had handed over to a sports correspondent.

'Well, Jeff,' the man explained, 'the news on Tipper O'Reilly doesn't sound good, I'm afraid. The facts are a bit sketchy at the moment, but our unconfirmed information is that this year's Derby-winning jockey had a near fatal fall from the Derby winner Citizen over a week ago at the training track in Moscow. He is believed to be in an unnamed hospital in Moscow. There have been protests from the Irish embassy as to why they have not been kept more fully informed about Mr O'Reilly's condition. But the Russians, as you know, often take a cavalier attitude to diplomatic protocol, especially concerning individual foreign nationals working in Russia. Citizen himself is reported to be unscathed and now, as we gear up for Royal Ascot this week, the question on everyone's lips is, who will partner the great Black Russian in the St James's Palace Stakes the day after tomorrow?'

Ana froze watching the screen. It was filled with footage of Tipper's Derby triumph and him walking back through a storm of acclaim from the crowd. 'Doesn't sound good' and 'near fatal fall' – what did that mean?

Ana grabbed her phone and dialled Sam's number. But he didn't pick up.

74

Shalakov fully intended to be the star of Royal Ascot. Afterwards, according to his plans, Citizen would never see another racecourse again. His job would be done and he would be the most eligible stallion in Europe. With such a good pedigree his earning potential would be twenty million pounds per annum in Europe, and half as much again if they shuttled him down for the southern hemisphere covering season.

Tipper's injuries could have been a lot worse. He had a broken nose and broken left forearm as well as severe concussion. Citizen's kick had split his helmet right down the middle but the protection had done its job and there would be no long-term brain damage. The doctors had heavily sedated Tipper and stood back, waiting for the bruising around his brain to repair itself.

Sinclair, too, was left with a headache. With Tipper out of action, who was going to take the Ascot ride? The problem was complicated by

Shalakov's attitude. First he wanted a Russian jockey, which Sinclair found the bottle to say was out of the question. Then it had to be a top Ascot jockey, but not one who'd ever ridden for either O'Callaghan or Wang Chung. That ruled out most of the best freelances.

Shalakov and his people looked like a flock of overweight king penguins as they shuffled around the paddock in their top hats and tails, waiting for Citizen to appear from his saddling box. Sinclair had solved his jockey dilemma by snapping up the young English star, Alfie Bradstock, who it seemed had never been legged up on any of O'Callaghan's or Wang Chung's horses. Alfie was unusual because he was just about the only good young English jockey around, most of the latest crop being Brazilian, Czech or Mexican.

But, until Bradstock walked out into the paddock he had never sat on Citizen. There simply hadn't been time to fly him out to Moscow to get to know the horse. This wasn't unusual, though. Every day jockeys ride horses they are strangers to.

In the paddock Citizen was in a particularly heavy strop, and had begun sweating profusely down his neck and flanks. Sinclair sensibly deployed two men to lead him, both of them hanging on to Citizen's bridle as he arm-wrenchingly tossed his head. No one could explain why he was so keyed up, though in fact the reason was simple. In all the pressure and excitement of the build-up to one of Ascot's greatest races, the noise of the crowd was buzzing like a swarm of bees inside his head, as it had after he'd won on President's Day in Moscow. Sinclair had been so busy basking in the attention that came with being the Black Russian's trainer, he'd totally overlooked the countermeasure that Tipper had used so successfully at Epsom. He'd forgotten to put cotton wool in Citizen's ears.

Sinclair chucked Alfie up into the saddle and told him to go to the start as quietly as possible after the parade. Citizen had never seen such a riot of colour packed behind the paddock rail. His eyes bulged in their sockets. The adrenaline flooded his veins. The serried ranks of top hats, far more than at Epsom, scared him. But even more damaging was the cloud of women's perfume wafting past his nostrils. As Citizen inhaled the women's scent a flood of testosterone started to course through his veins. He was on the very edge of eruption.

Jameson's health had not been good, so he didn't travel to Ascot. But he took his normal seat to watch the racing in Night Vision – a big slice of chocolate sponge cake in one hand, a smouldering cigarette in the other. Tipper, just out of hospital and with one arm in plaster, had insisted on being there too. He was in a lot of pain, his arm was throbbing like hell, but he'd refused to keep taking the mind blurring analgesics the doctors had been giving him.

'That stuff they gave me in the hospital made me off my face,' he complained.

A slightly grumpy Captain Maine joined them. He hadn't been invited to attend in person by Ascot Racecourse, so a stiff gin and tonic with Jameson in Night Vision had been his only invitation for the royal meeting that year. It wasn't exactly lunch in the Cavalry and Guards club, but it would have to do.

Jameson didn't like what he was seeing in the paddock.

'Look at him! He's upset. He's losing it.'

'Why's he in such a lather?' Maine asked.

'It's the crowd,' said Tipper, who was getting as agitated as Citizen. 'Where the fock are his ear plugs? I can't see them. Can you see them?'

Maine and Jameson gave a non-committal grunt. None of them could see them.

Alfie was relieved to be first out of the paddock and into the tunnel under the grandstand. At least for a few seconds they'd be away from the noise of the crowd. But it was a lull before the storm. Citizen came out of the tunnel onto the track like a cork out of a bottle. To make matters worse, the crowd gave a huge roar when they saw him. The towering glass stand echoed the noise back onto the track. Had the sound been muffled by earplugs, or had Tipper been there to reassure and calm him, all might have been well. But poor Alfie Bradstock had no chance.

As he felt his feet touch the grass Citizen's head plunged forward, forcing Alfie to slip his reins in the same way that Tipper had before his accident on the training track. This gave Citizen his head, and with all that open space in front of him he took immediate advantage. He careered off up the track, past the crowd and away from the grandstand. Alfie tried to gather his reins in and steady Citizen, but as soon as he pulled on his mouth Citizen chucked his head in the air. Alfie tried again, with the same result. It didn't matter what Alfie did, he could not impose his will. Citizen was out of control.

Citizen didn't actually know what he was doing. The cocktail of hormones pouring through his blood stream was sending him crazy. His endocrine system was in spate. Any sense of self-preservation that the horse might have possessed was being suppressed. Citizen was running away in blind panic, and his pumped-up hormonal system made sure he was doing so at a suicidal pace.

Alfie hadn't been so frightened since the age of six, when his pony had taken off with him down Wantage High Street. He had never travelled so fast on a horse in his life. They soon reached Swinley Bottom, on the far side of the course, having covered a mile of track going the wrong way. Citizen was still flat out and not stopping. Alfie's arms and legs by now had turned to jelly. He was a helpless passenger.

The crowd, who'd abandoned their strawberries

and cream to cram into the stands, realized they were witnessing a disaster. There was no chance now of Citizen talking part in the race. He would be – he probably already was – utterly exhausted.

'Bollocks,' was all Tipper could say as he looked up at the big screen.

'He's blown it,' Maine sighed, resting his face into the palms of his hands. 'He's bolted. He can't win after this.'

Jameson said nothing, but his fists were clenched and eyes full of moisture. He wasn't thinking about the race at all. He was waiting for the engine to fail. It would be beating faster than it ever had in its life. Beating itself to destruction.

Alfie was still desperately trying to steady Citizen as they tore up the hill. But it was nothing to do with his efforts when suddenly Citizen's stride faltered. Alfie gathered the reins to get a pull on him. But the horse gave a violent lurch to the right, his head went back, and the terrified jockey had a brief sight of an eyeball filled with blood. Then Citizen's legs buckled, and he crashed to the ground like a boulder. Alfie was lucky to be thrown clear. The colt was stone dead before he hit the grass.

Jameson stared at the screen without blinking, mesmerised. Maine buried his head in his hands.

'Oh my God,' he muttered. 'I can't believe it. Just can't believe it.'

'This is appalling,' the television commentator

wailed. 'This is a tragedy. The brilliant Derby winner has collapsed. They're rushing over with a horse ambulance . . . they're erecting screens . . . but surely, surely, Citizen – the Moscow Express, the Black Russian – surely his brief reign as the greatest horse in the world is over in the most disastrous circumstances.'

Tipper was trying to get his thoughts in order. Citizen had collapsed at Ascot. Was he dreaming? Was he still in his hospital bed? No, this was a real nightmare. He looked from Jameson, to Maine, to the screen. It showed the faces of shocked racegoers, then cut back to a long shot of the course. The camera slowly zoomed in on a cluster of vehicles and people, gathered round a small fit-up enclosure of green canvas.

'Why didn't he put the ear plugs in?' Tipper moaned. Jameson just shook his head. He didn't know why Sinclair hadn't done that, either. Maine just stared at the scene being relayed by the TV. He knew what the pictures meant.

'This wouldn't have happened if I'd been there,' Tipper said to neither of them in particular.

'Well, that isn't strictly true,' Jameson said without explanation.

'It is. He wouldn't have run away with me. I would have got him settled,' Tipper replied.

'Hmm. Maybe not today you wouldn't have. Even if you hadn't been injured.'

'But I knew him better than anyone.'

'Well, if you come with me, back to Xanadu,

485

you might understand. But we have to go now.' Jameson now had a crazy, mad-looking smile across his face and his eyes were staring at Maine without blinking. 'I think you'll find the visit very revealing, Captain.'

'What are you talking about,' Maine hissed.

'Come with me and I'll show you,' Jameson replied stubbornly.

Maine's military background warned him against doing so. You didn't just go wandering off behind enemy lines without a good exit plan.

'I don't think that would be appropriate for a man in my position,' he pointed out. 'I can't just go walking into Shalakov's laboratory without permission. Even if it's at your invitation. Not appropriate.'

'Hang on a minute. What exactly are you saying, Doc?' Tipper asked.

'Come with me and I'll show you. I'm not telling you here,' Jameson insisted stubbornly.

'Fock it, Captain. We're going. I want to get to the bottom of this. And so should you if you want to do your job properly. Come on,' Tipper insisted.

'It's not . . .' Maine was interrupted.

'You'll have to drive, Captain,' Jameson added stubbing out his cigarette.

'Why?'

'Because,' Jameson smiled, 'I never learnt to and he can't with a broken arm. Have you got your car here?'

'Yes, but . . .'

'There are no buts, Captain,' Tipper now interrupted. 'It's your duty. You're in charge of racing in this country. I think you know it's your job to come and see what he's got to show you. Whatever the fock it is.'

Jameson lit up another cigarette and blew the smoke into the air towards the TV screen. 'That's right. It's your duty.'

Tipper stood up from his chair.

'Come on, Captain. We're going.'

75

The journey to Xanadu was largely silent. Tipper was devastated. Everything that he'd been working towards had now collapsed. He hadn't only been dwelling on Citizen's death. Which wouldn't have happened if he'd been riding him. He was also churning with the thought that Ana had probably never loved him. It was eating away at him.

Maine had very mixed feelings. He was dreading what he was going to be shown. It would be the end of his posting in Russia. But Tipper had been right. It was his duty to find out.

Jameson said nothing. He knew this was the end.

When they were a mile from Xanadu Jameson told Maine to pull over.

'You'll have to get in the boot, Captain. A bit undignified, I know, but you don't have a security pass. They won't look in the boot when they see I'm in the car. Tipper, you'll have to drive the last bit. You can do that with one arm can't you?' Jameson asked.

'Jesus. Can't you drive at all?' Tipper asked.

'Never sat behind a steering wheel in my life,' Jameson confirmed.

'Bloody hell!' Maine said with feeling.

'Keep quiet in the boot,' Jameson added.

'What do you think I'm going to do?' said Maine truculently. 'Sing a bloody opera?'

Both the guards in the grey, square concrete gatehouse smiled at Tipper and Jameson as they let them through the gates. They liked Tipper. He'd always had a wave and a smile for them on his way in and out, even though he didn't speak a word of their language.

As they got to the laboratory entrance, Jameson showed Tipper the exact spot to leave the car.

'It's got to go where the cameras won't spot us.'

'But security know we're here.'

'They know two of us are here. And that's all they're going to know. In fact they won't see any of us again in a minute. Just follow me in as if every thing is normal.'

'I still don't get it,' Tipper mumbled.

Jameson led him into an area he'd never seen before. There was a bank of TV screens covering the stable block. Jameson sat down at a keyboard, lit a fresh cigarette and started to type in codes.

'Jesus, Doc, I hope you know what you're doing.'

'I invented this system. Of course I know what I'm doing. In one minute the guards will still have the correct time and date super-imposed on their screens, but the pictures they're watching will be clean.'

'How do you mean clean?'

'Clean. Five hours for each camera with nothing happening in the shot. It will look like the place is empty.'

'But won't they wonder where we are?'

'No. They've seen us come in here. Those cameras don't reach further than that door. D'you think I'd have designed a system that spied on me?'

Jameson took a draw on his fag and pressed the shift key.

'Hey presto! It works. Let's get the Captain. He's probably a bit uncomfortable by now.'

Maine was more than a bit uncomfortable as he unwound his large frame from a foetal position.

'Follow me,' Jameson said urgently. 'We haven't got all day.'

Tipper and Maine followed Jameson back through the ante-chamber into the stable block, where Citizen had spent the winter. The block was deserted. All of the horses were at the training track in Moscow. Maine was amazed, though, by his first sight of the buildings, and the scale of the Xanadu operation.

Jameson bustled on as fast as his lungs would let him through the stable block and along the tunnel towards the indoor gallop.

'Bloody hell, this is incredible,' Maine exclaimed

when he set eyes on the mile round indoor gallop. 'When the hell was this built?'

'Years ago,' Jameson told him. 'We used to grow things in here. It's heated in the winter. Come on!'

Tipper couldn't think for the life of him where Jameson was taking them. They were heading for the closed doors of the tractor shed; the doors that Citizen used to pull himself up by when he was younger. By the time Jameson got to the doors he was wheezing terribly and so breathless he couldn't speak.

He stood for a moment with his eyes shut, his shoulders rising and falling as he fought for breath. Then he touched the biometric recognition pad and the doors slid silently open. Tipper peered through. What he saw, with not a tractor in sight, was another stable barn, identical to the one in which Citizen had lived.

All the boxes were open and vacant, except for one. Jameson shuffled across to it, lifted the latch and pulled open the door. Tipper followed him inside. There was a big, black horse chewing on his hay net.

'Jesus Christ. I don't believe it.'

He walked towards the horse who was more interested in his hay net than him. Tipper knew who it was before he ran his hand down his neck. He turned round to Maine nodding.

'It's Citizen,' Tipper said in bewilderment, turning to look at Maine.

Jameson grabbed a packet of mints from the cupboard outside the stable and handed them to Tipper.

'Give him some of those,' Jameson said triumphantly.

Tipper held out his hand with a mint on it. Citizen walked across the stable and licked the mint off his hand. Then Tipper pulled his ears affectionately and stroked behind his ears. He nuzzled Tipper's coat to find some more mints.

'It's him all right. No doubt about it.'

'Bloody hell,' Maine muttered to himself.

76

'I don't want to be a killjoy,' Maine said dryly as Tipper kissed Citizen's muzzle and wrapped his good arm around his neck. 'But now what? If this horse is Citizen as you say? And it would appear he is. Why the hell have you brought us here to show him to us?'

'I would have thought that was pretty obvious, Captain,' Jameson said in as blunt a tone as he could muster. 'You two have got to rescue him.'

'Jesus. You must have run a ringer at Ascot today,' Tipper interrupted.

'I'll come to that,' Jameson said dismissively. 'This horse will be shot the minute Shalakov gets back here. Probably by him personally. We might only have about three hours to get him out.'

Tipper snapped out of his celebration embrace.

'Let's just get him in a horse box and fock off quick,' Tipper suggested, as if it was that simple.

Jameson shot this plan down.

'There's no chance. Even if we bluff our way

493

out of the front gates in a horse box, how far will we get? The border's hundreds of miles away.'

Tipper's arm was now throbbing. But instead of distracting him the pain focused his mind.

'Okay,' he said. 'We'll fly him out. There's a runway there. Is there a spare horse plane?'

'No. There's only one. It's gone to Ascot,' Jameson replied flatly.

'And even if it hadn't,' said Maine acidly, 'I wasn't aware that you hold a pilot's licence.'

Tipper ploughed on.

'Never mind about that. Someone to pick us up, that's what we need.'

'Don't talk bloody rubbish, Tipper,' spluttered Maine.

'It's not rubbish at all. I know just the person.'

Tipper was focused on his plan. 'It's like this. My cousin Sam works for Dermot O'Callaghan. They have planes coming out of their ears. I'll ring him.'

It took seconds for Tipper to flip open his phone and press the keys that connected him to Sam. His cousin immediately started gabbling about the death of Citizen, but Tipper cut him short.

'Citizen's not dead, Sam. He's here, alive and well.'

'Are you pissed, boy? Didn't I see him keel over on Ascot racecourse? The whole world saw it.'

'No, they didn't. That's what they thought they saw. Really he's alive, and he's still in Russia.'

'This is bollocks. What was the horse at Ascot that died?'

'That was . . . another horse.'

'For God's sake get on with it,' groaned Jameson beside him. 'We haven't got all night.'

'You mean, a ringer?' gasped Sam. 'You ran a fockin' ringer in St James's Palace?'

'Yea. Something like that Sam. Only now Shalakov's on his way back to kill Citizen and cover his tracks. We got to stop him; tell O'Callaghan we need a horse plane.'

Once Sam had got the message things happened fast. An excited O'Callaghan rang Tipper back minutes later, and was passed over to Jameson, who gave him the co-ordinates of the runway at Xanadu. O'Callaghan was shouting instructions to someone called Ray on another line. Then he spoke to Tipper again. His plane was on its way.

Still in a state of unnatural clear-headedness, Tipper called Sam again.

'Look, there's one more thing. You've got to get hold of Ana. The Russians have someone on her, like a minder. You've got to get her away from him and safe, Sam. She's in danger. She's in London, near King's Cross station.'

He gave Sam the address. Sam didn't argue. He was already in his car driving back from Ascot races. He said he'd divert immediately to Central London, and do what he could.

77

Shalakov stared silently out of the window of his hospitality box, high up in the grandstand. He could see the great arch that spanned Wembley stadium on the horizon as he gazed across Ascot Heath towards Windsor Great Park. But it meant nothing to him.

Sinclair poured himself a stiff drink and looked around the box.

There was no sign of Nico. Ten minutes earlier he'd quietly taken his top hat and made himself scarce. The Nicos of this world know when to melt away. And something else had come up. Nico had an option to buy some nuclear data from an Iranian source. He had a buyer from Pakistan who wanted to meet in London that night. This deal was going to move him up to another level. It was good-bye Shalakov time.

Alexei C sat in a chair in the corner, saying nothing and looking at the floor. The top hats hanging from their hooks made the place look like a changing room in a Funeral Director's office – which was quite appropriate really because Sinclair was in the deep shit. This was thanks to an eagle-eyed journalist, who had remembered Citizen's use of ear plugs at Epsom and noted he hadn't been wearing them today. He'd raised the matter at the press conference Shalakov had reluctantly held. The General hadn't reacted, which worried Sinclair more than if he had. The best that could be hoped for was that the distressed Shalakov had not taken it in. Yet he did not appear distressed, only menacingly calm.

'We are leaving now,' Shalakov suddenly announced, turning from the window. 'We have some things to do at Xanadu. We will go straight away to the airport and take my plane.'

'I was thinking,' Sinclair said hesitantly. 'Perhaps I, er, should stay and fly back with Citizen's body? We don't really want the authorities here poking around inside the horse, do we? Best to get him away a.s.a.p.'

It was a good point, though Sinclair's motive was less the preservation of Citizen's genetic secrets and more the avoidance of a plane journey back to Xanadu with Shalakov. Shalakov thought about it. He didn't want anyone looking inside Citizen Number Two, that was for sure. On the other hand it would be folly to leave Sinclair at large in England. He snapped his finger at Alexei C and spoke to him in Russian.

'Alexei, you will stay with Citizen. You will

need Nico's help to make arrangements. Go and find him now. You will not allow anyone to touch the horse. I don't want to see a mark on him when he comes home. If they do anything to him, I will do the same to you.'

Alexei C nodded and left the box. Sinclair's hopes of avoiding an anxious flight home were crushed. He got up from his chair and wandered towards the door. Suddenly he wanted to be in another county, and as soon as possible.

'I'm, er, just going to the toilet,' he said as casually as he could.

'No toilet. Sit!' snarled Shalakov.

Sinclair hesitated then, with a shrug, returned to his seat. For a minute he thought the Russian might hit him. But only for a moment. He wouldn't dare hit me, Sinclair thought to himself. I know too much.

One hour after Ray Fine, O'Callaghan's pilot, had lifted the cumbersome horse plane into the air for its estimated three-hour flight, Shalakov and Sinclair were sitting on the runway at Farnborough in the General's sleek executive jet.

'I hope you have an enjoyable flight, gentlemen,' the Captain said. 'The weather between here and Russia is looking perfect. By my estimation we should arrive there in almost exactly two hours. Caroline is with us today to ensure you have an enjoyable flight.' Shalakov's jet could get to Xanadu in an hour less than the horse plane.

As soon as he'd got over the shock of seeing his horse die so very publicly, Shalakov coolly grasped all the implications. He had a healthy, sound, fertile Derby winner sitting in its stable at Xanadu who must never again see the light of day. He could never run in another race because he was officially dead. The tagging system that operated around the world meant he could never masquerade as another horse. And he could never breed because his DNA would give away his identity. Citizen Number Two may be worth a few tins of dog food, but Citizen Number One had no value at all, except to his enemies.

Caroline tottered along the plane with a half-kilo tin of caviar. After she'd served Shalakov, Sinclair helped himself to several heaped table-spoons, scraping out the last of it. Greedy bastard, Caroline thought to herself. She'd been hoping to finish the caviar herself.

Shalakov was enjoying watching his prisoner eat his last meal.

'Bloody O'Reilly,' Sinclair muttered in the direction of Shalakov. 'If he hadn't got injured the horse wouldn't have run off like that.'

Shalakov ignored him. But the remark acted as a prompt. Ana. It might be time to lift her and park her somewhere else; somewhere unknown and 'safe'. Shalakov picked up his phone and dialled Carter.

'We're moving the girl,' he said gruffly into his handset. 'One of my men will come and get her now. Make sure she's there. Accompany them to the place where she is going. Then your job is finished.'

Shalakov didn't wait for Carter to say anything before he cut the call off and rang Alexei C.

78

'Are you going to give us the full story, Doc?'
Tipper asked Jameson as he pulled out files and
files of paper from a massive safe in his office.
'Which horse did you run at Ascot today?'

'How much of the story do you want to know?
You'll be taking it with you anyway. I want you
to take all my research papers,' Jameson replied
deadly seriously.

'What d'you mean *you'll be taking*? Where the
bloody hell are you going?' Maine asked. He
knew he was in the wrong place at the wrong
time.

'Do I sound like I'm going anywhere? No. This
is the end of the road for me,' Jameson said matter
of factly. 'My lungs probably only have weeks left
in them. But my work has been hidden for too
long. You must take it. With Citizen.'

Maine wasn't particularly satisfied with that
answer. He was going to make sure he kept
Jameson right next to him.

'Jesus. We've got the best part of three hours, Doc. Spit it out. Which horse did you run at Ascot?'

Jameson paused, as if contemplating whether to tell them. Then he began his tale.

'I'd expected to work in Nuclear Science when I arrived here. In the West there'd been an obsession that Russia was only interested in having a huge nuclear arsenal and getting to the moon; but the Soviets had several more immediate problems, not least the recurrent famines caused by Lysenko's disastrous anti-genetics policies.'

'Who was Lysenko,' Tipper demanded.

'A lunatic with too many theories,' Jameson replied. 'Anyway a lot of stuff produced at Xanadu like fertilizers, pesticides and hormones repaired the damage. But only to a point. Then Shalakov persuaded the Politburo that genetics were the only way forward. We genetically engineered plants and animals so we could make them grow bigger and faster. And then we cloned them, and bingo, the food production problems were solved.'

'When were you doing this?' Maine asked incredulously.

'In the seventies,' Jameson said smugly. 'I concentrated on animals. I identified growth-controlling genes in sheep and cloned the first ram twenty years before the Edinburgh scientists produced Dolly.'

'You're joking?' Maine said sceptically.

'Oh no I'm not,' Jameson smiled. 'Then I took a new direction. I got a request from the Sports

Minister. Russia had been successful in producing Olympic athletes, but the Party Chairman wanted more gold medals.'

'Don't tell me you've been messing around with humans,' Maine interjected. Jameson ignored him. He'd never had the chance to tell unclassified ears this story.

'I had a huge budget,' he continued, almost boasting.

Jameson wasn't joking. And every word he was telling them was the disgusting truth. He'd spent two years mapping human DNA; three decades ahead of the Human Genome Project. His team produced thousands of human embryos from genetically modified cells; so they could see what deformities they'd be born with. Some of the clones survived longer than others but in the early days they were all grossly deformed or died soon after birth. It wasn't work for the faint hearted, but they got results. Eventually they were able to promise the Politburo twenty gifted sporting types annually. And three cloned copies of each.

Thirty full time surrogate mothers were selected along the lines of the Nazis' *lebensborn* programme. They had the privilege of gestating and nurturing triplet foetuses in Xanadu's maternity section. Two thirds succeeded in delivering viable 'units'. The effectiveness of the drug-induced hypnotism, used to make sure the mothers' maternal instincts didn't get in the way, was remarkable.

Maine and Tipper stayed silent while they were

being told all of this. Jameson regaled them with his life's work with relish. He didn't miss out on a detail.

The infants that were produced had bigger lungs and hearts, produced more growth hormone and were a lot more competitive than normal children. A zinc-sensitive promoter gene was added to the clones' DNA, capable of switching on and off the production of luteinizing hormone, which controls levels of testosterone. By varying the doses of zinc, Jameson had been able to boost or lower the clones' testosterone levels at will. This also speeded up their sexual development; puberty was normally reached at eight or nine and the clones were fully grown men by the age of fourteen.

'Jesus Doc. How could you do it?' Tipper half whispered.

'We pushed the physical training to the limit. And if a breakdown did occur, we had an indistinguishable understudy. But the nature-versus-nurture question was the bit that fascinated me,' Jameson said animatedly. 'The clones had different kinds of upbringing. And they were never allowed to meet each other. But the psychological conditions were deliberately varied. In Compound A, all the children were brought up permissively with kindness and tenderness. In Compound B they were accustomed to mental stress and constant discipline. In Compound C the regime was physical deprivation.'

Jameson was now looking at Maine for some

approval. He'd been in the army. Surely he could see the benefits of this. But he was getting nothing from Maine, who continued to sit in silence.

Jameson's clones from the three groups turned out very different in character. Those from Compound A tended to be spoilt, self obsessed and narcissistic; in Compound B they were characterless and bland; and in Compound C they were aggressive. The physical abilities of the clones were identical, but the extra competitiveness in Compound C gave that group the edge in performance. None of the clones suffered nature's inconveniences; like cystic fibrosis, colour blindness, leukaemia.

All the groups, however, shared one weakness, which was particularly prevalent in Group C; a major flaw that couldn't be ironed out. The testosterone switch, for some reason, occasionally got stuck in the 'on' position. There were some ugly scenes. One clone, Alexei C, wiped out four of his group in one night in a brawl in the sleeping area.

Besides being a threat to each other, they were a danger to themselves. Under the influence of uncontrollable hormone levels they pushed their bodies beyond the capacity even of their highly developed cardio-vascular systems. Dozens self-destructed through irreparable heart-failure.

But when the Berlin Wall came down, a rapid clear up operation was carried out at Xanadu to cover up the tracks of their human experiments.

The only remnant was Alexei C, who Shalakov kept for special assignments.

By 2000, Jameson had been moved back to further animal research. He was producing genetically modified and cloned pigs, sheep, cattle and horses; with hardly any problems. Then Shalakov proposed the Citizen Project.

The starting point, so to speak, of the Citizen Project, was that the mare and stallion had to have no markings. They had to be mono-colour. Jameson had discovered that some Friesian cattle they'd cloned although genetically identical, had different skin patterns. Probably due to the way they lay in the womb. So Stella Maris had been worth more to them than anyone else because she was mono-colour.

Once they'd selected Border Dispute, who was also mono-colour, they had to guarantee that the foal would be a colt. The solution had been a ten grand bung for Border Dispute's stud groom in exchange for a thermos of the stallion's frozen semen. Stella Maris had actually arrived pregnant at Xanadu, but was immediately aborted.

'Jesus. You're a disgrace,' Tipper spat. 'I knew there was something wrong with the way you went about things. But Christ, I didn't know it was this bad.'

'Tipper, let's hear him out,' Maine suggested forensically. 'This is going to be the only time he tells this story.'

'Indeed,' Jameson agreed, taking the opportunity to light a fag. 'Interesting though, isn't it!' he prompted Maine.

'Keep going,' Maine urged. 'If we ever get out of here on this bloody plane we might as well know about our cargo. If, that is.'

Maine and Tipper struggled to comprehend the next bit of Jameson's tale. Which was hardly surprising. They weren't scientists.

Using centrifugal force, Jameson isolated the male-producing spermatozoa in Border Dispute's semen specimen supplied by the stud groom – male-producing sperm weigh more than female – and then waited for Stella Maris's next ovulation. She subsequently got pregnant again. This time with a guarantee that the foetus would be male.

After thirty-two days gestation the male foetus was aborted, its head removed and the rest cut into small pieces. The cells in these pieces were genetically modified in much the same way as in the elite athlete programme a few years earlier, giving them the same testosterone switch, and the same superfast growth characteristics. Jameson borrowed the growth hormone gene from a Shire horse. He thought it would stimulate bigger muscles.

Twenty-seven live equine embryos were produced. Twenty-six were implanted in surrogate mothers – and the last was reserved for Stella Maris, herself. The vets had the devil of a job trying to deliver twenty-seven extra-large foals.

As it happened Stella Maris foaled last. And she produced Citizen I. One of the only two clones that came through.

'Tipper, it's amazing that Citizen I, who Stella Maris carried, was, the one you bonded with. Which won the Derby. The one that's in that stable,' Jameson enthused, dropping his cold hearted scientist's façade.

'Oh, it's amazing is it?' Tipper replied. 'Doc, you're a sick man. In more ways than one. Have another cigarette.'

Tipper's disapproval was water off a duck's back to Jameson. He knew Tipper was too emotional when it came to horses. But Maine, he still thought, would get it. Maine was a military man. He understood duty sometimes meant sacrifices had to be made. So Jameson concentrated his attention on Maine.

'We split the foals into two groups, but they started to fight. The promoter gene for the growth hormone was working perfectly, but for some reason, the luteinizing hormone promoter gene seemed to be random. We ended up with variable testosterone levels. I eliminated zinc, as far as was possible, from their diet to limit their testosterone production.'

Maine kept looking at him blankly.

'They galloped around their fields until they'd passed the point of exhaustion and their hearts burst,' Jameson said with frustration in his voice.

'Only two Citizens survived. One from each

group. Citizen 1, Stella Maris's Citizen, he was brought up in the kindness group. That's why he loved mints. That's why he trusted Tipper.'

'Jesus. What about the other one? The one I guess that died at Ascot today,' Tipper asked.

'Well you did a fair bit of work with Citizen II, as well. But so did that groom who used to watch you. I think he over-did the brutal regime we had him in.'

'What do you mean?'

'Well. We had two regimes of course. Like we did with the athletes. But I think the hard regime made him more prone to suffering a malfunction of his promoter gene. He freaked out on President's Cup day in Moscow. He tried to savage that horse in the Dewhurst stakes at Newmarket. And he finally blew up his heart at Royal Ascot.'

There was no trace of emotion in Jameson's voice at all. 'You know, I think it might have been the women's perfume on President's Cup day that flipped him,' he thought out aloud. 'And maybe that's what happened today. I wonder if there's any zinc in it?'

Tipper thought back over his time at Xanadu: the extraordinary training regime, the mood swings, the sudden recovery from injury.

'So much for the chamber mending his injuries. How did I fall for that, for Christ's sake?'

'Well the kriotherapy chamber works very well,' Jameson said defensively. 'But even that can't

509

mend nasty injuries in two days. Or heal cuts overnight.'

Tipper then thought about the mints.

'Jesus. There were days when he was in a strop and he wouldn't take a mint. That was the other fella then? He didn't *like* mints, did he?'

'Well, he didn't associate them with kindness. Because he'd never known any.'

Tipper shook his head in bemusement.

'Jesus, some bloody mug I am. I've been riding two different horses and I didn't even know it.'

Maine had been thinking, rubbing his cheek with the palm of his hand. And his mind went back to the dope box when he'd seen the name 'Alexei C' in the neck of Shalakov's bruiser.

'I'm beginning to get this,' he said. 'You switched them every Sunday, right? That's why he was so bloody fresh every Monday morning.'

'Exactly. Sometimes I worried that Tipper would work out the symmetry of his mood swings: how every other Monday he didn't like mints and was unfriendly.'

'And the drugs?' Maine asked bluntly

Jameson laughed again.

'There were no drugs, except the ones the horse produced quite naturally for himself. We didn't need to use anything as childish as injections.'

Tipper felt a surge of anger.

'Jesus, Doc, this is all wrong! It's not natural. It's a crime.'

Jameson gave him a pitying look.

'Tipper, in science you have to prove and disprove theories, otherwise you can't move forward. That's all I was doing. And think of the upside. Would you have won the Derby without me? He's a scientific marvel. He's unique.'

He gave another creaking laugh.

'I cloned him, and I'm saying he's unique. That's a laugh, isn't it?'

Tipper and Maine weren't laughing.

Maine was thinking about his options. Was it too late to get the hell out of there? Reluctantly he realized it was. About two hours too late. But he still didn't trust Jameson.

79

Although they were dealing with the more placid of the two Citizens, Tipper doubted he'd be able to lead the horse out to the aircraft hangar. As soon as Citizen sensed the open space he'd be liable to have a buck and a kick. He'd never hang onto him with only one good arm.

'Captain, it might be best if you led him,' Tipper suggested.

'I doubt it. I've never led a horse in my life.'

'Jesus, it's not that difficult,' Tipper remonstrated.

'Remember, I've seen this one out exercising in the morning. I know what he can do. If I lead him and he gets loose, the game's over. Why don't you ride him out?'

'Ride him? Are you mad?' Jameson interrupted. 'Tipper's got a broken arm, for God's sake!'

'No, Doc. That's a good idea,' said Tipper. 'I can do that. And with me on top of him he'll keep his cool better, I think.'

The hour waiting for the plane dragged by for Tipper and Maine. But Jameson was still busy sorting papers. Any other scientist would have had the whole bloody lot on one disc. But not Jameson. He was a paper and pen man. What wasn't on his computer couldn't be hacked into by prying eyes.

Maine was tense. He kept jumping to his feet and walking up and down the room jingling the loose change in his trouser pocket. Tipper, with nothing better to do, counted the number of times Maine looked at his watch in the space of five minutes. It was fourteen times.

Jameson fished a fag packet from his pocket, found it empty and threw it into the bin. He immediately opened another.

Tipper's brain was jumping about. 'Citizen might slip around on that concrete and tarmac out there. Why don't we put the kriotherapy chamber boots on him, Doc?'

'Not a bad idea, Tipper.'

'They'll also dampen the noise of his hooves in case anybody's about. By the way, what are we going to do if someone is about?'

'No one is about,' said Jameson, taking a deep drag of his cigarette. 'No one's allowed to be about at this time. The rest of the scientific staff are working in other buildings, or else they're in the accommodation block. The guards on duty will be in the gatehouse. They won't hear a thing. But if anyone does . . .'

Jameson walked over to his desk, opened a

drawer and reached inside. When he brought his hand out it was holding a handgun.

'Where did you get that?' Maine demanded.

Jameson held the gun in the palm of his hand, studying it as if he'd never really looked at it before.

'I've never fired it. I bought it from a guy in Moscow. A peculiar person, who only had one leg. He said he'd lost the other in Chechnya. He took this from a dead Chechen.'

'I think I should have it,' Maine said firmly. 'I can't believe you know how to use it. I'm trained to.'

Jameson thought about this proposition. Maine was probably right, but he was holding onto the gun anyway. He tucked it into his jacket pocket.

'I guess you were also trained never to give your gun away too, Captain,' Jameson said sarcastically.

Maine didn't argue the point. Instead he took another impatient walking tour of the room.

'How the hell did I get involved in this bloody mess,' he grunted, checking his watch once again.

'But you are, Captain,' Tipper pointed out. 'I've got the one arm and the Doc's not well. We need you. Come down to the tack room. We got to get his saddle and bridle, and the boots. It's just down the corridor.'

'He goes where I go,' Maine stipulated nodding at Jameson.

'Relax will you?' Jameson asked. 'Will he load onto the plane okay?'

'Should do,' said Tipper. 'He's been on one before. But the pilot might have to turn the engines off.'

'Will there be time?' asked Maine sceptically. 'The guards will have heard the plane landing. They'll send someone out to check, won't they?'

'Well, they may think it's Shalakov landing,' Jameson wheezed.

They collected the tack and went to Citizen's stable. There was still half an hour to wait and it felt like an eternity. Tipper's arm was hurting. He kept swallowing the pain-killers and talking to Citizen. They agreed they'd get to the hangar five minutes before the plane was due to arrive. Maine tacked Citizen up under Tipper's instruction and fitted his padded boots.

When the time was right Maine legged Tipper up into the saddle, and they slipped out of the back door of the stable block.

'If someone sees us we're sitting ducks,' Maine complained, struggling along with Jameson's loaded suitcase.

'Relax,' Jameson said, though he was panting himself. 'There's no one about this time of the evening. We get to the hangar and we're fine.'

Citizen was in a hurry. He was excited. Tipper wasn't going to win a battle of wills with one arm. So he let Citizen walk as fast as he liked. They soon left the other two behind. Maine was sticking close to Jameson, even if it did hold him up.

'Get a move on,' Tipper urged the other two

between his teeth. Maine replied with a few expletives. They looked like remnants of a defeated army as they straggled down the concrete road towards the hangar. Maine had lifted the case onto one of his broad shoulders, but its weight made it impossible to move quickly anyway. Jameson was wheezing like an asthmatic in a hay field. Tipper, talking away reassuringly to Citizen all the while. Riding like a cavalry man, his stirrups right down and one hand on the reins. With his other arm plastered and in a sling, he looked like a war casualty.

80

Ana was feeding the baby when Carter ended his phone call. He had a strange look on his face, a stressed-out look.

'What's the matter, Alan?' she asked looking up from the baby. He didn't answer immediately, just glanced down at the newspaper he'd been reading. Then he looked at the baby, and from him to Lara, playing on the floor with a puzzle. At different points in his life Carter had done some pretty hardcore things to people. But they had deserved it. All had been fair in love and war. But he'd never handed over a mother and her small children to a bunch of gangsters. Which was what he was about to do. He'd certainly never bonded with an innocent baby and his defenceless mother before. But there was no messing with these Russians if you wanted to stay alive.

'We have to leave, Ana. You'd better start packing now.'

Ana's stomach lurched.

'Packing? Why?' was all she could say.

'Shalakov wants to see you. Could be good news,' he suggested unconvincingly. Ana just looked at him.

Carter looked shifty and awkward. 'I'm just doing my job, Ana. You'll be fine. They'll look after you. But you need to get packed. No fuss, all right?'

Lara saw her mother open a suitcase. 'Where are we going, mama?' Ana wasn't listening. Her mind was racing.

'Where are we going?' Lara repeated.

'On a trip,' Ana said, glaring coldly at Carter.

'You've probably got half an hour,' Carter said bluntly. He picked up his keys and went to the front door. 'And don't try anything. I won't be far away.'

He shut the door behind him and took the lift to the ground floor. Ana's accusing eyes unnerved him. He wanted to wait for Alexei C in the open air.

Tipper had told Sam the street and the name of the apartment block. But he didn't know the number of the flat. He parked across the road and crossed to speak to a man who was hovering outside the entrance, smoking.

'Excuse me pal. Do you live here?' Sam asked.

Carter immediately picked up the Irish accent.

'What do you want?' Carter asked.

'I need to find a bird called Ana, who lives here. She has two small children. It's urgent, really urgent.'

'Oh yes? Urgent? Why's that?' asked Carter giving nothing away.

'It's a personal thing, like. But if you don't know her—'

'I didn't say that.'

Carter hadn't expected this development. A knight in shining armour, come to rescue Ana. He could easily punch the guy's lights out. Or if he didn't, Alexei C would. Because Carter saw a car, with Alexei C at the wheel, pulling up thirty yards down the street.

Then he surprised himself.

'Look pal,' Sam was saying, 'do you know her or not?'

'The twelfth floor,' Carter murmured through tight lips. He was keeping an eye on Alexei C, who still had not exited his car. 'The door on the right when you leave the lift. You'll have to get a move on. You've probably got about three minutes to get them out of there.'

Sam didn't wait for an explanation. He was gone in a second. Meanwhile Carter watched Alexei C climb out of his car and lumber up the road towards him.

Sam was shaking when he pressed Ana's doorbell. Something about the guy downstairs had frightened the wits out of him. When she didn't answer the door Sam banged on the door and shouted.

Carter greeted Alexei C with a cordial smile and

a nod of the head. Alexei C just jerked his own head in the air and looked upwards.

'Afraid the lift is broken,' Carter told the Russian. 'Kaput. We'll have to walk. It's only twelve flights.'

Alexei C grunted and shouldered past Carter. He located the swing doors that led to the fire stairs and began methodically climbing. Alexei C rarely did anything in a hurry which, Carter reflected, was rather a good thing under the circumstances.

Ana was thrown into confusion by the sight of Sam through the spy hole in her door. She assumed it was Carter, or one of Shalakov's men. She opened the door a crack.

'Open the door, Ana. We've got to go. Now!' Sam was shouting.

Ana was even more confused. It even occurred to her to wonder if Sam was working for Shalakov.

'What are you doing here, Sam?' she asked, still hiding behind the door. 'How did you know where I was? Who has sent you. Are you working for Shalakov?'

'No, Ana, don't be daft. I'm here to get you out. Tipper's idea. So get the kids. There's no time for a debate.'

Alexei C was already up to the fourth floor. Carter, following, looked up at his back, his bulging arms and tree-trunk legs as they trudged mechanically up the stairs. Carter stopped on the eighth floor and pretended he needed a breather. Alexei C stopped too, but he was not even slightly short of breath. Carter knew he'd already blown the second payment due from Shalakov on this job. Too bad. What he needed now was an exit strategy. As soon as it became clear that Ana had gone, would he be able to outrun Alexei C? But if he cut and ran too soon, Alexei C would know something was up. He needed to buy Ana as much time as he could.

Sam had got Ana, clutching the baby, and Lara into the lift just as Alexei C reached the twelfth floor. He pressed the button inside the lift as the Russian walked past it. Alexei C heard the lift move and he stopped in his tracks. Slowly he turned to Carter. His brain engaged gear. Why was the lift moving if it was broken?

Carter spun around. He went to leg it back down the stairs, but Alexei C was too quick for him. He grabbed him by the arm and pulled Carter towards him. Carter was trained in close combat, but Alexei C had the flat of his hand under his chin before he could react. He jerked his hand upwards and Carter's neck snapped with a distinctive crack. He was dead before he hit the floor.

Alexei C took off down the stairwell as fast as his massive legs would take him.

81

Ray Fine had a pretty good run in the horse transport plane. He'd worked out where he was landing and was grateful this was June and it was still daylight. Apart from a couple of minutes lost dodging a storm, he was bang on time. He had, however, raised an eyebrow during O'Callaghan's briefing.

'Ray, you won't have time to mess about. This is no ordinary job. There'll be no time for tea and biscuits. Get down, taxi to the hangar and get the cargo doors open. They'll be ready to load the horse. You just ensure he's on board and fly straight out of there.'

'How will I know which hangar to taxi to?'

'There's only the one, I'm told. It's not Heathrow. It's a private strip in an industrial complex of some kind.'

'I only hope they maintain the runway.'

'Don't worry about the runway. They're in and out of there with horses all the time.'

Ray had a feeling that he hadn't been told the

whole story, but O'Callaghan was a top man and he had Ray's unqualified respect. Besides, Ray had flown aid flights into Darfur and landed on plenty of crap, makeshift strips. This, he thought, would be a picnic by comparison.

Tipper got Citizen to the hangar without bother. To start with the colt was confused by his new surroundings. He'd never walked out of the back of the stable block before. He'd been out to the hangar to fly to Paris for the two-year-old race, and England for the Derby, but that had always been in a horsebox from the training track. This was a totally new experience for him. And although he was used to walking into the krio-therapy chamber with the padded boots on, he'd never gone for a walk anywhere else in them.

The walk from the stable took them a very long twenty minutes, with Maine, Tipper and Citizen reaching the hangar about a hundred yards ahead of the toiling Jameson. In the vast empty space of the hangar the only thing they found was Shalakov's car. Lowering his burden with relief Maine tried the driver's door. It was open. He looked at the ignition to see if the key was there. No key. Pity, he thought. The car could have been useful. He tried the glove pocket. Maybe there was a spare key. Or a gun. No such luck. Shit. He would have liked the reassurance of a weapon.

'No key,' he told Jameson, who had finally caught up with them.

'You're catching a plane, not a lift in a car,' Jameson replied.

'When is Shalakov due back?'

'How the hell would I know?'

Tipper had Citizen constantly on the move, walking him around at the back of the hangar. He just wanted to keep his mind occupied. Any minute now he might blow a fuse and fire Tipper out of the saddle.

It was Maine who heard the rumble of the plane first, about a minute before it landed, and he knew enough about planes to realize this wasn't the noise of a horse transport. As the sound increased Jameson hobbled to the door and peered out. Shalakov's executive jet was skimming in over the treetops. A minute later, to his horror, it had landed.

'Who the hell is this?' Maine shouted at Jameson. 'It's not a horse plane.'

'Who do you think it is? Bloody Shalakov of course.'

'Christ,' Maine groaned. 'Give me the pistol. At least I know how to use it.'

Jameson drew out the gun but, instead of giving it to Maine, he pointed it at him.

'No. Come near me and I'll shoot you,' he growled with as much venom as he could muster. 'I'll deal with this. He won't be surprised to see me. You get behind the car. And tell Tipper to stay right at the back of the hangar, in the shadows.'

The pilot could see only Jameson as he taxied

the jet into the hangar. Maine crouched out of sight behind Shalakov's car, five yards from Jameson. Tipper and Citizen were in the shadows at the back of the hangar. Tipper could feel Citizen tensing up under him as the noise of the jet echoed through the metal building. Maine thought about rushing Jameson to get the gun. But Jameson was crazy enough to shoot if he tried. Maine looked back towards Tipper and gestured for him to keep out of sight.

'When is the horse plane due?' Maine shouted, as the jet got closer to them. The noise of the jet taxiing into the hangar was now deafening.

'Now. It should be here now,' Jameson called back. He still had the pistol in his fist, holding it behind his back out of sight from the plane. 'I'll stop them getting off this plane. You help Tipper get the horse onto the other plane as soon as it shows up. Do anything else, and I'll shoot you.'

'I love you too,' Maine shouted sarcastically above the noise of the jet.

'Just do it,' the scientist said calmly, focussing on doing what he had to do.

The pilot brought the jet to a standstill about twenty yards from the car. The door opened and steps folded down automatically. When Sinclair appeared in the doorway of the plane he saw Jameson standing at the bottom of the steps. That was no surprise. But the gun in his hand – that *was*.

'What the hell are you doing with that?' Sinclair shouted.

Jameson waved the gun in the air.

'Don't try and come down those steps or I'll shoot you,' he barked. 'Stay on the plane.'

Sinclair couldn't really hear what he was saying, but he'd never had a gun pointed at him before and he didn't fancy it much. He retreated backwards into the fuselage, where Shalakov was preparing to disembark. Shalakov immediately clocked Sinclair's body language and looked out of one of the portholes.

'Jameson's gone mad,' he roared. 'Get that pistol off him, you idiot.'

'Me?' stammered Sinclair. 'I can't. He'll shoot me.'

Sinclair was still framed in the doorway, blocked in the narrow exit by the comely Caroline, who was stationed between him and the galley. Shalakov shoved Caroline without ceremony out of the way. Before Sinclair could retreat Shalakov had grabbed him by the neck with one hand and got his burly body behind him. With one good shove Sinclair was sent flying head first down the steps.

From where Jameson was standing it looked as if Sinclair was diving on top of him. In that second he shut his eyes, pointed the gun and pulled the trigger. Sinclair was unlucky to be caught by such a blind shot, but caught he was. The bullet entered his skull just above his eyes and exited it near the base of his neck. He was dead before his body landed on top of the scientist.

When Jameson opened his eyes he had the

remains of Sinclair's head resting on his chest: blood, hair and a shattered skull leaking out more blood. Jameson wrestled with Sinclair's dead weight. He needed to get to the gun, which had spun away out of his reach. He heaved Sinclair's bloody body off him and sat up, gasping for breath and looking up the plane's steps. Shalakov was standing there with a grim smile on his face. He reached behind his back for something in his belt and his right arm jerked outwards. Jameson instantly felt a blow in the chest that knocked him over backwards. Shalakov never missed from that range. His throwing knife, which had kept him alive in Afghanistan, had embedded itself in Jameson's heart.

82

Tipper could see what was going on from the back of the hangar. He'd heard the shot and knew something had happened to Jameson; but he couldn't see Maine and he didn't know whether he was now left to face Shalakov alone. Citizen had jig-jogged and ducked from side to side when the jet came into the hangar. But in spite of the racket from the engines, he hadn't totally freaked out. They were still obscured in the back of the hangar, but with no obvious means of escape, Tipper now felt like a cornered rat.

Maine had rolled under the car. He heard Shalakov shout to his air crew to stay where they were, and saw him walking cautiously down the steps of the plane. He bent over Jameson's body, pulled his knife from the chest and wiped it on Jameson's hair before putting it back in its sheath. Maine thought Shalakov would remain suspicious, but wouldn't expect to face any further danger. He would have simply assumed Jameson had taken leave of his senses.

But in the next instant everything changed. The engines of his own plane had whirred and whistled into silence and now Shalakov's ears picked up a different sound. He spun round and marched towards the open side of the hangar to peer at the sky. The approaching aircraft looked like a lumbering crate of a machine compared to Shalakov's sleek jet. It was unmistakeably a horse plane, but not *his*. He wasn't expecting that until tomorrow at the earliest. So whose then was this other horse plane? And why was it landing on his runway?

Shalakov stood in the entrance of the hangar. He watched the aircraft pull up at the end of the runway and start taxiing towards him. Shalakov assumed it must be something to do with Jameson. Had the fool planned to spirit away Citizen I? He'd always thought that, for all his brilliance as a scientist, Jameson was a romantic imbecile when it came to the creatures he created.

Tipper was aware that O'Callaghan's plane had landed. He didn't know where Maine was, but he knew he had to do something. Looking around, he spotted a substantial length of chain lying on a work-bench. Something like an extended bicycle chain. Tipper's mind cast back to his drunken fantasy the night after the Derby. He'd lassoed Shalakov with a whip and dragged him off his feet. Just like he used to lasso buckets when he was a kid in Dublin. This was at least a chance.

It wasn't exactly a rope but it would have to do. Grimacing at the pain, he slipped his left arm out of its sling and put the reins into it. Then he leaned over to his right and grabbed the chain.

It was about nine feet long. Tipper swung it through the air to get a feel of it. Citizen suddenly shot sideways, alarmed by it swinging past his ear. Tipper squeezed Citizen's sides with both his legs and got him to walk forward. I'm only going to have one chance at this, Tipper told himself, trying to get the feel of the chain. I've got to get the rhythm right. After a couple of practice swings he gave Citizen a good kick in the ribs and sat down in the saddle. Citizen responded and leapt into a canter towards the entrance of the hangar. But Tipper needed him to go faster. He squeezed Citizen with his legs even harder and the horse quickened again.

Shalakov couldn't hear a thing. The combination of the horse's padded boots and the plane taxiing up to the hangar masked the sound of Citizen's approach. Shalakov was still staring out of the hangar towards the horse plane. Twenty yards from him, Tipper started swinging the chain. By the time he got to him the chain was on its third rotation.

Shalakov never realized his danger. The chain struck the back his neck. Its kinetic energy then wrapped it tightly around his throat. Shalakov gave an astonished cry and grabbed at the chain; but Tipper held onto it firmly with his good arm. Citizen's forward momentum snapped it taut. Shalakov was yanked off his feet, tumbling like a bowling pin.

Tipper held onto the chain as long as he could. By the time he had to let go, Shalakov had been dragged head first out of the hangar and onto the tarmac. His body lay still. His head was at an unnatural angle, his neck lacerated.

Maine scuttled out from under the car and ran towards Jameson's gun. For some reason, he felt responsible for Jameson's suitcase, and went back for it. Lugging the suitcase, he stumbled after Tipper, who'd kept going towards the horse plane. Passing the prostrate Russian oligarch, Maine didn't need to ponder the diagnosis. Shalakov's eyes were wide open, but absolutely dead. He'd been garrotted.

By the time Ray Fine had taxied according to his instructions up to the hangar and dropped his loading ramp, he'd seen some strange sights. A lunatic on a horse was dragging a man's body out of the hangar, while another bloke staggered out after him with a suitcase. What the hell was going on here?

It took Tipper a couple of furlongs to pull Citizen up. Once he'd dropped the chain he'd grabbed the reins with his right hand but Citizen had been panicked and wanted to keep running.

Looking back Tipper could see the tall, ungainly form of Maine staggering across the tarmac. He'd run straight up the loading ramp into the plane and dropped the suitcase with a thump.

'Don't turn the engines off,' Maine was shouting at Fine. 'We've got to pick up that horse and get the hell out of here.'

Ray regarded the crimson-faced captain uncertainly.

'He'll never ride that horse up that ramp, not with the engines going. He won't get him near it. That's impossible.'

'He'll have to. Security will be here any minute.'

'Security? What do you mean? What is this – the Wild bloody Geese?'

Maine nodded at him.

'Something like that. Stay in the cockpit and be ready to go.'

Tipper was turning Citizen in a wide arc, so that he was circling the plane. Gradually he tightened the circle, coming nearer and nearer to the plane. He was terrified the guards from the front gate would appear and start shooting.

He was right to be. Shalakov's pilots had radioed for back-up. And it was on its way, in the form of two jeeps full of armed guards, scrambled from the front gate.

Tipper's left arm was screaming with pain and completely useless. The roar of the engines was deafening, disorienting. How could he ever get Citizen up that ramp through that noise?

He saw Maine running down the ramp towards them.

'He'll have to turn those engines off,' Tipper shouted.

'No time,' Maine yelled back. 'Give it a try. They'll be here any second.'

The jeeps were now in sight of the plane, racing towards them from the far end of the runway. Tipper squeezed Citizen to go forward but he would only jink from side to side. Next thing he would plant his front legs.

'They're here!' Maine shouted, waving his arms. 'Come on, Tipper.'

In desperation Tipper turned Citizen away from the plane. With the back of his heel he kicked him in the belly and got him to trot about twenty yards away.

'Where are you bloody going now?' Maine bellowed.

Tipper turned Citizen and urged him forward. Citizen suddenly seized the bit in his mouth and started galloping towards the plane. Tipper gambled that as soon as he was faced with the ramp Citizen would jink past to his left, as he had done once at the racetrack. So as they cantered towards the ramp he gave him an almighty kick with his left foot and roared at the top of his voice.

Citizen went to jink but, feeling Tipper's kick, straightened up at the last moment and jumped onto the ramp. With his padded boots to stop him slipping he scrambled to the top like a champion three-day eventer, and disappeared inside the plane. Maine ran up behind.

'Go! Go! Go!' he shouted at Fine. 'Shut the ramp in the air. We haven't got time to wait. They're on us.'

The guards were now two furlongs away, and

in range, but they didn't really know what the hell was going on. They got to Shalakov's body and stopped to check. This gave Ray Fine the extra time he needed. But there was one problem. The wind was in the wrong direction for a conventional upwind take-off. If he taxied down the runway and turned around he'd be a sitting duck when the security men started shooting. He would have to go at once, downwind. No problem, he told himself. He'd done it a lot of times off potholed strips in Africa, with bullets ripping through the skin of the plane. At least this was a long runway.

He opened the throttle to maximum with one hand and pushed the button to shut the loading ramp with the other. He didn't want to spill his load out of the back. His only hope was to get as much speed as possible up and lift her nose with the wing flaps at the last moment. He was going to get no help from the wind.

As the ramp was drawn in and the cargo doors closed the plane thundered down the runway. Ray checked his gauges and focused on the fir trees at the end of it. At the last possible moment he pulled the stick back and the flaps angled upwards to lift the nose. They were counteracted by the following breeze trying to push the plane back down. For several seconds the aircraft seemed uncertain whether to fly or plunge to earth. Ray waited for the smash of the undercarriage on the trees. But it never came. They cleared them by feet. They were off.

83

Tipper's problems were far from over. Citizen was well and truly terrified by now. He'd sensed Tipper's urgency and trusted it instinctively, but loose in the plane he was liable to do himself a fatal injury unless Tipper could calm him down. There was a padded box-like structure in which the horses normally travelled, but they were invariably put into these before take-off. To attempt to do so in mid-flight, with an extremely fractious horse, was madness.

But Tipper had no choice. Sweat was pouring down Citizen's neck and he was lashing out with his hind legs. If he caught the fuselage of the plane he might break his own leg, and they'd have no option but to euthanize him with the bolt gun. The quicker Tipper could get him into the padded crate and secure him the better. But if he tried to get him in too quickly he was likely to panic even more. He just had to give the horse a chance to recover his composure.

The padded crate was designed so that horses didn't have too much room to throw themselves around once inside, making it quite claustrophobic. Citizen's previous experience of it, however, combined with his regular sessions in the krio-therapy chamber, probably saved his life, as these had accustomed him to being confined in small spaces. Inch by inch Tipper nudged Citizen into the crate. Maine stood behind them ready to shut the back of it. Citizen's ears were pricked, and his eyes rolled. He planted his feet, relaxed and shifted a few inches forward, then planted again. Finally, he was far enough in for Maine to force him the rest of the way by closing the crate. The worst of the danger was over.

Maine slumped into one of the shabby passenger seats and watched Tipper soothing Citizen. The adrenaline was starting to run out of him now, and he was shattered. He was too old a soldier for active operations.

Maine knew he was now going to have to eat a large chunk of humble pie, which would be served up gleefully to him by the British Racing Board. They were going to love his humiliation at having unwittingly presided over the biggest scam the racing world had ever seen. As the regu-lator of Moscow racecourse he would have to carry the can with the international racing author-ities. His credibility would be shot to pieces. He was finished: not only in horseracing, but any other walk of life. He'd always be the official who failed to notice that the star of his show had a double.

But, though prospects looked bleak to Maine as the horse plane made its way across France, he was torturing himself unnecessarily. Dermot O'Callaghan had left his guests at Ascot rather unexpectedly in order to fly to Ireland. He considered Maine had played an important part in saving his bloodstock empire, and Dermot O'Callaghan always made sure good deeds, like bad ones, were answered in kind.

Tipper's arm was throbbing like hell as he tried Sam's number on the plane's satellite phone. He wasn't picking up. He left a message and rang off to nurse his throbbing arm. Every pulse of blood that pumped past the injury caused a heavy, dull thud of pain. Tipper was even more exhausted than Maine, but sleep was impossible while he didn't know if Sam had got Ana and Lara to safety.

Worse doubts lurked in the depths below these worries. What would Ana's feelings be? If there was another man, she might just have focked off with him – with their baby and Lara. The whole operation suddenly started to feel futile. He was going to be stripped of his Derby win. His girl might not be there. If he'd left Citizen at Xanadu and just walked away at least he could have remained a Derby winning hero. His instincts had taken over. But had he just destroyed himself?

He glanced across at Maine, who was looking very red in the face.

'You all right, Captain?' Tipper asked.

'I'm fine. Yourself?'

'Jesus, my arm has felt better. I'd better take a couple of those pills. Lucky I brought them with me. Jesus that was bad about the Doc. I never saw anyone killed before. Now I've seen two.'

'I should think it's three. I doubt any of them suffered.'

'Think so? Jesus, I can't believe the Doc shot Sinclair.'

'I wouldn't shed too many tears for Sinclair if I were you.'

'Why's that?'

'Well, he set you up at Chester, you know. I've heard the recording. He told the Racing Board you were going to stop Fighting Talk.'

Tipper considered this information for a few moments then shook his head fiercely.

'The dirty bastard. Why the fock would he want to do that?'

'Because they wanted you in Russia. They reckoned if they threw enough shit at you, you'd go.'

'But that was a while before the job came up?'

'Come on Tipper. They planned this for years. You were just the last piece of the jigsaw.'

'What about Shalakov?'

'Dead as a kipper. You garrotted him. Where the hell did you learn to do that?'

'When I was a kid.'

Tipper brooded on this for a while, but his conscience was clear. He thought about what

Jameson had told him last night. And what he'd admitted to when they were waiting for the plane. The human clones Shalakov had killed at Xanadu. The hundreds of deformed embryos he'd allowed Jameson to create.

'Hey!' said Tipper, snapping out of it. 'He's some horse, you know. I couldn't ride one side of him, had to trust him. But it was like he just knew what to do. Can you believe he went up that ramp? I didn't think he was going to.'

Maine nodded.

'I thought you had no chance. Those guards were onto us. It was incredible.'

'I must be some dopey bastard, Captain. How didn't I realize that there were two horses?'

'Well how would you realize? They were identical for God's sake.'

'I know. But you'd have thought I'd have sensed the difference. They were different in their characters.'

'I think you did feel it. But you were led to the wrong conclusions. Individual horses, I mean everyday ones, don't always behave the same way from one day to the next either.'

Tipper nodded.

'What'll happen to Citizen now, Captain?'

'Good question. I'd say you better ask Dermot O'Callaghan.'

'I hope Sam got Ana out, Captain. They wouldn't do any thing to her in London, would they?'

Maine knew perfectly well what the answer to that was. But there was no point telling Tipper right now. He wouldn't back Sam's chances.

When the lift doors opened Sam had burst out carrying Lara. Ana was on his heels with the baby. There'd been no time to take anything else with them.

'We can't hang around, Ana,' Sam said in the lift. 'We're in deep shit if those bastards get hold of us.'

Ana didn't need telling but Lara wasn't enjoying the game, and was struggling to get free of Sam.

'We've left Mr Sponge Bob behind,' she was wailing. 'Mama, we have to go back. Mr Sponge Bob.'

Alexei C had hurled himself down the stairs in pursuit of the lift. He knew what Shalakov would do if he failed this task. When the lift reached the ground he was more than half way down. As Sam and Ana ran for the outside revolving doors, Tony her warned-off neighbour came pushing in.

'Ana. What's going on?' he said. She looked panic-stricken.

Ana stopped and faced him. She wanted to explain to him. Sam yelled in panic.

'We haven't got time, Ana. They're right behind!'

As Sam spun back round his mobile phone spilled out of his jacket pocket and spun across the reception carpet. Sam was oblivious of his loss in the panic.

Ana looked at Tony for a moment longer, her face chalk white, then turned and hurled herself through the doors. Seconds later Tony saw Alexei C running from the stairs towards the revolving door. Tony stepped into it and jammed it with his feet. The thug could neither get at him nor get through the door. No matter how he jerked the door backwards and forwards, Tony didn't shift. He didn't have the first idea what an incredibly dangerous thing he was doing, but it enabled Sam and Ana to get to Sam's car and drive off.

'Now what?' Ana asked. 'What the hell do we do?'

'Is anyone on our tail?' Sam wanted to know. Ana looked behind them. The road was clear.

'We're okay, I think. But where are we going Sam?'

Sam was trying to concentrate on the road, and on the rear-view mirror. He wanted to make sure they were safe. What he was afraid of most of all was the sight in his mirror of a car full of Russian hoods coming up behind. He drove for several minutes and saw nothing. Then he relaxed a bit.

'Where are we going?' Ana asked.

'Well Ana,' Sam replied. 'That's your decision.'

84

Ray Fine was a mighty relieved man as he straightened up for Tipperary's illuminated air strip.

'Belts on boys. Home sweet home,' he shouted over the tannoy to Maine and Tipper as he made his final approach. He brought the plane down to earth with the lightness of a ballerina. Tipper checked Citizen as they taxied. He hadn't turned a hair.

A horsebox was waiting for them up by the hangar. Not far away was a private jet.

'Looks like O'Callaghan's here to greet us boys. You're very honoured,' Ray added with a touch of irony.

Tipper and Maine had taken it in turns to sit up in the cockpit with Ray. He'd saved their lives and gone well beyond the call of duty. But that was Ray Fine. He'd do anything for O'Callaghan. And he never asked any questions. He hadn't even asked who Citizen was. Or why he was being evacuated. As Ray always said, he'd been around long enough to work only on a need-to-know basis.

Tipper knew O'Callaghan by sight. And it was his face that he saw when the loading ramp was lowered.

Citizen was deeply suspicious as Tipper led him down the ramp. He hesitated before every footstep.

'Thank God, he went up it quicker than that,' Maine said, shaking his head.

'Good evening, gentlemen,' Dermot O'Callaghan said genially, his right hand resting in his blue suit jacket pocket. 'What kept you? We've been waiting six months for that phone call.'

'You just can't get a signal in Moscow these days,' Tipper replied dryly.

Tipper took Citizen off the runway onto the grass. He let him have a pick. There was no worry he'd get loose now. He looked as exhausted as the rest of them.

'Captain Maine?' O'Callaghan asked, offering him his hand. 'We owe you a big debt. And we always pay our debts.'

'It got pretty messy back there,' Maine said. 'There will be repercussions.'

'Nothing we can't handle,' he replied.

O'Callaghan had given the situation his full attention as soon as he knew they'd made it out. The obvious thing to do with Citizen was to go public. The upside on the value of his horses, and their stallion potential, would be immediate once Citizen had been rubbed out of the form book. Which he'd only be if the cloning scam was unveiled. Then Translation would be the Derby winner retiring to stud. But O'Callaghan wasn't a man who did the obvious; until he'd weighed up the less-than-obvious. And that was going to take him a few days.

'Any news on Sam and my missus, Mr O'Callaghan?' Tipper asked.

'We haven't heard, Tipper. He's probably getting no phone signal. It's desperate over here at the moment.' O'Callaghan was sort of telling the truth. He hadn't heard. Sam's phone had been diverting to voice mail.

'Okay, this is the plan,' O'Callaghan said. 'Tipper, you need to lie low with the horse. Sam should be meeting you at the stud. And Captain Maine, will you come back to London with me? We have things to discuss.'

'What are we going to do, though?' Tipper asked. 'They'll come after us, won't they?'

'Well at the moment they don't know who to come after. Or where. We do nothing, and we say nothing. By the way, how many knew there were two Citizens?'

'Difficult to say,' said Maine. 'But three of them are now lying in a pool of blood.'

'Oh dear,' said O'Callaghan smoothly. '*That* messy, was it?'

'Whoever else knows,' Maine went on, 'they won't want to be shouting about it, I don't suppose.'

'Right! Let's get this horse loaded on the

544

horsebox and be on our way,' O'Callaghan called decisively. 'Tipper, best to say nothing about Citizen or yourself to the driver. Careless talk costs lives.'

Tipper and Citizen were driven towards Fethard by a time worn driver who understood the rewards for seeing nothing, hearing nothing and most importantly saying nothing.

'Where we heading?' Tipper asked him.

'You'll see soon enough,' the driver replied dourly.

Tipper recognized McCarthy's pub in Fethard as they drove past. He looked at the wall he'd sat on waiting for Sam when he was a kid.

'Looks quiet in there tonight,' he observed trying to get some conversation out of his man.

'Very quiet, so it is,' the monosyllabic driver agreed.

'Do the funerals still go the long way?'

'They do.'

The driver swung the horsebox round the right hand bend at the top of the street and drove down past the old walls. Tipper thought about him and Sam taking turns to lug his bag along the road.

'See they haven't mended the castle yet.'

'No.'

'Polish builders. Probably got held up on another job,' Tipper joked. The driver didn't laugh.

Further along the road Tipper recognized the turning on the left down to Kiltinan Castle.

'Jesus. That place would do for me,' he wished. 'Does Lloyd-Webber still own it?'

'He does.'

'How much further, pal?'

'Couple of minutes.'

Small world, Tipper thought to himself. They were within spitting distance of the stud where he'd worked with Sam when they were kids. He gave up trying to talk to the guy. He was only trying to take his mind off Sam and Ana, anyway. Why hadn't they rung? What had happened?

It was pitch black when the horse box swung into the avenue lined with horse chestnut trees. Tipper couldn't believe it. He could see the big white barn now in the headlights.

'Jesus, who owns this place now?'

'O'Callaghan,' the driver said reluctantly. 'He only bought it recently. It's deserted.'

The drive was full of holes and the bumps jolted his arm.

'This is where I'm to drop you off. And then go. God knows where you'll put the horse?'

Tipper gingerly climbed down from the lorry and took the torch from the cab. The big wooden doors into the barn weren't locked. Tipper swung them open and peered into the barn.

He found an old light switch by the entrance. Miraculously a dim light on the wall came on. The barn looked a bit different from how Tipper remembered it. There were a load of wooden pens down each side and it smelt of cow manure.

'Jesus, someone's had a load of cattle in here,' he shouted to the driver.

At the end of the barn was a stack of straw bales. Tipper pulled the strings off one of the bales with his good arm and started to kick it around to make a bed for Citizen. He wanted to make it comfortably deep. Then he found an old bucket in the yard and filled it up with water. Citizen had drunk well on the flight, but he was still going to be thirsty.

'I think he's had enough of ramps for one day,' Tipper observed as he let him feel his own way down the ramp to the ground. When he let him loose in the barn Citizen had a good old sniff of the water bucket and suspiciously eyed up the strange-smelling straw.

'You're not sure about our white barn, are you mate? Nor was your mother when I brought her in here bleeding all over the place,' Tipper told Citizen.

'I'll be off then,' the box driver said standing in the barn entrance. He'd been told to ask no questions. He'd done his job. If they wanted a man and a horse dropped off in the middle of nowhere, that's what they got.

'Cheers, pal. Go steady,' Tipper called after him.

The white barn fell very quiet when the noise of the horse box disappeared out of the end of the drive. If Sam and Ana and Lara had been there, Tipper would have been very happy. This was his spiritual home. This was where he'd first felt real pride. This was where he'd learnt to understand horses.

He lay back in the straw, hardly keeping his eyes open. Citizen came over to investigate him. Tipper reached up and gave his ears a rub. Then tears started to pour down Tipper's cheeks. He couldn't bear the ironic agony that he and Citizen had made it back to Tipperary. But Ana wasn't there and she obviously wasn't coming. He finally had to accept it. Exhaustion then got the better of him. He let his eyes shut.

Tipper's recurrent dream in Russia flooded through his exhausted head. He was lying in bed half asleep with Ana, as the little body tunnelled its way into the bottom of their bed and snuggled up between them. And then, from under the sheets, poked a little sleepy head that wanted a cuddle, while he and Ana rubbed noses.

But the dream didn't seem to be quite the same this time. There were no sheets, just straw every-where. Ana was kneeling next to him stroking his forehead.

'Tipper,' she was whispering. 'Tipper.'

The dream felt so real this time. Tipper's eyes flickered but the dream was still going on. Ana was kneeling next to him. She bent down and kissed him. Then she rubbed his nose with hers.

'Hello,' she smiled.

Tipper opened his eyes. He was momentarily disorientated.

'Ana.'

'Are you all right, Tipper?' she asked softly. But she didn't have the confidence to touch him. Ana lifted up Lara who was half asleep and put her between them.

'Look who's here. Sweetheart. It's your daddy. D'you remember him?'

'Jesus,' Lara said sleepily.

'Where did she learn that,' Tipper laughed. Then he looked Ana straight in the eye. 'I'm only all right if you'll have me back.'

'Tipper, we have to discuss things. You might not want me.'

'I swear I didn't know anything about those birds.'

'I'm not talking about that.' Ana looked down at Lara. She looked like she'd dozed off.

'Tipper. I never told you the truth. About my background. How I ended up in Newmarket . . .'

'You don't need to tell me Ana. I already know,' Tipper interrupted. Then he stroked her hair with his good hand. 'Ana. I love you. And I'll protect you from now on.'

Tears welled up in Ana's eyes. 'I'm so sorry Tipper,' she whispered. He pulled her towards him, rubbed her back and kissed her head. Her face was pressed up against his jersey.

'I didn't know how to tell you. And then everything between us happened so fast.'

'Shush Ana. It's finished. You'll never have to worry about him again.'

Ana clung tightly to Tipper. Not for the first time in that barn, an elated feeling washed over him.

'I don't care who the baby's father is, Ana.'

She stroked his good arm then leant behind her. She picked up the sleeping bundle and put him on Tipper's lap.

'You are the father, Tipper. You are.'

'Jesus,' Tipper smiled broadly. 'What's he called?'

'Well he was called Alan after someone who helped me. But now you're home. So I guess it's Frankie Lester?'

What's next?

Tell us the name of an author you love

and we'll find your next great book.